MONKS' COURT

KINGS COURT

Books by Katherine Wigmore Eyre

AMY

THE CHINESE BOX

THE LUTE AND THE GLOVE

MONKS' COURT

MONKS' COURT

a novel

by

Katherine

Wigmore

Eyre

APPLETON-CENTURY

New York

APPLETON-CENTURY
AFFILIATE OF
MEREDITH PRESS

Library of Congress Catalog Card Number: 66–14957
MANUFACTURED IN THE UNITED STATES OF AMERICA FOR MEREDITH PRESS

*To Mary Abbot
and Patricia Schartle,
gratefully*

MONKS' COURT

ONE

"No! And do stop pestering me, Ritchie. Please."

The young woman, both pretty and chic in black chiffon and pearls, pulled away a hand as the London cab pushed through the tangle of after-theater and supper-club traffic, and the man sitting next to her shrugged. "The Widow Collier, in a narrow bed all the rest of your life?" he inquired, an eyebrow lifting. "Is that the future you have in mind? Of all the nonsense! Of all the waste. It's ridiculous. Idiotic. And you know it, Mag."

"Don't call me Mag. And straighten your tie."

"It wasn't that much of a clinch. But if you say so . . ." The man looked amused and put a hand to the collar of his dinner jacket. "How's that? And now tell me why you object to 'Mag'? Wasn't it always that when we were children? Mag and Ritchie—to say nothing of its being 'darling' at one stage, as I so often recall when to the sessions of sweet, silent thought—and all that."

"You still spout poetry?"

"Only when the occasion or the company warrants. You used to like it, along with a lot of other things about me. Which brings us back to 'darling.' A nice ring to it, don't you think? So why not let's put it back in circulation?"

"We don't happen to be children any longer."

"But why did you look me up if you didn't want us to get back on the old basis? I wondered it, first thing, when you telephoned last week, and I've been wondering it all the more, each time you've let me see you. Seven evenings and four lunches together ought to add up to some kind of score in my favor. Come on, Mag, tell me what you had in mind, your real reason for calling?"

The young woman stirred uneasily in her corner of the cab, and played with the catch of her black satin bag.

"There was no especial reason—not really."

"How did you know I was in London?"

"How could I help it, with the papers full of interviews and pictures? '. . . another highly successful, swashbuckling, lusty historical novel by the brilliant young newspaper correspondent turned fiction writer . . .'"

"I hardly imagine you're one of my fans."

"Well . . . no. Your kind of book is more for men, don't you think? But oh, it's wonderful! Imagine you having two best sellers in a row."

"Nothing to it, once you've got the knack. A simple twist of the wrist. But I'm glad you're impressed. And that's why you dredged me up? Because it might be interesting to give the once-over to a home-town boy who has made good?"

"In a way."

"How long will you be here?"

"I have no definite plans."

"Neither have I. I'm the bird-of-passage type. A free soul.

No ties, no obligations, and no wish to take on any. Not unless you give me the nod."

"I can't imagine you ever settling down, Ritchie. From what I've read, it's pretty much Moscow one day for you, and Karachi, or Bangkok, or Saigon or Zambezi the next. How does it happen to be London now?"

"I'm working on another book. A sea story. I need some Royal Navy data. But it's my turn for questions again. What brought you here, Mag? Anything, or anyone, in particular? Not that I want to pry—much! Though you've got to admit I've skipped a questionnaire up to this point." The man's lively blue eyes were suddenly serious. "It hasn't been easy. I've held back on a thousand questions. I've had the feeling all along you'd turn and run if I tried closing in. But there's so much I want to know."

"And so little to tell you, Ritchie." Margaret Collier half sighed, half laughed, ruefully. "As to why I came to London . . ." She hesitated. "I don't quite know. It was just that London seemed to be indicated. Boredom had set in at home. Boredom or restlessness. You could call it either. Whichever it was, I wanted to get away."

"It doesn't sound like you somehow. The great American Sisterhood of Unattached, Floating Female Travelers—you're the last girl I'd have expected to join up."

"A lot of us don't belong by choice, Ritchie."

"Sorry. That was stupid of me. How long, by the way, since Allen's death? A car accident, wasn't it?"

"Yes. Driving back from the golf club, a year ago."

"Any children?"

"No. I'm entirely alone. Mother and Father are dead now, too."

"Beaux? Dozens of 'em, I'd say."

"You flatter me. But there's no one."

"Your own fault, that's easy to see. The chilly, choosy sort. You've all the signs of it, my sweet."

"And why shouldn't I be choosy, as you put it? Having a man around the house isn't an essential. Not in my opinion, at least."

"No? The animals came in two by two, remember? And a girl like you without a man in her life doesn't make sense."

"It's my affair, isn't it, if I choose not to marry again? And don't bring up the subject again. A husband doesn't interest me at this point. Neither do proposals, as I should think you'd know by now. And Ritchie, if I have to ask you once more to stop trying to kiss me . . ."

"All right. All right. It's a matter of viewpoint, the whole thing, I expect. But just the same . . ."

Conversation lapsed, and the cab driver, who had already taken his fares across the river and back, and been directed to circle the spraying, lighted fountain in Trafalgar Square, was directed again.

"Carlos Place, please."

Turning eventually into Berkeley Square and then into Mount Street, he drew up at a small, quietly expensive looking hotel, its window boxes bright with late spring flowers.

A doorman in a glossy, cockaded coachman's hat and polished boots and, despite the muggy, wilting heat, impeccably correct in his closely buttoned, fawn-colored greatcoat, helped Margaret to the sidewalk while Richard Page, consulting the cab meter, took out his wallet.

"On the warm side, isn't it, madam? Let's 'ope we'll have rain before morning. We could do with a bit of cooling off, wouldn't you say?"

"Rain would be lovely." Margaret turned to Ritchie then, and her smile was forgiving as they walked into the hotel.

"I've cooled off already. So let's be friends. I had a wonderful evening. It was perfect—when you were behaving."

"Then you'll let me see you soon again? That's my girl! I'll telephone first thing in the morning. Meanwhile, Mag dear, you'd better do some thinking. Cliché or not, time does march on, and no one can afford to throw his life away. You and I have wasted too much of ours already—oh, yes, we have. And can you give me one single reason—just one, mind you—why we should miss this second chance? Why we shouldn't pick up where we left off? Or rather, where you broke things off?"

"There you go again, Ritchie, being a nuisance. We were only children, I tell you."

"I never did understand what happened."

"Didn't you? Neither did I exactly. I only knew it couldn't go on."

They said brief, reserved good nights under the eyes of a brass-buttoned lift boy. Ritchie watched the cage ascend out of sight, and as he walked through the lobby and out the hotel door he was reflecting that the perfume Margaret wore now was a more subtle and doubtless more expensive variety than the girlish favorites he remembered her using.

Her clothes, too, were decidedly different. Sophisticated. In the Baltimore days there had been southern-belle overtones, particularly in summer—fluffy things, for swinging in hammocks, and wide straw hats, worn at the garden parties her mother—and Allen Collier's mother—had doted on giving. He could remember jodhpurs, too, when they rode together, and linen shorts when she'd come wading across the creek that was the boundary line between her parent's country place and the run-down, mortgaged farm that his father ignored to read law books without ever practicing law.

All long ago in retrospect, if not in time. And the hurt and the humiliation, the anger she was responsible for decently buried. Along with them, that ardency of his, he had hoped. Damn her, for disinterring it again. Damn her—his

Mag—for giving him another look at those eyes of hers, those topaz eyes.

That was how he had always thought of them—as deep topaz. The lashes were darker, and thick enough and long enough to be the glue-on kind. And her hair, all that soft, shiny stuff—damn her for making him crazy to reach out and touch it again. It was still the color of the sand in the creek bottom, bright-streaked by the sun that had glinted through the water on those hot summer days.

As he walked away from the hotel, Margaret was letting herself into her bedroom with a key from her evening bag. Too bad of Ritchie, she thought resentfully. Not fair to presume on the past.

So much had been stirred up this evening. So much looked back on that might better have been lost to sight. And none of it relevant. None of it part of things as they were now. None of it mattering now, when you came right down to it. The truth was, very little of anything mattered lately, except her own growing concern for the emptiness of her life. Loneliness was dreadful.

The bedroom was stifling as Margaret stepped into it, and switching off the lamp a chambermaid had lighted earlier, she went quickly to the windows and opened them wide and pushed aside the chintz curtains.

There. That was a little better. She stared out into the night, turning a number of things over in her mind.

That was London out there, huge, gray, grim, impersonal London. The London that had drawn her here, all across the ocean. It hadn't frightened her in the least on her two former visits, once with a school group, and once with Allen.

Was it a mistake to come alone? It would seem so. And why had she chosen London for this trip instead of any other place? She had told Ritchie she didn't know. Was that entirely true? Hadn't she given way to a kind of compulsion?

Hadn't London reached out in a curious and almost frightening way, demanding her presence and refusing to let her go anywhere else on the spring trip she was considering? A silly thing to say. She had chosen London, chosen it of her own free will, merely because London *was* London, a superb, marvelously interesting city.

Quite naturally it frightened her a little, and depressed her, if she let herself dwell on the fact that she knew no one in the entire city, not a single person, except Ritchie. No one, that is, whom she knew nearly well enough to impose on by turning up unexpectedly just at the beginning of the Season.

Margaret sighed in the darkness as she considered the few Londoners she had ever met. None of them had been more than business acquaintances of Allen's, and their wives were the sort, she was certain, who took the Season seriously, with their plans made well in advance.

And what was she now, without Allen, but an Extra Girl —spelled with capitals? It would be awful to push herself onto them by telephoning or writing notes; she knew she would be a nuisance, an awkwardness, with people feeling bound to scurry politely around making last-minute, highly inconvenient arrangements.

Anything but that! And she wouldn't feel too sorry for herself—or she'd try not to. London on her own could be perfectly well endured. She had come because, perversely enough, she had longed to come, felt she *had* to come, and now she was here, she'd stick it out.

She had the shops and the theaters, the music and the ballet, didn't she? She had the parks and the squares, and the charming, charming window boxes, crowded now with the last of the daffodils and primroses, the hyacinths and freesias that in another month would give way to geraniums and lobelia and hydrangeas.

She had the Tower and the Abbey and all of the city's domes and spires and the clangor of its bells. And think of the gray river, curving down to the Pool and the Isle of Dogs, and up to Hampton Court. She had the Mall and the palaces and the Queen's soldiers marching and the sentries at St. James's. And to make her ashamed of her self-pity she had the Chelsea Pensioners, one-legged or blind or faceless, in their scarlet coats with the pinned-on medals.

Too, she had the city's chimney pots, hundreds of them, black and sooty with coal smoke, and a roost for pigeons and swallows and starlings, to remind her this was still Little Dorrit's London, and Mr. Pickwick's, and Becky Sharp's and all the rest.

More than that, tonight she had those people, silhouetted just now against lamplight in the windows over there across Mount Street, directly opposite, to take her mind off her loneliness. Speaking of theater! This unexpectedly glimpsed bit of staging offered a London play at its best; one of those drawing-room comedies she adored. And she'd be in the choicest of center stalls, no less if she gave way to a sudden and completely inexcusable impulse to bring the actors into even sharper focus. She ought to be ashamed—and she was —but . . .

Margaret reached into the black satin bag she still held and took out a little pair of gold and mother-of-pearl opera glasses.

The ground floor of the soot-grimed building that fronted on Mount Street was given over to small shops filled with expensive antiques and old porcelains, its upper floors to flats.

The flat at the top was brilliantly lighted, its windows

flung open, its curtains as widely pushed aside as the curtains in Margaret's bedroom.

Could anything be more entertaining? Grasping at the chance to be diverted, Margaret ignored her scruples and frankly stared.

The Leading Man was obviously that handsome West End type in evening clothes who was standing by a table set out with a tray, and pouring wine into thin-stemmed glasses. The Leading Lady was, of course, the woman sitting on a crimson damask sofa drawn up to a marble hearth, one of her white, heavily ringed hands, the nails long and scarlet, reaching for something off a little plate.

A *pâté de foie gras* sandwich, or caviar, or smoked salmon on brown bread, Margaret decided, beginning to enjoy herself hugely, and without compunction. And the wine being poured was certainly the best of champagne. It had to be champagne. The plushy look of the drawing room with all that damask, and its thick white rug, and the glamour of the two principals definitely called for it.

Glamour—an overworked word, but so exactly right in this case. Exotic, too, was applicable, in the woman's case. Appreciatively, Margaret studied every detail of the woman's Oriental pajamas. A superb brocade. A gorgeous green. Jade green, with the narrow legs of the pajamas slit provocatively high on the side, and the collar subtly seductive with its close, frogged fastening.

You knew her throat and shoulders would be white. With the masses of her black, sleek hair pulled away from small ears and piled on top of her head, long green pins thrust through it, you expected her to give off an aura of musk or some other heavy, pervasive Far Eastern perfume. And yet there was a distinctly European look about her, too. More than that, the look of a cat.

Critically, Margaret made the comparison. Yes, a cat's

face, with that slight fullness at the jawline and those curiously round eyes that should have been almond shape, you would have thought, and that surely would prove to be green on closer inspection, with the pupils a vertical, feline slit.

Claws? Sheathed, in such delightful company, you imagined. Amused at herself, Margaret adjusted the glasses to bring the man closer. On second glance, "handsome" was inadequate. "Distinguished looking" was far more like it. As she watched him he gave the filled wine glass to the woman and then poured a glass for himself. She shifted her glass in a smiling, suggestively intimate salute, but before he responded the man pulled close the heavy folds of a pair of curtains that matched the damask of the sofa.

End of Act One. And just at the most intriguing of moments.

Margaret laughed outright. The bad luck of having to miss the next scene of so delightfully urbane and entertaining a play. She had been cheated; the box office owed her her money back!

"Risqué" was an old-fashioned word you never heard any more, but it fitted this particular play perfectly. Without any doubt, those two were lovers, weren't they? It was much, much more interesting to think so, at any rate, than not.

Fortunate, that cat-faced woman, to have so fascinating, so personable a man to make her London night exciting. Ridiculously enough, Margaret envied her. But there was something about the man—something terribly attractive. Something—something disturbing—absurd as it sounded.

One thing was certain, he wasn't a man to forget easily. Curious, how every detail of his appearance stuck in the mind.

Margaret went over them, one by one, with her glasses still on the windows opposite, on the faint chance the curtains might again be pushed aside.

Taller than average, he had been. Lean-faced, with a boney high-bridged nose. Not too young a man; his dark hair was thin at the temples and graying, and he limped, noticeably, and used a stick. The limp could well be a wartime souvenir and not necessarily have anything to do with his age. Lots of Londoners in their thirties and early forties limped.

His eyes? She couldn't tell, at that distance. Her overall impression was of an Englishman at his best, with that assured carriage, in spite of the stick, that way of holding his head, that intangible—and infuriating—air of upper-class arrogance that seemingly was inbred in every Britisher of her acquaintance. They still thought they owned the earth, the insufferable creatures, and nothing would ever convince them otherwise. That was part of their charm, their really devastating, spectacular charm.

Margaret sighed again, and drew her own curtains.

Oh, the ghastly men she seemed fated to sit next to at dinner parties! The dull, dull men at home, introduced to her by her married friends with the kindest intentions in the world. Any male, any male at all, was forever being produced in the charitable hope that poor dear Margaret, who was much, much too nice and too young and attractive a girl to be left high and dry, would find someone to settle down with again.

So far, a lost cause. Her friends ought to have seen the light by now; they ought to give up. It would be so much simpler for everyone. Ironic, that even Ritchie couldn't change things now, and Ritchie was a thousand times better company than any other man she knew, and always had been.

But did she want Ritchie now any more than she had wanted him a few years ago? A terrifying boy he had been, like a rushing stream, a torrent, she used to think, sweeping everything before him, determined to carry her along with him.

A boy who wouldn't listen to "No." Not with good grace. And he was like that still, it seemed, all these years later.

Margaret yawned and began to undress, and wondering with both vexation and wry amusement if a girl alone always regretted the lack of a husband most keenly when a zipper stuck halfway down her back. Useful, that's what a husband was—and precious beyond price.

When the zipper was conquered, she put on the lacy nightgown that lay folded at the foot of her turned-down bed. She brushed her hair and her teeth and wound her blue leather traveling clock; but it was too hot to get into bed, and she went to the windows again.

One of those sultry, heavy nights that weighted you down unbearably, she thought, with another yawn, a night that left you headachy and all out of sorts. If only it would rain.

Dong. Dong. There was Big Ben striking. And down the river, at the Tower, a watchman, swinging his lantern, would be crying, "Two o'clock, and all is well."

Its striking two o'clock meant that the couple across the way, in the flat over there, hadn't many hours left before morning light would filter through whatever crack it could find in those intriguingly drawn curtains.

How had they spent their evening earlier, before their champagne supper? Had they gone to the theater, as she and Ritchie had? Afterward, had they, too, danced and had supper and then taxied along the Embankment and crossed a bridge to get a breath of air on this hot night, to look back at London's lights, watching their reflection in black, glassy river water?

Had the man kissed the woman in the dark closeness of a cab, as Ritchie had tried to kiss her this evening? And now, if they had finished their wine, would they go to bed together?

The question kept recurring to Margaret, and when she

had turned from the window, with hope of rain given up, and gotten into her own bed, she was still asking it.

In spite of her yawning, her eyes would not close, and she made a firm resolution to give up after-dinner coffee. A demitasse was not worth the turning and the tossing, she decided wearily, not worth the rumpling of the luxurious, cool-to-the-skin feel of the embroidered linen sheets and pillow slips with which only the best of London hotels still indulged their guests.

Or perhaps it wasn't coffee after all. If she had been strictly truthful with Ritchie she would have confessed the true reason for looking him up. She would have confessed this aching, miserable loneliness of hers. Ritchie was someone to talk to, aside from chambermaids and waiters and porters and doormen. Ritchie would take her out of herself.

Strange, the way the loneliness had mounted, mounted, the past weeks since her arrival. And now, seeing those two across the street was making the loneliness hurt more than ever.

Allen would be sorry—Allen, who, in his own fashion, had cared a great deal for her, and who had never for a single moment let her feel anything but looked after and protected, or wanted her to be anything but happy.

Those two . . . It seemed she could not forget the expression on the man's face as he filled the woman's wine glass. A thin-lipped intensity to it, a kind of grimness almost. A man might well look like that if his mind had been made up to something momentous, his purpose irrevocably set.

Perhaps they were not lovers in the accepted sense after all. Perhaps he was merely going to propose. Men always seemed to take proposing with the most painful seriousness.

And she ought to be ashamed of herself to have watched them through her opera glasses like a female Peeping Tom. Guiltily, Margaret reproved herself. Spying was horrid. All the same, she wished she knew what had happened after those curtains were drawn. Were they, or weren't they, lovers tonight? Two people in one another's arms. Two people in bed together—with, of course, the possibility of their being nothing more exciting than a happy married couple.

So very, very odd, her not being able to get them out of mind, Margaret reflected drowsily. Especially the man—the cat-faced woman's husband—if he was her husband.

There was a rumble of thunder that brought her sitting up, suddenly, and a streak of lightning, vivid against the predawn sky, and then a hard beat of rain and a stir of cooler air, with the chintz curtains blowing wildly.

The crimson damask curtains across the way would blow, too, those drawn, concealing curtains.

She fell asleep, at last, lying on her side, with the hand that wore Allen Collier's solitaire and gold band under her cheek. Her hair, the bright hair that Ritchie Page thought the color of sun-gilded creek sand, fell in a plait over her pillows. The dark lashes, thick enough to be the glue-on variety, were heavy crescents against creamy skin. Her mouth, drooping at the corners, and without the bravura of lipstick, was disconsolate.

Once, she stirred.

"I'm here," she murmured in her slumbering. "I'm here. I came. . . ."

TWO

She was running her bath water two mornings later when the telephone rang, as it had rung every morning of late. She answered it with an eagerness that surprised her and had to admit to herself that she was not in the least irked at being addressed as Maggie again, or even Mag.

Ritchie was sweet. Well, not sweet—that didn't fit him—but a dear.

". . . not ringing too early, am I? . . . I've missed you since our last binge. That's a workingman's life for you. . . . Yes—yes, I got a lot done. A chapter out of the way. Are you free this morning? I have a man to interview at the Maritime Museum, so what about going down to Greenwich with me? We'll have beefsteak and kidney pie and some good brown ale at a pub I know, and go all out for Merrie England. You're on? . . . Good. I'll stop for you about eleven. And wrap up. It will be cold as the devil on the river."

He called for her in a taxi and they caught an excursion

boat at Westminster Bridge, and in spite of the weather chose outside seats, well forward. The wind was a cutting blast, the water and the sky pewter gray, and Margaret, with a yellow tweed coat close around her, thrust her gloved hands deep in her pockets.

Spring in England. Unpredictable spring. With windows open and curtains pushed aside only two airless, stifling nights ago.

"You are amazingly good-looking, Mag, my love, even with your nose blue and your eyes streaming," Ritchie told her as they drank the coffee he had brought up from the cabin's buffet bar. "A stunner, in your quiet way."

"Nice of you, but I'm not your love, as I've told you before. And besides, I don't believe a word of it. I'm not nearly as fond of looking in mirrors as I used to be."

"Gone off, have you?" Ritchie made a slow, critical study and shook his head in disagreement. "I wouldn't say so. I wouldn't put you in the old-hag class exactly. You've got a while yet."

His easy, brash nonsense amused her. Decidedly pleasant, she thought, to have the company of an attractive man. Ritchie was right. She had been too choosy, too aloof, since Allen's death, and she had been foolish to cut herself off from people. "People" being "men." Especially when she so much enjoyed a really entertaining man.

The trouble was, she wanted too much from life, she now knew, and always there was that unrealistic, foolishly romantic streak that invariably made her draw back and freeze, and that spoiled things for her, time after time.

But how terribly she missed not having a man around—the right man—for keeps. Not all the missing had to do with— well, with making love, either. Not by a long way. It was masculinity in general that she craved, the masculine aura. Shaving soap . . . bay rum . . .

Even a man's clothes could give pleasure. They could hurt, too. Allen's dark-blue pinstripes, his flannels, his evening clothes, his Sulka smoking jacket, his Jäger bathrobe, his quiet, good ties had brought back too much when she had to empty his closets after the car crash.

The black, polished shoes he wore to the bank every morning. The golf shoes. The patent-leather evening pumps. Putting away his hats had been the worst; just the conservative correctness of their brim width was Allen all over again.

Dear Allen . . . Already the tiniest bit stuffy as a young man, would he have become pompous? But enough of that.

It was a narrow, swift cruiser, as gray as the river, cutting across the bow of the excursion steamer, which put the final, abrupt end to her useless reveries.

"Good heavens!" she exclaimed, half indignant, half laughing, as icy, flying spray from a white wake stung her face and wet the front of her coat. "Who are they—those men in uniform—and what's their hurry?"

"They are some of the River Patrol boys on official business from the Watling Street Station. It's over there, on the London side," Ritchie explained.

"A River Patrol—oh, exciting. Are they after a murderer, by any chance?" Margaret laughed. "I adore murder stories, and all those fascinating Scotland Yard inspectors. Why don't you write a good, thrilling detective novel, Ritchie, and make a few more million dollars overnight?"

Ritchie laughed too. "It's an idea. But I couldn't turn out anything morally satisfying to the public, I'm afraid. I'd be too soft toward the villain. It can't be much fun, having the Yard on your tail."

"Oh, but a murderer would deserve being caught. And speaking of murder, did you see the papers this morning? I was in a hurry—I only glanced at the headlines. It wasn't in the *Times*, needless to say! The lift boy had a copy of one of those awful, sensational sheets. The woman was a well-known dancer, I gathered, though I didn't recognize her name."

Ritchie cupped his hands against the wind and lighted a cigarette, then tossed the match overboard. "You haven't been to that Oriental revue at the Viceroy? She was the top feature. Honorine Duclair. The troupe is on a world tour. Opened about a month ago."

"Poor thing. Who did it? Do they know? Where was it, at the theater?"

"At her flat."

"In Soho, I suppose?"

"No. As a matter of fact, her flat is on Mount Street, right near your hotel, judging by the address the papers gave. I read an account in the *Daily Mail*—not too badly written, if I do say so, as an ex-reporter. That's what I'll always be, I expect, at heart. A newshound, with my nose quivering to sniff out the real dope on a story, no matter how sensational. Once reporting gets in the blood. . . ."

His smile was amused and reminiscent, and a little bitter. "I used to run my legs off when I was a cub, chasing after this sort of story—to keep eating, believe it or not."

"You didn't mind the sordidness?"

"It was news. And it sold. This one will sell, too. It's got everything—an exotic Eurasian dancer, a swank address—with question mark, Who pays the rent?—and champagne, a cozy little champagne tête-à-tête."

"Champagne? A Eurasian? When was it, Ritchie? When did it happen?"

Margaret's voice was startled and interested, and Ritchie looked at her surprised.

"She was done in Tuesday night—late. Toward morning, actually. Tuesday was the evening you and I went to the Savoy, remember, and drove around afterward? And it's the night I took a vow to leave you strictly alone for a while and get back to my typewriter. Black Tuesday! But here I am, with the vow broken. Mag, Mag sweet, if only . . ."

Margaret was not listening.

"A flat on Mount Street . . . Tuesday night . . ." Her eyes were horrified. "Near the hotel? Then I saw her. Oh, Ritchie—oh, how dreadful!"

"You saw her?" Ritchie's blue eyes were incredulous. "What do you mean, you saw her? You couldn't have. How on earth?" .

"But I did. I know I did. I was looking out the hotel window, my bedroom window." —Margaret's words tumbled over themselves, a torrent, rushing out in shock and pity— "It was just before I went to bed. The lights were on across the street in a top flat. And there was a woman with black hair—and very white skin, white hands."

"How could you possibly tell whether she was white-skinned with the width of Mount Street between you—and through rain—to say nothing of drawn curtains." Ritchie's laugh was frankly scoffing. "Any day, Little Bright Eyes."

"The rain hadn't started. The windows were all open. Her curtains weren't drawn—not until later. And I had my opera glasses. I had them focused. It wasn't very nice of me, but watching the two of them was like watching a play, I thought, and—"

"The two of them?" Richard put the question sharply. Now he, too, was interested. "You mean, someone was with the woman?"

"Yes. A man. A man in evening clothes. He was pouring wine."

"Good Lord! A young fellow? A boy?"

"No. Not a boy at all. A man, I tell you. Fortyish, perhaps."

"You'd be willing to swear to that? You'd go on oath it wasn't a boy?"

"Swear?" Margaret echoed it uncomprehendingly. "Yes,

certainly I'd swear to it." Quickly she added, instinctively on
the defensive and uncomfortably aware of it, "But why do
you ask? Why should it matter whether or not I'd be willing?"

"Because the police happen to be holding a boy for the
murder; a French boy, just a kid, as far as I can gather from
the papers. The Duclair woman had made a monkey of him
for a few weeks, and then, well, dumped him. Showed him
the gate."

"And the police think . . . ?"

"They are a long way from being sure of it. He's got an alibi
of sorts: the night porter at his hotel 'thinks' he remembers
the boy stopping by at the desk for his key and going up to
his room around ten o'clock that night. The police say the
woman was killed some time after midnight. Her maid, who
sleeps out, found her in the morning."

"How . . . ?"

"How was she murdered? By strangulation. There were
some fingerprints in the flat—a lot of them—but none of
them were the kid's, and if you saw the woman alive with an
older man after midnight, the police will let him go. It's the
bloke you watched pouring champagne who will have some
tall explaining to do."

Ritchie drew hard on his cigarette and then exhaled with
extraordinary satisfaction. "By God, Maggie sweet, you've
made a scoop. A man around forty! And all but caught in the
act. Little Bright Eyes, did I say?"

"Strangulation! How dreadful."

"Not too bad, actually. There are worse ways."

"Was she . . . was she on the sofa . . . ?"

"They found her slumped on the floor. She struck her head
on a brass hearth rail, going down, and—" Ritchie checked
himself. "You can fill in for yourself, I imagine."

"Her head . . ." Margaret shuddered. "I don't want to think about it! And it couldn't have been the man I saw."

"The police won't agree. Reading between the lines, I'd say they were only picking up the boy as a front until a real lead turns up."

"But Ritchie, it couldn't have been the man I saw. There's some terrible, terrible mistake—some sort of mix-up in time, maybe. Or do you suppose some other man could have come into the flat later? He simply couldn't have done it!" It burst from Margaret vehemently. "He was too—too decent looking, too—"

"Too clean-cut and upstanding a sort?" Richard was jeering tolerantly. "You haven't gotten around enough in this naughty world, my dear innocent babe. The Little Lord Fauntleroys can turn into killers like that"—Richard snapped his fingers —"given sufficient provocation. So can any man, if he happens to blow his top. You'd be surprised."

"No, Ritchie, no—you are all wrong." Margaret was indignantly, fiercely defensive now. "Little Lord Fauntleroy. I never heard anything so silly. He wasn't like that at all. If you'd seen him—I can't describe him, but a top Englishman —truly top—you could tell. . . ."

"Wore an Old School tie, did he? A toff, eh, what?"

"Laugh at me all you like; but you are wrong, you are wrong." Her voice shook with inexplicable rebelliousness. "And I shan't listen to you. He couldn't have done it. And don't keep saying he did."

Ritchie's teasing stopped abruptly. "What's got into you, sweet? Simmer down. Lord, you're white! I'm a dog not to realize this could be a jolt, you in on a murder! Of all the damnedest twists. Hang on, and I'll bring you more coffee."

He raced off, and as the boat plowed steadily downstream through the gray, strong tide that washed the stone pilings of arched bridges, Margaret sat with tightly clenched hands, fighting a sudden nausea and shrinking from the remembrance of herself at a hotel window.

"In on a murder . . ." She repeated it unbelievingly. "A murder. And I stared, and stared, and made up a play, and enjoyed myself, while it was being planned. And I . . . I liked the man."

The nausea worsened. With morbid, dreadful curiosity she wondered if death had been unbearably painful for the Duclair woman. Ritchie had said there were worse ways, but. . . . How long after the curtains had been drawn had the man looked down at her, slumped on the carpet, in her green pajamas?

A discolored, swollen face? A bruised temple? Blood . . . ? Oh, wretched, wretched luck, to possess an imagination . . . the champagne glass, fallen from her hand, lying on the carpet, too? Champagne, and a trickle of blood, mingling . . . and he, standing there . . .

Margaret refused the coffee when Ritchie came hurrying back. "I'd disgrace you if I tried to drink it. I'd be sick. I know I'm acting like a baby, but—" She stopped to draw a deep, unsteady breath of sharp, bracing air. "Will they hang the boy . . . or whoever did it?"

"It's not likely. Capital punishment is on the way out in England. But he'll get prison; a dose of that'll be worse, to my mind, than any gallows."

Margaret drew another deep breath and then another. The boat reached the Greenwich landing before she could announce cautiously, "Everything seems to be under control, I think." She attempted a wan smile. "It serves me right. The number of murder stories I've lapped up."

"But you've a weak stomach when it comes to violence in real life? No need for apologies, though. You've got lots of company, I expect. Which doesn't mean you ought to take this so to heart, sweet. It's just a couple of strangers involved, after all. None of it any skin off your hide. And there's also the chance you've had a nasty knock for nothing; we'll buy a paper when we get ashore, and then look in a telephone book and check that address on Mount Street. A laugh, if you'd focused those glasses on two other Mount Street champagne drinkers!"

"Not a laugh—I'd thank heaven!"

But ten minutes later there was no doubt about the proximity of Honorine Duclair's flat to Margaret's hotel, and Ritchie had to lead her forcefully through a door that announced The Bell and Anchor was fully licensed.

"Sit down. You're going to have a brandy."

"I loathe brandy."

"Don't argue, paleface. Now drink up."

She sipped obediently, and even gratefully. She mightn't like the taste, or the fumes, but perhaps certain horrors would recede a little. But no food, positively. It would gag her.

Ritchie ate the beefsteak and kidney pie and drank his bitter ale, and then they walked along over cobbles to the palace and the museum, and while Ritchie had his interview with the curator, Margaret wandered up and down between rows of uniformed dummies in glass cases, and looked at Nelson's cocked hat and his baby shirt, and at cannon and ship models and swords and battle flags, blankly and unobservantly.

The man in the flat—he was all she could see. The man who had handed the wine glass to the woman in the green brocade Oriental pajamas. The Englishman she had thought about and thought about, time and again, since that hot, fateful night.

The impelling Englishman, pulling her further and further along so curious a path. The one man in London out of all Londoners, magnetizing her. The one man, anywhere . . .

Ritchie joined her at the end of an hour, and they sauntered back to the docks, where Richard inspected a sandwich stand dubiously. "A ham and mustard, Mag? A raisin bun? I don't imagine so." She ought to eat, though, he maintained concernedly; nothing helped more than to eat when you felt rotten, and just because the Duclair woman was dead, there was no point running around all hollow inside.

"Don't joke. It sounds hard as nails, Ritchie."

"I am hard, Mag. A man gets that way, kicking around, and on his own. And I've got a hide that would make a rhinoceros look like a complexion-soap ad." Richard looked down at Margaret, and his smile was sober and sorry. "Some of it is your fault, you know. If you'd let me stick close—taken me in hand."

"The influence of a good woman?" Margaret laughed and gave his arm a quick little squeeze. "Dear old Ritchie. And just where would you be now if I'd hung on to your coattails? Not on top. You would have been much too busy playing house with me."

"A lot of fun, I should think. But the top *is* nice, once you get there. Some climb! But I made it, by God . . ."

"The view is worth it?"

"It's worth the world."

They boarded their boat, and Margaret was again drawing in deep breaths of air. The wind was sharper, the sky and the sea were even more bleakly gray than earlier, and huddled in her coat, she stood by the rail, uncommunicative and withdrawn, her eyes on the city's darkly etched outline.

Huge, sooty, city of stone, so old, old, and having pulled her to it from home all those miles away, what was it offering now? Nothing but disillusionment. Even worse, a sick revulsion.

Evil so close and so unrecognizable, that night. Ugliness, sordidness—and she blind to it, and refusing, even now, to open her eyes.

Cold, gray London, swallowing up people, allowing people to be lost, one from another.

Oh, for some sun! And no more of this chill in her bones. This strange, unwholesome, morbid chill.

A ticket to the Mediterranean, that was what she would buy, a plane ticket, to sun and blue, blue water, with London and a flat on Mount Street left behind and forgotten. So easy. By tomorrow, if she chose.

The boat had passed under Tower Bridge in a churning of tide water, dirty with yellowed, oily foam and the flotsam and jetsam of ships and tankers and barges, and was heading toward the Westminster pier, when Ritchie, previously as silent as she, and smoking another cigarette, broke in on her unhappy, depressed musings.

"Still upset? Aren't you taking the thing much, much too seriously? You're a big girl now; it's time you learned that if you stumble over something ugly, you've got to give it a good swift boot out of your way. Yes, yes, I know murder isn't pleasant, but once I've taken you to the Yard and you've made your statement, the whole thing will be finished, done with, as far as you are concerned. So don't you see? Honest, Mag, it's just not that important—"

"My statement?" Margaret looked at him bewildered. "You weren't serious?"

"Certainly I was serious."

"No, no, Ritchie. I don't want to—"

"Like hell you don't want to!" It exploded from Ritchie. "You'd let that French kid they're holding run the risk of coming up for trial at Old Bailey, with you standing by, not opening your mouth? Of all the—" With an effort he reined in his indignation. "You don't know what you're saying, Mag. You're crazy. You can't do that to the boy."

"You said yourself the police aren't sure. And they can find out for themselves. They don't need my help."

Margaret stated it flatly, and with finality, but Ritchie reached for one of her hands. "You know you don't mean a word of it, sweet. And I wish you didn't look so undone. Frightened, are you? The police aren't bogeymen." He might have been calming an alarmed child. "All you need do is tell the Yard exactly what you told me—that you saw a man, not a boy, in the Duclair woman's flat, late Tuesday night—or Wednesday morning, technically. That's all you know, and that's all they'll be interested in. What the devil is your objection?"

"It's—" Margaret floundered. "It's—" Hurriedly she tried to supply a reasonable, plausible excuse. "The publicity. The papers. The photographers. It will all get back to Baltimore."

"Rot. You aren't that important. At most, you'd get an AP line or two that ninety-nine out of a hundred people won't ever see."

"They'll drag me into court." Margaret stumbled along, lamely. "I'd die if I had to get up in public and say I'd been staring—peeping—"

"Don't be an idiot. What if you were staring?" Ritchie asked it impatiently. "The break of a lifetime for that French kid, I can tell you, that you had those glasses of yours handy."

"It's no use, Ritchie. I shan't make a statement, and I don't want to talk about it any more." Margaret's eyes were defiant, her lips set. Ritchie looked at her with curiosity.

"You really mean you aren't going to lift a finger for that boy? I wouldn't have thought it of you. And incidentally you're leaving me in a fine spot; you can hardly expect me to keep my mouth shut."

"Do what you like." Margaret flung it at him. "Run to Scotland Yard, if that's the way you feel; but I'm not going. Not unless I have to. Not unless you interfere, and I'm dragged there. Oh, Ritchie, Ritchie, keep out of it. Please, won't you let it drop?" Her eyes searched his distressedly. "Don't look so—

so righteous. So conscientious. It's not the least bit your affair. Oh, if only I'd had sense enough to keep still. I wish I'd never said a word."

"So do I. I don't enjoy being disappointed in you, Mag. Or ashamed of you, I ought to say."

She was ashamed, too, and yet she *must* keep silent for a while, anyway. Already she had done harm enough.

The launch came alongside the wharf. When it was made fast, they stepped out onto the planking and climbed the landing stairs to the street level. Ritchie waved down a cab.

"You take it. I'm walking, thank you," Margaret told him stiffly.

"Being a little childish, aren't you? It's blocks and blocks to your hotel."

"I enjoy walking."

"Have it your own way."

Ritchie shrugged and got into the cab.

And Margaret started off, her back straight, her head high. All she could think of was a tall Englishman, walking with a stick, and a young French boy.

"Just a kid," Ritchie had put it. A pathetic, foolish boy, running after an actress years older than himself. The woman, with her white skin and in those narrow, slit-legged, fitted pajamas had looked to be what—in her late thirties?

And if the police changed their minds, if his alibi didn't hold up, they would put the boy away for life.

No. Not that. She was letting her imagination run away with her again. She was exaggerating. There wouldn't be life imprisonment unless evidence could be piled on evidence against him. But he'd come to trial, all the same. He was certain to be tried; so far, whom else did the police have for a suspect? No one—yet.

A boy, a mere boy. His whole future would be ruined, even if he was dismissed from the courtroom by a verdict of "Not

Guilty." A lack of circumstantial evidence would get him off. There would be a smear, though; there would be notoriety, like a brand.

Nothing could be more unfortunate. Awful for him. But surely, before things went that far, the police would find whoever had really done the murder. And just as surely, clever Scotland Yard didn't need her help. Though if they did, if she were convinced they did . . . There must have been clues, left behind by—by whoever it was that murdered Honorine Duclair, strangled her.

Thought of the French boy and the tall Englishman was something she could not walk away from, and it still plagued her when she had crossed the Horse Guards Parade and the Mall and cut through the cobbled stableyard of St. James's Palace. She was shivering as she came onto Piccadilly, and then told herself firmly that the shiver was only because of the raw chill of this gray, bleak city built of grimy stone and brick and plaster and stucco.

At her hotel on Carlos Place she stopped at the porter's desk to ask for a theater ticket. "Something for this evening, please. Something light."

Any play at all would do so long as it made her forget the French boy who was going on trial for murder, she was thinking as she rode up in the lift to her room. She would be thankful if it made her forget the Englishman, too. Forget his quiet, resolved expression, when he had limped to the damask sofa with a wine glass in his hand. Forget how, when the glass was offered, he had reached out and drawn crimson curtains close.

Obtuse Ritchie—but thank heaven, with all your heart, for that same obtuseness. Would the true reason for her halting, fabricated excuses, her adamant refusal to testify in the French boy's favor dawn on him eventually?

Never. There wasn't the slightest danger of it. Not in a thousand years would he suspect her of that swift, bewildering determination to protect the man she had stared at through her opera glasses. He would no more suspect it than he would ever, ever, be able to understand her instinctive, unshakable belief that the man was not a murderer. A murderer? It just wasn't possible. It simply was out of the question.

Ritchie would never dream she could be so absurd, take so quixotic a stand. An unbalanced stand, from his viewpoint. Or, at best, stupidly ridiculous. Cheap, even. Was that what she was, cheap?

It would seem so, if she were honest and made a thorough examination, a careful analysis of her private daydreams lately, her nighttime reveries. And even the loneliest of women could not be excused for romanticizing to such a maudlin extent.

A complete stranger, a man she had seen only through opera glasses. She had better take herself in hand. Yes, and without delay. It was a sincere self-admonishing. Margaret meant every word of it. But before she took off her street clothes and started to change for the theater, she telephoned down to the desk.

The evening papers sent up, please. Which—? All of them. Sitting on the edge of her bed she waited for a bellboy's knock at her door. In one or another of the papers there would be a further account of the Mount Street strangling. In one or another, perhaps in all, more about the murderer.

The wait was endless. Margaret began to move restlessly around the room, straightening the magazines on a table, picking up an emery board to smooth fingernails that didn't need it. When at last she heard the thud of the lift stopping she hurried out into the corridor.

"Thank you." She snatched at the papers. "I'll want all the morning editions sent up, too. Early. As soon as they're out."

Back in her room she tore open copy after copy. Being late
to the theater meant nothing.

A few lines, somewhere. Even a single line. But something.
Let there be something.

THREE

The telephone was ringing insistently. Margaret, finished with a leisurely breakfast, and in a white crepe lace-trimmed slip, her comb in her hand, hesitated before she turned from the dressing-table mirror to answer. It was certain to be Ritchie.

Reluctantly, she picked up the receiver. Exactly what she had dreaded—Ritchie interfering, Ritchie being difficult.

". . . and I've made an appointment for you." It was stated with infuriating calmness and with total disregard for anyone's viewpoint but his own.

"That's inexcusable of you, Ritchie. I told you—"

"You couldn't possibly have meant all that tripe. Good God, haven't you got it through your head yet that the boy will get off in five minutes once you speak up? How would you like to be in his shoes, implicated in a murder mess, when you've had nothing at all to do with it?" The calmness at the other end of the telephone wire took on impatience and a hint of heat. "Murder isn't exactly a laughing matter, you know,

Mag. You're in this up to your neck, and you've got to realize it."

"But I told you—"

"Telling me isn't what counts. It's telling the authorities. And if you have any doubts about who you saw, man or boy, you're going to have a chance for a second good look, to help make up your mind. The French kid will be repeating his story at the Yard this morning, and if you're in the parking lot at the entrance gate when they bring him from the precinct station, you'll see him."

"The parking lot? How can the public use Scotland Yard's parking lot? No one would let me in to begin with, and besides—"

"You can't crawl out of it that way, Mag. They'll let you in, all right. And I'll come around for you at eleven sharp. The Yard is expecting you. I gave them your name and outlined the whole business."

So it was out of her hands. In a way, Margaret was relieved. She had known that she must do something about the boy. Nothing was worse than indecision, she conceded, privately, nothing was more exhausting. A long night of tossing had been wretched. And she wanted to do the right thing. She knew she did, in her heart. Bless Ritchie, actually, for taking a load off her. Only he should not have been so high-handed. She would have decided to speak in her own good time, without his prodding. Was she certain of that, though? Quite certain?

She began folding the pages of half a dozen newspapers that were scattered, open on her bed. Nothing new last evening, and now nothing new this morning. Nothing she was looking for. Just the same story, cut to fewer lines. ". . . strangled . . . a severe contusion on the left temple."

She was quiet, a little distant with Ritchie when he met her at the lift door and helped her into a cab, and after a glance at her face he made no attempt at conversation as they drove toward the Embankment. Just as they reached the entrance to Scotland Yard he consulted his watch, and at his order, the driver pulled up inside the gates a little to the right of the main door, and it was then that Ritchie put a hand over one of Margaret's and held it firmly when she tried to pull it away.

"Ready? They'll be bringing him along any minute. You'll be able to see him full face, and you'll see him walk. Take your time about it. This is the big moment. And remember, it's important. It's big stuff." Richard's voice was quietly serious. "A hell of a lot depends on you, Mag. Life or death —a living death—and I'm not fooling."

A police car drove through the gates seconds after his grim, factual reminder. Margaret's heart began to pound uncomfortably. She had to force herself to sit forward on the cab seat for a careful scrutiny.

An officer and then a boy got out of the police car. A boy, in truth, Margaret saw. A pathetic, white-faced boy who looked as though he had not had a night's sleep since the murder in Mount Street, and whose big, liquid eyes were full of shock and fright.

He was slight and short, with a head of thick, curly black hair, worn too long, and brilliantined. A rather stupid-looking boy, an unengaging adolescent as unlike as could be to the man she had seen in Honorine Duclair's drawing room.

Richard was studying her face as she sat back in the cab, her silence telling him all he needed to know.

"It wasn't he? You are positive?"

Margaret nodded, saying nothing.

"Then come along. We'll go in now. Of all the lucky kids!"

Richard took Margaret's arm when they had gotten out of the cab. He gave their names at the Yard door and they were admitted into a severe, repressive hall, and ushered by a constable to a hard bench. They had a long ten minutes' wait while Richard twirled his hat in his hands and looked at Margaret now and again. She was still silent.

The boy would go free, she was reflecting, her thoughts curiously torn. The shattered-looking boy who, whether or not you liked his looks, had innocently been caught in a net of sordidness and terror. In five minutes he would go free, Ritchie had said. Well, technically not five minutes, but soon, anyway.

The tall man, limping a little, with a stick, whom she couldn't seem to forget no matter how hard she tried, would be the wanted one now, thanks to the testimony she'd be making all too soon.

Curious and troubling, out of all proportion, to so deeply regret that a choice between them had been inescapable.

One or the other, a murderer. And after all, she did have a conscience. She had to help the young French boy. Dreadful, though, the feeling of having stabbed the limping Englishman in the back. She could imagine his eyes, sorry and surprised, just before she betrayed him.

Could she somehow find the courage to get up from this bench and walk away? They couldn't force her to talk, if she chose not to, the "they" who were Scotland Yard. She wasn't a criminal. She couldn't be held. And now was the time to walk away.

Margaret half rose, but Ritchie was standing also. The constable was beckoning, authoritatively. They followed him into a lift and then along another hall and into a small, plainly furnished room that looked out on stone cornices and window ledges smeared and gummed with the droppings of gray gulls. Beyond was the cold river, wind-whipped and scummed with dirty white foam, and noisy with the whistling and tooting of tugs and barges and launches, the deep long blasts of cargo vessels.

Two old-fashioned, cumbersome oak desks crowded the room. A police sergeant was typing at one. At the other a mild-looking, middle-aged man, tilting back in a swivel chair, frowned, consideringly, while he absentmindedly stretched the rubber band he had slipped from a bundle of papers.

My dossier, Margaret thought. The records. Already, the case has begun. "The Case of the Man in the Window." Already, they are lined up against him. Because I have given him away. I wish he knew how I regret it. I hope he knows I couldn't help it.

The mild-looking man had gotten to his feet.

"Mrs. Collier? Mr. Page?"

"Yes," Richard answered for them both, crisply.

"I am Inspector Downs, and this is Sergeant Dickson, who will take your statement, Mrs. Collier. I understand you have some information for us regarding the Duclair murder. Correct?"

"Yes, Inspector. Mrs. Collier happened to be—" Again it was Ritchie answering.

"I'll hear from Mrs. Collier herself, please. Would you get on with it, Mrs. Collier?"

"I was at my hotel window." Margaret's cheeks flamed as she went on. "I . . . I was looking through my opera glasses. . . ."

When she had finished, the Inspector was still stretching his rubber band into cat's cradles. "Hmm . . . Interesting. Very. Not the French lad, at all? I hardly thought so. Tell me, Mrs. Collier, would you recognize the man in the flat if you saw him again?"

"Yes." With an effort, she brought it out. "That is—I think so."

"Not a distinctive type, was he?"

The sergeant's hands paused on the typewriter keys, waiting. Margaret's answer was evasive, barely audible. "I—I only saw him for a moment."

"But you can give me some sort of description?" The Inspector asked it without emphasis. "For instance, what color was his hair, Mrs. Collier?"

"I—I'm not sure."

"Black, brown, blond, red, gray? It would be a help if you could remember."

"There was some gray—I think." The typewriter keys clicked. "I—I could be mistaken. I told you, I only saw him for a moment."

"So you are not entirely positive about the gray, is that it? What about his height? Was he short, or tall, or average, would you say?"

"Tall. Very tall." It was said before she could catch it back.

"And the color of his eyes? You were not close enough to see, I fancy."

"No."

"There was nothing in any way out of the ordinary about his general appearance? No blemishes, no scars, nothing of that sort?"

"No."

"That's all then, Mrs. Collier, if you'll just look over your statement. And if we may have your signature . . ."

Margaret took the typed sheet the sergeant handed her. She had not said anything about lameness, about a stick. Should she? She couldn't. . . .

Inspector Downs had dipped a pen in a Victorian silver inkwell. He presented it to her and a little hurriedly she signed her name.

"Thank you, Mrs. Collier. And that young Frenchman will thank you, too, I'll wager, when he hears what you've done for him. He's not a bad sort. A love-sick puppy with too much money to spend, but this scare will straighten him out. It's been a stiff lesson."

"How did he get mixed up with the Duclair woman?" Ritchie asked. "Out of his depth, wasn't he?"

"Very much so. As I got it, he saw her dance in Paris and followed her here and took to hanging about the stage door at the Viceroy. Apparently it amused her to play him for a while, and then she got tired of him and tossed him out. It was her dresser at the theater who gave us the tip the boy might have had ideas. Our picking him up was more or less of a gesture. The inflamed young Latin who just might be guilty. But the woman had a number of men after her, and we'll sieve them all in due course."

"And come up with the right one fast, I wouldn't be surprised," Ritchie commented. "You Yard gentlemen have acquired quite a reputation, Inspector."

"We do well enough." The Inspector pushed a buzzer on his desk. "Before the constable shows you out, Mrs. Collier, just one thing more. May I see your passport?"

Margaret opened her bag. The Inspector thumbed through the little green book she gave him and returned it when he had written a number on a pad of paper.

"On holiday?" he questioned pleasantly. "How long will you be stopping in England?"

"I'm not sure. I haven't any real plans."

"You'll let us know, will you, before you leave? A matter of routine, you understand, our wanting to keep in touch with you."

"Yes, of course."

Margaret's response was nervously quick.

The Law and the Crown. No one could escape their reach, their grasp, not even the most innocent of persons, such as

she. Innocent except for her sin of omission, her leaving out
any mention of lameness and that stick.

They would get it out of her if they wanted badly enough.
No one could stand up against them for long.

A murderer would not have the slightest chance of escap-
ing prison. It was a stark fact made clear as day in this small,
unimpressive room, and with the mild-appearing man opposite her somehow managing to underscore it as he played
with his rubber band.

The buzzer brought the constable, and Margaret followed
him to the lift, wondering if she looked as guilty and afraid
as she felt, and then she and Ritchie were outside the building and through the gate, walking toward Whitehall. Ritchie
took Margaret's arm again.

"Not bad at all, was he?" he asked cheerfully. "I knew it
wouldn't amount to a row of pins."

"It will be horrible if they find the man I saw. Horrible . . ."

"Picturing yourself on the witness stand in Old Bailey, are
you? You're in a stew about nothing, Mag. At most they'd ask
you to sit in when they parade him in the identification room.
But say I'm all wrong about it; say they do bring you into
court. What of it? The point is, you've done the only decent
thing, speaking up. I know you too well, Mag sweet. You'd
hate yourself, keeping shut. Let's forget it all now, and have
lunch."

"Lunch doesn't interest me. I'm not hungry."

"Nonsense. I've reserved a table at the Berkeley Buttery.
How does Dover sole strike you, and a bottle of Chablis?"

"If you'd just listen, Ritchie. I'm not hungry. And anyway,
you've been much too extravagant this week. All the lunches
and dinners and plays, and going dancing—"

"You've got a plutocrat in tow, darling. I'm rolling. The

best sellers and a Hollywood sale, to say nothing of a syndicated column. I've got it made."

"And you're enjoying every penny of it?"

"Why wouldn't I? Lord, when I look back. Hog meat and hominy, in a manner of speaking. Served up on what was left of Great-granny Page's company dishes. I hated being poor. Poor and proud. The family always trying to keep up a front, and always on the fringe of everything. And when you think I'm slated as guest speaker at a Royal Naval College lunch that's coming up this summer—"

"Which means the most, the money or being a celebrity?"

"It's even-Steven. You won't catch me giving up either. I'm riding high, and nothing—and no one—is going to knock me out of the saddle."

"You were always sure of yourself. I envy that."

"I still am. A great thing, self-confidence. The greatest, possibly. Let's talk about food, though. We've got sauce to decide on, and dessert. Melon, or an ice, do you think, or something vulgarly nouveau and splendid, rolled up to our table, flaming?"

He was amusing; in spite of herself, Margaret was diverted. And he was strong, too, a quality she admired.

When they were seated at their very choice table and Ritchie had discussed the sole with an attentive waiter and a light white wine with the sommelier, who knew him by name, he turned his attention to Margaret.

"There. That's done. Now let's talk about marriage. Ours. When are we going to take the plunge? Tomorrow—if I can get a special license?"

"Silly. I'm not ready to marry anyone. I've made up my mind on that subject and I've no intention of changing it, so you might as well save your breath trying to talk me into anything different."

"I'll never change my mind either. And what I want, I get. Nothing has stopped me yet."

"Obstacles don't count?"

"No, frankly. They can be hurdled. By the way, to digress a moment, I like that bonnet of yours. Very nice. I'm glad you wear hats. I wouldn't want my wife going around with her hair looking like a haystack or lacquered like a Japanese doll's."

"As I'm not your wife yet, and probably shan't be, ever, as I've said before, it's not terribly vital to me whether you appreciate my hats or not. But thanks for the compliment anyway."

"We'd have some good laughs and an all-around bang-up time of it together if we were married, Mag. Why not break down and say Yes? You like me. You like me more than a little. And you'll be sorry one of these days, when you wake up and find yourself a lonely old woman."

"There's no immediate danger. Anyway, I'd rather be the loneliest woman in the world than marry again unless I fell in love—terribly in love."

"Waiting for something big to come along, are you, the all-out, smasheroo stuff?"

"I'd give anything for it to happen that way." Margaret looked wistful as she took off her gloves and unfolded her napkin. "Just once, before it's too late."

"Just once?" Richard asked pointedly. "It wasn't that way with you and Allen then? I've wondered."

"Allen was the finest, kindest man in the world." Margaret declared it with quick loyalty. "And I miss him. There's not a day I don't miss him."

"That doesn't answer my question, Mag."

"It's none of your affair."

"I suppose not. But tell me something. Where do you expect to find this fellow you've dreamed up, this wonderful guy who is going to make you go all dewy-eyed over him?"

"I don't expect to find him anywhere."

"But you believe in holding the thought, is that it?"

"You can make fun of me all you like." Margaret laughed. "It's not worth a quarrel. And now, Mr. Ritchie Page, as long as our fish is here, I'd like to stop arguing and start eating before it gets cold."

"Go ahead—though I thought you weren't hungry? Fall to, my little trencherwoman; you shall have your lunch, with further quizzing about your naïve hopes and dreams postponed, for the nonce. But let me ask you this: Could you look me in the eye and honestly say you have forgotten a lilac thicket behind that broken-down, deserted old summerhouse in my mother's garden that we used to call 'our place'? Could you say we weren't in love?"

"In love! We were nothing but children."

"A stock remark of yours lately, but as I recall it, we were growing up rather fast toward the end, weren't we? Or need I jog your memory?"

Margaret blushed, vividly.

"So you haven't forgotten? And I'm a cad, am I, to cause the lady's face to turn bright red? Cad. I like the word. Short and to the point, no matter how outdated."

"You are impossible—as I've told you before."

"I'd have taken on the Marine Corps single-handed to keep you that last summer. Or a pack of wild cats. What was the real reason, Mag?"

"I told you then I didn't know. It had to stop, that was all."

"You could have made something out of me, Mag."

"You have made something out of yourself, haven't you?"

"Hmm—yes. Yes, as a matter of fact, I have. In my own inimitable way. But if you'd—"

"That's enough, Ritchie." Margaret's smile softened her warning. She began to make conversation about inconsequentials, with a careful avoidance of any more references to the

past, and Ritchie, she saw with relief, was amenable enough
to let her have her way.

If only he wouldn't look at her as though he wanted to eat
her up. If only he weren't the sort of man whose hands a
woman could imagine touching her, even if they were deep
in his pockets, or tied behind his back!

When lunch was over, he put down his coffee cup and
announced he must go back to his flat and his desk.

"Where may I drop you, Mag?" he asked as she picked up
her bag and gloves.

"Don't bother, Ritchie. I'm going to wander. I'll probably
wind up as usual in Shepherd Market, poking through all the
lovely junk in the antique shops."

"Until this evening, then. You are having dinner with me,
you know."

"Ritchie, I'm not—"

"Oh, yes you are."

He flashed the irresistible smile she remembered so well.
"Eight o'clock, and wear that black, floaty rag you wore the
other evening that I liked so much."

"Honestly, Ritchie—can't a woman choose her own
clothes?"

"Do as you're told. No back talk. And be ready at eight."

"Ritchie . . . !"

"The black number, Mag. I'm counting on it. It 'sends me,'
as they say in the vernacular. Really sends me, baby."

Margaret was laughing when he jumped into a cab. You
had to laugh when you were with Ritchie. It had always been
that way.

They had laughed together in the lilac thicket, even when
they had exchanged the first of those kisses, when her inex-
perience and his had caused them to bump noses, and miss
one another's mouth. Eventually, their aim had improved.

She had known, in those days, that she would never forget

what white lilac smelled like—all around her in that concealing world of white blossoms in spring, nor the smell of green,
heart-shaped leaves, powdered over with dust or wet with
rain in full summer.

Together, there, she and Ritchie had been close in thunder-
showers. In Ritchie's arms, her heart had beaten fast. But it
wasn't the thunder that had frightened her, it was Ritchie's
persistence. Ritchie was the one who already had grown up.
The last time he had kissed her, on an afternoon toward the
end of that lovely summer before he went away for always,
she had learned a good deal about boys.

To have been so young . . . Margaret's reminiscent smile
was a little pitying.

Ritchie had crushed his mouth on hers. Held her too tightly,
too close.

"If you think I'll ever let anyone else come along . . . let
anyone else ever kiss you . . . if anyone did . . ."

She had tried to push him away.

It was only when she began to cry that he let her go.

Left alone in the quiet, leafy tent, she had cried her eyes
out, an overwrought child, frightened and ashamed by her
half-knowledge of what she had stirred in Ritchie and Ritchie
had stirred in her.

After that, Ritchie, furious, hurt, proud Ritchie, hadn't
come near her again. Within days he had enlisted for his
army service—a wonder it wasn't the Foreign Legion—instead
of finishing college and waiting to be drafted, which would
have been sensible. But who ever had expected the entirely
sensible from Ritchie? After that, there had been New York
and his years on a newspaper. Then, at home, in Baltimore,
and everywhere else, people had begun to hear about him.
The reckless, outspoken correspondent and columnist, here,
there, and everywhere, sending in his reports on all the
troubled parts of the world, all the places there was turbu-

lence and violence. You were apt to read his coverage of the Olympics, too, or his witty writing up of a Dublin Horse Show, or of French road races. And now, amazingly, a terrific talent for turning out books.

As for her, in those few short years that exciting, amusing, brilliant Ritch had crowded so full to overflowing . . . ? Nothing but college and parties and a foolish little time-killing job selling clothes, and then Allen.

He was the antithesis of Ritchie. Perhaps that was why she had married him, or because he and his family and her family had wanted it so much; perhaps because so many girls of her circle had already become brides in white satin. Certainly some of all that had entered into it. And their marriage had worked —to a point. Allen had been devoted and kind. Allen had thought only of her. Allen had believed in carrying a wife on a cushion.

Whenever Ritchie had come to mind he had seemed, in comparison, a rough, headstrong, passionate boy with whom she could never have been happy.

Walking along, looking into shop windows, opening her purse to buy the little luxuries, the small treasures she could never resist, Margaret remembered her husband with affectionate gratefulness, and with the glad, conscience-free knowledge that she had made him contentedly, quietly happy.

And she had been reasonably content herself. It was just that—just that . . . She couldn't make up her mind that it should be Ritchie, attractive to her though he was now, all over again, but if there could only be someone. . . .

She'd want a life with more meaning to it, if another chance came her way. A less marshmallowy life than she had led with Allen, sometimes wondering if she had lost her true self for ever in the fluffed-up nothingness.

How spoiled she had been! How little she had given of herself. Committee meetings. Board meetings. There had been plenty of those, and she had been the girl who sold the most tickets for the hospital ball and the girl who wrote the biggest check for every charity—or whose husband did. That was the extent of it.

Was it entirely her fault? Not all. She had simply been what Allen wanted her to be. Now and then she had worried —as she still did—about her purposeless, useless life. No one had ever really needed her. Not even Allen. She had allowed him to mold her to his ideal of a conventionally satisfactory wife, but almost any other pretty, nice girl with the same background as hers would have suited him as well.

Not to be needed. It meant a perpetual state of hanging, detachedly, in space. Perhaps it would have been different if they had had a child. But Allen had been determined that their children would come later. And there had been no later after all.

Oh, to be everything to someone. And not because of her face and figure that meant so much to Ritchie in the old days, and that meant so much now; not because you were the malleable wife material that had been important to Allen; but because the essential *you* had value.

There was a dreamer for you. . . .

FOUR

It was not too difficult to dismiss the Englishman from her thoughts. Margaret admitted it to herself one afternoon a few days later as she sauntered with Ritchie along Albemarle Street. She had given in, she was allowing Ritchie to monopolize her, and she was enjoying his persistence. In other words, Ritchie had become a delightful habit that she had no immediate intention of breaking.

Such a really satisfactory escort. How extremely pleasant, for instance, to have him notice and approve the new brown suit she was wearing that had arrived only that morning from Norman Hartnell, and the brown satin cloche that did so much for her. All the small but vastly important attentions, too, such as the lily of the valley spray that was pinned to her small sable neckpiece.

"I like my heartthrob dressy," he had announced as he took her around to a flower shop in South Audley Street. "I like the all-prettied-up look."

His heartthrob! Ridiculous of him. And that engaging smile, the quirk of those eyebrows. But she really mustn't let him get ideas. It wouldn't be fair. On the other hand, give thanks for him a thousand times over. What in the world would she have done without him to beau her around these past two weeks? The evenings, especially, would have been awful. Oh, of course, a woman alone in London could always dine at her hotel, and go to a play afterward by herself, conventionally enough—which might be satisfactory if you were an old lady, but . . .

Ritchie could get away from his desk in the daytime, too, pretty much as he chose, once his syndicated, weekly column was out of the way. Work on his current book could be fitted in at his convenience, too, he had said; authors went stale if they let their writing bully them. Nice for her, that relaxed viewpoint! Could anyone be better company on a London stroll?

Ritchie loved exploring out-of-the-way corners, an alley, a mews, a square, as much as he enjoyed Bond Street. He knew all the wonderful shops. He enjoyed long, serious discussions with the proprietors about old maps or stamps or military prints or guns, or about marmalade or mutton chops or Stilton cheese, for that matter.

Even buttons interested him—so long as they were British regimental tunic buttons. And displays of Victorian mechanical toys excited him wildly. "I've already got Wellington on his wind-up charger, but if I could come across Nelson's flagship, bucketing along over tin waves, with all sails set and the Union Jack flying, the ambition of my life would be fulfilled," he had said once, laughing, as they rummaged through the exciting rubbish of an open-air stall in Petticoat Lane.

Ritchie enjoyed strolling through picture galleries, too, which was more than could be said for a lot of men, Margaret thought when Ritchie stopped in front of a window to read the announcement of a showing.

"Eighteenth-century portraits. Let's have a look. I've got a bare wall or two in my flat, and an Army or Navy officer might be just the thing."

They walked into a small shop given over to pictures and antiques, and at first glance Margaret found the pictures of no particular interest. None of those lining the wall would be worth spending much time over; the artists had obviously been mediocre. The sort, probably, who had jogged on horseback through the shires with paints and canvas in a saddlebag, glad of lodgings and a few pounds in payment for their efforts.

Their subjects were typical; country squires posed stiffly with their dogs and horses, women with small simpering mouths and large bosoms, wooden-looking children in blue-sashed muslins or nankeen breeches, holding a flower or petting a tame rabbit or saying "Tweet-tweet" to a bird in an elaborate cage.

No naval or military subjects for Ritchie, and nothing special enough even as a conversation piece for her to consider buying or to glance at a second time. Except—except that one —the next to the last in the row.

Margaret stood, frozen, staring. The artist had painted a young man in riding clothes, crop in hand, with the Queen Anne facade of an old stone and brick manor house as background.

Dark hair grew back from his high temples and was caught at the nape of his neck with a black ribbon. A thin, bony nose lent hauteur and breeding to his narrow, dark face and gave it a strength that belied the curve of a mouth which hinted at tenderness, hinted at vulnerability.

The eyes? Dark gray? Smoke gray? Rain gray? London gray,

at any rate! Because he was the man in the flat, the man who had drawn close a pair of concealing crimson curtains.

It couldn't be. But it was. A younger man, yes, or seeming to be younger, but the same man. Without question the same man.

"Ritchie! Look! Ritchie, it's the man in the flat!"

It burst from her involuntarily as the first fiercely crashing wave of recognition broke over her, inundated her. The man in the flat. There was no retracting it. Realization of what she had cried out, and of consequences, came too late. Ritchie had already turned from a curio case and the pair of dueling pistols that had taken his eye, and was coming to stand beside her.

"The man in the flat?" He repeated it incredulously. "What was that, Mag? What did you say?"

"The portrait!"

"I don't get you, sweet."

The intensity of her stare drew his attention to the portrait, but only for a wondering but quick and superficial survey. Then, greatly amused, he put an arm around Margaret's shoulders, lightly.

"My adorable idiot! You and your Gentleman Friend, the West End toff! Still on your mind, is he? I thought I'd put in enough hard work lately to make you forget the whole unpleasant business. It's time you did, you know. There's no percentage in harping on things like that." His reproof was gentle, and then he was purposefully teasing Margaret. "Top Hat Johnny and this fellow here one and the same man? Sure, sure, why not? Honestly, Mag, now I've heard everything."

She was not listening. Her eyes were still fixed.

Ritchie glanced at her sharply, and then studied a printed card that was thumbtacked under the portrait.

" 'Portrait of a Gentleman,' " he read aloud. " 'Artist unknown. Price, seventy-five guineas.' Too bad he is nameless. It would simplify things a lot if we knew who he was, since you are so certain he dropped into that flat in Mount Street so recently."

His scrutiny was on Margaret again, even more sharply.

"You don't really think this is the same man? If you do, you'll end in a nut house."

"I know." Margaret laughed, weakly, and a little quickly. "I'm an idiot. A prize idiot." She forced herself to laugh again. "It was just at first—just something, when I looked— something about both men being dark. This one and—and the other." She swallowed. "They aren't a bit alike, actually. Not a bit." She reiterated it, emphatically. "And you are right, Ritchie, it's time I stopped thinking about—about the mur- derer—whoever he was."

"It most certainly is, if even coming across a dark-haired man in an old portrait is going to upset you."

Richard gave her shoulders another brief hug. "If you don't think you had me worried, going all glassy-eyed, and turning to stone!"

"I feel such a fool."

"Never mind. All is forgiven. And come look at these duel- ing pistols. They're beauties. I might just buy them, if the price is right."

"In a moment, Ritchie, as soon as I've gone down the line here."

Richard hurried back to the glass case and became engaged in conversation with the shop owner. The instant he left her Margaret's eyes were on the portrait again, her gaze riveted, her blood seeming to run faster, all her senses roused.

The man in the flat.

Ashamed and horrified, she knew herself to be far more drawn and fascinated than repulsed. The murderer. It was the only true word. The murderer. Or, as Ritchie would put it, the killer. A killer. And when he had slipped out of the flat, a woman lay slumped on the carpet.

That swollen, blackened face. The bruised head. The trickling blood. No—don't think of it.

But how could she stop thinking, and why wouldn't her stomach turn, when here, in front of her, the killer was again standing? How had he got there, in that gold frame, to draw her to him, to shackle her, all over again? Who was he, looking out at her with those compelling, enigmatic eyes that wouldn't let her go?

"Portrait of a Gentleman."

She read the gallery's stereotyped labeling, knowing an utter frustration.

"Portrait of a Gentleman." The tantalizing, maddening anonymity of it drove her gaze to the portrait again as though her straining, burning curiosity could drag an answer from the man who was watching her in unrelenting silence.

Was there something inscribed, faintly, at the top of the portrait? Yes. A name and a date were there, obscure, barely discernible, but there, in the upper right-hand corner of the age-darkened canvas, and not impossible to decipher for anyone who was sufficiently interested to look closely.

"Sir Hugh Vane. Monks' Court, Salop. Anno Domini 1780."

Now she knew. Guessing was at an end. But 1780? His portrait painted in 1780? Impossible. Why, it was only a week ago that she had seen him.

The absurdity of her protest almost made her laugh. An explanation was obvious, even though startling and astonishing. She must be staring at an ancestor of the man in the flat. But of course! By an amazing trick of coincidence the man in the flat was, to her eyes at least, the twentieth-century counterpart of the Georgian gentleman looking back at her.

Two Vanes; the phrase "Portrait of a Gentleman" could apply well enough to them both, but in one instance a tag reading "A possible murderer" would have to be affixed. The majority of people would think him that. . . .

Margaret's glance flew to Richard. Was he still engrossed in those dueling pistols, still talking to a salesman? Greatly hoping so, she brought her eyes back to the portrait.

Vane. His name was there for anyone to read. Anyone, she modified, who wanted to find it badly enough, who searched for it hard enough. The man in the flat would never be safe again if Ritchie's interest was roused ever so slightly.

How easily he could be traced now. She need only persuade Ritchie that what she had to say was worth listening to without scoffing. She need only point out the painted-on name, so faint but so damning, there on that old, cracked canvas.

A Vane. Look up that family name. Trace it, in whatever ramifications it might branch. Find a present-day Vane who had been in London on a certain night, and confront him.

Ritchie—and Scotland Yard—would know precisely how to go about the tracing, the pinpointing, the confrontation.

It wouldn't be a case of stabbing just Someone in the back, a sort of phantom Someone; not any longer. If she gave him away to Ritchie, if Ritchie chose to pay attention to her, she would have delivered a Someone who was flesh and blood into the hands of a judge and jury.

Ritchie had laughed at her just now, and if she called him over again, he would laugh even harder. But if he gave her time to explain carefully and make her point, he would listen. Ritchie had imagination. Ritchie would think it all a fantastic, incredible coincidence, but on second thought, he would see the excitement, the importance, of following up her crazy supposition for all it might be worth.

A family named Vane could be sorted out, investigated, interviewed.

Fun, that was what Ritchie would call the dreadful pursuit. Fun. And even if at first he didn't take the coincidence

too seriously, and balked at calling in Scotland Yard until such
time later as any developments might warrant, he would be
off on the scent himself, sniffing harder and running faster
than any policeman. What had he called himself? A reporter,
first, last, and always.

Who knew Ritchie better than she? Who better understood persistent, tenacious Ritchie, who never was willing to
let go, who never let obstacles stand in his way?

In a panic Margaret turned from the portrait. No more
lingering and staring and surmising. No more giving way to—
to charm—to magnetism. Ritchie might well think the portrait worth another look, curious as to why it claimed her
absorption, and he might well discover the lettering in that
upper right-hand corner. But she'd come back. Nothing could
keep her away.

Richard was reaching for his wallet and the dueling pistols
were being wrapped when she walked over to him. He had
forgotten the portrait, forgotten her exclamation, she saw,
thankfully; the Someone, whose name was Vane, had nothing at all to fear.

Albemarle Street was cold and blustery when they left the
shop, and people were putting up umbrellas against the first
splattering drops of a threatening downpour, and rushing to
queue for buses, and hailing cabs.

Richard was concerned for Margaret's new hat, and as he
hurried her along, with his pursuit of a taxi vain, her quietness, her preoccupation, went unnoticed by him until they
had reached Carlos Place and her hotel; but over tea in the
charming flower-filled drawing room, he asked, solicitously, if
she were tired.

"Not in the least. Why?" She was on the defensive at once.

"Not coming down with some sort of bug? One of those
virus things?"

The persistence she knew so well put her nerves on edge.

"I'm fine, thank you." She emphasized showing her annoyance. "Perfectly fine."

"You don't look it." The comment was blunt, and Richard's observant glance lingered. "How about a spot of rum in your tea for a bracer?"

She accepted the suggestion meekly. After the first cup of tea it was easier to make the imperative effort to chat and smile. You could not be too careful with anyone as quick and astute as Ritchie, not if you had something to keep to yourself. The carefulness proved exhausting. When Richard finally left and she went upstairs, her head was aching.

A long, difficult evening was in prospect; how would she ever get through cocktails and the theater and a late supper? It was her feeling of guilt, the weight of her knowledge, that was to blame for a splitting head; why not admit it? To tell Ritchie was the only right thing to do. Speaking up for that French youngster had been the only right thing, too, and hard as it had been, the relief, afterward, was worth it.

She would feel a hundred times better now if she spoke up again. Otherwise she would know herself to be over her head, morally and legally, in the deepest of murky waters. Couldn't she even be held for aiding and abetting a criminal if she did not give the name "Vane" to Ritchie and to Inspector Downs, and let them start their manhunt?

On impulse, Margaret reached for the telephone directory on her bedside table and began to turn the pages. Vane. Any number of them. No Sir Hugh Vane, though. But that didn't mean much. Sir Hugh Vane's riding crop, in the portrait, and the words "Monks' Court" plainly indicated the countryside. Where was Salop, though? North, south, east, west? A county, was it? A shire? For all she knew, it wasn't in England at all. It could be in Scotland or Wales. Or Ireland, or on the Isle of Man, or anywhere else in Great Britain.

She closed the directory and began to put out her clothes for the evening. When she bathed she did her hair, brushing it to a smooth gloss, knowing she was a little vain about its color and sheen, and taking pains with its arrangement. Agreeable to think that Ritchie—or any man, for that matter—would approve the result.

Before she went downstairs again in the frothy black chiffon that was Richard's favorite, she unpinned the wilting lilies of the valley from her suit jacket and put them in a glass of water from the bathroom. He was a darling to have bought them for her. Ritchie was altogether a darling man. And she? Soberly, Margaret regarded herself in the mirror. A neurotic, that was what she was, a neurotic with a well-deserved headache brought on by her own criminal and conscience-pricking avoidance of doing what was right.

Her mouth set stubbornly. A conscience could be controlled. All she need do was put her mind to it.

Cocktails at the Ritz bar, a play at the Haymarket, and supper at Mirabelle's went fairly well for her. Richard inquired again, tactlessly, if she was certain she felt entirely up to snuff, but she managed to answer him without snapping, and there were plenty of moments between them of good conversation and of laughter. Inwardly, Margaret congratulated herself now and again on her show of gaiety, her surface enjoyment. She even let him discuss the possibilities of finding a flat, not necessarily in London—no use getting in a rut—but any place in the world, when they chose to move on, which might be fun to do, before too long. A nice flat, suitable for a married couple who needn't worry too much about finances. Due, she was certain, to a very pleasant and extravagant champagne, she went so far as to express an interest in antiques when Richard inquired her taste in decor.

It was necessary then to snub him when he asked what her ideas were on double beds, but she could laugh, even when she was wondering if the evening would never end.

Eventually, when Richard had said good night at her hotel lift, and Margaret was in her room, she turned out the lights and went to the windows on Mount Street, and pushing aside the chintz curtains, looked out into the dark.

Where was he, where had he taken cover, the man who had made her his unwilling but fascinated captive? Whether or not his roots, his Vane family roots, were in the country, whether or not the limping, tall Englishman, the descendant of Sir Hugh Vane, was also a country squire, a present-day country squire, the fact remained that he had been in London for one night at least in the past week.

Out there, somewhere. He had all those streets and squares and crescents, those quiet mews, to hide in. He had those tall old houses for refuge, those clubs, looking out on Park Lane and St. James's Street and the Mall. He had the hotels, the flats, the shabby-genteel bed-sitting rooms, squalid lodgings along Cromwell Road, he had tenement rooms, like rat holes, along the wharves.

Here, in London? Deep in the countryside, somewhere? Where was he, the man who held her in bondage? Where?

FIVE

In the days preceding the visit to the Albemarle Street shop, it had become a pleasant certainty for Margaret, on awakening each morning, to know the telephone would ring. She had even begun to time her bath to avoid the rush to answer dripping and swathed in a towel.

Lovely, to have an attractive man interested in you. Terrific, to like the man, to like him very, very much. To be, in fact, on the brink— But would Richard's attentions mean quite so much to her, would they mean anything at all in the future, now that she had seen the portrait of Sir Hugh Vane? The question was worrying her when the telephone rang the morning after their supper at Mirabelle.

"How's my beautiful? In a bucolic mood, I trust, because we are going to have a picnic lunch on a bench in St. James's Park." Richard announced it authoritatively.

"Are we? You are giving Orders of the Day?"

"I am. The sun is out, in case you hadn't noticed. Nothing

exactly blistering about it, and you won't need dark glasses, but it's out. Though you'd better bring your umbrella, to play safe. And meet me at Fortnum's at twelve to help choose some food."

She gave in. But why not? she asked herself as she got in her tub. What else had she to do all day? One thing she had settled, lying awake until all hours: no weak, maudlin, shameful return to a shop where Sir Hugh Vane would look at her out of those dark-gray eyes.

She soaked, reflectively, and when she had dried herself on one of the hotel's big, soft towels, warm from its rack, and done her hair and put on a dressing gown, her mind was made up about something else.

No more telephoning down to the desk for a copy of every available paper, no more searching through feverishly while your breakfast tea got cold in hopes there would be some news about the Duclair case. Just a line. Just a tantalizing mention of him. Perhaps his name among a list of the Duclair woman's followers for her to single out, and guess about.

She contented herself with the London *Times* when it came up with her tray, and gave her entire attention to the Court Circular, ". . . the Queen at Windsor . . . Princess Margaret at a First Night . . . the Queen Mother, wearing blue lace, a blue, flowered hat, at a Horse Show. . . ."

Forget Sir Hugh Vane, and in putting the portrait out of mind, make it that much easier to forget his double. Try, at least. Make an honest effort.

She met Richard at noon, and assisted by elegant clerks in striped trousers and neat cravats, they bought lobster mayonnaise, a small crock of *pâté*, another of Stilton, salty biscuits, two apples, and a bottle of chilled white wine. All of it was packed for them in a wicker hamper fitted with plates and cups and cutlery and large linen napkins.

With Richard lugging it, they strolled the few blocks along Piccadilly and down St. James's Street and across the Horse Guards into the park where they found a bench by the lake. Pale but determined sunshine filtered down on them through the new green leaves of a tall elm tree.

Richard put down the hamper and opened it.

"Posh, eh what? And deuced expensive, old thing," he remarked with satisfaction as he began taking out plates.

"You really shouldn't . . ."

"It's worth the investment. We'll be using it often once the weather settles—if it ever does," he said. "We'll be tooting all over the place. Brittany, for instance. Or Austria."

"Quite the tour manager, aren't you? How you do love making plans for other people. And how can you leave London to go off on these delightful little excursions? Don't you ever work?"

"I work damn hard—in spurts. But I'm fed up on town at the moment. Oh, for the song of the cuckoo, tra-la, and all that sort of rot. Here, take your plate. Eat up. And try the wine."

"Speaking of the country, Ritchie," Margaret began as casually as she could, "speaking of getting out of town, where is a place called Salop? Did you ever hear of it?" She took a sip of wine. "Salop—S-a-l-o-p."

"It rings a bell. I'm not sure, though. Let me think. I've a vague idea it's another name for Shropshire. An old name. I don't know whether or not it's in use any more."

"I see. . . . And where is Shropshire?" Margaret sipped her wine again. "Near London?"

"No. Quite a stretch away. Up north. Why?"

"I was just wondering. There's so much English countryside I've never seen."

"We'll give it a look, some day. But there's a chance of better weather on the Continent, this time of year. By the way, did I tell you I have a new car? A beauty. A special order, bright red Jag."

"Heavens, Ritchie. Why bright red, of all colors?"

"Freud could explain it easily. Call it compensation for a toy automobile I asked for one Christmas and didn't get."

"And now it's a status symbol?"

"Right. A terrific, gaudy, unmistakable assurance to myself that in the end, what old Richard wants, Richard gets. You've always been up there, on top, since way back, don't forget, and naturally you take a different slant."

"Is the top the only thing that matters?"

"Yes. Well, almost. And I'm planning to camp there permanently. It's the planning that counts. And if I had you, up there alongside of me, honey, I'd be King of the Castle."

"None of that, now, Ritchie; behave." Margaret discouraged him lightly as she passed her plate for lobster. "And to get back to motoring, I've never driven a car in England; I wonder—would the left-hand side of the road business, and all the rest of it, be frightfully difficult to get on to if a person were new at it?"

"There's nothing to it. But you're not thinking of buying a car, are you?"

"I might. Or rent one." She did not look at Richard. Seemingly, she was intent on the lobster. "Hmm—good!"

"Why waste your money either buying or renting? All the driving you'll do this spring will be with me, toots.

> *It was a lover and his lass, with a hey and a ho, and*
> *   a hey nonino,*
> *That o'er the green cornfields did pass,*
> *In the spring time, the only pretty ring time,*
> *When birds do sing, hey ding a ding;*
> *Sweet lovers love the spring."*

"You and your poetry. And if you think I'm going to spend the spring in that ridiculous show-off car of yours. . . ."

How certain he was of her doing just that, Margaret thought as she laughed at him and ate her salad. How coolly, complacently certain. But as always, why try to argue with him? And the chances were, he was right.

She brave enough to rush off on a wild-goose chase that would lead to heaven knew where? She brave enough to take a chance on whatever might lie ahead for her in the unknown depths of a place called Salop? Not brave, though; crazy was the word for it. She would be out of her mind.

They finished their lunch, and when Margaret had packed the debris into the hamper, Richard took charge of it.

"Time for me to get back on the job. May I drop you anywhere? No? Then I'll hop a cab to my rooms and leave this for Mrs. Rump to cope with. She's my daily."

"Mrs. Rump? Oh, Ritchie. You're making that up. No one is named Rump."

"This Cockney gal is. And she comes, complete with a smell of gin and a purple velvet hat, to cook my breakfast every morning and tickle around with a feather duster. Speaking of breakfast reminds me: I'll be telephoning you on and off, but I'm afraid I can't suggest dinner or anything of the sort for an evening or two. I've got to knuckle down at my desk and do a little homework. My agent has been sending cables to find out how my manuscript is coming along. Rather sharp little billets-doux that I can't afford to ignore. So can you survive the next twenty-four hours without me, do you suppose, while I pound out a couple of chapters?"

"I may just manage."

"Don't try too hard. I hope you'll find the going tough, my sweetest Peg. Miss me like hell, will you? Make a project of it."

Richard pulled Margaret close and kissed her, swiftly and hard, and flashed her one of his audacious, difficult-to-resist smiles, and then he was off down a path to the Mall and a taxi.

Margaret sat alone on the bench for a little while, idly observing the last of the daffodils, the masses of newly opening tulips that crowded close to the lake's edge. Who could ask anything lovelier than a London park in spring? But Ritchie had wearied of London, it seemed. Ritchie wanted the Continent.

Spring did queer things to people, it seemed, stirred up all sorts of restlessness, and he would get his way about those motor trips, doubtless. And why not? It was only sensible, wasn't it, to give in, give up, and accept gratefully all that Ritchie was offering her?

Spring. Spring in Brittany. Spring in Salop . . .

Margaret got up abruptly.

Salop, a name so barely discernible on dark canvas, Salop, a name half obscured, and yet there, waiting to catch her eye. Salop, there to be read, like a sort of signpost. It was the strangest sort of feeling, she thought, as she walked back to Piccadilly and crossed over into Albemarle Street, to know she was absolutely mad and, at the same time, not to care too much, not to be overly concerned about her lack of sanity.

Inside the antique shop, and standing in front of Sir Hugh Vane's portrait she reflected, with resignation, how much simpler everything would be if only his eyes would let her go, if only he would have compassion and loose his hold on her.

To be free of him would be to forget, sooner or later, his living double, his mirror-image. And when that came about, would there not be a chance ahead for her and Ritchie to be happy, the miraculous second chance that was a gift from the gods and given to so few men or women?

Every chance in the world, but the man whose eyes were

meeting hers from the dark canvas had no intention of letting her go, it seemed. Praying to be free, struggling to be free, calling on all her willpower, summoning all her common sense was useless.

Two men—one a portrait, one its living replica, and she was captive to them both.

As she stood gazing, the greater was her realization that she was caught fast, the greater her consuming curiosity, her burning desire, to know more about the man in Honorine Duclair's flat.

She stood for a long five minutes in front of the portrait and then she went over to the gallery manager's desk.

"About the portraits . . . I was wondering . . . were all of them bought by you from their original owners?"

"Yes. They are all from various private sales."

"Then could you tell me—"

"I'm sorry, madam, any transactions we make are strictly confidential."

"But—but this is rather important, and—"

"I'm afraid I can't help you. It's the policy of the gallery, madam."

"You couldn't make an exception?"

"It would be quite impossible." The manager was adamant, and himself curious. "A particular portrait interests you?"

"There's one I—I rather like."

"Perhaps you'd consider buying?"

"I'll think about it a little more."

She would indeed think about it, she reflected, as she was escorted courteously to the door.

Half a dozen different ideas presented themselves and were discarded as she walked back to her hotel, and then, as she stopped at the desk for her room key, she suddenly knew exactly how to discover whether there were any Vanes still living in Shropshire, and if so, how to go about finding them.

Or rather how to find one member of the family in particular.

Ask the head porter where a person interested in family history should go for information. How simple. The head porter of any good English hotel traditionally knew the answer to any question put him.

Thousands of Americans were eager to look up their British antecedents when they came to England. So, to the head porter, the sort of question she would ask was probably routine; he could answer it as easily as telling her what time the Guard changed at Buckingham Palace, or if the National Gallery were open on Sunday.

Only she wouldn't be tracing *her* name, *her* antecedents. It would be the descendants of Sir Hugh Vane, including every branch, who would be under scrutiny. A monumental project, possibly. It could take forever. Or then again, perhaps there were no Vanes at all of Monks' Court, Salop. Not one left in the whole world, nor any Monks' Court.

A family that had died out, a house that was a pile of tumbled bricks, or a mere weed-grown, rubble-filled excavation; if that was what she found, courtesy of the head porter's help, then where would she turn? It was a bridge she would cross when she came to it. And family or no family, house or no house, she was going to find the whereabouts of the tall, limping Englishman whose eyes, painted on canvas, were so deeply, so unfairly troubling.

He had no right. . . .

She was Margaret Collier, a perfectly sane person, a completely conventional, entirely sensible and responsible young woman. Why, why should she be enmeshed in all this?

And all because she simply happened to look out her hotel window.

Act One. The woman, smiling.

Act Two. The woman so dead, so horribly dead.

Margaret wondered if the sick revulsion mounting, mount-

ing in her was apparent in voice or manner as she put her
questions to the porter. Evidently not; he was as incurious
and as helpfully informative as she had expected.

"Somerset House, madam. Open from ten to five weekdays.
Closed Saturdays and Sundays."

She thanked him profusely. Such a thoroughly nice, helpful man! And if Somerset House on the Strand gave her the
information she was seeking, and if it turned out she wasn't
too much of a coward after all, he could doubtless advise her
about hiring a car.

It had begun to rain, she saw, as she turned from the desk.
The doorman outside on the curb had put on a caped rubber
coat and was holding a big umbrella for incoming guests.
Spring, yes, but capricious spring. That was England for you,
and the sun might not emerge again for days.

What would driving to Salop be like, in this weather? With
practicality she considered her packing as she went up in the
lift, and then remembered she would be alone that evening,
without Richard's pleasant company, and that she had intended to ask the porter for a theater ticket.

She telephoned to the desk when she got to her room. Any
play, except one of those she had already seen, she stipulated,
as she had done on a previous evening. Any play that was
light. No—no, she didn't care to see the dancers at the
Viceroy. The Oriental Revue was still on, she had read in
the papers; an understudy was dancing Honorine Duclair's
role.

She put the telephone receiver back on its hook with relief
that a portion, at least, of the solitary evening ahead would
be taken care of, and with the optimistic hope that after the
theater sleep would come. There would be no danger of her
lying awake until all hours thinking about a man named Vane,
or about the morning, when, first thing, she would begin her
private searching of family records.

Now if only the afternoon would be over with and if she could make herself stay away from the window—she mustn't let staring at the flat opposite, across Mount Street, become a thing with her.

Such a blank-looking flat, with its curtains still closed, as they had been ever since the double of the man in the portrait had drawn them.

It was all too easy to imagine; the sprawled, inert woman, the blood, her dreadful head. And she had been so alive so short a time earlier.

> The grave's a fine and secret place,
> But none, I think, do there embrace.

A gloomy two lines. And she had derided Ritchie for his verse-quoting, but here she was, doing it herself.

Had the Duclair woman done any last-minute reflecting about death? Had there been time? Was death by strangulation swift or slow? And the man who had murdered her? Was he sorry, now? Or merely thankful the police had not yet caught up with him?

Remembering the limp and the cane she had neglected to mention to Inspector Downes, Margaret wondered, amazedly, at herself. Margaret Collier had always been so entirely on the side of the law, so scrupulously ethical.

She settled herself in a comfortable chair and took a piece of tapestry out of an embroidery bag. Poor Allen, who had never gotten his bookmarker. Now it would go to some friend or other for a Christmas present, she supposed, if she ever got it done. Threading a needle with a length of gold wool, and pushing it in and out of the little canvas squares, she tried, valiantly, to forget the tall, lame Englishman, and to convince herself she was entirely content with her secure world. When rain was pouring down outside, who wouldn't enjoy the prospect of afternoon tea, coming shortly, with cress and tomato sandwiches, served in the chintz-hung suite of a luxurious London hotel? And what was more, if she really needed to reassure herself, there was no reason on earth for the depression sweeping over her. How many other women were half as fortunate as she? Very few.

First there had been Allen to give her devotion and security, and now there was Ritchie, offering a different kind of love, to be sure not so quiet nor protective a love as Allen's, nor, of course, could she yet know the full reach of it. But love all the same, plus a dividend of excitement and laughter and a realization she was alive, alive.

What more could the most demanding woman ask? Nothing, one would suppose.

Then be grateful. Margaret was severe with herself. But the loneliness closed in on her, the depression cast her into darkness, and submerged by vague longings as unsubstantial as they were painful, she knew what she already possessed was not enough. Not nearly enough.

SIX

The plane trees in all the misty squares were dripping, umbrellas bobbed over bowler hats, galoshes flapped, the gaseous smell of wet soot and a hint of the river was in the air as Margaret's taxi skidded through the early-morning traffic along the Strand and left her at Somerset House.

She was the first visitor through the doors when they opened to the public, and her eagerness, her impatience mounted inordinately as she paid a small fee, asked a few questions, and began delving in the files opened for her inspection.

How simple it all was, she marveled, with mixed emotions. How readily accessible the information you were seeking, how courteous and helpful the attendants, how extraordinarily easy to pry into other people's affairs. That very ease was disconcerting, though. It meant that anyone who cared to try could find the particular Vane whom she herself was tracing. Ritchie, for instance. Or Inspector Downs.

The Vane family of Salop, along with thousands of other families, was documented, here in Somerset House; their births, their deaths, their marriages, their last wills and testaments. Generation after generation was linked, in all its branching. Fathers and mothers, sons and daughters, brothers and sisters, husbands and wives, and the legal inheritors of each. All you needed was patience.

At the end of an hour and a half Margaret closed a thick book of records. A Sir Hugh Vane existed today, a Sir Hugh Vane, Baronet, last male survivor since the death of his father and a brother, of the Vanes of Monks' Court, Shropshire, a widower with a daughter.

He was alive, he was real. But could she find him? Was it logical or only wishful thinking to presume him at Monks' Court, his family estate? A fox gone to earth, somewhere up north in Shropshire? One fine day there would be hounds after him. Inevitably, hounds. A pack of them, sniffing, running, and giving tongue when they picked up the scent. Ritchie, one of the hounds, Ritchie the newsman, would want to be first in at the kill. And he would be, if she went to him now, and if he listened instead of laughed.

Perhaps it was only natural he should laugh. Should she be laughing, too, at her own expense, sheepishly, and ashamed of her foolishness? Was the man she had seen in the Mount Street flat truly the double, the mirror-image of the man in the portrait? Were they truly both Vanes? Or were they merely two oddly fascinating men who had no connection whatever between them except in her imagination?

Imagination could lead you along all sorts of roads. Hers had always been lively and easily stirred. Was she now allowing herself to concoct the silliest sort of sensational fiction? Probably.

But she was going to Shropshire, nevertheless. She had to go, just as she had been compelled to come to London. She could not stop herself. Recognizing the fact, Margaret accepted it. Leaving Somerset House, she took a cab to Regent Street, ate a bite of early lunch at Liberty's among a crowd of women shoppers having their elevenses, and then bought a mackintosh and scarf and driving gloves, and three ties for Ritchie.

She spent some time and thought on her selection of a pearl-gray silk, a maroon knit, a green-and-brown small-figured foulard. To please him seemed vitally important. She must let Ritchie know she had been thinking of him this morning. She must let him know, if only by this smallest of gestures, how fond she was of him. And when she came back to London, she would make every effort to make up to him for her sudden and unexpected running off.

The coming back went without saying. Of course she would be back. What could possibly keep her away longer than a scant week at most when her only purpose was nothing more than to assure herself that the murderer of Honorine Duclair was, without any doubt, a man named Vane?

A single, brief—though careful—scrutiny would be enough. How she would manage it was something else again. She had no idea, at the moment, how to go about it. But she would think of something. And it was only fair to make a try, the only fair thing for everyone concerned.

With it put this way, Margaret felt a sense of virtue. Wasn't it the only decent thing to give the present-day Sir Hugh Vane of Salop the benefit of a doubt before she went to Ritchie with her fantastic deductions? Think of the injustice of it if she prattled to him and to Scotland Yard before she was certain, before she had made that careful, vital scrutiny.

It would be outrageous of her, and there could be serious consequences, if she should take it upon herself to make a murder charge based on nothing more substantial than the evidence she now possessed. A glance through opera glasses, and a Georgian portrait!

One could be sued for libel easily if the present Sir Hugh became sufficiently irked by loose, irresponsible statements. But if one went to Shropshire and made certain, absolutely certain, that the Vane who was the sole living descendant of the Vane looking out of that portrait in Albemarle Street would stand vindicated—surely he would be; she knew it— And with one's feeling of guilt evaporating, conscience clear, this absurd obsession for an unattainable, arrogant Englishman, glimpsed only once, the width of a street away, would disappear.

To forget was Margaret's sincerest hope and almost prayer as she took a proffered pencil from the haberdashery clerk and struggled over a note to be enclosed with Richard's ties. Oh, dear. What to say, exactly? How keep from sounding as mad as the well-known Hatter? It was impossible to explain things in a few short lines. The full explanation, her justification, would have to wait until she came back. Would that be too late? Ritchie might not be interested in explanations by then. He might be through with her. He was bound to be hurt by her running off, just at this point, when he had every right to think she was beginning to listen to him, and he also was certain to be furiously angry. He had a temper that would flare like a match.

Margaret hesitated, and sighed. It was all so difficult. She would not like it if there were no more Ritchie in her life. She would simply hate not having him.

The clerk was waiting. Margaret began scribbling, and then had to ask for another card, as her message lengthened.

> Ritchie dear—
> I shall be out of town this week on a private matter. I _must_
> leave. There has been so much, lately, that has made my

life become "curiouser and curiouser," as Alice put it,
but I keep telling myself that Alice came safely out of
the rabbit's hole, and I refuse to doubt that I shall also.
Though in my case the rabbit's hole looks, at the
moment, to be more of a fox's hole.

Have I mystified you completely? I am mystified myself
at what I am doing, and why. But when I get back I'll be
able to tell you all about it. I'll telephone. Take me to
dinner, will you, if you are still feeling rich, and are not
too cross with me? I'll wear my black dress for you,
the floaty one.

> Yours,
> Maggie

There. It was done. And if Ritchie was not willing to wait
for a full, understandable explanation, well, then—good-bye
to Ritchie.

She thrust the two scrawled-over cards at the clerk, and left
the shop. Instead of taking a cab she walked back to the hotel,
wanting to give her jumbled thoughts, her indecisions, time
to clarify. She could still telephone Ritchie. She could go to
his flat and tell him the whole story, and make him see,
clearly, and without hurt or annoyance, her reason for wanting to go away for a few days.

It was such an entirely sensible reason; surely he would see
her point?

What if he scoffed, though—if he tried to talk her out of
it? He would kiss her, make love to her, and she would
weaken. Against her will, against every instinct, against the
strange tide of curious longing, inexplicable desire, rising in
her to hurry, hurry, off to Shropshire, she would stay behind
in London.

And if she did, would or wouldn't she be sorry all the rest
of her life? Who could say? What was to be, would be. What
better way to look at things? And as Ritchie himself would

say, in a bad moment, very likely, "Keep your chin up and plow ahead."

She was doing the latter certainly! In just a little while now she would be on her way to a town in Shropshire called Ludlow.

The Somerset House records showed that the Sir Hugh Vane of today had been baptized in Ludlow's parish church of St. Lawrence, and it stood to reason that Monks' Court, the Vanes' family seat, must be near Ludlow. Ludlow was a starting point, at least. She had to begin her search somewhere.

She still did not know her own mind when she had reached the hotel, but she went to the head porter's desk and asked about the hiring of a car. The procedure was simple, she discovered, and before she knew it, she was letting the porter make arrangements.

Such an efficient, brisk head porter, she thought, bewildered, as she took the lift to her room. It was all his fault. He had pushed her into it, settled things, when all she had done was put a question or two.

Continuing to blame the porter, she started to pack a suitcase.

Only a few things, she decided, but warm, and of course right for the country. Several sweaters and blouses. An extra tweed skirt. A casual beige knit to change to in the evenings, and a long yellow wool dress, very simple, but especially comfortable if the inn should prove freezing. The brown velvet sandals that went with it. Walking shoes. Night clothes. Her tapestry. Paperbacks.

An hour later, at a telephone call from the desk, she went down to the foyer, her new mackintosh, with the price tag only just removed, buttoned over her tweed suit, the scarf from Liberty's around her hair like a turban, pigskin driving gloves pulled on.

A uniformed chauffeur, cap in hand, was waiting for her at the lift door.

"Mrs. Collier?"

The car-hire agency had sent him, he explained, to see her safely through the London traffic, and out of town onto the Great North Highway. Ludlow was a day-and-a-half journey, if Mrs. Collier chose to take it slowly on unfamiliar roads. And might he just check her driver's license? Very good. This was a folder with all the necessary hire papers. Would she sign, here and here? Yes, she would be billed on her return. And she would find road maps in the car.

The same ease of procedure, the same readiness to help that she had met with at Somerset House, Margaret thought, with resentment. Well-meaning people, everywhere, who did not realize they were facilitating her jump off the deep end. And that signing of papers! Reminded of the statement she had signed at Scotland Yard, Margaret followed the chauffeur out to the street curb.

Off to Shropshire in search of a possible murderer.

Ritchie, Ritchie. Hold me back. Don't let me go, Ritchie. Was it presumptuous to do a little praying? Just let Heaven be kind when—or if—she came face to face with the present-day Sir Hugh. Let him bear no faintest resemblance to the man she had seen in the flat. And please, Heaven, let the man in the flat, murderer or not, become nothing more to her than a figure in a montage, with only her imagination and the darkness of a London pre-dawn for background.

Margaret watched her bag being put in the boot of a small car, let herself be helped into the front seat, and watched the chauffeur switch on the ignition.

Ritchie—

It still wasn't too late before she took the road north. But he wasn't at hand to hear her, she must remember. Deliberately, she had chosen to leave Ritchie behind.

As to who and what waited ahead, and how so deep a sense of foreboding could be explained . . . Margaret buttoned the collar of her coat higher as she felt a queer little shiver like —what was the expression?—"someone walking over your grave."

SEVEN

Three hours later the rain had become a steady downpour, and Margaret, clutching the steering wheel of her little rented car and peering through the blurred windshield that the inadequate sweep of a wiper failed to clear, was thoroughly convinced of her own insanity.

To attempt this unfamiliar, risky English driving. To hurtle along on wet, slick highways. To attempt anything as foolish, anything as futile as running away from Ritchie!

And it *would* prove futile. However many miles she put between herself and London, Ritchie would follow her. Ritchie, not willing to wait, would come after her, demanding an immediate explanation. That was Ritchie for you. He could find her easily enough. She had made no attempt to hide her destination. The hotel's car-hire people could tell him where she was going. Her direction in general, that was, and the name of the Ludlow inn that would be her headquarters while she drove about looking for Monks' Court.

Perhaps he would not follow her immediately. He had his manuscript to get out of the way; but in the end, he would come, in the end he would take her back to London with him.

No use to try and fool herself. No use to play the ostrich, with her head in the sand. Ritchie was exciting. Ritchie had tremendous physical attraction. Ritchie could be very, very entertaining. And she happened to be an extremely lonely woman who had wearied of staying a widow. Maybe she wanted him to follow.

It would very likely not be Ritchie, after all, to whom she would say good-bye. Far more probably it would be farewell to—to the Someone her ridiculous, unrestrained imagination had conjured up, to her own undoing.

She drove faster, dangerous though it was, to put London and Richard still farther behind her.

Once she even glanced anxiously into the rear-view mirror with a tense, wrought-up feeling that she was being followed, and then forced herself to laugh at the idea. Liberty's Delivery Service was not that good! Ritchie wouldn't have the ties and her note until the morning, and even if he took time from his desk to telephone her this evening, the hotel would give him a proper, noncommittal, "Madam's room doesn't answer, sir," and he would merely suppose she was entertaining herself by going to a play.

She was glad to be diverted from thoughts of pursuit, and her ultimate surrender, by a signpost announcing the village of Little Wendling, and she pulled up outside an inn called The Blue Boar.

A glass of sherry and dinner, and a night's sleep would put things in their right perspective. She wasn't insane; this was an eminently sensible journey she was making, and, above all, Ritchie wasn't pursuing her.

She had two sherries and discovered she was really hungry, but a slice of grayish lamb floating in pale gravy and brussels sprouts followed by a pink blancmange left her unsatisfied.

Going to her room she unpacked a Penguin novel from her suitcase and tried to read until the single, small ceiling globe made her eyes begin to blur.

There was nothing for it but to hope sleep would come. She turned out the light and curled up determinedly. Dozing for a moment, she wakened, and then dozed and wakened again.

Would the rain never stop pelting against the windows? Seemingly not. So many long, dreary miles away from London. So far to have come, and for what?

The small hours of the night dragged on, and again her sanity was a concern. She, Margaret Collier, bent on seeking out a murderer; how could it be true?

When at last she fell heavily asleep, a hand was stretched out to the other pillow, where her last drowsy reflection told her Allen ought to be. Everything so pleasant and easy, nothing in the least complicated, if Allen hadn't died. Kind, clear-thinking Allen, who would have hated seeing her so mixed up now, so irrational in thought and deed.

She woke from the horrid half-asleep, half-awake hours when the alarm of her little traveling clock whirred. The rain had stopped, she saw with relief, and a breakfast of tea and toast and marmalade, with bacon and eggs, made facing the day possible. When she drove away from The Blue Boar, she was cheered by a hope the sun might come out. At noontime when she stopped for petrol again, and a sandwich, a glance at her road map showed her she was well north, now, and veering west. There was little or no traffic as she drove on, and she made herself concentrate on the countryside. She made herself pretend she was merely an American tourist, seeing the sights of rural England for the first time. Because this was Shropshire, now, according to the map. This was Salop.

It was postcard countryside, leafy with larch and birch and beech trees, green with meadows where red cows grazed. Everywhere there were bluebells. Everywhere brooks rushed and gurgled. Occasionally a church spire or a broken stone tower thrust against the opaque, watery sky, where ragged windblown clouds were massed. Thatch-roofed cottages appeared, their small gardens crowded with yellow and brown wallflowers and rank-smelling cabbages, and with fat sows and piglets wallowing in rain puddles.

A yellow-haired child, swinging on a gate, waved as the car passed, and a farm boy touched his cap to Margaret as she slowed to pass his cartful of barnyard manure, his plodding, shaggy-fetlocked team.

There were bands of sheep blocking the way, silly-faced ewes and skipping lambs with heavy, sodden fleece; there was a shepherd with a crook then, and a clever, heel-nipping, Border collie to start them moving. There were apple and pear orchards aureoled with bloom. There was lilac hanging over stone walls, heavy with buds waiting for a week or two of warmer weather before they would open.

The lilac was a reminder of Ritchie for a moment. Would the package from Liberty's have reached him yet?

The car was beginning to climb a gentle grade through rolling hills. When it reached the crest, Margaret was looking down into a green valley where the slate roofs of a small town clustered close to a tall turreted church tower and the square Norman tower and battlements of a ruined castle. Perhaps this was Ludlow. She braked the car and looked at the map. Yes. Which meant that Monks Court was somewhere near.

There was room on the hilltop to turn the car. She could go back the way she had come. It was not yet too late to patch up things with Ritchie. She hesitated for a moment only, and then she drove on, steady of purpose, and fighting the sense of foreboding that still troubled her, fighting her conviction that Richard would follow her, Richard would defeat her. And yet in a way hoping he *would* find her. After all, she might need him.

She was on an old, arched stone bridge then, where the River Teme met the flow of the River Corve, and when she had crossed to the far side, she was on a small road leading into town and a narrow street that was crowded with cars and bicycles. Driving with nervous carefulness and intent on keeping left, always left, instead of right, she passed the Market Place her map had told her to expect, with its stone Butter Cross, done in the baroque manner, and a line of black-and-white Tudor and Jacobean houses in plaster and timber, with leaded casements and sagging, jutting second stories that needed each other for support.

The car-hire chauffeur had recommended a fifteenth-century inn, The Feathers, and when Margaret had found it, half-way down the main street of the town, she parked in what had once been an old stableyard. A boy in a leather apron took her suitcase, and when she had registered, she followed him up the inn's winding, worn oak stairs, black with age, to her room.

Here she was, as near to Monks' Court as she knew how to get. She had carried her mad idea through this far, yes, but what should she do next? She washed in the bathroom at the end of the hall, and combed her hair in front of the mirror that hung over the basin, and meeting her reflection, asked it bewilderedly, "Where do I go from here? Have you any idea at all?" There was no answer forthcoming, and she went downstairs.

A coal fire burned in the low-ceilinged, heavily beamed lounge. Old pewter tankards and trenchers hung over an oak tallboy. Pots of red geraniums bloomed against the glass

of the bow windows. A cheerful group of guests were order-
ing drinks from a barmaid in the adjoining taproom.

In a comfortable chair, and over a glass of sherry, Margaret's tension eased, her doubts and apprehensions gradually
lessened. She told herself there must be hundreds of upper-
class Englishmen in London, all with a look of breeding,
that certain something about them. A good many of them
were tall, surely, and there certainly must be more than one
with a limp. More than one who knew the Duclair woman
intimately enough for after-midnight visits. She simply had
made an understandable mistake. People often rushed up
to perfect strangers, thinking they recognized a friend, and
then had to back away, feeling foolish. And she had romanticized idiotically over that portrait. Those dark eyes *had* been
fascinating—but really! So now make up for your foolishness
by being intelligent and sensible about the whole thing.
There was no point at all in jumping to conclusions. It could
so easily have been someone else.

When she went in to dinner, Margaret found the freshly
caught salmon, the duck with applesauce, the little boiled
onions, and the bacon savory more than appetizing enough
to make up for last night's meal.

After coffee she went to her room again, knowing she
would fall asleep as soon as she closed her eyes. No tossing
and turning tonight. No worrying, and puzzling. Everything
would work out.

EIGHT

She felt wonderfully rested when she woke, and self-confident, and she smiled a little to herself as she went down the hall in her dressing gown, with a bath towel over her arm.

Such a nice little dream she had to remember, involving Ritchie and herself—an intimate dream. One of these days she would tell him about it, one of these days after she had been to Monks' Court, and settled once and for all whether or not it was Sir Hugh Vane who had murdered Honorine Duclair.

She dressed quickly, drew a lipstick over her mouth, and picked up her handbag. She would eat breakfast, and then again there would be questions to ask at a porter's desk. Or no, better yet, she would go to the post office. More chance, that way, of hiding what she was up to from Ritchie if by any chance he did follow her here to Ludlow and The Feathers and start, in his newspaper's way, to ask questions of his own.

The name Vane was her secret now until she had seen Sir Hugh with her own eyes and come to her own firm, final conclusions. Not that she liked the idea of keeping things back from Ritchie, but it could not be helped for the present. Soon she would make a clean breast of everything to him. He would forget his hurt and anger at her running away. He would laugh, entertained by the story of her absurd high adventure that had proved to be no adventure at all.

"Some sleuth!" she could hear him say.

Then her obsession would be over. Down with silly fancies and far-out imaginativeness. Up with common sense.

She would have Ritchie, and she wouldn't want anyone else.

Margaret finished her breakfast, inquired for a post office, asked her questions, and then got into her car. Monks' Court was twenty miles or so away, and she was ready to assume the role of an American interested in old houses, old gardens. Not at all a bad plan—and the only one she could think of. In one way, it shouldn't be too difficult a part to play. Her garden club card from home and her National Trust card were in her wallet. Membership in either group gave you entrée almost anywhere, and in the rare case where visitors were not welcomed, all anyone need do was adopt the brazen, thick-skinned manners of so many American sightseers and calmly refuse to accept a snub.

She had seen intrusive women pushing and clamoring to get in, time and time again, no matter how firmly doors were closed to them. She didn't want to be like them, she didn't want to be unattractive or embarrassing, but the fact remained they generally succeeded in edging in somehow.

Encouraged by the thought, and following the directions she had easily obtained, Margaret drove out of town, back over the bridge, and along a road that followed the Teme for some ten miles.

More lush meadows. More sheep. More red cattle, grazing. More churches and bell towers and thatched cottages. Dovecotes and bee houses speaking of a summer to come, of a cooing and humming.

At a sharp fork she branched left, and after another ten miles she again took the left turn, this time into a muddy, rutted lane sunken between hawthorne hedges interlaced with coarse-growing brambles as impenetrable as strands of wire.

On and on, interminably; how much deeper must she penetrate this lonely, silent countryside? She would have been glad to hear a sheepdog's bark or the baa-ing of lambs, and enormously grateful for the voice of a shepherd or a farmhand.

Wasn't there anyone around anywhere? No animals, even, to make things less—less ominous? Though ominous was an exaggerated word, of course. But this was the most remote, most desolate stretch of driving she had ever done, and she didn't like it, not one bit, Margaret admitted frankly. But when the lane came to an abrupt end at a pair of rusty, closed iron gates set in a high, forbidding stone wall, she was almost sorry.

Now what? Get out? Try to open the gates? She sat irresolute a moment. This far and no further? All the way from London, only to turn the car around, if the narrow lane permitted, and go back defeated? Was she that much of a coward?

She shamed herself into getting out finally, and by putting all her weight against the gates and shoving hard, she managed to open them just enough to squeeze the car through with only a slight scraping of each fender. When she had managed to drag them shut again, she drove on. After a few yards she came on a small, deserted-looking stone house half hidden in overgrown thickets of greenery that, she supposed, a lodge keeper might once have lived in. Still farther along, driving under tall, crowding rhododendrons that were trees rather than shrubs, she passed the ruins of an ancient tower, and then a small crumbling-walled chapel smothered in rankly growing ivy.

She was on what in other days, perhaps, had been a graveled, well-tended driveway, winding through parkland, but now the drive was as rutted as the lane outside the gates and full of weeds, and the massive, old trees that bordered it made a dark, oppressive tunnel closing around and over her and shutting out any view of what lay beyond them on either side.

There was another jolting, muddy mile of the solitary, overhung drive, and then, at the top of a rise from which dark, mist-wreathed mountains could be seen against the sky, a stretch of rough, unmowed turf that had once been lawn came in sight, suddenly, and a large house whose bricks had faded to a soft, rosy red.

Margaret pulled on the brake of her car and jerked it to a halt, a wave of excitement sweeping over her.

The house that was the background of the portrait in Albemarle Street. Monks' Court. Monks' Court, Salop, where, in only minutes, now—she did not dare put the rest of the sentence into words; she could not bear it, she thought, simply and without pretense of self-deception, if for any reason at all she had to turn back without sight of Sir Hugh Vane.

All eagerness, in spite of the pounding of her heart, she released the brake and drove on again, a little too fast, regardless of ruts and splattering mud, and drew up at the entrance.

A proud house, it struck her at once; as proud now, in its obvious decay, as ever in its days of prosperity, but a melancholy house. People had been sad here. She did not need to be told it. The sadness hung in the very air.

To intrude struck her as almost shocking, the worst sort of vulgar insensibility. So terribly sad . . . Old dark yew trees seemed mourning sentinels at each side of shallow steps that led to a wide sweep of terrace. The steps were moss-grown and little used. The sunken, uneven paving of the terrace was cracked and weed-crowded. Two leaden urns on lichened stone pedestals spilled weeds instead of flowers, and the basin of a stone fountain was choked with rotting leaves and coated with green slime.

A heart-tearing house. Thinking it, Margaret got out of the car and as she mounted the steps and crossed the terrace and lifted the tarnished brass knocker of a heavy carved door, she scolded herself. There was nothing to be afraid of— not really. . . . She let the knocker fall. There was a hollow echo, and then the silence that followed was absolute. An empty house? She lifted the knocker again, and after a moment's wait she started back to the car, half thankful to escape from the house and leave it to its melancholy, pitiful dissolution, half disappointed.

The whole trip useless, she questioned resentfully, and with a feeling of being somehow cheated. Nothing gained. Nothing settled. Now it wasn't something she could put away from her, with thankfulness that it could be forgotten and a sense of satisfaction that she had accomplished what she had so timidly attempted.

She had reached the foot of the steps when she heard the door open behind her. Quickly, she whirled, conscious again of her heart's hard thumping.

An old woman, as short almost as a child but broad and sturdy-looking in her neat printed cotton dress and white apron, and with tightly braided, thin white hair that showed pink scalp at a center parting, was inspecting Margaret out of black eyes, bright behind steel-rimmed spectacles.

"Yes, madam?"

The inquiry was that of a well-trained, courteous servant.

A funny little gnome of a woman, but with a pleasant, comfortable, kind look about her, Margaret thought. The scar was a pity, though, that long, puckering scar on her right cheek, just missing an eye. Not a scar to put one off, however; she was likable at first sight. Her employers were lucky. This was the old-fashioned, family-retainer type that hardly existed any more.

She hurried back up the steps.

"Is this Sir Hugh Vane's house?"

"Yes, madam."

"Is he in? You see—you see, I'm an American, and I was driving by, and—" Hastily, awkwardly, she began fabricating. "I—I am writing a series of articles." It was not easy. Lying was new to her. "Magazine articles, about English houses and gardens, and—and I thought—"

"I am sorry, madam, Monks' Court isn't open for show."

"Oh."

She was at a loss for a moment, and then she asked, with more wistful entreaty in her voice than she knew, "Mightn't I just ask Sir Hugh? If I explained it was rather—rather important?"

The old woman hesitated, and Margaret pressed her advantage.

"I'd only take a moment of his time. And I've driven such a long way."

"Sir Hugh is in the stableyard, madam. You could go around, if you like, not that I'm saying 'twill do you much good."

"Thank you. Thank you very, very much."

The woman closed the door, looking gratified at such fervently expressed appreciation, and Margaret was left to ask herself if she were brave enough to go on with her role of article-writing tourist. She would feel such a fool, so cheap and silly, trying to lie, if Sir Hugh turned out to be a man she had never seen before, a perfectly nice, respectable Englishman whose privacy she was so outrageously invading. And if she *had* seen him before, what then? She would want to turn and run.

But face him she must.

Margaret got in her car, and with the thought that the stables would be well back of the house, she followed the drive that curved now away from the stone entrance terrace until, through the arch of an enclosing brick wall, she saw a cobbled yard.

The sound of the car started a frenzied barking and yapping, and as she parked and turned off the motor, wishing she knew whether the dogs were safely leashed or kenneled, a man appeared in the archway, and after a long, cool survey, limped toward her.

No, oh, no! Don't let it be him!

Margaret's inward, protesting plea died before it reached her lips. It was too late now for praying. He was who he was, and there was no possible mistaking him for anyone else.

She grasped the car's steering wheel, her hands trembling with sudden panic. Terrified, she longed to feel the car move, turn, and plunge ahead, carrying her along the dark, menacing tunnel of closing-in trees and shrubs that was the driveway through the rusty gates of Monks' Court to escape and safety.

NINE

She fumbled frantically with the ignition switch. The motor caught, only to sputter and fail. Trapped and helpless, Margaret felt the gray, cold eyes on her, appraisingly.

He was one of those impossibly arrogant Englishmen, she thought with a surging resentment almost as strong as her terror. Exactly the type she had guessed him to be the night she stared at him through her opera glasses, the type who would continue to stand there, contemptuously, icily silent, until he had forced her, humiliatingly, to speak up and explain her intrusion.

She couldn't just sit and sit. She would have to say something, she thought wildly. Horrible, this state of panic-struck immobility, like a rabbit hypnotized by a snake.

"I am Margaret Collier, Mrs. Allen Collier." She offered it weakly. "I'm an American—"

"So I supposed."

The brief statement, cutting in on her explanations, implied that her Americanism was obvious, and undisguisable even by a Liberty mackintosh and scarf.

"I—I am touring England, Looking at old houses. I'm writing a series of magazine articles." The lie, repeated, was far harder to tell this time and sounded transparently false to her ears. "I thought I'd stop—so many English houses are open."

He broke in with chilling sarcasm. "You were expecting the 'Open April first to October first' sort of thing? Two shillings, sixpence, with tea, for adults, one and six for children? Was that what you had in mind when you drove in?"

"I—"

"You are not missing anything, however." The man's thin, hard mouth was bitter with a faint smile. "Monks' Court isn't worth an admission ticket. Not these days. Rather too shabby now for any American's taste, I should think, and with too many bare spots. The best of the pictures and furniture have been sold." The smile touched his mouth again. "Shipped to the States, for the most part."

"I—"

Again he refused to let her finish.

"You weren't told at the front door that the place is closed to the public? I shall have to give stricter orders. And when you drive out may I ask you to close the gates, the way you found them?"

It was dismissal, humiliating, scathing dismissal.

Margaret fumbled with the ignition switch again, her face burning. That cool distaste, that insufferable sarcasm—but just wait until she got back to London, just give her five minutes with Ritchie and with Inspector Downs. What of Sir Hugh Vane's arrogance then? Would it last him out to the end when a prison gate clanged shut behind him?

Unconsciously, Margaret's hand flew to her own throat. He deserved a rope, but . . .

Confused and torn by conflicting thoughts, conflicting emotions, she turned the switch once more, but her hurried, flustered efforts were useless, and the car refused to start.

"Flooded the motor, have you?"

The man limped closer. "I suggest you let it drain before you try to turn it over again. And if you're frightfully keen on having a look round, you may as well, now you are here. I'm Hugh Vane, by the way. As far as visitors are concerned, it's only the general run of tourists I find obnoxious, the weekend hordes of trippers, strewing their lunch papers about and then going away feeling cheated of their money's worth."

It was, in effect, a stiff-necked apology, offered belatedly to an attractive woman. Margaret was certain of it as she tried, hurriedly, to think of an excuse to get away, and then made a show of consulting her wristwatch.

"It's late. I didn't realize—"

"The gardens aren't worth your time, but there is a Norman chapel that's fairly interesting."

"It's almost noon—I—"

The protest was futile. To her horror, Sir Hugh said, "Let's see what we can do," and limped around to the other side of the car, opened the door, and with the help of his stick got in next to her.

What was there to say? An unbelievable situation; how would she cope with it?

When the car started at last, Margaret began driving mechanically, an automaton at the wheel, with the man next to her not bothering to make conversation, but when they reached the ruined tower and the ivy-smothered chapel she had passed earlier, he directed her to pull up to the side of the road.

"Just here."

In spite of his lameness he was out of the car quickly, and opening her door. "This way—watch the brambles."

There was nothing to do but get out and follow him. If she had had her wits about her, fast enough, would she have waited in the driver's seat until he had gotten out on his side, and then made a dash for it, with her foot on the accelerator, hurtling the car at top speed toward those iron gates she would need to drag open, and into the lane?

Margaret asked it of herself as she dodged thorny, clutching branches and steadied herself from being tripped by gnarled roots and matted vines. The answer that honesty demanded of her came as a bewildering shock.

Her first instinctive and frantic impulse to get away, to escape, no longer existed. In its place was an unreasoning, insane desire to stay on here at Monks' Court and find out more and more about its owner, sickened though she still was by her instant recognition of him—and frightened.

". . . and the chapel is all that is left of the priory that gave Monks' Court its name."

Sir Hugh was following up his apology with a guided tour, she realized. ". . . all that heap of stones was a Saxon castle once that later 'marched,' as we say in Shropshire, with Ludlow Castle against Welsh border uprisings. Wales is just over there, you know, where those mountains are."

She managed to murmur that it was all extremely interesting, and as though she were acting out a part in a bad drama, she followed Sir Hugh through the thick, nail-studded door of the chapel. For a moment, as she came in from outside, there was only indeterminate dimness and then, slowly, stone pillars took shape, a carved rood screen, and an altar.

With the chill of a worn stone floor under her feet, the chill of damp stone walls striking through her raincoat and tweeds, a dank, musty smell peculiarly distasteful to her, she shivered, glancing around her.

St. George and the Dragon, in old, old leaded glass over the altar. Tattered, time-rotted silk rags that were banners hanging from stone beams. Brass and marble memorial plaques on the walls. More plaques sunk in the floor. Margaret shivered again, all the colder at the reminder of a crypt under her feet.

"Do effigies interest you?" Sir Hugh moved toward a shallow niche in a side wall enclosed by a high grille, its wrought-iron palings terminating in arrow points. He turned a heavy, rusted key, and when the grilling door swung open, it revealed a dais that supported the carved stone figures of a knight in armor and of a woman in a long robe, her hair coifed under a wimple, lying on their biers.

Again Margaret made an effort for some sort of response and she moved forward through the gloom to stare at the silent, oblivious figures.

"Hugh Vane?" she read out uncertainly from a worn inscription.

"Yes."

To herself she was thinking, "Another Hugh. Now I know of three," and found herself wondering if the man lying here in stone had been, like the other two, the possessor of dark, rain-gray eyes.

Quickly, as though the living Sir Hugh, standing next to her so close, could know her thoughts, she put a hand on the woman's tomb with the sort of stereotyped interest a bona fide tourist would be expected to make.

"Catharine Vane, wife of Hugh . . . I don't know Latin well enough to translate the rest of it. What beautiful carving."

She noticed only then that the woman's wrists, crossed on her breast, were without hands, and it gave her the chance to make another tourist comment.

"What a pity her hands are gone. But I suppose stone as old as this couldn't be expected to last forever."

"The hands were never there."

Sir Hugh, a guide again, was giving his tour conscientiously. "And that inscription on the side, *Amare est donare*, means 'to love is to give.' The story is that when her husband went off to the Crusades he was captured by the Saracens, who sent a messenger with word that the price of his ransom would be her two hands, cut off in the presence of the messenger, to be carried back by him to Constantinople."

"How terrible! The cruelest thing I ever heard."

"It was a worthwhile bargain, in her opinion evidently. At any rate, the Saracens lived up to their part of it, and she got him back."

"What a ghastly story!" It burst from her spontaneously, as, for an instant, she was wrenched from her daze. "The awful pain! How could she bear it?"

"How much a person can bear seems to be in direct ratio to how much has to be borne—or to how much one happens to care about this, that, or the other thing."

He made the observation impersonally, but there was something about it that made Margaret glance at him with oddly aroused curiosity. There was only a profile; Sir Hugh had turned from the grilled vault. "Shall we go?" he asked abruptly. "Even the most dedicated of American sightseers must find it too chilly here for lingering, I should think."

They got back into the car and Margaret drove to the house, prepared to have Sir Hugh get out at his door with another implied, if not verbal, dismissal, but to her astonishment, and with an unpleasant feeling of being cornered, she heard him extend an invitation to lunch.

"Old Pell, who sent you around to find me at the stableyard, I presume, will be giving Cherry and me cold meat and salad in a few minutes. Cherry is my daughter."

"You are very kind," she stammered, "but—"

"It would please Pell enormously. She is forever after me to have guests. And Cherry would enjoy meeting an American. We are a dull lot here; we see very few people. So do stay. Will you, Mrs. Collier?"

Stay? Of course she wouldn't stay. Margaret was entirely sure of it. Accept a luncheon invitation from a murderer, even though she was finding him, to her everlasting shame, so devastatingly attractive and intriguing? Never! She wasn't that much of a fool. Nor had she the courage.

"Then there is the Adam drawing room I could show you, Mrs. Collier. Even though it's had its day, unfortunately, may I offer it as an inducement? And, incidentally, the foundations of the house are early fourteenth century; a Tudor reconstruction followed, and then the present one. All of which could provide excellent magazine material, now I think of it. Hardly fair to your editor or your reading public to pass up the opportunity, wouldn't you say?"

Was he being sarcastic again? And did he or didn't he believe her lies about the articles on British houses? You couldn't tell, Margaret realized, baffled. You only knew he was dangerously intriguing. You only knew an irresistible urge to stay—and stay.

A magnet was what he was. She had felt the pull at her first glimpse of him in Mount Street. She had felt the pull again, standing in front of a mere portrait, whose eyes and mouth, the double of this man's eyes and mouth, had held her and refused to let her go.

"You will stay?"

"Yes." Incredulously, Margaret heard herself murmuring an acceptance.

"Then shall we go in? We almost never use the front door any more, but Pell would be shocked if I took a first-time guest through the kitchen garden and side entrance. She's a stickler for form, Pell is, and I shouldn't dare face her disapproval."

It was all easily, lightly put. When the door opened after

a loud persistent knocking that told Margaret the old woman was perhaps deaf, Sir Hugh ushered her into a stone entrance hall almost as cold as the chapel.

"Mrs. Collier will stay for lunch, Pell. Will you show her upstairs in case she'd like a wash before we sit down?"

The long stone-floored hall, rugless and bare-walled, stretched to a graceful stairway. The old woman led the way up it, and when she had shown Margaret a bathroom at the end of another long, cold hall, opened the door into a large bedroom and hurriedly flung wide the casement windows.

"There, now, madam, you'll have a nice bit of sunshine. And I'll just hang madam's coat here in the wardrobe and then I'll get rid of these dust covers."

When she had gone, with a bundle of muslin covers under her arm, Margaret looked around her.

The whisked-away covers and the opened wardrobe had released a breath compounded of mothballs and dried lavender and verbena; certainly a much pleasanter smell than that of the chapel, she thought, and it was a wholly charming room.

A chinoiserie paper covered the walls. The wide-planked, dark oak floor, polished to a gleam, slanted a little, and was gently hollowed at the threshold. Its only rug, an oblong of worn needlepoint, lay beside a walnut four-poster bed whose canopy and coverlet were of the same faded yellow linen that hung at the windows. An armchair, slipcovered in the linen, was drawn up to a small escritoire, and another chair, cushioned with yellow striped silk, stood in front of an antique walnut dressing table that was strewn with a miscellany of pretty little tortoise-shell boxes and amber glass perfume bottles.

It was a pity so delightful a guest room should give off so unmistakable an impression of long disuse. Thinking of it, Margaret wondered a little why Sir Hugh had never brought a second wife to Monks' Court. A house like this, and a man like its owner, would want more than a daughter for chatelaine, one would think.

Not that it was any of her concern.

She untied her scarf, and opening her bag, took out comb and lipstick and powder compact, and then straightened her stockings. Each move was made with deliberately delaying slowness. What a fool, what a fool, to have set foot in Sir Hugh Vane's house. How could she possibly encounter him again?

Pale, benign spring sunshine flooded through the open windows of the bedroom. She stared at the stir of curtains in the light breeze and at the lifting light and shadow that seemed to bring a flock of little birds on the Chinese wallpaper to life, to flutter their wings, and make the yellow peonies and slender-stalked bamboo sway. Forced to it, against all volition of her own, she at last walked out and toward the stairs.

Dreading her next sight of Sir Hugh, she yet moved along the hall like one enslaved. At the top of the stairs she paused to glance down, her fear briefly subservient to a terrible, shaming eagerness, and then, as she saw Sir Hugh waiting in the hall below, looking up at her, she gripped the banister rail.

There he was, the killer. Having murdered once, a man murdered again easily, it was said. What if she failed to play out her role of tourist-writer successfully? What if, in any manner, she gave herself away? Dropped the smallest, smallest hint inadvertently?

Margaret drew a deep unsteady breath and clung harder to the banister as she took a first step down the stairs. The answer was simple, hideously simple, staring her in the face.

Sir Hugh would find it essential to commit a second murder, and this time she would be the victim.

TEN

"Shall we go in to lunch?"

Sir Hugh led the way across the square, empty hall, and Margaret followed, the heels of her lizard-skin pumps clicking on a black-and-white marble floor.

"If you'll go ahead, Mrs. Collier."

The parquetry floor of the dining room was rugless, and the blank wood-paneled walls showed here and there the marring outline of pictures and mirrors that had been removed, and, Margaret guessed, sold. It occurred to her, too, that the ugly modern fixture dangling from the elaborately plastered ceiling might well be the inadequate substitute for the chandelier that had once graced the room.

The only furniture in the enormous and extremely cold room was a small table of no particular value and several nondescript chairs which were isolated in the embrasure of a long window that looked out on a walled garden, paved, like the entrance terrace, with broken, moss-grown bricks, and with its once formally maintained paths edged raggedly with old, dying-out boxwood.

A young girl was standing by the table.

"May I present my daughter, Mrs. Collier?"

The perfectly courteous "How do you do?" was indifferent, the expression on the thin, small face unresponsive.

She was one of those unfortunately difficult, gauche girls, perhaps eighteen or nineteen, who had not yet found herself. Pretty, though, in a dark, sulky way. A nice little figure, and the jodhpurs suited those long slim legs to perfection. And nice hair, falling straight to her shoulders, with the slightest turn-up of its ends, and a blue ribbon band to keep its dark swing out of her eyes.

The outdoor sort, obviously. Her small hands scrupulously clean, but rough-skinned and unmanicured, and that faint aroma clinging that was unmistakably doggy. Dog soap. Dog disinfectant. Dog flea powder.

Heavens, what eyes. Huge, with lashes out to there, a shade darker than her hair, and the eyes themselves of the same indescribable color as her father's, a reminder of rain or fog or smoke.

Not happy eyes; Margaret was wondering why, as Sir Hugh drew out a chair for her and the three of them sat down and unfolded big, monogramed damask napkins that were darned as carefully as was the tablecloth and worn as thin as the silver forks and knives and spoons at each place.

"I hope you are not too cold, Mrs. Collier," Sir Hugh said civilly. "It's something of a barracks in here, I'm afraid." The gray eyes swept the room with wry expressiveness. "The last London buyer picked fairly close to the bone."

London—now was her chance. But to seize it would be madness.

Margaret's hands tightened together in her lap. Desperately she tried to hold back a question, even while she knew with terrified fatalism that she would ask it, would have to ask it.

"Do you go to London often, Sir Hugh?" Her mouth was dry once she had asked it, and for a long, agonized moment, the question hung in the air as she waited for an answer, not daring to look at him.

"Do I often go to London?" Sir Hugh repeated the question as Pell came through a swinging door from a pantry, pushing a loaded trolley that she wheeled into position beside him.

He uncovered a silver platter. "What have we here, Pell? An omelette? Oh, excuse me, Mrs. Collier, about London, no, I shouldn't say I go often."

"Have you been there—lately?" Margaret struggled on. "What did you think of the weather these last ten days? Were you there for—for the heat? For any of the thunderstorms?"

He was not to be caught. Her clumsy, childish attempt at a bracketing of any calendar date was to be a failure, she knew at once.

"The weather has been wretched everywhere lately; but that's our unpredictable English spring for you, a storm one day, and sunshine the next." He said it casually as he served the omelette and some peas, and passed a plate to Margaret. "Shall you have enough, Mrs. Collier? I see we've salad and cheese, to finish with, but that seems to be it. Pell is crushed, she told me, not having earlier notice of a guest. She'd have liked nothing better than doing what she'd call 'a proper meal' in your honor."

"Nothing could be more delicious than this omelette, and you have no idea what a treat home-grown peas are, or that lovely-looking young lettuce, after so many hotel meals."

It sounded forced and fulsome, Margaret thought, but she had to say something.

"The credit belongs to Cherry. She has taken over the vegetables almost entirely now that we've only one man for the garden. She does very well, I think."

The girl looked pleased, almost pathetically pleased, it struck Margaret, as though praise from her father might be all too rare.

"Do you look after the dogs, too?" She asked it on an impulse to be kind. "I heard them when I drove in."

"Those were Father's dogs. I only look after my own."

"What do you have, sheep dogs?"

"No. Setters." The girl's brief answer could have been called curt.

"English, or Llewellyn?"

"English."

"Black and white? Or with lemon or liver markings?"

"Black and white." The girl lapsed into silence that was almost sullen, leaving Margaret at a loss, but Sir Hugh filled the conversational gap.

"My daughter chose to start a breeding kennel this year instead of going on with her schooling, Mrs. Collier. Not with my full approval, but I suppose we all have a right to a difference of opinion."

The sarcasm under the accord was apparent, and the girl flushed.

"School! When I could be here?" It burst from her resentfully, and then she bit her lip and looked down at her plate and was silent, her face dark and closed.

There was a moment's uncomfortable silence, with Sir Hugh looking both decidedly annoyed with his daughter and vexed with himself for having baited her. Were father and daughter often at odds with one another? Unfortunate, especially as the girl had no mother.

Sir Hugh took a wine bottle from the trolley and filled the
glass at Margaret's place and at his daughter's, and then with
his own glass full, lifted it with a formal little salute.

"This ought to be champagne, rightfully, I suppose, but in
any case, here's to your magazine article, Mrs. Collier. Success!"

Was it barely concealed jeering? Margaret neither knew
nor cared. She was staring at the glass in his hand, unable to
tear her eyes from it, and, to her horror, unable to check a
flow of words that suddenly were babbling, pouring out irra-
tionally, disconnectedly, dangerously.

"Champagne. Are you especially fond of it, Sir Hugh?
Some men like it and some don't, but it's a favorite of almost
all women, wouldn't you say? I mean, not just American and
English . . . I—I've never seen a woman refuse it, have
you?"

"No, I can't say I have," Sir Hugh admitted quietly.

"It's—it's a big-city wine, too, wouldn't you say? A New
York or Paris—or—or London sort of wine?" Margaret's
reckless words rushed on in full spate. "A late-in-the-evening
wine, especially, after—after one has gone dancing, or—or
after the theater."

Sir Hugh helped himself to more omelette.

"Do you enjoy the theater, Mrs. Collins?" he asked. "I
hear there are several successes on in London now?"

"Yes—" Margaret brought it out faintly.

There was another awkward pause, with Margaret as mute
as Sir Hugh's daughter until Pell brought in a coffee tray, and
then, as she accepted a cup and said an automatic "Please,"
to sugar, and "Black, thank you," she got hold of herself. The
babbling was under control now, checked as suddenly as it
had started, like an attack of hiccups. And the hysteria was
controllable, too, with some effort, and she was reasonably
sure neither of the Vanes could possibly have guessed her

shock and revulsion at the sight of that raised wine glass.

Her hand was trembling only imperceptibly as she stirred her coffee with a spoon so thin at the shaft it was ready to snap. She was again able to start a conversation. The chatty American female; well, it was one role Sir Hugh Vane would believe, at any rate.

"You fish and shoot, I expect, Sir Hugh?" That sort of thing, and "What about you, Miss Vane? Do you ride?"

She babbled on, establishing the fact that she was a widow by such phrases as "My husband, who used to play golf," or "My husband used to enjoy bridge."

The girl contributed almost nothing beyond either shy or sullen monosyllables—Margaret was uncertain which—but Sir Hugh met her at least halfway, reservedly, but with *savoir-faire*, and at moments Margaret almost enjoyed herself, with the stripped, bare dining room becoming as unlikely as a dining room in a dream, and her own enjoyment surely that of some other woman, who was not remotely herself, sitting at this table.

It had to be a dream: she, Margaret Collier, sitting at lunch with a murderer. She, Margaret Collier, rejecting all decency of behavior, dismissing all caution.

Sir Hugh was offering her a cigarette, and she took it. As he leaned toward her, holding a match, her heart began its hard, erratic pounding and lurching again, and once more her hands were cold, their palms wet. She dropped the cigarette and stood up, unceremoniously. "If you'll excuse me, I've stayed much too long."

The girl stared in surprise, and Sir Hugh's eyebrows raised inquiringly.

"I'm sorry—I must get back to my hotel. I have bags to pack."

"You are stopping in Ludlow, I suppose?"

"Yes." It escaped her before she thought. Now, if he suspected her knowledge, he could come looking for her, he would know how to get at her, if he chose.

"I leave tomorrow," she added hurriedly.

"More touring?"

"I—I'm not certain."

"But you haven't seen the house yet. And what of your magazine commitment, Mrs. Collier?"

"I—"

"If the house doesn't tempt you sufficiently, would you consider coming back for a look at a new litter of puppies? You'd be delighted, wouldn't you, Cherry, to show them to Mrs. Collier?"

The girl glanced at him quickly, as though she had not heard correctly, and then it was clear she was struggling with both sulky resentment and a pathetic eagerness.

"I didn't know you thought them worth looking at, Father —but if Mrs. Collier wants to come. . . ."

Margaret wished the girl's face hadn't lighted up; it only made everything more difficult. Why should this strange girl's unhappy eyes touch her so? Why on earth should it matter whether or not she disappointed the child?

"I—" It was impossible to flounder on with excuses, and equally impossible to say simply, yes, she would be back.

The girl's expression darkened. She gave an ugly little laugh. "You mustn't feel you have to come, Mrs. Collier. The dogs aren't anything at all special—they aren't in the least important. Are they, Father?"

She put her napkin on the table and walked, quietly enough to the door of the dining room, but then she was running; Margaret could hear her, the length of the long, bare-floored hall, and a door slamming.

"I apologize for my daughter's manners, Mrs. Collier." Sir Hugh's eyes were cold, unrevealing, but his mouth had narrowed. "As you may have gathered we don't see alike on her being home. I wonder, are all girls her age as difficult nowadays? Or is Cherry unique? I wish I knew."

They had left the table and were crossing the hall, walking toward the front door and the entrance terrace.

"A great many of them have a difficult adolescence, Sir Hugh."

"You couldn't reconsider another visit—for my daughter's sake, Mrs. Collier?" They were on the driveway, and Sir Hugh opened the car door. "Is lunch again tomorrow quite impossible?"

The gray eyes that she could not read, and that she had avoided meeting as much as possible all morning long, were on her, steadily.

"I—"

She was furious with herself for the foolish, ineffectual stammering that was all she could manage.

"You'll come? Splendid! Cherry and I will count on it, Mrs. Collier."

Calmly, swiftly, he had put words in her mouth. He would tell the child she was coming. Oh, a clever, clever man! A—a kind of devil to know so well that she couldn't disappoint that difficult touchy child.

As she drove off Margaret was vowing to herself that nothing on earth could induce her to look back, but before the car had gone fifty yards along the weedy drive she gave in.

He was standing by the terrace, leaning a little heavily, almost wearily, on his cane, and with something unmistakably expectant about his waiting, as though he had every confidence she would have to look back.

How insufferable. Margaret's face burned, and as she made the car fairly leap ahead, a tide of hot, suffusing shame washed over her. Loathing herself, she determined fiercely to be on her way back to London early the next morning.

Lunch at Monks' Court again? Never! And this time she meant it. What had she been thinking of? Let the girl be disappointed. What was she but a sulky, disagreeable, bratty little thing, anyway?

Never mind. Never mind. The morning was over. She had gone to Monks' Court, she had found out what she wanted to find out—or rather what had to be found out for the sake of her own consuming curiosity, and in London, there would be Ritchie waiting.

More lies would be necessary, though, and explanations plausible enough to satisfy Ritchie. To tell Ritchie the truth would be beyond her. Let Scotland Yard do its own ferreting out; Sir Hugh's future was their affair, not hers.

And she and Ritchie would go dancing again, and go off on motor trips, as he had wanted, and it would be easy to put out of mind both the portrait of an eighteenth-century baronet and his double of today.

Easy? It was possible, of course, that she might have to work at it. But that was no real problem. She would let Ritchie kiss her as often and as hard as he liked, for one thing, which would help. Right there was the root of the whole thing, a psychologist would tell her: she was longing for a lover.

And she was, she was. Though not just any lover. But then Ritchie was not just any lover.

It was disgusting, it was degrading, but why not be honest with herself for a change? The truth, the whole truth—it was the oath every witness had to take, facing a judge. But don't start thinking about a judge. Think about anything, anything else, and in a hurry.

Think about Ritchie again. Darling Ritchie. But marry him—now?

Margaret's foot pressed harder on the accelerator pedal in a desperate, hurrying attempt to leave Monks' Court, and the master of Monks' Court, behind her physically as well as in her thoughts.

Even the long driveway, with its jolting ruts slowing her, was conspiring to keep her captive. The dark, smothering shrubs and trees seemed to reach out to clutch at the car, bending down, bending over her, to close her in. They, and that man on the terrace, that man with the inscrutable eyes, pinning her down, were allies.

She'd never get away—insane, insane, to have come in the first place.

And that babbling—her babbling, that had added to her flimsy, transparent lying.

What was he thinking? How much did he suspect? It was impossible to guess. All Margaret knew was that her fear was growing, growing, monstrously.

But why, then, in heaven's name, should the pull of a magnet grow stronger every minute, no matter how many miles she put behind her?

She had reached the iron gates. Beyond the lonely lane there would be the lovely, quiet English countryside, all bluebells and hedgerows. She would be safe. There would be farm cottages deep in wallflowers, there would be shepherds and little springtime lambs, and her terrible fear would evaporate.

The trouble was, she longed to turn around and go back.

The realization was complete. Stunned by it, Margaret tried to tell herself that at least she was being honest, if nothing else. She had faced the truth, now, and accepted it, and knew where she stood. She knew, too, that it would never be she who betrayed Hugh Vane's visit to Honorine Duclair's flat.

Not to anyone, anyone. It wouldn't be she who was even remotely responsible for an imprisonment—for life—if she could help it.

Turning into the quiet lane beyond the gates of Monks' Court, Margaret began to drive even faster, with the little car careening wildly, recklessly over the muddy ruts.

Ritchie wasn't stupid. She reminded herself of it again, and knew, all at once, that a telephone call to an antique shop in London ought not to be delayed a minute longer than she could help.

A few questions asked at her Carlos Place hotel and then at the car-hire agency, and he would know she had come to Ludlow, if he cared enough to find out and perhaps to follow her, but that was not where the danger lay. Ritchie had been a reporter. He was used to snooping, and to putting two and two together. Logically, he might very well start reconstructing their last day together in London, going back every minute of it, thinking over every word she had said in stubborn, typically Ritchie-like determination to find any possible reason for her running away from him. Ritchie had never liked being thwarted.

If he remembered what she had let escape her in that gallery in Albemarle Street, and on a close, searching look read "Vane" and "Salop." . . . She must buy the portrait over the telephone and have it crated immediately and sent to The Feathers. The all-important, single clue lost to Ritchie. That is, if she was still in time, if already she was not too late.

ELEVEN

The High Street was clotted with Market Day traffic the next morning as Margaret drove out of The Feathers Inn garage. The car horn that she tooted nervously and constantly competed with the rumble and clatter of cart wheels bumping over cobbles, the grunt and squeal of hogs and pigs, the loud moo-ing and baa-ing of cattle and sheep, the hiss of geese, the cackle of chickens, and the stop and start of heavy trucks and goods vans, the screech of estate wagon brakes, the ping of bicycle bells.

Her tooting was mechanical. She was almost completely oblivious to the confusion and noise around her, to the permeating smell of animals and poultry, truckloads of cut flowers, crates of silvery salmon, fresh bread and hot meat pies, fish and chips, petrol fumes.

Nothing else was of interest to her, nothing else was worth a thought, except going back to Monks' Court.

It had been little or no use to fight against a return. She

had known when she drove away through its gates the day before that already she was defeated.

"A fatal attraction." How many times had she read or heard the phrase? Hundreds. Now she knew only too well what it meant. She understood, too, why moths proverbially flew close to candle flames: the moths couldn't help it. The answer was as simple, as rudimentary as that. There was no escape possible. They might hover and vacillate and then attempt retreat, but in the end, they fluttered close again and closer, cruelly, fatally drawn to the flame, and then eventually met their entirely predictable destruction.

She, too, would be destroyed.

There was one thing to be said about a fatalistic viewpoint —you began to experience a numbing, dulling acceptance. What was to be, would be. Margaret reflected it with a degree of calmness.

She felt completely detached from the every day world. She was almost a spectator, resignedly, although with astonishment, watching herself performing a grotesque, fantastic mummery. And she recognized another of the mummers. In green brocade pajamas. The curtains back of her crimson. The bubbles in her wine glass golden.

And the color of her lover's eyes?

Margaret wrenched at the steering wheel just in time to miss a farmboy on his bicycle pedaling out from a side street with a crate of cackling hens strapped on the handlebars.

She ought not to be at the wheel of a car this morning, she knew guiltily, and equally as guiltily she was remembering the careful scrutiny she had taken of herself in her bedroom mirror before leaving the inn.

Those gray, dark eyes on her . . .

Enough lipstick? Too much? She had gone to great pains blending in and wiping off, until she was satisfied. Her caramel-brown suede hat that rolled up in front to show some of her hair would pass muster, she felt, and she had been well enough pleased with the London tailoring of her gray flannel suit and the well-polished, correct country look of her low-heeled alligator pumps. Gold earrings? A gold clip? She had decided in favor of them.

As she drove on, Margaret, feeling guiltier than ever, left the town behind her. The little car crossed the river, climbed the grade, and reached the fork in the road where she could turn either left or right.

She made her choice deliberately, but with a sick, gone feeling in her stomach, and after the miles of narrow, hedged lanes and muddy ruts and bracken and bluebells, she drove through the iron gates that, once she had closed them behind her, would never let her go.

Oh, yes, she could shove the gates wide again and turn around. Physically, it was perfectly possible. But she wasn't meant to; she was meant to drive on, until she reached the lonely, sad house ahead, just as she had been meant to look out her window that night in London.

It was fate, and what could she do about it? Nothing. She was convinced of it, but in spite of her resigned acceptance, fear and shame mounted, mounted in her as she drove to the front entrance of the house and, parking, saw Sir Hugh limping toward her from the direction of the archway leading to the stableyard.

"Our watchdogs announced you." He smiled and opened the car door. "I'll take you around to the puppies first, and then we'll tour the house. That is, if Cherry lets you get away. She is looking forward to seeing you immensely, I know, though she wouldn't think of admitting it."

"The kennel project sounds fascinating." Was it, or wasn't it, a tactful remark?

"Yes. And it could be worked into something very much worthwhile, financially."

"Then why . . . ?"

"Then why make it an issue, is that what you are wondering, Mrs. Collier?"

"I'm sorry—it's not my affair, but—"

"But you are sorry for my daughter? So am I, for that matter. Not that she doesn't irritate me."

"School wasn't a success? She didn't want college?"

"No. And she ought to be with young people. She ought to get away—take a job in town. She's too much alone here." He hesitated. "Monks' Court doesn't offer the most normal environment for a moody, introspective sort of girl."

"She'll marry one day, very likely."

"I sincerely hope so."

His concern was that of any father for the happiness of a difficult young daughter, and Margaret, confused and wondering, followed him through the archway, her conception of him shifting and reshifting, kaleidoscopically.

He was leading the way across the cobbled stableyard, where, in the rear of what she took to be a long-disused coachhouse, a bent old man in patched corduroys, rubber boots, and a thick woolen muffler was hosing a wire-fenced dog run.

At their approach, two mastiffs hurled themselves against the fence, barking loudly and ecstatically.

"Down, you chaps!" Sir Hugh ordered emphatically. "And that's enough noise. Down, I say! That's better. Good dogs, good dogs."

A Vane worshiped by those great slavering dogs. As a child she had been around dogs enough to know that much. Her father's hounds had been exactly as wild with joy when they saw him.

A reserved, cold Vane, unable because of that very coldness to reach his daughter. But how could you explain this other side of him?

He was making an introduction. "This is Chubb, Pell's brother, Mrs. Collier, who shares the vegetable-growing honors with my daughter, and keeps us going, generally."

"Good morning."

"And this is Mrs. Collier, Chubb, who has come to have a look at Miss Cherry's pups."

"Morning, ma'am."

The old man snuffled and spat, and touched a finger to a shapeless, dirty tattersall-check cap.

He had his sister's black, observant eyes, Margaret noticed, a surly, uncouth man, though, with nothing of Pell's well-trained manners and natural agreeableness.

After a pleasantry from her about the vegetables that received no response but a grunt, Sir Hugh pushed open the divided door of a stable that adjoined the coachhouse. Passing a harness room hung with old cracked leather and tarnished brasses, he led Margaret along a row of box stalls, empty except for one at the far end, where a black-and-white bitch was lying on bedding straw.

A litter of fat puppies was clambering over her, and Cherry, at a workbench stocked with bottles and swabs and eyedroppers, was mixing a bowlful of some antiseptic-smelling solution. She was intent on the process, with no time or interest for more than a perfunctory "Good morning" at first, but when Margaret began exclaiming over the puppies she put the bowl aside, and wiping her hands on her twill breeches and pushing back a lock of hair, volunteered a tentative advance.

"This is Court Lady's first litter."

"She's a beauty!"

"She'll do." It was remarked with a carefully assumed casualness.

"Her puppies are adorable! Absolutely adorable!"

The girl searched Margaret's face, consideringly.

"You may hold one if you like."

She picked up a squirming puppy and thrust it in Margaret's arms. "Here."

It was entirely unexpected, and for some reason infinitely touching.

Margaret patted the puppy, praising it extravagantly, letting it slobber and lick her enthusiastically, but when it began to wet her suit, she put it down, laughing.

"Give her back to Court Lady!"

The stable passageway was narrow, and as she brushed against Sir Hugh the awareness of his jacket sleeve was disconcerting. She drew away a little, and as though he, too, might have been conscious of their nearness to each other, Sir Hugh turned.

"We shall just have time for a look at the drawing room before lunch, Mrs. Collier," he said abruptly. "And Cherry, I'll expect you to join us for a sherry," he called back. "Don't be late, please." His glance over his shoulder was critical. "I suggest you change."

He ought not to have said it, he ought not to speak to the girl that way, as though she were a child in the nursery. Margaret was quickly resentful, for the girl's sake, but as Sir Hugh walked away, his right leg dragging, his cane indispensable, and as they again passed the row of empty stalls and came out into the stableyard, where the only horse in sight was a little rough-coated farm pony, she knew a quick, unwilling moment of pity for Cherry Vane's father as well.

No more riding and hunting for this twentieth-century baronet of Monks' Court. He was too lame, as well as too poor.

"The gardens offer nothing, unfortunately," Sir Hugh was remarking when they had crossed the yard. He nodded toward a long vista that could be glimpsed through a second archway in the wall, framed by an *allée* of tall cypress.

"An Italian bit, once, and farther on, beyond where it's turf now, there's a lake." He shrugged. "As you can see, lawns don't take to neglect."

Reluctant pity stirred in Margaret again. She could imagine terraced greensward, smooth as velvet, instead of coarse, rough turf, going down to the lake. The cypress would have been pruned columns instead of shapeless, gloomy masses.

A fountain would have spurted, there would have been goldfish and floating lotus flowers; now, there was nothing to look at but rusted pipes and a basin as cracked and lichened and drearily leaf-filled as the basin on the entrance terrace. A row of moss-stained, broken statues—a Diana and an Appollo, a Psyche and a Pan, a winged Mercury—standing in niches in the thick, dark cypress, struck her as depressing beyond words. To live here—to look out on this every day . . .

They reached the side entrance of the house that Margaret remembered from the day before, and when they were in the empty, echoing hall, Sir Hugh threw open a door opposite the dining room.

"The mantel and what is left of the plaster work are its only present merits, I'm afraid."

There was a musty, close smell to the long room down which she stared and a chill that was almost as unpleasant as the dankness of Monks' Court's ivy-smothered chapel. It was empty of all furnishings.

The faded, pale-blue damask paneling was marred, as the dining room walls were marred, by the outline of removed pictures and mirrors, and there were streaks of water stain. The ceiling, too, was stained by leaks, and, like the dining room, robbed of its center chandelier. Mold was creeping over the elaborate scrolling. Chunks of white plaster had broken loose from a garlanded frieze and lay shattered on the oak floor, where, in places, the joints of the intricate parquetry, warped with the drip of water, had sprung apart. In the recesses of three long, shuttered windows, more splitting, fraying damask hung in swagged draping.

At the far end of the room a white marble mantel was silhouetted, its carving a classic design of wheat sheaves.

"The ultimate in Adam, so I'm told. I'm waiting for an offer on it from New York," Sir Hugh commented indifferently.

There seemed no fitting remark to make in turn, and standing there awkwardly in the depressing quietness of the room, Margaret thought she could hear mice scrabbling in the walls.

"Have you had enough of a look, Mrs. Collier? Taken enough mental notes? We could tour the rest of the house, but it's all like this, more or less. You can see for yourself that the general public would have the right to feel done out of their two-and-six worth."

"If your house had a ghost, you could charge pounds and pounds, instead of shillings." Margaret said it with a nervous little laugh, wishing the room—the whole house—were not so movingly sad, so heavily weighting, with its emptiness and decay. "Americans adore ghosts. Does Monks' Court happen to have any on hand?" There was a barely perceptible pause, just long enough for her to regret the silly, trivial question.

"Yes."

"You could guarantee it? From personal observation?" The inanities seemed to blurt of their own accord, and the pause, this time, was chilling.

"There is one I know, intimately."

"Catharine Vane, with her braids hanging down, weeping for her hands?" The nervous, uncertain laugh was forced. He was making fun of her, of course.

"No." Sir Hugh's reply was level-voiced, emotionless. "The ghost I have in mind happens to be that of a little boy, Mrs. Collier. And I doubt if he would show himself to anyone but me—not even to an American no matter how many pounds were paid. He is shy. He always was."

What was she supposed to say, after that? What *was* there to say? In a silence broken only by the scrabbling mice, Margaret turned when Sir Hugh turned and followed him through the door that he closed behind him.

"We'll just go along here now, Mrs. Collier. You've no objections to sherry and a fire after that freezing drawing room, I take it?"

He was briskly, politely concerned with her comfort as he led the way along the hall. "We won't wait for Cherry. She hasn't the least idea of time—or, I should say, she deliberately ignores it when she's down at the stable with those dogs of hers."

"She is a very pretty girl." Margaret seized the conversational opening gladly.

"Is she? I hadn't noticed."

"Oh?"

"My wife, Cherry's mother, is dead. And I'm not much of a father. It has been Pell who has brought up my daughter, not I."

It was explained to her concisely. And coldly, Margaret thought, with her pity for Cherry Vane quickening as Sir Hugh opened another door off the hall and showed her into a room that she saw was not only a library and estate office, but a repository of family heirlooms.

And a room of how many yesterdays, she wondered, a room unchanged in decor for how many years? Heavy brown curtains whose velvet had lost its nap hung at the windows, their worn, floor-sweeping folds looped back with tasseled gold cords to permit a view of the Welsh hills, and of the now neglected sweep of entrance lawn and driveway.

Books lined two of the wood-paneled walls, many of them bound in handsome, gilt-stamped leather, none of them new.

Military maps hung on another wall in company with tarnished crossed swords, a grouping of antique fowling pieces, the World War II service revolver of a British Army officer and, surprisingly, a child's toy drum, its sticks thrust through a lacing of scarlet cords.

Only over the mantel was there bare space of any size—a faded square and a hole left by a picture nail.

Margaret dragged her glance from the mantel to a globe of the world, painted with dolphins and mermaids, standing in one corner of the room, and to a long-case clock with a brass pendulum in another, ticking raspingly, and then to a tall, glass-fronted secretary against the fourth wall.

Every shelf of it was crammed with military and naval souvenirs: medals, epaulets, tunic buttons, cartridge cases—and they were only part of the jumble. Sealing-waxed parchment scrolls. Several pocket-size books that might be diaries, and ribbon-tied packets of old letters.

Wouldn't Ritchie love to rummage!

Automatically it occurred to her, and then, as her eyes went everywhere but back to the mantel, her attention was caught and held for an instant by an incongruously modern filing cabinet, piled high not only with farm journals but with a large assortment of newspapers—London newspapers?—and by a ponderous desk centered with an enlarged, silver-framed snapshot of two children. Two little boys; two little boys, near in age, wearing very English white sailor suits, in an old-fashioned wicker governess cart, driving a fat Shetland pony. Brothers, you could guess from their resemblance; was Sir Hugh one of them?

She turned from the desk to the stone hearth, where an old, almost blind, hunting dog, lying stretched out, had lifted its head from its paws when Sir Hugh opened the door and was now feebly thumping its tail while Sir Hugh, leaning down, patted it and rumpled its ears.

"Did we wake you, poor old duffer?"

The dog put its head on its paws again to snooze content-edly, and Sir Hugh pulled a worn leather wing chair closer to the fire. "Sit down, won't you, Mrs. Collier? I'll give this log a poke."

He sat down opposite her then, in another shabby high-backed chair.

"Your writing interests me; may I hear more about it? Which magazine is going to publish your article? Or a series of articles, is it? And what other English houses have you written up?"

The unexpectedness of it left her speechless for a moment. Magazine . . . ? Houses? No names came to mind, with those unreadable eyes on her, so steadily and unrelentingly waiting an answer.

"I—I—you see—" Desperately, she tried to think. "I free-lance." To avoid his eyes she leaned forward in her chair and put her hands out to the blaze of the fire. "And I haven't been in England very long—I—I'm just starting to write."

"Free-lancing? You aren't a newspaper woman, by any chance?"

"No—"

"How did you hear of Monks' Court? I am extremely flat-tered, naturally, but somewhat surprised at its being written up, with so many older and far handsomer houses to choose from. But my dear Mrs. Collier, you're shivering. That beastly drawing room. I shouldn't have inflicted it on you. Let's hope the sherry will help. I'll fetch it directly."

The old dog opened its rheumy eyes again as Sir Hugh left the room, and closed them, and once more, slept. So much here at Monks' Court that was caught up in sleep, Margaret thought, rubbing her icy, trembling hands and wishing they would steady themselves. Not only this old pointer on the hearth but the decaying gardens where the fountains were stilled, the bedrooms upstairs along that hall where so many doors were shut, the drawing room, its quiet disturbed only by scrabbling mice, the chapel, where the third Sir Hugh of the triumvirate she had been fated to know lay beside his handless Catharine.

The somnolent world of Monks' Court; the dreamworld of Monks' Court, with herself trapped in the dream. And, as in all dreams—all nightmares—the dreamer, struggling to waken, struggling desperately, was helpless.

TWELVE

Slowly the warmth of the fire, the ticktock of the clock, the wheezy, snuffling snore of the old dog brought a vestige of common sense to her thinking, and her submissive, numbed waiting for returning footsteps and the sound of a door opening showed itself to Margaret for what it was, a humiliation, a degradation not to be borne.

Where was her courage—the courage that had brought her here? Where was her pride in herself as a thinking, intelligent woman who could look after herself, defend herself, in any situation? And what of her curiosity, her insatiable, driving curiosity to find out more about this mysterious baronet of Monks' Court?

Was she giving up now? Would she run, even if she could, even if he let her? And where was her ingenuity in thinking up a way to stay on here until her curiosity was satisfied? Pull yourself together, she told herself. It's all you need do. And stop cowering. Get up on your feet!

She was out of the chair and making a pretense of looking at the swords on the wall when Sir Hugh came back with a silver tray, but as she turned toward him and saw him lift a decanter, his filling of a glass was, for a second time, overwhelming and her fear close to hysteria.

A tall, limping Englishman in a London flat pouring wine.

Her hands clenched. The nails cut into her wet palms. He would come closer, closer. Oh, God . . .

"Is there to be a magazine article about Wellington, by any chance, Mrs. Collier?"

"Wellington?" She repeated it senselessly as she took the offered glass.

"This happens to be a relic of the Peninsular Wars." Sir Hugh touched the hilt of one of the swords. "Or perhaps you—and your readers—would be more interested in this one? It was used at the Battle of the Boyne. Note the Toledo blade and the inlaid ivory grip."

Determinedly, Margaret ignored the sarcasm of the pedantically offered description.

"And this one?" she asked, to have something to say.

"It came from Macao. It's an officer's presentation sword."

"Macao reminds me of the lovely Chinese Chippendale wallpaper in your guest room. Have the Vanes always had ties with the Orient, like so many English people? A fascinating place, from what I've heard, that never lets go its hold on you."

The Orient. Her nervously rattled off comment was no sooner made than Madame Duclair the Eurasian was again uppermost in Margaret's mind.

"You have heard correctly, Mrs. Collier. The Orient is unforgettable."

If there had been a pause before Sir Hugh's entirely expressionless agreement it was infinitesimal, and he was indicating a short, blunt, double-edged weapon.

"Medieval. The oldest of any of them, and—"

"Have you ever considered selling the swords?" She interrupted with an inspiration so daring she could not believe it was she herself speaking. "Or all those other things?" She nodded toward the secretary. "They look marvelously interesting. And your books. They are extremely valuable, I should think. Have they ever been catalogued?"

"Not that I know of. Certainly not in my father's, nor my own days here."

"Then—then would you consider letting me make a listing?" Ice water seemed to gush through Margaret as she asked it. "I have a friend who is a collector. A beginner at it, but he has a good deal of money, and if all this could be itemized and described and priced—"

"The greater part of the furnishings of Monks' Court are already in the market, it's true, Mrs. Collier, as you seem to have noticed, but not all of them. There are some things not even American dollars can buy. Unless the pinch worsens, that is."

She was scarlet at the whiplash of it, and the faint smile she had seen the day before curved his thin lips again.

"There is no need for embarrassment Mrs. Collier. I can quite understand your supposition that I am seriously in need of funds. And how right you are. But fortunately my situation isn't completely hopeless at the moment—although there is always the future to consider. My daughter's future, I should say. Taxes, you understand—and death; the two inevitables."

Death. A heavy, echoing word; not one she cared to dwell on. Margaret looked at the swords again, avoiding Sir Hugh's eyes.

He was silent for a moment, and then slowly and consider-ingly he asked, "Would a serious cataloguing project appeal to you personally, by any chance, Mrs. Collier? You'd take it on yourself?"

As she quickly faced him, her eagerness undisguisable, try as she did to hide it, he went on, "You have made me realize that an inventory might not be a bad thing, whether or not I am ever forced to sell. It would be something of a job, you know, and might take an uncommon lot of time. And you'd find driving back and forth to town every day an exhausting nuisance, but you'd be more than welcome to stay on here until you got through with it. It's the practical approach—if your friend's collecting interest warrants the amount of work you'd have to put in. Ludlow is almost twenty miles away, you know. Twenty English country miles can seem three times that many in wet weather."

Both exultant and terrified, she was gauging him now, but his expression was unreadable. Stay on? He meant it. He was making possible the carrying out of her reckless plan. But did it only mean that his curiosity about her had been aroused? He, too, might have secret doubts and misgivings.

That sharp-edged question, for instance, as to whether she was a newspaper woman. He had reasons of his own, did he, for wanting to keep her here. He wanted to study her. He wanted to discover the true purpose of her coming to Monks' Court.

Well, then, let him try. He wouldn't succeed; there was no possible way for him to find out. For a brief instant, Margaret was full of confidence, and proud of the courage she had sal-vaged, proud of the "pulling herself together" she had ac-complished against such odds. Her chance to stay: here it was, handed to her. And when she had discovered what had to be discovered, she'd go back again to Ritchie.

If only this old, sad house were not so quiet, so remote, so crowded with secrets. And then it had a ghost. Not really, of course. She didn't for a minute believe it.

Margaret, averring it stoutly, banished from her thinking the supernatural. It was the owner of Monks' Court, not his house, that would put her to the test. She glanced into the challenging, cold eyes of the man opposite her, but in seconds she looked away, hastily, and once more put her hands to the fire.

"I ought to get back to London." Weakly, she offered it.

Sir Hugh put the tray on his desk and unstoppered the decanter.

"London can wait."

It allowed of no argument. "I shall send Chubb to town for your luggage."

"But my clothes—the packing—and my bill."

"We have a telephone, Mrs. Collier. It can all be arranged quite simply."

He was refusing to let her go.

More than that, he was the magnet again, drawing her, against whose attraction any will of her own was helpless. Caught, and moving in a trance from which there seemed no hope of awakening, Margaret picked up her handbag and opened it.

"This should cover my bill, whatever it is." She held out two five-pound notes. "And will you ask your man, please, to tip the chambermaid or the housekeeper, whoever packs for me?"

The hands she held out to the fire were still cold, and when Sir Hugh filled a glass and offered it, she lifted it to her lips hurriedly, unsteadily.

"Old houses have their drawbacks. I hope you won't miss American heating arrangements too much."

Sir Hugh's grave concern was mocked by a twisted smile. "A matter of accustoming oneself. Perhaps, if you stay long enough . . ." He glanced toward the door. "Come in, Cherry."

She had brushed her soft dark hair and obediently changed from jodhpurs to a skirt and cardigan, but she had joined them only under duress, Margaret suspected, as the girl accepted a glass of sherry and sat down on a cushion by the hearth, with the toe of one shoe a back scratcher for the old dog.

She was elaborately disinterested at first in her father and Margaret. She might as well have been alone in the room. But when Sir Hugh, refilling his own glass, casually announced that Mrs. Collier would be staying on to do some cataloguing—"rather a sound idea, it struck me, when she mentioned having a friend very much in the collector's market"—her large, clear eyes fastened on Margaret disconcertingly.

"London has plenty of shops; why does your friend need to come into private houses to buy?"

"No one is buying or selling anything, Cherry." Sir Hugh's rebuke was swift. "This is a question of an inventory, nothing more. It's time we got around to it. It has been on my mind."

"If it was on your mind, Father, why have you never spoken of it? And why shouldn't I get at it now, if it's important? Why do we need—a stranger?"

"You're being shockingly rude, are you not? And as I have asked Mrs. Collier to take over, and she has most kindly consented, the matter is settled."

"But Father—"

"That's enough, Cherry."

The girl checked a quick retort, but the eyes that were so like her father's in color, yet lacked any masking inscrutability, were bright with swift anger.

Or was the brightness a springing of hurt, hot tears?

In any case, the girl was jealous, a daughter longing for so much more from her father than she got, and miserable when someone else caught his interest.

That touching little incident with the puppies in the kennel might never have occurred, Margaret realized uncomfortably. From now on, she would very definitely be *persona non grata* to Cherry Vane.

Awkward, to put it mildly! A ridiculous situation. Grotesque under the circumstances. Margaret went into lunch when Pell appeared to announce it, pitying Cherry but berating herself.

Fool, fool, that she was, she thought as she sat down. Why was she stubbornly determined to stay on here in this depressing, decadent house, with only a blood-chilling, enigmatic-eyed man and a sensitive, sullen girl for company?

But there was Pell in this sad, blighted house, too. Give thanks for Pell. Margaret exclaimed it to herself with a grateful clutching at straws as the old woman wheeled the trolley through the dining room's swinging door and Sir Hugh began to pass plates.

The sight of grilled kidneys and tomatoes and bacon was almost ludicrously reassuring, and after that, rice pudding helped, too. The pudding was custardy, and full of raisins, and thick country cream was passed with it, to be poured from a Staffordshire pitcher in the form of a cow, and it was all very English, very substantial, with Pell in her cap and apron a kind of symbol, bespeaking all things safe, all things sane.

The good, solid food and a glass of hock warmed and emboldened her, and when lunch was over she was capable, without visible tremor, of allowing Pell to put a telephone message through to The Feathers' housekeeper arranging for madam's bags to be packed and madam's bill to be totaled. Chubb was despatched in an old, battered, mud-splashed Land Rover.

After Sir Hugh had escorted her outside and shown her where she might garage her own car in the stableyard, Margaret, with an excuse of enjoying a walk through the gardens, started off by herself through the archway that led to the cypress allée.

Uncomfortably, she was reviewing a parting question Sir Hugh had put to her.

"You have pencil and paper, have you? If not, I shall be happy to supply you."

"Pencil and paper?"

"You take notes, don't you, for your garden articles?"

"Oh, yes, of course." She had opened her bag hurriedly. "I have everything, thank you."

Had Sir Hugh believed, even for an instant, that her little brown leather address book was anything but just that, and blank as far as garden or house data went? With no hope of it, she had hurried off, feeling his eyes on her, knowing they were following her.

She strolled in the lonely, neglected garden until a chilly shower drove her back to the house, and Pell answered when she had let the brass knocker drop loudly several times.

"Your luggage is here, madam. I've unpacked for you."

"Thank you. Am I to have the room I was in yesterday?"

"Yes, madam."

"I'll go up, I think."

"Certainly, madam. And I'll just come along to show you the light switches along the hall and in the bath, so you'll not be left stumbling about in the dark later."

The dark, at Monks' Court, would not be pleasant, Margaret reflected uneasily.

When she had followed Pell up the stairs and reached the top landing, the long hall ahead seemed to stretch endlessly past one closed door after another.

"This is the guest wing, madam." Pell volunteered the information as though she had sensed Margaret's curiosity about the shut doors. "In the old days, when Sir Hugh's mother and father were alive—in their younger days, that is —there was always a lot of coming and going, but it's been very different these twenty years or so since the war."

She opened the door to the room done in chinoiserie and yellow linen, and as she went to the windows and drew the curtains closed, she asked, apologetically, "You don't mind, madam, even though it is a bit on the early side? What with dinner to start, and the table to lay, and Sir Hugh's drinks tray to put out, and supper for myself, I shan't be getting upstairs again this evening. I'm fairly on the hop, this time of day, and the unpacking put me back some'at. Not that it isn't a treat, madam, a guest stopping, and it's only a pity, as I was saying to Chubb when he came up with the bags, that there's only one of me, instead of half a dozen, to do what's needed in this big house to keep everyone comfortable."

She was turning down the bed then and putting out Margaret's nightgown and robe and slippers. "I hope you've no objections to take things as you find them, madam, now you're staying on."

"Everything is very nice indeed."

"It's kind of you to say, I'm sure. I don't mind telling you it's a worry to me, madam, things all at sixes and sevens and gone to pieces through no fault of Sir Hugh's, with his needing to put the little money he's got into working the land, if he's to hold on to it, with nothing left for keeping up the house. Changing times, they're something I could do without!"

"Have you been with the Vanes a long while?"

"I came from the village as scullery maid when I first went out in service, madam. My auntie was cook here, and she spoke for me, and for Chubb, who got put on as gardener's boy. There was a proper staff indoors and out, those days.

After, I was nursery maid, put to fetching trays for the children's nanny."

"The children?" Margaret thought back to the records at Somerset House. "Sir Hugh had a younger brother, didn't he?"

"Yes, madam. Master Jarvis." Pell settled a fold of the curtains.

Was it only her imagination, Margaret wondered, that made the brief statement seem a disinclination on Pell's part to further discuss the brother? An odd, chill little interim passed, and then Pell, obviously surprised at Margaret's knowledge of the Vane family, asked, "You saw the plaque to Master Jarvis in the chapel, did you?"

"Yes." Ashamed of the lie that covered her slip, Margaret quickly changed the subject. "This is such a big house— where are Sir Hugh's and Miss Vane's bedrooms?"

"Across the landing, madam, quite some way along, in the west wing."

"Where do you sleep?"

Pell looked surprised, again. "The staff's rooms are in the attics, madam." What she meant was, *naturally* in the attics. Where else had servants ever been expected to sleep in this Queen Anne manor house?

With only one servant to occupy them now, the attics would be as lonely as this shut-up guest wing, Margaret reflected, but the difference was that Pell had nothing to be frightened of, up there. Pell was used to the house. But down here, for a stranger, it would be a different story when dusk came on, and the hall filled with shadows, and the floorboards and the wainscoting began to creak.

"The switch is just here, madam, for your bed light, and there are matches in the nightstand drawer for the candle— the electricity fails now and again, the wiring not what it might be, and too costly for Sir Hugh to have put right."

There was a pair of silver candlesticks on the dressing table, too, Margaret saw, and she picked up one of the little tortoise-shell boxes, knowing she would find more matches.

"Does the electricity go off very often?" she asked, wishing at the moment that she were anywhere but at Monks' Court.

"Now and again, as I say, madam; it's not only the house wiring, it's all of our power system that wants replacing. But we manage quite nicely, with lamps for me in the kitchen when needed and lamps in Sir Hugh's library. They're a bother, lamps are, as you may know, madam, what with the cleaning and filling, so we don't have them everywhere. And now, madam, if there's nothing more required, I'll be going along."

Lamps in the upper hallway, with their cheerful, steady glow. Margaret hoped so as Pell left the room. One needed light in a murderer's house. Lamps in the children's rooms? There had been a Master Jarvis and a Master Hugh, living in this cold, sad house once; the two little boys in sailor suits.

She began to wonder, for no reason at all, where their nursery had been. In this wing? She felt certain of it, although she could not possibly have explained the certainty. It would be further along the hall, probably, much further, past all the other guest rooms, so that children, playing, could not disturb their elders.

At the very end of the hall? Around the turn, beyond the huge, old-fashiond bathroom with its wooden-rimmed, claw-footed tub, and its hot-water heater and marble basin? Beyond what Pell had referred to as the W.C.?

She had noticed, vaguely, a paint-scuffed door, some sort of service door opening from a back passage. A door to a serv-ant's stairway? Perhaps the stair Pell once climbed, running nursery errands.

Odd—she could picture the interior of the nursery as defi-nitely as she had been able to place its location along the hall.

A coal grate, with firelight on a tall brass fender. A dappled gray rocking horse in a corner. Shelves of fairy tales, and derring-do books, and toy soldiers set out. A nanny, rocking and mending in a comfortable, shabby, chintz-covered chair.

Pell, a young Pell with a country girl's red cheeks, clattering teacups and milk mugs, plates of bread and butter, bowls of porridge, dishes of pudding. And the children . . . ? Could she see the children?

Margaret came to herself with a start, and a little hurriedly reached out to flick on the light switch. A bedroom like this, so apart from the rest of the house, so silent, except for the softly pattering rain, and so shadowy with its curtains drawn, gave you all sorts of ridiculous notions.

Forget the children. It was time to take a bath and dress for dinner. The question was, though, what should she wear? There was not much choice, she realized as she opened the door of the wardrobe where Pell had hung her clothes. Sweaters and skirts and blouses, wasn't that about it? But no, there was the yellow wool, the long-skirted, long-sleeved dress she had put in, just in case, for The Feathers.

As she went into the hall and gave a quick glance toward the passage that led, she was confident, to their nursery, the Vane children were uppermost in her thoughts. Master Hugh, who was Sir Hugh, now, and Master Jarvis. Standing in her yellow dress, which was warm gold under the single globe that shadowed rather than lighted the landing, she hesitated before starting down the stairs.

Master Jarvis—a little boy ghost, by any chance? She would scream if she saw him, if he conquered his shyness, and let her see him up here in this long hall, so close to the nursery passage.

To stay upstairs would be to risk sight of one brother. To go down was to face the other. A toss-up. The flip of a coin. Heads I win, tails you lose.

But Sir Hugh was a magnet. She had no choice whether to go down or stay. A magnet drawing her, drawing her irresistibly. Slowly, Margaret took a step forward. In silent desperation her every fear cried out: Ritchie! Come take me away. Come in time. Hurry, Ritchie!

THIRTEEN

There was sherry in the library again, with Sir Hugh in a shabby dinner jacket and his daughter in an equally shabby long black velvet skirt and tartan-plaid wool blouse.

The fire was burning, the old dog snoozed on the hearth, and Margaret, her hand once more unsteady as she held her glass, told herself it could all be the rerun of a film she had seen before. Even the sound track was the same; the dog's heavy snuffling, the slow, rasping tick-tick of the clock, her voice a shade too highly pitched, the flow of her forced attempt at conversation a bright, shallow stream of meaningless words. If only the girl would talk and not just stare at her out of those huge moody eyes.

It was a relief to go into the dining room eventually, where Pell was, and a relief to have coffee over with a little later so she could excuse herself and go up to her room.

The prospect of a long, shadowy hall to be faced, a long night to be gotten through in the lonely east wing was infinitely preferable to a stay in the library, sitting opposite a man whose steady gaze was as unrelenting as his daughter's. Because all that ghost business was utter nonsense—absurd. And as far as a long night was concerned, she had plenty to read—practically a bookshop supply of Penguins.

She would choose something light and relaxing to fall asleep over, that would be the wise thing to do; no murder mysteries, certainly.

She reached the chinoiserie bedroom with a self-control of which she was proud, but she was quick to turn on the lights and both to turn the key in the door and to bolt it. Which was silly, she realized with a little shiver. If there were such a thing as a ghost, keys and bolts wouldn't do a bit of good.

The soft pattering of the rain, which, if she were absolutely idiotic, she could think of as a child running in the hall, made the shivering a trifle difficult to control. It was the cold, of course, the chilly dampness of the room that was responsible.

She persuaded herself of it and got into bed, grateful but surprised to find a hot-water bottle warming the linen sheets. Conscientious Pell, trudging upstairs again on those unwearying feet of hers?

Or could it possibly have been the daughter? Had that sullen, resentful little creature felt bound in spite of herself to look after the comfort of a guest?

Margaret piled the pillows behind her head and pulled up an eiderdown puff. Opening a book about travel adventures in warm, sunny Spain, she read a few pages and then, beginning to feel drowsy, she turned off the bedside light.

It was a mistake. Both the darkness and the continuing patter of the rain were immediately highly distasteful. The child wasn't running lightly, she realized, listening; there was a small drag to the sound of his footsteps.

She closed her eyes tightly and told herself she would on no account open them to look if the pattering should seem to come any closer, and then she immediately opened them widely, ashamed of herself.

It had to be rain. She would defy the darkness and the soft pattering even while she wished the eiderdown and the hot-water bottle could make her feel warmer and snugger and not so ridiculously afraid.

Rain. It couldn't be anything else—except in a house like this one, so very old and so very sad. Not that the child out there was unnecessarily anything but happy. It was the drag of his footsteps that had pathos. But what was she saying! The drag was the rain, slowly ceasing. The pattering died away altogether after a time; slowly she was less shivery, and then she was asleep.

It was morning before she wakened. Someone was knocking at the door, she realized drowsily, someone was calling her name.

"Mrs. Collier. Mrs. Collier. I've brought your breakfast."

"One moment," Margaret called as she got into her robe and slippers and hurried to the windows and drew aside the curtains. Then she unbolted the door and turned the key, wondering a little embarrassedly what Cherry Vane would think of a house guest who considered it necessary to lock herself in with such elaborate precaution.

"Good morning." Margaret took the tray from the girl. "You shouldn't have bothered. It was very good of you."

"Someone had to bring it up," the girl said ungraciously with a "good morning" of her own. "Pell has the downstairs to put in order first thing every day as soon as she's finished with Father's breakfast. There's the sweeping and dusting and ashes to take out and fires to lay. That's the way we divide things, Pell and I—she does the housework and I do the outside things. There are the chickens and ducks besides the vegetables and the dogs."

"I don't in the least want to be a nuisance, my dear." Margaret put the tray on a small table, and then, as the girl started to turn away, she added uncomfortably, "I shan't be staying long. It shouldn't take more than a few days to list the books and the things in the secretary. As a matter of fact, the quicker I can get back to London, the better it will be."

Awkwardly then she changed the subject, intensely disliking the girl's resentful sullen gaze. "What a lovely morning after the rain. Just look at that heavenly sunshine!" On impulse she added, "Won't you come in and keep me company while I eat this delicious-looking breakfast? Do."

"I've the dogs to look after. I don't have time to come in."

"Those darling puppies. I hope you'll let me have another peek at them. Will you?"

The girl shrugged. "You know where the kennel is," was her answer as she walked away.

Of all the ungraciousness, of all the deliberate rudeness! With a flush of annoyance, Margaret sat down and attempted to enjoy a breakfast that was already spoiled for her. What was the use of trying to make any sort of approach to the child? She lifted a flowered-silk cozy from a brown teapot and filled a cup, and took a piece of toast from a silver rack. What was the use of wasting the smallest civil gesture on her, the smallest of well-meant approaches?

And yet—if she *had* brought up that hot-water bottle . . . Margaret wished she had asked Cherry about it, and while she ate and thought about Sir Hugh's daughter, she found her annoyance fading.

She finished her breakfast and dressed and made her bed, and then, with the tray and the hot-water bottle, she went downstairs to the kitchen, which she found when she pushed open the swinging door in the dining room and gone through a butler's pantry lined with cupboards full of glass and china and silver.

Pell was in the scullery beyond, wringing out a mop.

"You shouldn't have bothered, madam." She glanced disapprovingly at Margaret. "I'd have managed the tray when I came up to do your bedroom and the bath."

"Mayn't I look after them, please? As I told Miss Vane, I don't want to be a bother, and if you just show me where the cleaning things are . . ."

Margaret emptied the hot-water bottle into the sink as she spoke. "Do I thank you or Miss Vane for this? It was wonderful, finding it in my bed last night."

"Miss Cherry, she took it up, madam. Out she came, after dinner, to fill it from the kettle, the pipes not ever heating up like they should, and—"

"Did you ask her to take it up?"

"Ask her, madam?" Pell looked surprised.

"I mean, did she do it just to save you another trip upstairs, or did she think of it herself? Not that it's important," Margaret added lightly, "I just want whoever it was that thought of those cold sheets to know how appreciative I am."

She left the kitchen with the feeling that, though she had made something of a rather large mountain out of a very small molehill, at least her curiosity was satisfied. As she went back to the front of the house and knocked at the door of Sir Hugh's office, the last of her irritation was gone; fundamentally the girl was a nice enough little thing. Too bad that her own almost impossibly difficult stay at Monks' Court should be made that much more unpleasant by Cherry Vane's attitude.

Almost impossibly difficult? If she changed that to utterly mad, wouldn't she be closer to the truth?

At Sir Hugh's "Come in," she turned the doorknob.

He was sitting at his desk looking through a London newspaper, which he put down to say a coldly formal "Good morning" and then to fix her with one of the steady, scrutinizing glances she invariably lacked the courage to meet.

"I thought, if it's convenient, I'd like to start . . ."

She ventured it in a voice she could barely keep steady. Her right hand was pulling nervously at her wedding ring, slipping it on and off over her knuckles.

"The project still interests you, Mrs. Collier?"

"Yes."

"About this friend of yours, the collector—it wouldn't be simpler if he came himself to look through things and make me an offer personally?"

"No—no, you see—you see, he—he hasn't the time. He can't get away from London just now."

Her wedding ring slipped from her finger to the floor and she bent hurriedly to pick it up from the worn, faded hearth-rug.

"When you are quite ready, Mrs. Collier." Sir Hugh stood up and held out a key. "I suggest you start with the top shelf of the secretary. The military memorabilia is arranged more or less according to dates."

He limped to one of the walls of books and pulled a small library ladder over to the secretary.

"There'll be a certain amount of dust, but I'm sure you won't let it put you off. You have your pencil and notebook? Now then, in that envelope to the right, you'll find a few scraps of silk. It's all that's left of a banner we Vanes carried at Crécy. But you'll see the tags; everything's marked.

"There's really no need for me to point out things. Those bits of silk won't bring much, of course, but I'm afraid I shall ask rather a stiff price for the sword belt and dagger you'll find on the same shelf a little farther along. A nice example of chase-work, and if your collector friend is at all interested in early armor . . ."

Margaret walked to the secretary and unlocked its glass door, and with the steps in position and Sir Hugh waiting, there was nothing for it but to climb up and with a show of interest, no matter how obviously false, to take notes on her pad.

". . . the fifteenth-century gauntlet on the next shelf is supposed to have been given to a Vane by Edward the Fourth. He spent a good part of his time at Ludlow, and we were fairly helpful to him in a battle that took place just down the road a bit, at Mortimer's Cross—you pass the signpost going into town. The gold-thread embroidery and those amethysts sewn on—they're real, by the way—make it worth something. But of course a little thing like price won't stand in the way of an American, I expect. You might call his special attention to that goblet there, too. We've the same Edward to thank for it. One of the more pious of my ancestors had it blessed by the Bishop of Gloucester, and it was used in the chapel as a communion cup—but seeing that we badly need a new tractor. . . . It would make a nice golf trophy, wouldn't you say? I really shall have to ask a good round sum. And if your friend doesn't happen to be a golfer, his wife—if he has one—could always have it standing about for a flower vase."

She would have found his continual sarcasm detestable even if nothing else about him were abhorrent, Margaret thought as she scribbled names and dates on sheet after sheet of her pad.

It wasn't a crime to be rich. There was nothing to be ashamed of about being an American collector. What infuriating arrogance and superiority!

In a way you couldn't blame him, though, not with a spur in your hand that a Vane had worn at Flodden Field. Not when you remembered for how many years there had been Vanes in England.

Saxon Vanes, to begin with, established here in Salop long before William the Conqueror had come along.

He needn't have said what he had, though, he needn't have insinuated that it was she who would be her collector friend's wife, using a king's goblet—a communion cup—for a flower vase.

An American tourist. Didn't he know there were more than one kind? Didn't he have any conception of Americans who were neither crass nor stupid about their traveling and the way they spent their money?

She glanced at him with furious indignation. He had put down one newspaper and unfolded another. Nothing—not a line about the murder, if you could judge by his imperturbable face. Another surreptitious glance showed him occupied at his desk with an account book and with writing out checks.

Everyone wrote checks and had to keep accounts of some sort. The commonplaceness of it, to begin with, and then the stir of a very real interest in the contents of each shelf she was examining made her momentarily forget her fear of Sir Hugh, the memory of what he had done in Honorine Duclair's flat.

The seventeenth century; here it was, made real to her as she looked at an epaulet worn by an officer of Charles the Second, fighting for his king at the Battle of Worcester, and another worn in the Marlborough campaigns.

Wars—wars—wars—and always a Vane, fighting.

The eighteenth century, and the Georges, on this next shelf—the era the Vane of the portrait had known. A Vane with Clive in India, and a button off his uniform. The sort of button Ritchie would give anything for. A feather, described in faded ink as "From the Headdress of an Iroquois." A dispatch box used when the Duke of York invaded Holland, and a plumed, visored shako, bloodied at Waterloo.

Victoria's reign next, and a miniature of a Vane killed in the Charge of the Light Brigade. Another button from the tunic of a Vane killed at the Siege of Sevastopol. A Vane who had fought the Boers in Africa and written a letter to his wife before he was killed at the Defense of Mafeking. Enough of them getting home, though, to breed more Vanes. A Victoria Cross, won at Ypres in World War I.

A Distinguished Service Cross awarded in World War II. Margaret picked up a small leather case, her glance going again to Sir Hugh. This was his decoration? He must have been very young in those days. A boy. One of those proverbial English schoolboys who left their playing fields to sign up for the services.

The last of the Vanes a war hero? It was perfectly possible, of course. The most callous, the most cruel of men were capable of making good soldiers. Cruel. The man in the Duclair woman's flat must have been exactly that. To kill. She gave a little shiver.

The bruised throat. The discolored face, and the head that had crashed against a fender.

As though her silent questioning had somehow made itself heard, Sir Hugh looked up, disconcertingly, from his accounting.

"Your friend could go to any pawnshop and buy that sort of thing by the dozen," he commented, "so I shan't ask more than a pound or two for it. I couldn't, in all conscience. Better make a note of it, had you not, Mrs. Collier? 'All military medals and decorations to be had half price due to overstocked British market.' And do you realize you have been on that ladder for almost two hours? Why not take a turn in the garden before lunch? You'll have all afternoon for your labors—the entire week—as long as you choose to give us the pleasure of your company, for that matter. We are hoping that neither the demands of your editor nor of your collector will deprive us of your company in any undo rush."

She flushed crimson at the sarcasm in his voice, even while all her fears rushed back. What was he suspecting, what was he trying to get at? What did he hope to learn by this farce of hospitality, this chilling willingness to go along with her weak, faltering lies, her prevarications, that a child could see through?

Would he let her go if, as seemed likely, the last small remnant of her insane determination to stay on here failed her?

His cold eyes on her offered a discomforting answer. Margaret put the little leather case back on the shelf, and with her legs weak under her, got down from the ladder.

"Just leave your notes here on the desk, Mrs. Collier. And I suggest you put on your mackintosh if you are walking; our Shropshire weather isn't to be depended upon these late spring days."

He stood up, the newspaper in hand, as she left the room without a word, and going up to her room for her raincoat, Margaret thought about the newspaper and about the others open on his desk. Two that she had seen him scan, but there were more—a copy of every London daily. Not only the *Times*, which you might so well expect to find on his desk, as on the desk of any conservative Englishman, but those others —the papers she herself had snatched at and read so avidly, that attracted their readers with the sensational, the scandalous, and that would carry every detail of a West End murder case. Was he getting nervous? Was he wondering what clues the police were following?

She pulled on the mackintosh, tied the Liberty scarf around her head, and let herself out the side door into the kitchen garden with a nod for Chubb, who was planting a hill of potatoes. But was she in the mood for the garden? She didn't want Chubb for a companion. Something about him, something about his bright, scrutinizing eyes . . . and the garden was too near the house, she decided, much, much too near.

Quickly, with her hands clenched in her pockets, her step

determined, Margaret left the rows of vegetables behind her and struck off down the driveway past the chapel, past a little copse of beech trees. Skirting a field green with young oats, she took a path that led along the bank of a stream, rushing and eddying and then quieting to become a stretch of water where willows trailed long drooping branches in placid pools, marsh-marigolds reflected their glistening cups, and dragon-flies darted.

She took off her raincoat and spread it on the damp grassy bank and sat down, thankful for the tranquillity of the spot, thankful for solitude and a chance to forget, if only for a little while, Sir Hugh Vane and her unwilling enmeshment in his life.

Leaning against a tree trunk, she closed her eyes, with filtered sunshine falling on her face, a soft breeze, smelling of grass and water and new leaves, ruffling her hair that was free from the scarf she had loosened.

She had almost fallen asleep to the sound of gently murmuring water and of birdsong from the willow thickets when a surprised, "I say! Sorry if I've disturbed you. I hadn't an idea anyone was about," made her eyes jerk open, and she sat up straight, to stare at a young man with a fishing pole in his hand, a wicker creel slung over his shoulder.

"Lucky thing I didn't step on you." The young man laughed. "I've come to think of the stream being mine, all mine, these past few weeks, I'm afraid. The last thing I expected was to trip over a poacher—a female poacher."

"Isn't it you who are the poacher?" Margaret smiled. A nice young man, with a voice she liked and an attractive sense of humor. "This is the Vanes' stream, isn't it? And I didn't know there were any other Vanes, besides Sir Hugh and his daughter."

"I've been given guest privileges." The young fisherman's

hazel eyes were merry. "I'm absolutely in the clear, so if you were thinking of preferring charges you'd best give up the idea. But what about yourself? Guest privileges, too?"

"Not exactly. In a way, I suppose. I'm stopping at Monks' Court for a few days on—well, on business. And I've been taking a walk. But it was so still, so beautifully peaceful here."

"The Sleeping Beauty!"

There was nothing impertinent about it, there was only boyishness, and again a humor.

"I'm Robin Soames, by the way. And you know Miss Vane, do you?"

"I'm Margaret Collier. I've only just met Miss Vane."

Margaret stood up and put on her raincoat. The boy looked as though he might like to dwell a little on the subject of the Vane girl, but conversation along that line would be awkward. What could she possibly contribute except her opinion of Cherry's gauche rudeness, or possibly some comment on her pathetic situation that would be entirely out of order to this boy, this utter stranger?

"I shall be late for lunch if I don't go back," she explained.

"I'll come with you," the boy announced calmly. "They're used to me popping in at odd moments. Pell always says she might as well set a place at the table for me and be done with it."

So he was on such close terms with the Vanes, was he, this nice boy?

Margaret felt a stir of curiosity and interest.

"Do you live near Monks' Court, Mr. Soames?" she asked as they walked back along the stream bank toward the field and the driveway that would lead to the garden.

"Not too far away, at Denes. That's the village beyond Little Wendling. My father is the Vicar of St. George's. Though

I can't say I'm home any more, except on holiday. I'm in the Middle East, on my oil job, most of the time."

"It's holiday time now, is it? And you're enjoying yourself?"

"Immensely."

"How much longer do you have here?"

"A fortnight."

"I expect it will go all too fast."

"I'm afraid so."

The boy stated it briefly, and with a certain grimness, and Margaret dropped the subject of holidays with the private reflection that those merry hazel eyes did not preclude the boy's having moments of unhappiness.

Good heavens, he wasn't enamored of the Vane girl, was he? Not that moody, jealous, sulky child so obviously with eyes for no one but her father, who, seemingly, couldn't care less about her? She wondered it as they started toward the house together. A love affair gone wrong? If that were the case, the girl was an absolute idiot. Imagine letting as attractive a young man as this slip through her fingers!

But then you never knew, you could never tell. Women were unpredictable. Take herself, for example, her own stupid, foolish self who had turned Ritchie down so flatly. And for a man she didn't even know existed—at least not when she and Ritchie had first started seeing each other again in London. The then nonexistent man had been nothing but a kind of dream-figure, no more substantial than the vague, ephemeral longings her loneliness evoked. And yet she had said No to Ritchie over and over again.

Margaret sighed. The boy walking along next to her, deep in his own thoughts, glanced at her.

"A problem? It sounded like it."

"Rather a big one, actually."

"No solution in sight?"

"Not at the moment."

"Jolly rough, coming up against a stone wall." He commented it sympathetically.

"Extremely rough, indeed." Margaret agreed simply, and sighed again.

FOURTEEN

Once more Pell proved herself equal to a last-minute guest. She was tremendously pleased at seeing Robin Soames. It was a continual Master Robin this, and Master Robin that when they sat down in the dining room and she trundled in her cart.

"More of the beef? Another helping of Miss Cherry's lettuce? Will it be ale for you, the pale bitter, as usual?"

Oh, yes, Pell was on his side, that was clear.

He was a young man with poise, for all his boyishness, and ignoring the fairly obvious stiffness and reserve of the other three at the table, he chatted easily and naturally.

But Sir Hugh liked Robin Soames and had been glad to see him; that had been evident in the quickly outstretched hand on first seeing the boy before lunch, evident in a momentary smile on his tight, narrow mouth.

"I've missed you this past week. Have the fish been biting? Is that what's kept you away?"

"Well, yes sir, partly." The boy glanced at Cherry, and then added, quietly, "I wouldn't want anyone to think I was underfoot."

"Rot! You're always welcome, Rob. By me, at any rate."

There was the dig again, the disapproval of his daughter. The girl's face darkened, her soft mouth took on its ugly sullen look.

She was eaten up with jealousy, Margaret had decided, filled again with pity for her. The girl couldn't bear the thought of her father's liking for Robin Soames. She couldn't bear anyone to be liked by her father, anyone to hold his interest in the smallest degree, when she herself lacked—or seemed to lack—even a modicum of her father's affection or approval.

The greatest pity, her attitude, because Robin Soames was mad about her; he couldn't take his eyes off her, and it was in the inflection of his voice, in every word he spoke to her.

She had better be careful; a young man with any pride wouldn't put up with disinterest and rebuffs forever. One of these days he was likely to stay away for longer than a week, and perhaps not trouble to come back at all.

And such a suitable young man for her, it would seem. Someone of her own world, in the first place, with whom she had grown up, who knew all about the decay of the Vane fortunes, presumably, and was not only willing to marry a girl with no money, but was able to—a young man with a profession that automatically held out prospects.

Margaret considered Sir Hugh's daughter with more than a little curiosity as she ate her lunch. Someone ought to open a window and let a breath of fresh air blow through her life, if she wouldn't open it herself.

Her devotion to her father was perilously close to the unhealthy; didn't she realize the slow but certain suffocation ahead for her, the atrophy of everything that was a normal part of girlhood, of young womanhood? Hadn't she anyone to straighten her out?

Wondering it, Margaret decided to put a question or two to Pell sometime, carefully, discreetly, not in any prying sort of way. Pell was too loyal, too devoted a person to satisfy a stranger's idle, impertinent curiosity. Pell, staying on here, doing the work of a staff of six indoor servants. Pell staying with a sinking ship. Pell, with that livid scar.

The old woman was passing cheese and crackers, and she had to nudge Robin Soames's elbow to turn his attention from Cherry. Would she fish with him tomorrow morning, he was asking. And his mother had sent an invitation for lunch afterward at the Vicarage. She wanted Cherry for dinner, too, for that matter. ". . . and I'll drive you home, unless you'll bring your toothbrush and spend the night?"

"I shan't be going at all. Not fishing, either." Cherry stated it bluntly.

"Why not?" The boy's direct hazel eyes were on her.

"I've got the chickens and ducks and the dogs, as you very well know."

"Couldn't Chubb cope this once?"

"Chubb has enough to do."

"I could gather the eggs, and I could feed Court Lady, if you'd let me," Margaret offered quickly, but with astonishment at herself. Why on earth should she bother? "If it's a question of vitamin drops for the puppies, I could give those, too." Lightly, she added, "I'm an old hand at that sort of thing. My family always had dogs."

Cherry's eyes, surprised and wary and suspicious, measured Margaret, and for a moment she had nothing to say. Sir Hugh, too, was without comment as he glanced at Margaret, but Robin burst out with a pleased, "Thanks awfully, Mrs. Collier! That's splendid, isn't it, Cherry?"

"It doesn't mean I'll go."

"Most certainly you will. It's all settled."

Robin ate his cheese and crackers and resumed an agreeable conversation with Sir Hugh and Margaret, calmly ignoring Cherry and her black, scowling displeasure, her lapse into sulking silence.

When the meal was over they left the cold, bare dining room, and Margaret planned to excuse herself and go to her room. Robin Soames could argue it out with the Vane girl. Sir Hugh could retire to his library and his searching of newspapers, or to his account books.

And she? She could stare out the window of the chinoiserie guest room, trying, trying to understand what quirk of fate had brought her to Monks' Court, while she listened—yes, actually listened, afraid to look over her shoulder—for the sound of a small child's feet in the hall, the sound of a child's laughter.

That was how far she had come along this dangerous, fearful road. A ghost upstairs, a murderer downstairs. And something holding her here, refusing to free her, refusing to let her go her way and forget she had ever laid eyes on this cruelly beautiful house that was slowly making her part of itself. Impregnating her with the very essence of all its desolation, all its sorrows, all its secrets, all its unanswered questions.

She was ready to slip upstairs when Pell, at the open front door, called to her. "If you've got a moment, madam. It's a parcel just come for you, sent out from The Feathers, in town."

"A parcel?" Margaret stared blankly at the large crated square Pell had leaned against a wall, and then a shock of realization struck.

The portrait! The address of the sender was printed clearly in black letters at the top right-hand side of the parcel, and Robin Soames was looking at it interestedly.

"The Camberley Galleries," he read aloud. "You've been

giving way to temptation, have you, Mrs. Collier? You and my mother would enjoy knowing each other, I suspect. She's combed every antique shop in Shropshire, and a good many others. You'd think we had enough old family stuff without acquiring any more. Its' the fun of rummaging, and the excitement, she says. This looks like a picture. Is that what you bagged?"

"Yes." There was no point in denying it. The shape of the package gave it away. Or should she have said it was a mirror? A mirror could be that shape.

"Did you stumble on an Old Master?" Robin was teasing her boyishly. "Is it one of those missing Rembrandts that's sure to turn up one day for a pound or two?"

"No. No, it's not a Rembrandt." Margaret attempted a smile. "It's—it's just a picture," she finished lamely.

It would have been the natural thing to suggest then that Robin cut the heavy cord of the package and tear off its brown paper wrappings.

She could see the waiting expectancy on Robin's face, followed by a slight surprise when she turned abruptly to Pell.

"I'll take it upstairs. I'm just going."

"Oh, but madam!" Pell was too well trained to allow a guest to carry packages. She was already lifting the picture.

The tiny awkwardness was over. Robin was turning to Sir Hugh. "If you've quite done with this week's *Illustrated News*, sir, my father would appreciate a look. I was to ask you for it. He told me to thank you for being good enough to share it."

They went into Sir Hugh's library, and Margaret and Cherry were left in the hall.

"Would you like to explain now about Court Lady's feeding?" Margaret asked, for something to break an uncomfortable, growing silence. "I could go out to the kennels."

"Do as you please. There's no hurry. And I mayn't be going tomorrow. Robin needn't be so sure he can run things."

"He's very nice," Margaret offered, gently.

"Did I say he wasn't?"

It was impossibly rude, but Margaret tried again. "He's fond of you, isn't he? Very fond, I should think. It's not every girl who is as fortunate."

"*Fortunate?*" The girl flung it back at Margaret bitterly. "But whether I am or not, what concern is it of yours, Mrs. Collier? None, let me tell you. None!"

She pushed past Margaret in a rush, and at the far end of the hall the side door that opened on the kitchen garden slammed hard.

Margaret's own temper flared. An impossible girl. That's what you got, was it, for trying to be kind. Well, you wouldn't waste your breath another time, and it was the boy who deserved sympathy. Undoubtedly Cherry would mope all afternoon, and send him home without another glimpse of her.

But Robin seemed to have plenty of quiet determination. He appeared in the doorway of the library just at that moment and Margaret took stock of his firm chin, his strong mouth.

"Is Cherry about, Mrs. Collier?" he asked with a glance up and down the hall and toward the stairs.

"She went out the side door."

"Thank you."

He hurried off, and Margaret started toward the stairs.

"Not cataloguing this afternoon, Mrs. Collier?"

Sir Hugh was in the doorway now, his steady gaze, without warmth, without expression, causing her knees to weaken under her. It might as well have been a direct command, she realized helplessly, and shamed and sickened though she was by her humiliating submission, she followed him into the library.

Hour after hour the long afternoon dragged by as she scribbled notes on the contents of the last shelf of the secretary and began a listing of books.

Great Battles of the World—Sawyer, 1850
Military Decisions—Cooper, 1792
Britain's Cavalry—Dawson, 1820

It began to rain again, and the library was dim, with shadows that the single lamp on Sir Hugh's desk did little to banish, and deathly silent except for the drumming against the windowpanes and the ticktock of the tall clock and an occasional soft plop when a fragment of burning log broke off and fell into the ashes on the hearth.

Sir Hugh, at the desk, was deep in farm journals, Margaret saw when once she found the courage to steal a glance at him.

Involuntarily she gazed up at the blank, faded square over the mantel. It must be there the portrait of a Georgian Sir Hugh had once hung. The size of the square was right. She could imagine him looking down on her, as he had looked at her out of the canvas in the Camberley Galleries.

That thin, proud face, its hauteur softened by a sweet curve of the mouth, the dark, compelling eyes; how well she remembered the portrait! And later, when finally she was able to go upstairs—if ever she were released from this dark, silent, somber room—she would tear away the wrappings and gaze her fill.

"You are wondering about that empty space, Mrs. Collier?" Sir Hugh, with his farm journal put down for a moment, asked sardonically. "You have noticed a number of them about the house, I have no doubt. Had I known you were in the market for period portraits—as well as militaria— we might have struck a bargain. Do you, or does your antique-minded friend, have a large collection?"

"No." It was barely more than a frozen whisper.

"Come now, Mrs. Collier! Whoever heard of an American not buying up everything in sight?"

He paused, and through the hush of the room his voice cut significantly.

"It just so happens the Camberley people bought the last lot I sold. Rather a coincidence, your patronizing their gallery. It couldn't be one of my family portraits you bought by any remote chance?"

"It isn't a portrait at all." The whisper this time was only just articulated. "It—it's a still life."

He didn't believe her, she knew, any more than he had believed her other lies. Margaret bent her head quickly over the notes.

His eyes were on her for a long, considering moment—she could feel them—and then at last he spoke. "It may be as well if I ask Pell to put the sherry bottle on the tray when she brings tea. You look a trifle white, Mrs. Collier."

FIFTEEN

She found the wrapped portrait leaning against the foot of her bed when she went upstairs to change for dinner, shaken and fear-ridden and tormented by a secret, growing shame she was determined not to expose, not to face.

Adamantly she kept her eyes away from it as she pulled off her skirt and cardigan, and brushed and coiled her hair, and put on the yellow wool dress.

Sherry, forced on her, and a cup of tea, and then the books again, and the cataloguing; she was exhausted with the strain of the afternoon. And now to go down, and somehow get through dinner. It was asking too much, too much. Those cat-and-mouse tactics of his. Sadistically, he was waiting, surmising, drawing conclusions unhurriedly. In his own good time . . .

The Chinese gong sounded, and she forced herself to go along the hall and start downstairs, but at the landing she faltered, and paused, with Sir Hugh looking up at her as he had looked up, and waited, the night before.

Her grip on the banister rail whitened her knuckles. Slowly she took another step down.

It is all part of some plan or other, some cruelly thought-out scheme of his, she thought numbly. It is all part of a game to him. He enjoys knowing I am afraid. He enjoys knowing I can't meet his eyes. It entertains him to watch me hesitate here on the stairs. He enjoys my floundering, transparent lying. But when he has had enough—when the game wearies him . . .

All through dinner her stiff lips framed meaningless, forced words. It would be too ghastly, an impossibility, to sit at a silent table in that gaunt, stripped dining room where even Pell's hot mutton broth could not dispel the chill, and where Cherry, sullen and mute, stared at her out of those enormous eyes, and Sir Hugh chose to let conversation come from her, if there were to be any at all.

And she could be in London, if she weren't such a fool. She could be sitting opposite Ritchie at a table for two in a smart restaurant, laughing and enjoying herself. And safe. Oh, a most lovely word, *safe.*

If only she knew what Sir Hugh was thinking, behind those enigmatic eyes. If only she knew the extent of his suspicions.

True, he had nothing concrete to go on, nothing more than those stupid, entangling lies of hers that had helped him guess so quickly that she had entrenched herself here for some curiously private and personal reasons of her own. But a murderer naturally would be on edge with guilty apprehensions, on guard for danger from any source, no matter how unlikely.

A murderer, ready to kill twice, once he knew he was threatened. Then why didn't she turn and run, while there was still a chance? Margaret asked it despairingly of herself as she toyed with Pell's good dinner and then swiftly refused to listen to the answer, her eyes feverishly bright in her pale face, her yellow dress a soft glow in the candlelight, her hands not entirely steady as she cut meat and raised a wine glass to drink thirstily.

After coffee in the library, Cherry took a pack of cards from a drawer of the secretary and sat down at a small table. "You wouldn't care to play, Father?" She offered it diffidently, and as though she fully expected Sir Hugh to decline, but nevertheless her eyes were hopeful.

"I'm sorry. I have got desk work."

Sir Hugh opened his big account book, and the girl, too proud to plead, set out a row of cards for solitaire, with her expression less sullen, then, to Margaret's eyes but with more of rebuffed hurt in it.

She looked inexpressibly lonely and touchingly young. Margaret instinctively spoke up, as though to console a child.

"Do you play cribbage? Or, if you like, shall we have a game of casino?"

"I've started this now."

The brief reply was like a slap in the face. Margaret flushed, and stood up.

"If you'll both excuse me, I'll go to bed. Good night."

The girl got to her feet, with a conventional automatic politeness, and Sir Hugh, standing, bowed slightly and expressed a formal hope that Pell had made the guest room entirely comfortable.

As she went upstairs, Margaret was wondering if it was always that way in the library, evening after evening, between the two of them? Not exactly pleasant. Tragic, in its way.

Margaret hurried a little along the hall of the guest-room wing, and locked and barred her door quickly, with a nervous attempt to laugh at her relief as the bolt shot home. Undressing and getting into a robe and slippers, she cut the cord of the securely wrapped portrait, and eagerly pulled away its brown paper.

The face looking back at her from the canvas struck her with the same impact as before. The dark eyes held her, as they had held her, magnetized, in the gallery. As the eyes below held her. The sweetness of the vulnerable mouth was there, as she had remembered it.

This Vane here, and the Vane in the library; two men who were one, in their strange duality, and she captive to them both. It no longer was possible to turn a deaf ear to that question: Why not run, why not escape while you can?

She knew why; she knew all too well why. And what was terror, what was shame and degradation weighed against her reason for staying? Nothing. Less than nothing.

Putting out her hand, Margaret traced the lips of the portrait. Two men who had been metamorphosed into one, with the Sir Hugh downstairs a murderer wholly abhorrent to her —or who would be abhorrent if she were sane. Which she wasn't, evidently.

With the dark eyes of the portrait on her she remembered the evening at The Feathers where, sitting in the lounge, she had made her first real attempt at rationalizing her belief in Hugh Vane's innocence. Those hundreds of other Englishmen—anyone of them a man who could have filled Honorine Duclair's wine glass and limped across to a brocade sofa.

The feeblest of explanations. She might as well give up, if that was the best she could do. And to argue with herself that someone else had killed Honorine Duclair, to keep longing for a scapegoat, to dream of any loophole in the case against Sir Hugh was to push reality farther and farther away from her.

But think how huge London was. Think how many, many people . . . Margaret wrenched her gaze from the unrevealing eyes that held hers so bafflingly, and carried the portrait to the tall armoire that served as the guest room's closet, thrusting it far behind the rack where her clothes hung. She would think of a better place tomorrow. Storage in a London warehouse would be best of all. Out of sight, out of mind. If it were in storage, you wouldn't think about that curving, tender mouth you knew could harden. Or not so much, perhaps.

She turned out her light a moment later and got into bed, glad of the puffy eiderdown and gladder still when her feet touched the hot-water bottle that again was taking the iciness from the linen sheets.

Cherry this time, too? Was it her way of making amends for her morning rudeness, her childish apology that pride kept her from putting into words? She owed an apology for this evening, too, poor youngster.

Were they down there still, father and daughter? A page turned in a book, a card turned up and put on top of another, and nothing but silence between them? Silence everywhere in this desolate house of so many empty rooms. Except for the sound of the rain—that pattering, pattering.

It *was* the sound of rain, wasn't it? She reached out to the commode that held a bedside lamp, switched it on and left it burning reassuringly, and shut her eyes. Slowly the welcome warmth of the bed helped her to doze, and then to sleep deeply, and when she woke in the morning it was with thankfulness that neither the portrait of a man with a tenderly curving mouth nor the fancied scampering of a little boy along the hall had troubled her rest with bad dreams.

How different things looked after a night's sleep. Even Cherry Vane might have wakened this morning with a change of heart toward the Soames boy. Pell would know. And there was so much, still, that might possibly be gleaned indirectly from Pell if once one started her off by asking a few red-herring questions.

When Pell knocked, and she had unlocked and unbarred the bedroom door for her, Margaret asked as casually as she could, "Are Miss Cherry and Mr. Soames going fishing this morning?"

"It's a pleasant, soft day, madam, which means a chance for a good catch, but as to whether Miss Cherry will let Master Robin have his way, that's another matter."

Pell's face was troubled as she put down the tray and took the silver lid from a plate of bacon and eggs.

"I wondered—it seems too bad. She'd be so much happier, I should think, if—"

"She doesn't know the meaning of the word 'happy,' madam. And never has. Not since she was old enough to think one way or another about it, that is."

"Mr. Soames has been interested in her for some time?"

"Ever since they were little things, madam, him in his knee breeches, and she in pinafores; it's always been Miss Cherry, that's the only girl he ever set his heart on."

Plainly it was a relief for Pell to talk, and Margaret ventured further.

"She seems devoted to her father."

"And always has been, poor young lady. I can see her now, madam, toddling across the lawns to him—it was lawns to be proud of, in those days, I can tell you—with her arms out, the lamb, and then him just turning away."

Pell hesitated and straightened a toast rack in line with a little dish piled with butter pats. "Between you and me, madam, more than once I've said to her, 'It's not what Sir Hugh is making of his life, it's how you go about making yours, Miss Cherry, that counts.' Time and again I've been at her."

"I'm sorry for her."

"As well you might be. It's a wicked shame, Sir Hugh drawing into himself like he has, or putting up a wall, you might say, all around him to keep her out. And Miss Cherry is wasting her days trying to pull it down, in my opinion. Turn to Master Robin, that's what she ought do, and leave Sir Hugh to his own ways. But there, madam, I've stood about talking too long; your tea will get cold if you don't pour out, and I've got a loaf to take out of the oven."

Abruptly she turned to leave and then paused with an arthritic, hard-working old hand on the doorknob. "Sir Hugh has had his troubles, as well I know, madam—and we're not all alike, each of us takes our bad times different."

Loyal Pell, too fond of them both to let a stranger think she had been criticizing the Vanes.

But there it was, put concisely—a wall built, and a daughter shut out. She mused over it as she drank her tea.

This strange, intriguing house, this fateful house, where you were held fast, as though tightly embraced, by its decaying, cold enchantment, where you waked each morning with something new to wonder about and puzzle over and to a devouring, fearful curiosity as to what the day ahead held.

This morning? The dark, silent library again and the farce of her note-taking. Sir Hugh's chilling scrutiny. More of her terrified, evasive lies that came so awkwardly, so unconvincingly, to her tongue.

No. She couldn't. Not until she had gotten out into the sunshine first.

Margaret put on thick shoes and a tweed skirt and cardigan, and when her bed was made and the hot-water bottle taken down to the kitchen, she glanced into the entrance hall. The library door was closed. There was no one in sight.

As quietly as possible she tugged at the heavy front door and scurried across the broken, mossy bricks of the terrace and down the cracked, sagging steps, past the weed-grown urns and along a stretch of gravel to a curve in the driveway that would put her out of sight of the house.

All those shuttered, blank windows. But from any of them, he could be looking out through a tilted slat. She knew all about windows, and spying, unobserved eyes, didn't she?

Now and then she glanced back uneasily, and as the dark tunnel of trees closed over her, she hurried a little faster, the dark boughs a symbol, now, of all her crowding, closing-in uncertainties and fears.

Hurry. Hurry. And don't stop. Hurry through those iron gates ahead, to the lane. A farm cart would come along, or, at the crossroads, a truck, to give her a lift.

The Feathers' telephone, then. Not having a purse with her wouldn't matter. Ritchie would pay the toll for a hundred long-distance calls. Even if he were angry. And the anger wouldn't last. Not after she had explained.

Ritchie was like Robin Soames. Always there had been only one girl on whom his heart was set. Affairs? She didn't doubt it. Ritchie liked women. And Ritchie was a man of the world. But always, Margaret Collier at the back of his mind, unforgotten, and meaning the most to him. It was a humbling thought, and the temptation to rush on was great, but when the chapel came in sight, she contrived an excuse for slowing her pace.

She would stop a moment and sit down on that pile of stone rubble that once had been the battlements of a Saxon keep and catch her breath. The faint sunshine, visible now that she had come out from under those oppressive trees, would be pleasant to feel at her back. And it was only a little way to the gates. She could be through them in minutes.

That is, if she wanted, in her heart of hearts, to hear the grate of their rusted hinges, their slow, heavy drag on gravel as they closed behind her. A moment of stark self-revelation was upon her, she realized with a jolting suddenness.

Never, never would she leave Monk's Court of her own

will. The portrait's unexpected arrival had put an end to any further self-deception. You knew last night that escape was forever beyond you, she thought, when you lost yourself in the dark depths of the portrait's eyes, when you traced those lips.

Didn't you, Margaret, didn't you? Own up. For this once, be honest. She cried it silently, her self-contempt like a lash. Admit to what every fiber of your fundamental, intrinsic honesty tells you is the truth. Admit that when you traced the mouth of that long-dead Vane on canvas, you were longing, longing for it to be the mouth of a living Vane. Admit your irrevocable commitment to him. Admit he is the love of your life, for whom you have waited all these years—for whom you have been so lonely and whom you had given up hope of ever finding until a London night when he was silhouetted in an open Mount Street window.

Her instantly recognized, brutally ruthless, shocking love, whom London, beckoning so strangely, so insistently, had given her. Yet Ritchie had been in London too.

A longing to gaze again at the portrait seized her. Two Vanes who were one, yes, but the eyes of the portrait didn't frighten her, the mouth of the portrait lacked harshness. She could look and look and lose herself in rapturous imaginings without cowering terror and without revulsion.

Closer at hand, though, than the portrait, there was another image of her love. Margaret got up and walked slowly over to the chapel where the stone effigy lay, waiting.

At the last moment she lacked the courage to push the door open and go into the dank dimness, and after a moment she went back to the stone rubble heap, gladder than ever of the sunshine.

All those men and women lying in there, nothing but dust and bones now, who had lived and loved and died exactly as men and women did today.

Vanes. For one of them, at least, loving had been hideously painful. To love is to give. Had the Catharine with bloody stumps instead of hands made her gift to a Hugh whose mouth had the same tenderness of the portrait or—

"So here you are, Mrs. Collier!"

As it broke so unexpectedly into her reverie, she gasped and jumped to her feet. This wasn't Robin Soames, coming down the stream bank, boyish and merry-eyed, and stumbling over her by chance. This was—this was a murderer. She was insane to think of him as anything else. She had lost her mind.

This was a man who had been in Honorine Duclair's flat the night she died, with a stemmed wine glass falling from her hand. This was the man who had filled the glass.

"Chubb told me you had started off this way."

"I—I was going for a walk along the lane." Margaret moved away, a little.

"The lane? You'll find it nothing but a mud puddle. And I couldn't offer you my company if you attempted it. The ruts would make it a bit difficult for me. You wouldn't consider sitting here in the sun a little longer? It's a fairly decent morning. Certainly the birds are appreciative. They've been racketing since dawn. They were at it when I went down to the farms to get my men on their jobs, and they haven't stopped since."

All of it so easily, pleasantly spoken, all of it so cleverly meant to disarm her. Margaret edged a little further from the stone pile toward the driveway, and the gates.

"Have you ever seen a blackbird's nest, Mrs. Collier? There's one just behind you in that thicket, I'll wager. I've not seen a spring go by, of all of them that I've ever spent here at Monks' Court, without finding a nest there, in that same spot."

He pushed aside new, green, concealing foliage with the

tip of his stick, gently, and there was a flutter of wings, and an excited, protesting chirping. "I've disturbed the female, but she'll fly back and settle down again in a moment. Come have a look."

Submissively Margaret glanced at blue, mottled eggs.

"I used always to hear a cuckoo calling from the beech copse on the other side of the chapel on soft, warm days like this, with the air full of moisture. We've got a country saying that 'the cuckoo, he likes a drop to moisten his throat, he do.' "

What was he up to, with his playing of games? What did he want of her? When would he pounce?

"What do you say we wait, and listen? If we sit very still . . ."

Sir Hugh rested his stick on the rubble and sat down. Like a puppet manipulated by strings, Margaret seated herself next to him.

Slowly, slowly, she was aware then that the silence that settled on them was very different from the silence of the library. A kind of peace descending, she thought, astonished, here in this ancient clearing where a tower had once stood, and where now there was a sheen of sunlight on yellow dandelions and cowslips thrusting from green grass, and where the warm, wet earth smelled fresh and alive.

"Cuckoo!"

The low, throaty call sounded, somewhere, distant, and Sir Hugh quickly touched Margaret's sleeve.

"Hear? It's a cock."

"Cuckoo! Cuckoo!" The call came nearer.

"Cuckoo!" Indescribably seductive and persuasive, it stirred Margaret beyond words. Her heart swelled in her breast. A lump closed her throat. Tears rushed to her eyes, hot and blinding.

"Cuckoo." The amorous call deepened and grew hoarse with the ardent insistency of its wooing, and then Margaret saw a gray bird, like a small hawk, fly over the chapel roof and ascend to the sky.

Frantically blinking back the embarrassing, foolish tears before they could fall, she forced a shaky, artificial laugh. "Exactly like every silly Swiss clock I ever heard!"

"And nothing more than that, Mrs. Collier? You won't elaborate on the English cuckoo when you write your garden and house articles?"

Had he seen her tears? Was he mocking her?

It did not matter whether or not his narrow-lipped mouth derided her or his cold eyes remained unreadable, she was suddenly, astonishingly, jolted into realizing. All of that was facade. Underneath was the real Sir Hugh.

And like the Catharine who slept in effigy inside that quiet, dim chapel, she, too, Margaret Collier, miraculously and out of the blue had a gift to offer a Vane. A sudden faith, a sudden belief in him again, born of the spring morning, born of sunshine and a bird's call. And though it was nothing compared to Catharine's two severed hands, was it entirely valueless as an offering made for love's sake? Surely it counted for something, had some small worth, at least, rising in her, welling up, overflowing?

Dazed, Margaret still clung with all her strength to common sense and reason. Once her gift was given, there would be no breaking free ever from the enthrallment of the dark inscrutable eyes that even now were searching her face. A pity she couldn't ask Catharine in there, with her handless wrists crossed on her breasts, whether the price of her giving had proved worthwhile.

What a coward she was, hesitating and haggling and so fearfully counting the cost of her gift! Catharine's generosity ought to put her to shame, though surely for her it had been easier, with her gift given to a Knight Defender of the Holy Grail?

This other man—this other Vane—was a mur——

Margaret caught back the word, hastily. Never that again in her thinking—if she could control the thinking.

The giving of her gift would not be easy, she recognized, with humbleness and honesty. Doubt and misgivings would assail her relentlessly. Tormenting puzzlement and baffled, futile conjecture would cast deep shadows. The brightness of this momentary revelation would dim as certainly as the sunshine that was warming her now would dim.

Faith put to a test, indeed, once the door of the library shut her in, once the pall of that deathly silence had fallen.

"Shall we go back to the house, Mrs. Collier?" Sir Hugh was reaching for his stick. "We're in for more rain from the looks of things. Clouds pile up surprisingly fast these spring days."

Margaret got to her feet, obedient and wordless.

SIXTEEN

Lunch was ready soon after they reached the house, and Cherry joined them at the table. Her face was darkly sullen, and Margaret, with a quick side glance, suspected she had been crying.

"You didn't go fishing?"

"No."

"Where is Robin?" Sir Hugh's eyes were on the empty place that Pell, evidently hopeful, had set.

"He's gone home."

"And why is that? Because you made yourself thoroughly disagreeable?" Sir Hugh's voice was controlled and even, but to Margaret it carried the cut of a lash.

"As disagreeable as always, is that what you mean, Father?" The girl gave a short laugh and unfolded her napkin.

There was no attempt on anyone's part to make conversation after that until, toward the end of the meal, Pell passed a bowl of strawberries and a pitcher of cream, and then, in desperation, Margaret attempted a neutral, safe comment that she hoped might smooth matters.

"English strawberries! Are they yours, Miss Vane, from the garden?"

"Yes."

"They're delicious. You forced them, of course?"

"Yes."

The girl really was impossible. Provoked, Margaret gave up any further tactful efforts, and lunch ended as uncomfortably as it had begun.

When they had left the dining room, Sir Hugh limped to a table in the hall where Chubb, after a bicycle trip to the village, had left a fresh supply of newspapers. Margaret watched him pick up a thick bundle and go into the library and close the door firmly behind him.

Cherry had darted toward the stairs, and started up them.

What would she do, spend the afternoon crying? Hadn't she a vestige of common sense? Didn't she realize what a prize she had in that charming Soames boy? She was the worst sort of stupid little donkey. But there ought to be some way to reach her.

Again Margaret tried. "Does the Vicarage have a pretty garden, Miss Vane?" she asked.

"Pretty enough." The girl tossed it over her shoulder as she paused on the stairs.

"To Americans all English gardens seem utterly charming."

"Do they?" Cherry turned and faced her, deliberately disinterested.

For a moment Margaret longed to seize her by the shoulders and shake her, hard, but instead she stated simply, "I know you would like me to leave, Miss Vane, and I'd like to leave myself—if I could. But as I have to stay on—rather in-

definitely—couldn't you be on speaking terms with me?"
Her attempt at a smile was apologetic. "This is such a very
big house to roam about in—and rather lonely for a stranger."

"Cataloguing books and making lists can't be so frightfully
important a job. If you don't like it here, why don't you
leave?"

"I've told you I would, if I could. It's—it's a commitment, in a way. . . ."

It was impossible to explain. What was there to explain,
Margaret wondered, unless she came out with the truth? And
how could she say to Sir Hugh's daughter, "I'm in love with
your father—I can't bear to leave—I haven't the willpower to
leave"? That, spoken out freely and honestly to an already
jealous, antagonistic girl?

The fluctuating pity that competed so often with irritation
got the best of Margaret. If only Cherry could be made to realize that Robin Soames could so easily dissolve her unhappiness once she gave him the chance.

"If you change your mind and decide to go to the Vicarage
after all, I'll be glad to drive you over." Margaret suggested it
pleasantly. "You could telephone Mr. Soames, couldn't you,
about changing your mind? I'm sure he'd be delighted—and
my car is just sitting in the garage—and I'm not doing a
thing."

The girl's enormous eyes flicked Margaret contemptuously.
"You had your terribly, terribly important listing to keep you
in my father's library, I thought. And besides, my plans
haven't changed in the slightest."

She went on up the stairs, her back stiff, her head high. Margaret watched her go, and then turned slowly toward the
library.

Sir Hugh's cold scrutiny would terrify her, she knew, and
like a candle flame in a draft, her newly lighted faith stood

every chance of being extinguished. But she entered the library, and Sir Hugh, getting up from his desk, closed the door after her.

As he moved from the desk, one of his newspapers fell to the floor, and Margaret stooped automatically to pick it up.

"Is there ever anything in the news these days except the Russians and the Chinese?" Like so many of her remarks, it was only an attempt at conventional comment.

"The usual hinted-at political scandals invariably come in for a column or two—or any other sort of scandal, for that matter." Sir Hugh's reply was as conventional, but the suavity was a goad.

"And there's generally a murder." As Margaret blurted it, recklessly, she went hastily to the bookshelves, careful to turn her face from Sir Hugh.

"True. People are addicted to murder, it would seem."

"Londoners more than—than other people?" Margaret voiced the question faintly.

"I haven't any statistics at hand, Mrs. Collier."

Sir Hugh seated himself again and opened another newspaper. "Motives being equal, I fancy however, there's little or no difference in a person's tendency toward violence, geographically speaking."

He began to read, and Margaret could hear the rustle of the newspaper as he turned pages. With cold hands she began taking dusty books from the shelves.

The Diary of Major Thomas Rutledge—published 1825.
The Sepoy Rebellion—published 1887.

She jotted down title after title, and as the rustle of newspaper ceased and she heard a desk drawer being opened, she guessed that Sir Hugh was at his accounts again, although she had not the courage to turn and look toward the desk.

By teatime the clouded-over sky had darkened the library, and when Pell came in with a tea tray she drew the curtains.

Sir Hugh switched on his desk lamp and got up to put a log on the fire. "Won't you come down off your ladder, Mrs. Collier, and pour?"

"If I may wash my hands first."

When Margaret came back into the library and sat down in one of the chairs opposite him and lifted the big silver teapot, she just managed not to spill as she filled his cup and her own.

Tea and bread and butter and spongecake with a mur—— That was a word she had vowed never again to say. And he wasn't—he couldn't be. Not even though she *had* seen him there that night.

"How is it going for you, Mrs. Collier? The cataloguing, I mean?" Sir Hugh asked pleasantly as he took his cup from Margaret. "I looked up once or twice from my papers, and you seemed engrossed. You are finding the work worth your time and effort?"

"I had no idea history could be so fascinating." Margaret, glad to grasp at any ordinary approach—even if only superficially—to what could be a most difficult half hour, answered him with an unfeigned eagerness. "The books, and everything in the secretary, from an epaulet or button, to that lock of soldier's hair cut off before the Battle of the Nile, makes it come alive. I've never had any real sense of its continuity before. But then, I've never been in a house like this before, either, where one generation has followed another, for so many years, with all of them—how shall I say it— touching hands, and never letting go."

"Well put."

"You must be very proud of your house and your land."

"I am." There was a grimness to the flat, unequivocating admittance. "And I shouldn't enjoy being the only Vane who hadn't succeeded in keeping it going."

"But surely you won't be!" Margaret's protest expressed

a world of simple, objective concern. "You work so hard, you make so many sacrifices, you are putting everything you have into your estate—Pell has told me."

"The results of which remain to be seen. Nothing, at the moment, is certain. There's no telling what the outcome will be."

He was right, Margaret agreed inwardly, with both fear and pain. Nothing, nothing, was certain about the future.

"Monks' Court is the most beautiful house I have ever seen."

Saying it, she broke the constraint of a momentary quiet that had fallen on both of them.

"You don't find it an anachronism? A white elephant to be gotten rid of as quickly and advantageously as possible?"

"I'd never get rid of it. Never!"

"You don't happen to be saddled with it, Mrs. Collier—which might make a difference in your viewpoint. But say you were in my position, wouldn't you sell it, and take a flat in London or Manchester—and a job of sorts—instead of staying on, pouring money down a rat hole, as it strikes me now and again that I'm doing?"

"I'd stay, and I'd work, just as you are working, and I'd spend my last penny on the place. I'd go down with it, if I had to, but I'd stay." Margaret's brown eyes were very bright, very earnest and expressive. "I'd feel chosen, and privileged if I'd inherited Monks' Court, and I'd feel obligated to hold on. I'd eat crusts rather than let it go. I'd be ashamed to be soft and choose the easy way. And I'd loathe a flat and a town job if this had ever been mine."

"My word, what a strong supported of England's Stately Homes!"

Would the sarcasm start now? Margaret waited in trepidation, but he was looking at her with nothing more than surprise and a faint ironical smile. "It's you who are the anachronism, Mrs. Collier, with that sort of outlook, just as I am. We are in complete agreement on the subject. My moments of doubt are always temporary. I know quite well that no matter what, I shall never voluntarily leave Monks' Court."

He laughed shortly. "A small journey, feet first, to the chapel, when I'm dead, is the farthest I choose to go. But look here, is there anything left in the pot? I'd like another cup if I may."

He helped himself to bread and butter.

"What else do we have in common, I wonder, Mrs. Collier? I've watched your handling of my books; you enjoy a good binding?"

"Your books are superb—most of them—inside and out. It's not only the bindings that are a pleasure to touch and look at, the engravings and the woodcuts are wonderful, and the bookplates—all those scroll and shell and acanthus leaf designs, and the plumes and the urns and the shields of arms."

"Are you an ex-librist?"

"I don't know what that is."

"It's a coined word for bookplate enthusiasts. I happen to be one of them."

"Your own plate—the Vane plate—is very handsome."

"Typography used to interest me when I was a boy. I once rigged up a press, fancying myself a young Caxton. And I was sent from the table more than once at school for showing up with inky hands and a filthy jacket. Extraordinary—I've not thought of that press in years. You've taken me back a long way, Mrs. Collier. Light-years!"

For a moment, with the glow of the fire playing on him, he looked younger, and Margaret could see a trace of the schoolboy he had once been, but all too soon he was disconcertingly and woundingly the Sir Hugh Vane she best knew, carved granite of face and scathing of tongue.

"I should like to believe your enthusiasm for my house and my books is genuine, Mrs. Collier." He put down his cup and pulled his chair from the hearth to face the desk again. "But you are doing an excellent job, my books need the dusting they're getting, even if your cataloguing, along with your enthusiasm, is a sham. What a lot of wasted energy, though, your scribbling all those notes. I hate to think of it."

He jerked open a drawer of the filing cabinet.

"These damnable, time-consuming quarterly reports. A pity you didn't apply for a position as secretary. I could do with one. And from your standpoint, fancy how much more you could find out about me, if you were serving in that capacity! Because curiosity, of one kind or another, has brought you here, has it not?"

Margaret flushed. "If you call an interest in an old house curiosity—"

"Oh, come now, Mrs. Collier." He was coldly amused. "You'll have to do better than that. Unless you choose to be honest with me, for a change? No? Your story still stands? Sorry I can't cooperate by being more gullible."

She had no retort, nor did Sir Hugh seem to expect one, and Margaret remounted the library ladder.

She and Sir Hugh could have become friends under other circumstances; they could have become congenial acquaintances, if nothing more, enjoying mutual interests and outlooks. Lacerating herself, she dwelt on the possibilities. Under other circumstances he would have ceased to see her as the impossible American. He would have forgotten she was a woman whose bold, pushing, intrusive ways had given her entrée to his house.

They could have shared a fire and evening lamplight whose

intimacy was untainted by fear or distrust and useless conjecture. They could have shared many unblemished springtime mornings, listened to the call of a cuckoo in lasting, quiet companionship.

But never any of that the way things were, and as they would be in the future when Inspector Downs made his final deductions. Sir Hugh Vane on trial. Which was only justice, wasn't it?

Torn and confused, Margaret attempted to go on with her listing of books, but when the dressing gong sounded and she went upstairs her head swam with protesting arguments and vehement defense.

If she could trust to instinct, trust to faith, Hugh Vane was incapable of murdering Honorine Duclair, whether or not he had been in the flat that hideous night, whether or not she had seen him, or some other man, through her opera glasses. Clinging to that premise, she would stay on here, a little longer, anyway, in hope of finding proof of his innocence. It was all very well to say that true faith, faith worthy of the name, had no need of proof, but it was proof, and proof alone, that would make her existence endurable.

And how would she go about a search for such proof? She hadn't the remotest idea where to start. One thing only was clear. To find proof of Hugh Vane's innocence was, necessarily, to have first found proof of someone else's guilt. X— the unknown quantity. Make yourself believe, with all your heart, there was an X. Begin with that.

Margaret had taken off her beige silk blouse and brown cardigan, and was stepping out of her tweed skirt when Pell knocked.

"Fresh towels, madam."

"I'm sorry you had to come up all those stairs."

"It's nothing, madam. And I'll be up with the hot bottle

later. Miss Cherry isn't to be counted on this evening from the look of things. She's shut in her room, and it will take all my talking to get her down for dinner."

"I wish she didn't dislike me so much. I expect you noticed she wouldn't speak to me at lunch?"

"It's not you in particular, madam, that she's against, poor lamb, it's anyone who'd come here, making three of it, when it's only the two she wants, her father and herself."

Pell sighed heavily as she turned down Margaret's bed and plumped the pillows. "She gets that black look on her face from her father, and her temper, too. Well, I remember how he was, as a boy. I couldn't forget if I tried—not with this." Pell touched her scarred cheek. "Threw a toy at me, he did, in a tantrum. One of his tin soldiers, it was, with a nasty sharp edge."

"How awful!" Margaret stared, horrified, at the jagged scar.

"It was my fault, you might say, madam. I shouldn't have teased him, saying I'd take his cricket bat away because of him being careless and spilling ink on the nursery rug. Cricket was everything to him, madam, and it wasn't my place to do the punishing, it was up to Nanny, she being in full charge, and me only the nurserymaid."

"But he could have put your eye out."

"It was a near thing, and let me tell you when the blood started running down my cheek, he was the sorriest lad you'd ever want to see. I can see him now, standing there like he was turned to a statue. The next thing Nanny and me knew, he was off to his room, locking himself in, and not letting us at him nor eating his supper that night. And then in the morning early out he comes, with his eyes all swollen up, to hug me and beg me to forgive him."

"And you did?"

"To be sure, madam. I couldn't have helped myself. He was the sort who could always get round you."

"Does he still have a violent temper?"

"There's Welsh blood in him, madam, and though it's only a drop, with that forever deviling you . . . But what with this and that, the past few years he's got so turned in on himself and quiet, there's no recognizing him for the boy who used to fly into those black rages."

"A bottled-up temper can be the worst of any—can't it?"

"It can, madam. And one of these days, I've always said, if there were occasion he'd . . ."

Pell would not let herself finish.

Tucking the sides of the eiderdown puff on Margaret's bed securely under the mattress, she looked at Margaret worriedly. "If I've talked too much, madam, it's not that I don't know my place, nor that I'm not fonder of Sir Hugh and Miss Cherry than any kin of my own. You'd never be thinking it, I hope?"

"Of course not. I know you are devoted to them. And I'm sure they feel the same toward you."

Margaret began to brush her hair. "It is too bad Sir Hugh didn't marry again," she commented slowly. "Too bad for his daughter's sake. A nice stepmother, when she was little, might have made all the difference."

"That it would have done, madam, but there was no young lady from any of the big houses nearby that took Sir Hugh's eye, and he never was one for going into town."

"And—and there was never anyone in London?"

"Not to my hearing."

"Does he go to London often?" Margaret coiled her hair and thrust tortoise shell pins in it. "I should think he'd be lonely here all the time. I suppose he has a club?"

She was putting her questions carefully. Pell just might realize she was being quizzed for a purpose and check her garrulous tongue.

"Most of the gentlemen that's in the country, like Sir

Hugh, have their London clubs, madam, same as they have their tailors and bootmakers. But working as hard as he does, like a farmhand more often than not, when he's not at his desk, he's got little time for them. Except for a day or so away last month, he hasn't been off the place for I couldn't say how long."

What had she learned? Anything?

As Pell, with a belated thought for dinner on the stove, hurried out of the room, Margaret frowned, consideringly. Sir Hugh hadn't been away from Monks' Court for "I couldn't say how long," and yet the woman whose flat he had gone to that night had been playing on the London stage for a month before her death.

Sir Hugh, who "hadn't stirred himself" had journeyed to London purposely on a certain date solely to murder a woman he'd had no recent dealing with?

A trip down, a trip back, and a rendezvous after the theater. It hardly seemed likely. And yet he had been there. And his temper. How many people outgrew violent black tempers?

She shivered, standing in her slip, and went to the wardrobe for her yellow wool dress and the high-heeled brown velvet sandals she wore with it.

The portrait was there, at the back behind her suits, she was glad to think, and a rush of anticipation warmed her. Later, she would take it out. Later, she would gaze and gaze, giving herself up to its fascination. To so much as reach out now and touch the portrait's frame would be to know a moment of pleasure.

Pushing the suits aside, she put out her hand, smiling a little at her own absurdity, and then she was staring into the depths of the wardrobe, aghast. The portrait was gone.

Frantically, she pushed clothes hangers aside, refusing to

believe it at first, and then she leaned against the wardrobe door, limp with shock.

Who? Why? Cherry Vane, in a fit of malice? A childish, spiteful Cherry, with no idea who the portrait was, and no interest in it, her sole purpose to make mischief, her one thought to get back at the attractive, young, rich American who was taking up so much of her father's time and attention?

Cherry Vane, or Sir Hugh? Far rather, the former. And it had to be one or the other. There was no one else. Pell didn't count. Pell wouldn't have done it.

It had to be either Sir Hugh or his daughter. A motive presented itself easily enough, in the girl's case, but Sir Hugh? Margaret tried to collect her bewildered thoughts. Sir Hugh had seen the portrait arrive. He had commented pointedly on the return address written so clearly on the package; the same gallery as the one to which he had sold a consignment of family pictures. Had it struck him as more than a coincidence? Was he determined to see what she had bought? And in finding out, had he some hope of puzzling through to a solution of what had brought her to Monks' Court?

The murderer, always on edge, always alert. The fox, ears pricked for the first baying of hounds. There was that ugly, preposterous word again that she had vowed never again to use. And never, never let yourself speak that name that Ritchie would use, "A Killer."

Ritchie and Scotland Yard, too, no doubt, as well as every reporter who seized on the story. "The Killer, known to be a man of uncontrollable temper . . ." Vividly, Margaret could imagine it. Vividly, too and nauseatingly, she could see a woman crumpled by a drawing room hearth, a pool of something dark staining a white rug to the crimson of the damask curtains.

A long way off she heard Pell sound the dining-room gong

again to say dinner was served. Sir Hugh was waiting for her with punctilious, formal courtesy. He seated her at the table, raised an eyebrow at his daughter's empty place, sat down himself, and pulled the cork from a bottle of wine.

Cherry appeared ten minutes later, her eyes swollen, and as she slipped silently into her chair, with no apology, Sir Hugh spoke to Pell, changing plates. "Don't bother with soup for Miss Cherry," he ordered, his mouth thin. "Just get on with the rest of dinner, please."

The girl turned a dull, ugly red under her dark Welsh skin. "Pell needn't bother with anything else for me, either, Father," she announced in a strangled voice, and throwing down her napkin, she pushed away from the table and ran from the room.

Sir Hugh ignored her. "Wine, Mrs. Collier?" he asked stiffly, and filled her glass, and then began to carve the mutton that a distressed Pell put in front of him.

There was no attempt at conversation by either Margaret or Sir Hugh, and by the time the difficult meal was over, Margaret's sympathy had again veered toward Cherry Vane. After all, she was very young. Remember that, and she lacked all power to more than temporarily annoy you. Don't let her get under your skin. And if it was she who had taken the portrait—not that you were about to ask questions of anyone —wasn't it exactly what might be expected of a girl so patently immature? Spite, that was what it was, babyish spite.

Where was she, up in her room alone, somewhere in this vast, unhappy house, crying again, torn with the affection for her father that was so completely one-sided, so coldly disregarded, torn with her ridiculous, pathetic jealousy? Poor, mixed-up little thing. But had she the courage to try to help her?

No, she didn't. And anyway, Cherry wouldn't listen. She was a stranger in the first place, an intrusive, rich American, whose collector's interest—at a price—in the Vane family possessions was a galling humiliation, and secondly, Cherry would think her an impertinent meddler if she attempted to be kind.

If Cherry were to be helped, it would have to be by someone of her own sort, her own background. Could the Soames boy be persuaded to come back, after the girl's apparently final dismissal of him this morning?

Margaret considered it, uncertainly. What if she put in a telephone call, or sent off a little note to the Vicarage? Should or shouldn't she interfere? What a simple and perfect solution, if only he kept on, stubbornly persevering, until blind and hungry little Cherry waked to the fact it was with him, and not her father, that she would find serenity, and happiness, and a complete fulfillment.

Was Robin Soames mature enough to handle the situation? But even if he were, wouldn't he be too proud to come back? She could get the Vicarage address from Pell. And even though it wasn't any of her affair . . .

She was still debating with herself when Sir Hugh got up from the table. "Coffee and brandy? Shall we go? It will be warmer in the library. Which reminds me. When the weather clears, you might enjoy a walk to our lake, and a look at our island, and its Greek pavilion. An early eighteenth-century extravaganza, by the way—if the eighteenth century happens to interest you."

"It does, very much." Controlling herself, she gave the quiet reply. What was he getting at? Anything in particular? The portrait was eighteenth century.

"This time of year the island is a mass of naturalized narcissus and cyclamen and freesia, and in full summer, the lake itself is clotted with waterlilies the color of thick Jersey cream. You ought to stay on and see it, Mrs. Collier."

"It sounds lovely, but—"

"Perhaps you will reconsider. Meanwhile, I'll speak to Chubb about putting our little rowboat in shape. Do feel free to use it anytime, if you care to."

"Thank you," Margaret murmured. A row on a lake would take her out of the house on some future day when to stay in became unbearable, she was thinking as she followed Sir Hugh to the library.

The rain that had threatened all day was now a persistent, quiet tapping against the windows, so heavily curtained in their faded velvet, and the wind in the chimney a sigh. Sir Hugh took up a poker and stirred the fire, and the suddenly leaping, bright flames struck a glint from the swords hanging on the wall, and the brass screws of the drum, and from the blue-black steel of the oiled service revolver.

He patted the old dog sprawled on the hearth, twitching in dreams, poured brandy, and sat down in one of the wing chairs.

Margaret put a coffee cup on the little table beside him.

They were as silent as they had been at dinner.

"It was not the pleasantest scene at dinner, Mrs. Collier." Sir Hugh spoke up abruptly. "My apologies. Needless to say, my daughter owes hers, though whether or not you'll receive them—"

"I'm sorry for her," Margaret stated with simplicity and frankness.

"Sorry? And why is that?" Sir Hugh asked sharply.

"It's not easy to be young and—and unhappy."

"The unhappiness is of her own making, Mrs. Collier. The average girl, with any common sense, would get away— make a life of her own. There's no need for her to stay on here. She's in no way trapped."

"But this is her home."

"She'd do better to make a home of her own."

"I entirely agree." Margaret murmured it emphatically,

and then, with Sir Hugh's eyes on her, she added quickly, "It's—it's such a big house—and lonely, I expect, for a young person." Her voice trailed off. She had not said "such a frightening house." But had he read her mind?

It was easy to think so, with his steady gaze never leaving her face. Hurriedly, she added, "Your daughter is very fond of you. To go away would be difficult for her, I expect."

"And I'm in duty bound, am I, to return her devotion?"

"Not all men would consider it a duty. Fathers are proverbially fond of their daughters, are they not? I've always heard so."

"I happen to be the exception, Mrs. Collier. And it's no good my daughter trying to find in me what isn't there."

Sir Hugh picked up his brandy glass. "My wife died in childbirth. A not unusual situation resulted. I became a young husband who couldn't forgive the child—a girl child at that—who was responsible for her mother's death."

"You held it against a baby!"

"She had Pell when she was little, and later, boarding school, and Swiss pensions for most of the holidays," the cold, level voice continued, ignoring Margaret's exclamation. "This is her first year at home. And though I have long since got over my early resentments and sincerely regret them—and am willing to accept the complete blame for our lack of closeness —the less Cherry expects from me, the better off she will be in the long run, and the less hurt."

"She is already hurt."

"The hurt could easily worsen, depending upon circumstances beyond my control. And just let me say this. If it's affection she's looking for, let her turn to young Soames. You have guessed his interest, I presume?"

"Yes. And you approve?"

"More heartily than you could ever imagine, Mrs. Collier. It would solve no end of things if she'd have him. The future,

for one." Sir Hugh replenished his glass. "The extremely uncertain future," he added evenly. He drank his brandy and
shrugged. "I'm not proud of myself as a father, but there it
is."

"You spoke of the uncertain future. Does it always pay to
look ahead? The present ought to count for something—
everyone ought to snatch at it. I feel that strongly—more
strongly all the time. I'm sure you could make your daughter
happier than she is now, if you'd try. As I said, I'm sorry for
her. Terribly sorry. And wouldn't it distress her mother if she
could know your attitude?"

"You are a sentimentalist, are you, Mrs. Collier?" For an
instant the expressionless mask was down and Sir Hugh
smiled with bleak amusement. "It's on the late side, I'm
afraid, for my daughter and me to come to any congenial
terms."

"Couldn't you make an effort not to be so impatient with
her?" Margaret leaned forward in her chair tense with the daring that let her speak out. "The smallest show of interest or—
or compassion would help." The firelight was coppery on her
yellow dress. Her hair was nimbused against the shabby
brown leather of the high-backed wing chair. "She is very
young. She had been crying when she came to dinner, and
earlier, I think."

Sir Hugh regarded her for a long moment.

" 'My Stay in an English Family,' is that what you'll be
writing next, Mrs. Collier?" he asked icily. "Will it follow the
'Old World Houses, Old World Gardens' series? You must
send me a copy."

Margaret put down her coffee cup.

"You are not going up so early?"

"Yes."

"Why? Is it because you are shocked at my unfortunate

lack of paternalism that you are running off and depriving me of your very attractive company? Or is there some other reason?" The dark eyes were mercilessly fixed on her. "I've wondered. You have no other offense chalked up against me?"

"No. No, I haven't—why should I?" Margaret stammered weakly, terror in her eyes as she grasped the doorknob and turned it.

"Why, indeed? Precisely what has been giving me some thought. I am glad my concern was unnecessary. You still insist on deserting me? Well, then, good night, Mrs. Collier."

"Good night." She breathed it with difficulty, and closing the door behind her, made herself walk. Then she ran in panic across the hall toward the stairs.

How long would he stay in his library, the brandy bottle in reach? Would the brandy, and the sound of rain against the window, and all the shadows of the room, bring the little boy ghost in, to visit him? Or would there be a different ghost, possibly? A woman recently dead, her throat bruised, her head bleeding? It depended primarily, didn't it, upon the guiltiness of his conscience?

A murderer. Was he? Did she or did she not in her heart believe it? Fear mounted, mounted; despite the struggle of her new-found faith to assert itself, fear battled for supremacy. And now the dimly lighted stairs to climb, which would bring her all too soon to the empty, deserted wing of this silent, isolated house.

How easily she could be disposed of, if by any chance Sir Hugh, putting his mind to it, puzzled out the "chalked up other offense" she held against him.

No one in the world who cared about her, except, perhaps, Ritchie, knew where she was. Oh, Ritchie. I have been such a fool.

She cried out to him again, as she had cried out before on the stairs, but Ritchie could not hear her, she remembered, her hands clammy on the banister. London was too far away.

Wretched with loneliness and apprehension, Margaret undressed and got into bed and opened a book. She read on and on, chapter after chapter, not so much interested in the book as anxious for an excuse to keep her bedside lamp burning. A lamp was company. A lamp made all the difference. Midnight settled on the house, bringing a cessation of rain and a quiet outside interrupted only by the drip, drip of trees, and inside by the creaking of old wood, which, though familiar to her now, was still something to be endured. This big, isolated house; beyond its four walls the stretch of dark gardens, and beyond the gardens the darker border hills that would be looming through thick night mists, spectral in moonlight paled by obscuring, scudding clouds. She read on, determinedly.

Suddenly the watchdogs in the stableyard were barking loudly for a startling instant and then as suddenly they were quiet. Probably a tomcat on the prowl had excited them; willing to suppose it, Margaret turned a page and yawned, and she had just made up her mind to turn off the lamp when a small sound in the passage jerked her upright, and intent.

Not the patter of rain—or footsteps—this time. A soft, dull thud as though something had been dropped just outside her door. She was staring at the door, and giving thanks for its big key and heavy bolt when the knob turned with a hard, loud rattling.

What on earth—? She was more astonished than frightened. At least no one was creeping up on her stealthily. Whoever it was may as well be sounding a tocsin!

The knob was rattled again.

"Who's there?" she called sharply.

There was no answer, but the rattling stopped instantly.

How very queer! It was almost as though in having called itself to her attention, wakened her, perhaps, a purpose had been satisfactorily accomplished.

"Who's there, please?"

There was still no answer.

She heard—or thought she heard—a louder than usual creaking in the hall that may or may not have been a stairboard, and when the little traveling clock on the bedside table had ticked away exactly three minutes, she heard the mastiffs start up their barking again before they once more were silent.

Had someone twice crossed the stableyard, going to and from the house, disturbing the dogs momentarily, but quickly quieting them with a command in a familiar voice? Cherry Vane, out for a late look at her puppies? Possibly. But what connection would Cherry have with a rattled doorknob, or that small thud? Pell? Correct, kind Pell would be the last person who'd prowl at midnight, disturbing and mystifying a guest.

And most certainly it hadn't been Sir Hugh. She could almost laugh, in an hysterical sort of way, at the thought of him creeping about, rattling doorknobs. He wouldn't be so lacking in dignity.

Could she have dozed off and dreamed the thud and the rattling? That was it, of course, and to prove to herself that she wasn't the least frightened, but only curious, why not get up and open the door and peer down the hall? Suppose there was anything as alarming even as a shadow, she could scream, couldn't she? Who would hear her was another question.

Anything was better than staring at that doorknob, completely bewildered. Margaret got out of bed, turned the key in the lock, drew back the bolt, and cautiously opened the door. Then, with a horrified gasp, she jumped back, instinctively clutching at the hem of her robe to keep it high off the floor.

A dead rat, a huge dead rat, lying so close to the threshold she had nearly stepped on it. A nauseating rat, its paws drawn up, claws gleaming in the dim light from the globe that dangled at the head of the stairs, its white, pointed teeth showing in an ugly grinning rictus.

Margaret slammed the door and bolted it and leaped back into bed.

A dead rat, over a foot long, grayish brown, thick-skulled, short-eared and short-tailed. The ugliest, most revolting creature she'd ever seen.

And for someone to have put it there—dropped it, with that soft thud—was the most disgusting sort of trick, a clumsy, petty trick. The trick of someone not quite normal.

She wanted to pull the covers up over her head. She wanted to make herself small. She longed for morning, and Pell.

She slept only fitfully the rest of the night, with the lamp left burning. When finally Pell knocked, and called "Your tray, madam," she sprang up and unlocked and unbolted the door again, and opened it, prepared to hastily avert her eyes. But there was nothing on the threshold.

"You saw it?" she demanded of Pell.

"Saw what, madam?" Pell put down the tray.

"That rat. That great, horrible rat. Someone put it there late last night. I heard them—I got up. They'd gone, but they'd left it—a huge, disgusting rat—"

"You are quite certain, madam?" Pell questioned it mildly and unargumentatively, as though Margaret were an overexcited child. "I shouldn't think it a likely happening. There's no rat at the door now, that's certain. A dream, could it be, madam, that mixed you up a bit?"

"No. I tell you someone put it there. Someone who came into the house. Someone who started the dogs barking—"

"The dogs? I can't say as I heard them, myself, but—"

Humoring her, Pell drew aside the curtains. "About the rat, madam. I can see rats are not to your taste, nor are they to my liking, either, to be honest, but we do have them, now and again, here in the house. It's the old stables, and the same story of no money to set things to rights. A proper cleaning out is what's needed, between the walls, and under the flooring. It puts you off a bit, does it, thinking you might see one of the nasty things scuttling about? I shouldn't wonder if you thought twice about staying on with us."

"The rat wasn't that big—the dream rat—if you say so." Margaret laughed, nervously.

"And you shan't be minding the wretched weather we're in for?"

"Not too much." With the uncomfortable feeling she was accepting a challenge, Margaret addressed the back Pell was keeping turned toward her. "It's only drizzling, now, and the sun is sure to come out to stay, one of these days."

"I'd not count on fair days ahead, madam. There's a storm due, Chubb says, the worst we've had in years. And if ever you'd known one of our Salop blows, coming off the mountains, with the wind howling and trees and wires down, and the stream flooding, and rain washing away the roads—weeks you could be kept here, cut off—and you'd find it lonely, with no telephone calls getting through, and no post to keep you in touch with your friends."

"I can see you don't need an almanac, with Chubb such a weather prophet. A little on the gloomy side, though, isn't he?" Margaret's question was put with false lightness as she lifted the silver cover from a rasher of bacon.

"I've never yet seen Chubb mistaken about what's to come, madam—and not only where weather is concerned."

They were trying to frighten her. Even Pell. Now they were all trying to frighten her.

SEVENTEEN

Another long morning, another long afternoon alone in the library. Another after-dinner coffee, with Sir Hugh sarcastic and enigmatic, Cherry Vanc unapproachable. Another midnight in her bedroom, listening to the creakings and the hard, persistent rain, listening for another soft thud outside her door, another turning and rattling of the knob.

Unsuccessfully, she again tried to lose herself in a book. Finally her eyes closed. When she opened them, it was just after dawn, and getting out of bed she pushed aside the curtains and opened the shutters Pell had closed against rain the evening before.

Clear skies at last! And a promise of bright sunshine later in the day. This was one time Pell's pessimistic brother had made a big mistake with his weather forecasting. What was more unlikely than a storm blowing up?

Eagerly, she drew in a breath of fresh morning air fragrant with the smell of drenched grass and leaves and soaked earth.

She heard a thrush singing its matins from a yew tree in the neglected garden, and it pleased her fancy to think the little yellow birds on the bedroom wallpaper were about to trill in unison among their bamboo stalks. And who would care to think otherwise than that the trickle of blue-green stream, like a flow of liquid aquamarines, was murmuring under its pagoda-topped bridges?

A lovely room, in a beautiful, captivating house. And to have wakened to so glorious a morning was to wonder at her cowardice, her doubts. Only too willingly she let them dissolve.

How could she stay on in this house unless she could see some of its beauty, rather than only what was decaying and melancholy and frightening? A wholly beautiful house, like a house in an enthralling dream, that was how she must make herself think of it. The thing to do was make yourself declare over and over that it held no danger for you. Say it enough times and perhaps you would believe it. Make yourself believe there was an answer, somewhere, to the dreadful riddle, "How can he not be guilty, when I saw him—where I saw him—that night?"

The morning air, so cool, so sweet, brushed Margaret's face like the touch of a hand, and in spite of herself, and the hope and the faith she was trying so hard to hold fast to, a long, tremulous sigh escaped her. So perfect a day's beginning! And to let doubt and terrible, unconquerable fear sully it!

Dawn was meant for lovers, wakening to each other. Only she had no lover. Nor ever would. She hadn't even a portrait, whose mouth, on canvas, she could trace, and in the depths of whose eyes she could lose herself, imagining them other eyes.

And who had stolen it from her, which cruelest of thieves? Sir Hugh, for some frightening, mysterious purpose, or his daughter, merely from petty, babyish spite?

Foolish, blind Cherry, who had a lover, or could have, if she so chose. Had she cried until she fell asleep last night? If she had an iota of sense she would start this lovely morning by begging, begging Robin Soames to come back.

Only two more weeks left of the boy's holidays, hadn't he said? Two weeks was nothing. Had the girl stopped to think? Had she any true idea of what she was letting slip through her fingers? How desperately she needed help. How pathetically she needed to have her thinking straightened out.

This perfect morning, this morning for lovers, thrown away, hurt, hurt. Even though for her it held nothing, its waste was a kind of stabbing pain.

How far away was the Vicarage? Margaret wondered with a sudden, considering interest. Ten miles? Would she find the lanes too muddy and rutted for driving? A face-to-face talk with the boy would be better than a hundred notes. As for a telephone call, it wouldn't do at all, with its lack of privacy.

The thought of wet, winding, narrow lanes was a strong deterrent, but at another idea, her face cleared.

The stream! The boy enjoyed fishing enormously, and with his holidays so soon over, he might be down by the big, quiet pool under the aspens and willows. He might be along the stream somewhere even now, casting while the river was still gray with mist, before the sun was high enough to strike through the trees.

There was a chance. And she'd hate to skid into a hedge-row or mire her car. Even if a farm cart should come along to pull her out, she wouldn't want to risk breaking a spring on her rented car.

The stream, by all means, for a first try. She glanced at her traveling clock. Only a few minutes past five. No one in the house would be up. No one would see her.

Hurriedly she got into a skirt and sweater and thick shoes

and snatched up her mackintosh. Tiptoeing along the upper hall, she tied her scarf over her hair and crept down the stairs.

As quietly as possible she unbolted the side door and slipped out into the garden where the broken statues stood in their cypress niches, and across the weedy drive to the fields below the house, and an orchard, and then the stream.

Her shoes were soaked, and squelching in mud. Wet, dripping orchard boughs drenched her. Wet, white pear-blossom petals, stirring in a little breeze, drifted down around her.

A brown hare, tall-eared and limpid-eyed, crossed in front of her, scuttling to cover in sodden bracken, and made her jump. She heard a lark, and wished it might have been a cuckoo calling.

Had Sir Hugh wakened yet to this pearly, misty dawn, she wondered, this dawn meant for lovers—this hurting dawn?

She came to the stream bank and hurried along it, telling herself she was on a wild-goose chase; but when the rapid, noisily chuckling water ran more quietly and she had reached the still, deep pool and the clump of silvery aspen and willow where she had first seen Robin Soames, she saw him again.

He was casting, and she waited until his line had floated into the eddy of a big rock before she called to him.

"Good morning! You're up early."

"And so are you, Mrs. Collier." The boy waved, and smiled.

"Had any luck?"

"Rather!"

"Mind if I watch?"

"Make yourself at home. Isn't that what you Americans say?"

He played his line for a few minutes and then it tautened, and he was reeling it in, with a glistening trout hooked.

"How's that? Not bad, eh?" He flashed Margaret a boyish grin, and when the fish was in his creel, with four others on a bed of wet grass and fern, he sat down beside her, and reached in his jacket pocket for a short, stubby pipe and a worn Morocco leather tobacco pouch and a box of matches. "You don't mind?" He puffed for a minute and then, as he put the pouch back in his pocket, he remarked quietly, "Cherry sent it to me one Christmas. We go back a long time together, ever since my first cricket bat and her first doll. Our going off to our schools, and her holidays away, couldn't spoil things. We used to write. Her letters were different, though, after she came home to stay. . . ."

His young hazel eyes were all at once sober and bewildered. "It would have been so tremendously right, if it had come off the way it ought—the way I counted on, until I got home, myself, this trip, and saw how she was trying to—to push me aside. . . ."

Margaret put out a hand and touched his sleeve. "You can't change her mind?"

"No. She sees things her way, I see them another, and she won't give an inch."

"Does she—forgive me, I'm only asking because I wish I could help—does she care at all for you? I mean if—"

"If she weren't such an ass about her father?" Robin brought it out bluntly.

"Well—yes—yes. Exactly."

"She would marry me any day if only I could get it through her head that she has wasted enough time trying to make him over. He is what he is, and it's only sensible to let well enough alone."

"Marriage would make a different girl of her, I should think, a happy girl."

"That's my theory. With me to look after—and a lot of jolly kids—she'd forget about trying to make Sir Hugh fit her idea of a father. You can't standardize people. We're all of us different, as I've tried to make her understand, time and again. We're not all cut from the same piece of cloth and—"

"Do you like Sir Hugh?" Margaret asked. "Is he liked, generally?"

"He's one of the deep, quiet kind, and not easy to know." Robin drew on his pipe reflectively. "But he's got people's respect, and I should think he'd have masses of friends if he'd let himself go a bit, and didn't work so beastly hard, and live so much like a recluse."

"You are too young to remember Cherry's mother, I expect."

"Right. But she and my mother were great friends. Each other's bridesmaid, and all that."

"Cherry will be a beautiful woman some day. Was her mother beautiful?"

"A stunner, my parents say."

"I—I suppose she is buried in the Vane chapel?"

"It just so happens she's the one Vane wife out of the lot who isn't. Her people took her to Devon, where they've a family place of their own. She'd been homesick here, the story was—something of the sort."

Homesick, when she had all this? Wondering, Margaret knew an odd, inexplicable gladness that Sir Hugh's beautiful bride was in Devon, and not at Monks' Court, waiting for her husband to lie down beside her. And yet maybe there was another reason. Maybe she had *wanted* to get away from Monks' Court.

She jerked her thoughts back to Robin Soames.

"Cherry sent you away finally—for good and all—yesterday? I guessed it because she looked so miserable. She had done a lot of crying, I'm afraid."

"She knows I want her to come with me when I leave. But if she won't listen . . ." Robin shrugged.

"Where do you go, to the Middle East, did you say?"

"Yes. Company headquarters are at a little village called Naasam."

Robin filled his pipe again, and this time held the pouch in his hand instead of returning it to his pocket and stared at it unhappily.

"I could get a Special License. We could be married before I leave. My parents would give the earth if Cherry would agree. They've got five sons, Mrs. Collier, and not a daughter or a daughter-in-law in the lot yet, and they've always thought it would be Cherry and I."

"Does she get on well with your parents?"

"She used to. And she would now, if she didn't stiffen up and pull away for fear they'll talk her into it."

"Tell me about the village. Would Cherry like it?"

"She couldn't help it." Robin's face brightened. "It's smashing! Oh, it's crude, and the house we'd live in isn't a palace, but it's comfortable, and you should feel the sun, Mrs. Collier, and see the desert—the light on the hills, changing every hour. Lots of pinks and purples—it would take a chap who paints to describe it. And there are date palms and fig trees and camels, and women at the well, filling their jugs. All of it is like an illustration out of a child's book of Old Testament stories."

He hesitated, and then laughed, with an engaging mixture of a kind of British schoolboy shyness and a man's ardor. "Do you know that bit from the Song of Solomon, Mrs. Collier— 'For, lo, the winter is past'? It goes like this: 'My beloved spake, and said unto me, "Rise up, my love, my fair one, and come away. For, lo! the winter is past, the rain is over and gone; the flowers appear on the earth; the time of the singing of birds is come, and the voice of the turtle is heard in our land; the fig tree putteth forth her green figs, and the vines with the tender grapes give a good smell. Arise, my love, my fair one, and come away." ' "

"And Cherry won't listen, even to anything as persuasive as that? How can she be so stupid? I can see her there in your Naasam, in the hot bright sunshine. And when I think of her father's cold, empty house! It's the dreariest place imaginable for a girl."

"It's not Paradise, Naasam, don't misunderstand me, Mrs. Collier." Robin's brief grin was in evidence again. " 'The good smell' of the vines gives way now and again to goat and camel stink—ever get a whiff? And there's sand in your teeth and your ears and your nostrils when the wind blows, as it does a lot of the time, and you're battling filth morning, noon and night. But Cherry wouldn't mind that part. She could take it. And I shan't be stuck in Naasam forever; we get shifted about every two years, and eventually I'll land in one of the big central offices. It could be Paris or Vienna or San Francisco or even London. But where we go isn't important; the big thing is just to get away, and let Cherry have a chance to take a proper look at her attitude toward her father."

"She is starving here." Margaret stated it flatly. "You can't give her up. You've got to keep at her. Please, won't you put your pride in your pocket?" Margaret's hand was gentle on the boy's sleeve again. "And may I call you Robin? You see, I like you, and—and the Vane family interests me very much. I don't know when any two people have—have troubled me as much for one reason or another." She paused, and then added slowly, "I don't like to think Sir Hugh is as hard and cold as he seems." She paused again. "I keep trying to think he is deeply sorry about—about the barrier between him and Cherry." Her voice was almost pleading as she went on. "People hide behind masks sometimes, don't you think? And are they not different, often, than we suppose? Different in so many ways?" Her voice was unsteady as she finished and Robin looked at her curiously.

"You've taken on the Vanes in a rather big way, I'd say."

"Yes. Yes, I have."

"Decent of you."

"They—they happen to have caught my imagination. And you will come back, Robin?"

"What good would it do?"

"Make her see Naasam. Make her find a life of her own. Your own. You can, if you try hard enough. And you've got to get her away. You must!" Margaret's voice shook with intensity. "You must, Robin."

She broke off quickly then under his again curious glance, and her words came lightly, almost naturally as she laughed.

"She would adore the goats and the camels, stink or no stink. Though leaving the puppies might be hard. Oh, dear, what about them?"

"No problem, Mrs. Collier." Robin's smile was rueful. "I've got all the details worked out beautifully—if only she'll let me do the arranging! I've got my mother to swear she'll take on the pups. She's as dog-crazy as Cherry, every bit. That's one of their great bonds. That and growing vegetables. Lord, the new peas and early cucumbers I've had to admire!"

"Then it's all settled," Margaret declared gaily. "All you need do is come back every day until she gives in."

"I'm to lay siege, in other words?"

"Exactly."

"I'm afraid it won't work. And I shouldn't care to hang about where I'm not wanted." His eyes were rebellious, his boyish mouth set. "I shan't come begging."

"You can't afford to get up on your high horse. You simply can't. You've got to keep coming back. It's your only chance. Take it, Robin. Promise? Oh, if you only knew—"

She broke off again abruptly. "I seem to be getting rather carried away. It's just that I like to see people happy. And now, I must go back to the house. Pell will be bringing up my breakfast tray and wondering where in the world I've disappeared to. Incidentally, she is on your side—as you doubtless know—and so is Sir Hugh. He told me he was. So, you see, with the three of us for you, besides your parents, you can't help but win."

"I'm not so sure. But anyway, you've bucked me no end, Mrs. Collier. I don't know how to thank you."

"Don't try. Just come."

"I'll think about it, at any rate. And here—take this along to Cherry for me, will you? She might like it for her breakfast. Tell her it came from the pool near the bend in the stream where we used to have picnics. She'll know."

There was a question then as to how she would carry the fish Robin pressed on her. A pocket of her mackintosh was the only solution, and Margaret was laughing hysterically as she took the path along the stream bank through the orchard and the fields to the gardens of Monks' Court.

Her Liberty mackintosh, bought for the pursuit of a mur——of a man she had seen in a window on Mount Street!

It wouldn't be goats she would smell of. And what had she written in her hurried, placating note to Ritchie from Liberty's, her last day in London? That "things were getting curiouser and curiouser"? Dear God—Alice's adventures had been nothing.

A fish in her pocket, squeezed in, dripping wet, to be daintily grilled for the daughter of a man in a highly suspect position. A man who would be tried, and perhaps serve a life sentence, once Scotland Yard got around to catching up with him. Margaret could see Inspector Downs playing cat's cradle with his rubber bands.

Robin Soames *must* come back, to take Cherry Vane away,

out of it all. Cherry needed a husband—and a change of name—desperately. And who else was there for her, and who better, in this away-from-everywhere countryside but Robin Soames?

When she had gone through the gardens, Margaret turned at the archway in the wall and went on to the stableyard. At the end of the row of empty stalls she found Cherry putting out the morning's meat and milk for the setter bitch. As she looked up at the sound of Margaret's footsteps, her eyes, enormous in a wan face and with shadows under them, were hostile and wary.

She wonders why I'm here, Margaret thought, and she hates me. She hasn't slept, from the looks of those heavy eyes and that pallor.

"Good morning." She said it with an effort, and hoped she sounded nothing more than casually courteous.

"Good morning," the girl muttered with the minimum of civility.

"Your puppies seem to have grown just these past few days," Margaret remarked with controlled pleasantness. "May I pick one up?"

"I'd rather you didn't."

"Oh. I suppose it frets the mother?" Margaret asked equably, and without visible annoyance. "I've been down at the stream," she went on. "Robin Soames was there."

"Robin?" The girl flushed, and her eyes dropped from Margaret's face and she became very busy stirring the bitch's food.

"He sent you this." Margaret dragged the fish from her pocket, once more struggling to hold back wild, hysterical laughter. "He said to tell you he caught it in the pool, by the bend, where you used to picnic."

The girl's flush deepened. Had she let Robin kiss her on any of those picnics? Undoubtedly.

"If he comes back to Monks' Court before he leaves for his job, I hope you'll be kind to him," Margaret persisted, and as Cherry stiffened, visibly, she added with gentleness, "Puppies are nice, but wouldn't you like babies even more? They are supposed to be rather special. Not that I know through experience. I've never had a child."

She left the stable then, with Cherry still silent, her eyes still averted, and let herself into the house through the side door and went upstairs reflecting how different the quiet, sad rooms and the long halls would be if Cherry married, and, on visits home from wherever Robin's job took him, she brought "a lot of jolly kids." The house needed children. Living Children.

She was thinking about the little boy Jarvis as she went along the upper hall and paused to glance down the passage that led to the nursery.

When she was back in her bedroom, changing her soaked shoes, Pell knocked, with her breakfast tray, and Margaret, still thinking about the nursery passage, wanted to ask a question, and began chatting in the casual, but interested manner she knew would start Pell talking.

"I was down at the river. It's so beautiful, there. I suppose Sir Hugh and his brother used to spend hours fishing, when they were children?"

"So they did, madam."

"Did they get on well? I mean, you spoke of Sir Hugh's temper. Did the boys quarrel much? An older brother, flying off the handle all the time, could make things difficult, I should think."

"Quarrel, madam?" Pell looked shocked. "Never. Master Jarvis worshiped Master Hugh, and Master Hugh thought the world of his brother. Took him under his wing, you might say, Master Jarvis being a delicate child. Not a hard word, ever, did I hear between them. And I wish, madam,

I'd not spoke about Sir Hugh and this—" Pell touched her scar. "It wasn't right, me speaking out as I did, and could have put a person against Sir Hugh most unfairly."

"I didn't give it a second thought—not seriously."

Almost believing she spoke the truth, Margaret poured a cup of tea. "Did your Master Jarvis die here at Monks' Court?"

"It was in China, madam. He and Sir Hugh were there some years together for a big company. A fever did it. One of those nasty, sudden-like foreign fevers, taking one off overnight, as Sir Hugh wrote us. And a blow it was, to all of us, I can tell you."

The Orient again. First in London. Now here. Would there never be any surcease from reminders of a Eurasian dancer? Had Hugh Vane known her out there? Had the brother? The brother who had once been a little boy?

Margaret buttered a piece of toast.

"Tell me—an old house like this, has it a ghost, by any chance?" She repeated the nervous little joke she had attempted with Sir Hugh. "Americans love ghosts."

"They're not what a person chooses to live with. But why do you ask about ghosts, madam? You haven't—seen anything?"

"No. Though sometimes the sound of the rain, and the old wood creaking, and—and my imagination—" Margaret laughed uncertainly. "Silly of me."

"I shouldn't say that, madam. There's plenty of queer goings on in houses like this that can't be explained. Though often as not it *is* the rain or the wind and the creaking." She smoothed her apron and did not quite meet Margaret's eyes. "Which isn't to say we shouldn't do our share of praying, if we think there's need, for any uneasy souls we know of. It's never amiss, madam, to get down on our knees now and again."

Pell hung up Margaret's pale-blue nightgown and robe,

set her blue satin mules under them, and closed the wardrobe door.

"Ghosts or not, this is a house that can do with prayers," she stated slowly. "And plenty of them. Not that I've got the second sight, as some have, but there's trouble coming, madam, worse than any the house has seen yet, in all the years I've been here. . . ."

"Trouble?" Margaret's spoon paused in its stirring of the tea in a flowered Spode cup.

"Worse trouble, madam, than any the house has seen yet, in all the years I've been here. It's in the air—thick enough, almost, to put hand to. And every morning and every night, first and last thing, I'm asking God's mercy on the lot of us under this roof. A matter of weeks it's been, madam, since I first took notice of it."

"Did it come on suddenly?"

"Not at the start. It was like the mists that close in on our mountains. A cold, creeping grayness, and then a quick settling down, dark and heavy, over the house. As I say, madam, I'm praying—"

Pell interrupted herself to look at Margaret's tray. "You're not eating, madam. The toast not touched. And nothing wrong with your egg, I hope? It was fresh from the nest not an hour ago."

"Everything is perfect. I'm just not hungry."

"The tea would settle you, madam, if it's a touch of stomach upset. Drink it while it's hot. That'll do it. And if it's all you can manage, I'll take the tray."

Halfway to the door Pell turned. "Like I said, I've not got the second sight, which would come in useful at a time like this when a person would wish to know straight out what was ahead, and stiffen for it, as you might say. But I'm like Sir Hugh, I've got my drop of Welsh blood. And all the Welsh have what we call a 'knowingness'—some has more and some has less, but it's in every one of us. And that's why you can believe me when I say there's trouble coming, certain as I'm standing here."

"Will it have anything to do with me?"

There was a tremor in Margaret's voice she could not control. She longed to scoff, to laugh outright; instead, her eyes were afraid as she stared at the old woman. "Am I mixed up in—in the trouble?"

Pell looked long and intently at Margaret. Then the black eyes, so bright in her scarred gnome's face, were pitying, and her answer came evasively. "You don't see the darkness of it yourself, madam, nor feel the weight?"

EIGHTEEN

A lot of rubbishy, superstitious nonsense, that Welsh knowingness. Firmly, Margaret dismissed Pell's forebodings once
she had gone, though it was difficult to explain the goose
pimples she had felt on her arms as the old woman put her
questions.

Trouble. Who knew better than she herself that it was
on the way? She hadn't needed Pell's eerie prescience to tell
her. And to stay on here was going to be the hardest thing
she had ever done. To say that faith gave one the courage of
a lion was only to repeat a false and silly fable. She'd be out of
here in minutes, as fast as she could go, if it weren't for X.
The X who had to be discovered. Strange, how now that she
had fixed on X, he seemed so real to her. She had come to
feel she was playing a game of blindman's buff. If she groped
long enough, she would find him. Meanwhile, nothing but
waiting, and wondering, and fear.

Margaret moved restlessly to the windows to stand there,

looking out over the garden. The Land Rover, with Sir Hugh driving, turned out of the stableyard. Would his farms claim him all day? How long had he waited for her to put in an appearance downstairs?

She could not bear the library that morning. She went down to the kitchen and asked Pell for a sandwich instead of lunch in the dining room and took a lonely, disturbed departure for the chapel and the broken ramparts of the tower where she had sat with Sir Hugh on another morning.

The lingering indecision which was as painful as a bruise took her to the door of the chapel. When she had lifted a heavy iron bar from its socket, she pushed the door open, to gaze through the moldy smelling gloom.

Catharine, lying there, brave Catharine. Brave at the last, at any rate. Had she, too, flinched, and shrunk from the giving of her gift of love? Hesitantly, Margaret walked to the grille and stood shivering in the darkness and chill, staring, awed and marveling, at Catharine Vane's effigy.

How deeply, deeply, she must have loved, how passionately, with both her soul and her body. Two hands gone. Two hands that had willingly, gladly been held out. How could she? Mutilation—truly the gift of gifts. More than life.

Margaret's wondering, almost envious, eyes lingered on the crossed, handless wrists, and instinctively she gripped her own hands tightly together, knowing, vicariously, the horror and the pain.

Her gaze went then to the effigy of Catharine Vane's Crusader husband. This Hugh, here in stone, had a mouth like the portrait. There was tenderness and warmth to it even in his deep sleep of a graven image.

If the present Sir Hugh Vane smiled—ever—would his thin mouth curve, too, and take on this same sweetness?

She reached out a hand to touch the stone mouth and

trace its curve, as she had touched the mouth of the portrait, and then she turned from the effigies and went out of the chapel, still shivering.

The sandwiches Pell had cut and tied in a white napkin had no appeal, but she sat on the stone rubble heap and listened for a cuckoo call that never came. Perhaps it was as well, she reflected heavily.

She was still sitting among the crumbled ruins when she heard a clatter of hooves and the rattle of wheels. As she hastily drew behind the concealing shelter of thickly clustered trees, she saw an old-fashioned cart, pulled by the rough-coated pony from the stableyard, with Pell slapping the reins, bump past on the rutted drive.

Pell, with lunch over, and her dishes done, was off to market in the village. And was the cart the same Edwardian governess cart of the snapshot on Sir Hugh's desk?

Unwillingly Margaret's thoughts flew to the younger of the two little sailor-suited boys in the picture. Master Jarvis, of course.

Only unhappy people came back, after death, as ghosts, she had always supposed. What had little Jarvis been unhappy about? Why did he haunt his brother? A boyhood feud, between them, perhaps, never forgotten? But as a revenant, why had a grown man at death resumed the form of a child again?

A curiously persistent idea began to nag Margaret. In one way or another Jarvis Vane was at the root of the trouble Pell had predicted, and that she herself saw so clearly in the offing.

Jarvis Vane the child, or Jarvis Vane the man? She gave the question more than a moment's consideration, with a suddenly quickening sense of its importance. To think of him as a man was to wonder again if as adults the Vane brothers had looked alike. And that little drag of footsteps along the hall, could it mean that Jarvis, the child, had grown up to limp like his brother? And if he had . . . ?

For an electrified moment tingling excitement gripped her. Like a zooming rocket, hope was a bright, dazzling flare. Two limping Vanes. Two tall, look-alive Vanes, who walked with sticks. One of them the man in the window on Mount Street, but the other, not. X no longer equaling the unknown. Jarvis was X. And to think that only now she had wakened to the potentialities of a Vane family resemblance between those two. Hadn't Jarvis as much right to it as his brother? And why shouldn't he, as well as Hugh Vane, be the double of the portrait?

But Jarvis was dead. She had more than Pell's word for it. She had seen the records in Somerset House. She was up against a stone wall of hard facts. With the bright rocket a fizzled, burned-out stick, Margaret opened Pell's white napkin and after a few disinterested nibbles at the sandwiches spread what remained of them on a slab of broken stone that would serve as a feeding table for any birds that might come. Then she started toward the house, only to turn abruptly back to the chapel. A plaque, Pell had said. She found it on the wall close to the niche where the effigies slept. Even in the dimness of the chapel its bronze looked new, its lettering recently inscribed. "Jarvis . . . China."

That much was enough. Margaret's return along the drive, under the dark trees, was subdued and reluctant. As she approached the house, she dispiritedly rejected any idea of going inside and of crossing its long upper hall to spend the rest of the afternoon in her bedroom. She was tired of reading, bored with her tapestry. Nor was she in a mood to sit waiting, listening, for a child's dragging footsteps outside her door. Even in the daytime you couldn't be sure when he might choose to limp along the passage.

Uneasily she admitted that Master Jarvis, the child Jarvis, for some reason or other was proving to be an extremely difficult little child to put out of mind. And, as inexplicably, Jarvis Vane the man, dead of fever in China, was entrenching himself deeper every moment in her thoughts. She would have supposed the plaque to put a period to further foolish, futile reflection on a dead man. But no. She was at it again. "In memoriam . . ." It implied that Jarvis Vane's body had not been brought home for burial. She could presume that, certainly. Was it because there hadn't been money enough to bring him back that he had been left to lie among strangers in so far away a land? It would be the only reason, wouldn't it, to an old family like the Vanes? Monks' Court would seem the one suitable resting place for any of its members. But what if—what if there had been no body? What if you could begin to think Jarvis Vane was not dead? You'd be out of your mind.

With her emergence from under the trees, a walk to the lake suggested itself to Margaret. A walk in the open. Any sky overhead, even though not of the brightest blue possible, would be preferable to the house. Perhaps a row to the island, too, with a glimpse of the Greek summerhouse, and a nosegay brought back for her dressing table.

But how did you get to the lake and find the boat Sir Hugh had mentioned? Pell could have told her, of course, but Pell had gone marketing. She'd have to look for Chubb. Margaret started for the stableyard but stopped at the kitchen garden when she saw Pell's brother down on his knees weeding around the young stalks of rhubarb that had begun to thrust through a mat of straw mulching.

"Good afternoon."

" 'ternoon, ma'am." Chubb's response was brief.

"Will you tell me, please, how to get to the lake?"

He sat back on his heels, and pulling a dirty handkerchief from a pocket blew his nose, his eyes, black and deep set in his weatherbeaten face, fixing on her.

The bright, unblinking gaze of a toad. An old toad, with a perpetual cold.

"Yon's the path." He pointed with his weeding fork in the general direction of the wide stretch of turf that had once been lawn. "Below the slopes, t'other side of the birch stand."

"And the boat?"

"You'll come on it."

With another blowing of his nose and a swipe against the back of an arthritic hand, thick and twisted as an old root, Chubb began weeding again, the fork discarded in favor of black, broken fingernails, grubbing deep.

Definitely an unpleasant, loutish old man—he needn't have been so short and unhelpful with his directions. But a faithful sort. Give him credit for that much. Plainly, he worked as hard as Pell to keep things going for Sir Hugh.

Leaving the kitchen garden, Margaret struck off across the turf and after a stone balustrade and bench had been reached, began descending a terraced hillside. So far, so good. And there were the birch trees ahead, a tall screen of silvery-barked trunks and new silver leaves.

The path, when she found it, led through bracken as high as her head, and around a bend into a secluded glade. The lake then came as a surprise, planned to be glimpsed unexpectedly.

Only a small lake, but entirely beautiful with its quiet, pellucid water a mirror for the uncertain blueness above, the gray of clouds. Utter stillness. No faintest breeze to stir either leaf or bracken frond. Not even bird song. An unreal silence, and an unreal lake, an unreal little island, out there.

Now a look for the boat Chubb had said she would come

on. It was easily in sight, pulled up on shore a few feet from the water's edge, its bowline tied around the slender trunk of a birch sapling, its single pair of oars lying across a center thwart.

A dear little boat, though all its paint was gone except for the faintest of lettering that spelled out the name on the bow: *Sprite*. For water sprite? Nice!

Evidently, however, Chubb had not put much effort into readying the boat for her use. Margaret eyed the covering of old leaves in the bottom, leaves that had fluttered down several autumns past from the looks of them, lying in a thick, sodden carpeting.

But they didn't matter. This was almost going to be fun.

With her spirits lifting, Margaret gave herself up to the diversion of the moment. She found it a small but enjoyable adventure to cast off the line, push the light skiff into the water with a few vigorous shoves and make a leap to board it, with the boat tipping excitingly as she reached for an oar and poled from shore.

When the boat was well afloat, she moved forward to the center seat and began rowing, vigorously, with the island as her goal. The lake was shallow near shore; she could see fish darting among lily roots.

"Lilies the color of Jersey cream . . ."

There was Sir Hugh's little temple, closer now, the marble pillars of its portico as white as the pair of swans that were floating serenely past her, as white as the drifts of flowers she could already smell. Or pretended she could smell!

Narcissus. Freesia. Cyclamen. To the Greeks the narcissus was the asphodel, hadn't she read somewhere? "Asphodel" had exactly the right classic ring; it suited the temple to perfection.

And the little island was Elysium, why not, where every goddess had a god? A delightful arrangement.

The fancy pleased her. To elaborate on it, to turn one of the swans into a Leda, and just to dream and drift a little, she rested her oars, idly watching the shimmer of drops that fell from their blades.

It was with a sigh that she reproved herself for her romanticism, the useless, foolish romanticism that had done her no kindness ever, and, of late, had served her so disastrously.

Then with unpleasant abruptness she was jerked from daydreaming to reality. The boat had begun to leak. The soles of her shoes were already damp from water just beginning to show in a steady seepage through the autumn leaves.

Exactly what might be expected of a Monks' Court boat. What else but rotting floorboards and split seams in need of caulking? For a moment or two it was only an annoyance; she would have to forego exploring the island, and she would have to put up with wet feet. She began to row with no sense of urgency at first, but with a little spurt when she saw the layer of leaves begin to rise, pushed up by the increasing seepage beneath them. The water was now around her ankles.

Concerned, she pulled in her oars and searched hurriedly under the thwart for a bailing bucket. Or a tin can would do; there must at least be a tin can! It would be standard equipment, you would think, for a leaky old sieve like this.

There was nothing. Nor would it have helped much now, she saw with alarm. No container could bail out fast enough against the bubbling rush of water that was pouring through the hull as well as the floorboards, like water pouring from a faucet—an intentionally turned on faucet.

Helplessly staring, Margaret saw why the water was rushing in so swiftly. Under the leaves auger holes were visible. Newly bored holes. There was no mistaking the newness. The raw wood around the boring proved it. And the leaves had been purposely left in the bottom of the boat, a thick covering on someone's tampering, until the boat would be launched and its unsuspecting occupant caught far from the shore.

She would have to start swimming. Already the boat was filling to the gunwales. Waterlogged, it would sink, its buoyancy lost, slight as her weight was.

She had the presence of mind to jerk the oars free from the rowlocks and to jump just before the boat capsized under her. Margaret was over the side, but at the first shock of cold water she was calling herself a brainless moron not to have pulled off her heavy walking oxfords and thrown off her mackintosh.

Snatching at a floating oar, she clutched tight with one hand, and treading water, tried uselessly to untie shoelaces with the other. Double knots; she had tied them for her walk too neatly, too firmly.

Clinging to the oar and kicking out with her feet, she made for a clump of reeds and rushes and cattails halfway between herself and the shore. Once reached, it would serve as a haven where she could struggle out of her binding, dragging-down raincoat. Already her hands were blue from the cold water and a grip on the oar more and more difficult.

The water could be melted ice; even when she got to the reeds, the shore would still be much, much too far away. No. None of that. Keep your head. The shore was no farther away than the length, and back again, of a swimming pool. You could do it. You could hold out.

It was just before she reached the reeds, frozen and exhausted, that her feet touched firm bottom. She was in shallow water no more than neck high. But her indescribable relief lasted only seconds.

The swans! A pair of them coming at her! The lightly gliding swans that a few minutes before had charmed her were turned now into fiercely honking, hissing attackers, their bodies heavy and low in the water, their black, webbed feet stroking rhythmically, like powerful pistons.

A nest in the reeds! She had disturbed their nest, threatened their hidden eggs, or their cygnets. There was time only for the flash of a guess before she was swinging her oar to fend them off.

As they swam close, they circled her, rising high now in the water for an onset, spreading strong wings, stretching long necks, thrusting out with orange bills. Margaret inched shoreward, the swans retreating, then advancing again, their sinuous necks snakelike, their vicious hiss and honk a terrifying assault of its own.

Her shoes could have been concrete blocks. Her arms had seemingly been pulled from their sockets. The oar was too heavy to lift again. Letting go of it, she staggered on through waist-deep water, her hands to her face and head for protection from the menacing bills that darted here, darted there, with every reptilian undulation and arch of white necks.

She was within a yard of the shore, agonizingly close to it, agonizingly far, when the honking and hissing, the terrible flapping of wings ceased as unexpectedly as it had begun. Surprised by a sudden, hard bombardment of rocks hurled from a thicket of bracken, the swans veered, and with their spread wings instantly furled, they were gliding majestically, serenely, to reestablish dominion over their reedy kingdom.

Her rescuer? Margaret stared unseeingly around her, exhausted almost to insensibility. There was no one in sight, and her strength gone, all interest, all curiosity deserting her, she dropped to the ground. Just to lie there. Just to know she was safe.

Those horrible birds. Those nightmarish birds. Part water-serpent . . . But she must gather herself together; there was someone she must thank. Someone nearby. That rustling sound—that almost inaudible rustling. Listen . . .

"Who's there? Who is it?" she called weakly, and with supreme effort raised her head to look toward the thicket of tall, coarsely growing bracken and gorse from which the rocks had been thrown. There was another rustle, and then she had a glimpse of a scuttling form, crouched close to the earth, before it took cover behind a farther shield of bracken.

The absolute silence that followed, enveloping the little glade with a curious sense of suspenseful waiting and watching, was as immediately terrifying as had been the honk and hiss of the swans, the sound of their wings.

To stay alone there, and to listen for another rustling, to feel concealed eyes, peering, would be to lose all self-control, all hold on herself.

With terror giving her back the will and the physical ability to struggle back to her feet, Margaret wrung what water she could out of her mackintosh and heavy skirt, and not daring to look to one side or another, set out on the path that would lead her past the birch trees and up the slopes of turf to the house.

The climb was steep; she questioned whether she would ever get to the top. With her endurance near an end, her teeth chattering, her shivering uncontrollable, the anticipation of a hot bath and dry clothes and a bed pushed all questions, all conjecture to one side.

Let her have time to think, time to sort out the happenings of the afternoon, and draw what conclusions she could. Let her have time to get warm!

She filled the tub, immeasurably grateful that Pell had already lighted the boiler for before-dinner baths, kicked off her soaked, pulpy shoes when the laces had been cut with her manicure scissors, and stripped, letting the clothes lie in a heap on the floor without the energy to pick them up. When she had soaked until her blue flesh was rosy, and had rubbed herself hard, with one of Monks' Court's old-fashioned, extravagantly big towels, and put on her deliciously warm dressing gown, she went quickly to her room and collapsed on the bed, with the silk puff wrapped around her, close as a cocoon.

To think, to reason, was still beyond her. The warmth was a soporific. Her eyelids fluttered and she fell into a light doze that lasted until Pell came into the room with her usual hot-water bottle to turn down the bed and draw the curtains.

"A nice lie-down, madam?"

"I was nearly frozen when I came in. And I've got some wet clothes; would it be too much trouble for you to hang them to dry in the kitchen?"

"Wet clothes?" Pell asked with astonishment. "When it's been so fine all day?"

"I went for a row on the lake." Margaret hesitated. "I had to swim ashore," she added quietly. "The boat leaked."

"You could have drowned, madam! I'm that sorry! Not a pleasant thing at all to have happened."

"It was very unpleasant." Margaret unwrapped herself from the puff, and getting off the bed, went over to the ward-robe, and as she took lingerie from a drawer, she kept her eyes on Pell.

"The boat was full of holes. Large holes."

"It's an old boat, the *Sprite* is." The brass curtain rings rattled on their rods.

"The bottom was covered with leaves. Sir Hugh mentioned to me that he'd ask your brother to clean them out. And if he had, I'd have seen—"

"Chubb gets behind, madam, with all he's got to do."

Pell finished with the curtains and went over to the bed. "A good, scalding-hot bottle, and there's nothing more of a comfort I always say." Pell smoothed the rumpled pillows. "You're wishing yourself back in London, I should think, after the afternoon you've had, madam," she commented. "The country can be a tricking place for town people, not up to its ways."

"What do you mean, tricking?"

"The lake, today, and you not being used to boats."

"I'm entirely used to them."

"Which isn't to say it couldn't be a bull loose in the lane, another time."

"Or a sow or a boar out of its sty, making for me?" Margaret inquired meaningly. "Which would be worse, that, or the swan attack, do you suppose?" It was a leading question, but Pell evaded a direct answer.

"I shouldn't enjoy either, Madam."

"And I expect you wouldn't appreciate a dead rat dropped at your door—even if it were in a dream?"

"I can't say as I would, madam."

Taking a little more time over it than necessary, Pell was folding the puff into an elaborate triangle at the foot of the bed as she added, thoughtfully, "Nor would a stirred-up beehive suit, either, nor I shouldn't fancy coming on one of Sir Hugh's dogs that had slipped its leash—not if I was a stranger to the dog, I wouldn't."

"I expect I shall have to take my chances. I'm not leaving, although I can see the country is dangerous. I'll simply have to keep my eyes open. People have been known to fall into wells, too, when the covers were left off—accidentally."

That ought to do it! She'd laid it on thick enough. And let Pell substitute "deliberately" for "accidentally" if she chose, and let her fully understand that Monks' Court had offered its dubious hospitality to a not entirely stupid or blind guest.

Margaret ran her hand through a pair of sheer stockings, as though in search of runs, her surreptitious glance still on the old woman's face. The kindest of faces. And yet as closed as Sir Hugh's face. Concealing much, you were certain. Telling you nothing. And there you were, left to guess what lay behind those black shrewd eyes.

Eyes like Chubb's eyes. Uncommunicative when they

chose to be. She was remembering that Chubb and Pell were not only brother and sister but a brother and sister with equally strong loyalty to Sir Hugh.

"Your wet things, madam?"

"In the bathroom. There's a pair of shoes, too, though they are probably ruined."

"I'll stuff them with paper and set them in the kitchen—not too close to the stove—and then with a rub-over with Sir Hugh's boot oil, they'll be none the worse, chances are."

"I hope you are right. Thank you very much."

"A pleasure, madam."

Pell left the room, and as she closed the door after her, Margaret felt a cold draft of fear and uncertainty as chilling as the lake water.

Pell had been hinting as strongly as her kindness allowed: "Leave Monks' Court, madam. For your own good, leave."

As she dressed, Margaret tried to visualize again the scuttling figure she had seen in the bracken thicket. Just that, it had been; a scuttling, unidentifiable figure, nothing more. It was impossible to imagine Sir Hugh hunched on all fours, concealed and peering. Nor could he be imagined, auger in hand, stealthily boring holes in a boat.

But he could give orders. And Chubb was at hand, the loyal but not very nice old man, the unblinking toad. She had an idea Chubb would stop at nothing. And Chubb could have been in the thicket, just as Chubb, in rubber overshoes, could have crept silently into the house after he silenced the dogs in the stableyard, and dropped the dead rat at her door.

She had been slow-witted to overlook Chubb. Chubb taking orders. Should she look on both incidents as merely two unpleasant but harmless attempts to frighten her away? Would there be more? And if the attempts proved unsuccessful, and she stuck it out here what other—and final—trick would be played on her? Someone wanted her out of the way. A determined someone.

After a last look in the mirror, Margaret picked up her embroidery bag and went downstairs. Hold fast to faith, she was reminding herself with each unwilling step. She would need every bit of it. Weak and faltering though it was, what else would see her through?

With gratefulness for the fire in the library and for the proffered sherry, she tried not to mind that Cherry had not yet appeared and that she was alone with Sir Hugh.

"The day passed agreeably for you, Mrs. Collier?"

"It was pleasant to see the sun."

She was ashamed of her answer. If she still possessed any hold at all on faith, why not come out with the truth about the afternoon? "I walked to the lake." It came out bravely. "I went rowing."

Bravely, she plunged ahead. "The boat leaked quite a lot. Someone will have to bring it ashore—I—I had to get out and swim."

"My dear Mrs. Collier!" Sir Hugh exclaimed with astonished concern. "I say, how unpleasant! I'm most frightfully sorry."

"I shouldn't have minded if the water hadn't been so cold." Margaret gave a nervous little laugh. "And I didn't enjoy your swans, either."

"They attacked you?"

His concern seemed genuine. Surely no one could pretend so cleverly. Surely he had nothing to do with leaks in the *Sprite*. Chubb, perhaps, but not he. She was determined to believe in him.

"I had wanted to see the flowers, too. The narcissus, especially." She was finding it surprisingly pleasant to chat relaxedly. "Narcissus seem so right for the little temple. Did you know the ancient Greeks called them asphodel? At least I think they did." She glanced toward the bookcase. "I may as well look it up and be sure."

"Which will you have, a dictionary or a mythology?" Sir Hugh followed her to the shelves.

"The dictionary will do."

He reached for a volume and handed it to her. "Here you are."

Opening it, she turned the pages and then began to read aloud. "Asphodel: the narcissus or daffodil. A white-flowered plant, genus Asphodelus, of the lily family—" She stopped abruptly.

"Yes?" Sir Hugh waited, inquiringly.

"In Greek mythology, the flower of the dead."

"So now you know. And on the best authority." Sir Hugh's comment cut through a moment's curious silence. "You look as though it lessens your liking for them, Mrs. Collier—does it?"

"No, not really—" Her answer was false and unhappy. The dead. A dead woman in particular, who though she suggested a scent of musk rather than of narcissus, found so many ways to make you think of her, make you never stop questioning.

Shrinking back from Sir Hugh's dark, inimical eyes, Margaret returned the dictionary to the shelf, the warming glow gone. Such a brief stay. Such a cruelly brief stay.

NINETEEN

Another day stretching ahead. The only way at all to make it pass was to keep busy, Margaret told herself from the top of the library ladder. She took book after book from its shelf, made her notation, and applied a soft dust cloth gently before replacing each volume. Sumptuous leathers, gorgeous gilding! A few cheaply bound editions. But interesting, all of them. She had the library to herself. She worked until noon and then got down to wash her grimy hands and to eat lunch, alone.

Cherry had not appeared for dinner the evening before, and now she was again absenting herself. Oh, well. A thoroughly impossible girl, as she'd thought from the start.

Margaret mounted her ladder again, with the handling of the books a pleasure that would have been greater had she not disliked the loneliness of the library that became more of a weight on her spirits as the afternoon advanced.

Now and again she looked down at Sir Hugh's desk and

discovered herself wondering how late his farm duties would keep him. Her eyes went once or twice to the silver-framed snapshot. Master Hugh—and Master Jarvis?

Such a shadowy room, this quiet library, with the sun gone off the windows and the old-fashioned lighting so very inadequate. Had two little boys ever played in here? It was not likely. This would have been a room sacred to their elders in the days when there was a nursery staff and Monks' Court had been formally run.

She could see the little boys here, all the same. No, that was silly. Not see them, but sense them. But that was not quite correct, either. Not "them." Only one. Perhaps being conscious of him here was because she had begun, upstairs, to be so often aware of him? Nonsensical, all of it! Including her frequent wondering why Jarvis Vane was supposed to return as a child ghost, when she knew, both from Pell and the records in Somerset House that he had died as a young man?

What sort of little boy was he? Did he look more, or less like his brother than the faded snapshot on the desk suggested? Not that she had any wish to find out from first-hand knowledge. . . . Margaret got down from the bench, abruptly, deciding she had done enough work for the time being. After dinner there would be another hour of it, unless she elected to go early to her room and put up with the solitude of the guest wing. A paucity of choices, it struck her.

A few hours later, when she and Sir Hugh went into the huge, candle-lighted dining room, there were only the two of them to sit down at the table.

"My daughter's manners leave much to be desired," Sir Hugh remarked with a glance at Cherry's vacant place. "I see we are to be deprived of her company for the second evening in succession, and without an explanation. Will you be writing anything on the subject of England's young people of today, Mrs. Collier? I regret Cherry doesn't offer the best example. You'll make due allowance in your article, I very much hope."

Margaret let the sarcasm go unanswered, but Pell, who was bringing in the soup, spoke up quickly. "Miss Cherry is at the stable, sir, as she's been all day, and yesterday the same. She sent word by Chubb, not five minutes ago, she'd be late in. She's got her hands full trying to feed the pups, the bitch being down with a fever for twenty-four hours, and now her milk stopping."

Margaret gave a little exclamation of pity. So that was why the girl hadn't come in to lunch, she thought.

"Chubb could take over." Sir Hugh ignored Pell's explanation. "He was handling dogs before she was born. A lot of nonsense. And if the bitch is in bad shape, why doesn't she get hold of the vet?"

"I asked the same of Chubb, sir, and he says it's because of the fee. She'll make do, she told Chubb, and it's only herself she wants handling the pups. She's got gruel hotted up, and some drops for Court Lady."

"Wants her own way as usual? I still say Chubb could manage. And the fee for the vet is hardly an insurmountable difficulty—not if she'd come and ask me."

"That she won't, sir. 'The kennel expenses are my own affair,' is what she told Chubb. And you know how it is with Miss Cherry, sir, once she's got her mind made up."

"I know quite well." The comment was curt. Abruptly, Pell dropped the subject of Cherry, and to the accompaniment of a few contrived remarks, stiffly exchanged, and of long pauses that to Margaret were infinitely uncomfortable, dinner proceeded through a roast course and dessert and a savory.

It had just come to an end, with a decanter of port put on the table in front of Sir Hugh, and a silver bowl of walnuts, when a telephone somewhere shrilled. Pell, hurrying away to answer, came back to say the call was for Madam.

"For me?" Margaret's surprise sharpened her voice. "You are sure?"

"It's for Mrs. Allen Collier they asked, madam, and as we've but the one guest of that name stopping—"

"Of course. Yes. Of course. And if you'll excuse me, Sir Hugh?"

He stood up to draw her chair from the table. "Show Mrs. Collier where the telephone is, Pell."

Margaret's heart was racing as she left the dining room. A call for her? Who knew she was here? Ritchie—ferreting?

"This way, madam. It's along the hall, under the stairs, in the Cloaks."

Margaret closed the door of a small closet jammed with an accumulation of cricket bats and tennis rackets in need of restringing, of balls that had lost their bounce, of fishing rods and waders and creels, of walking sticks and heavy, rough outdoor jackets and took the receiver of an old-fashioned telephone off the hook.

What did Ritchie want? What could she say to him? And the irony of not being at all sure whether she was glad, glad— glad or disturbed beyond measure at his calling!

His voice came over the wire with a familiar nonchalance and flippancy that made her see him.

Bright blue eyes, laughing. The thick shock of hair, not red red, more of an auburn. The broad shoulders, the long legs, the becomingness of his new Saville Row clothes.

"Tired of hotel life? Pretty swank sounding, this Monks' Court you've switched to. What is it, one of those paying-guest propositions, with the laird piped into dinner every night, and all that? No? And don't snap my head off, I know

you're not in the Highlands. You're in Shropshire, twenty
miles from Ludlow."

"How did you know I was here?"

"I did some detective work."

"Detective . . . ? What do you mean?"

"I called your London hotel and they put me onto your
garage people. And when I rang The Feathers they told me
where you were."

"It—it's very nice of you to call."

"Thanks—for nothing. Listen, Mag, when are you coming
back?"

"I don't know."

"What's keeping you? What's the big attraction?"

"I—I'm with friends."

"Friends? The plural, not the singular? Not a boyfriend, by
any chance?"

"Don't be cheap, Ritchie."

"My apologies. But you can't blame me for wondering, can
you? You're not an easy habit to break, as I was remarking to
a pigeon this morning. Yes, that's what I said. A pigeon.
There's one that roosts on a ledge outside my bedroom window. A filthy old so-and-so. I wish the dome of St. Paul's had
him back. But he's company, in a pinch, and makes a good
listener when I feel like unloading my troubles."

"Troubles?"

"My lonesomeness. And my acute dislike of the regrettably
monastic state into which you've plunged me."

"There are thousands of girls in London, Ritchie."

"Haven't you ever heard of what Henry James once called
'the horrible numerosity of London society'? He meant the
town was crawling with a lot of people he couldn't care less
about. That's how I'm feeling. So how about it? Come on, be
my Mag! Set a definite date for coming back, and make it
soon."

"I can't, Ritchie. I simply can't. Not just yet. You see—"

"I don't see anything. It's all clear as mud to me—at this point. On which unsatisfactory note we may as well end this conversation. But I'll be giving you another call one of these days. Good night, sweet. Don't forget you're still my girl. And don't let anyone else forget."

The voice coming over the wire from London deepened. "You will make it soon? Please do. As I told you before, we're wasting a hell of a lot of time."

"I have to hang up now, Ritchie. Good night."

Unhappily, Margaret put the receiver back on its hook.

Ritchie and his pigeon. You could laugh—or you could weep. It was awful to hurt anyone. Only a night or two ago she had cried out desperately to Ritchie, longed for safety with Ritchie. But now . . .

She could go back to him so easily. She need only ask the operator for a London connection. Do it. Do it at once. It needn't mean a betrayal of anyone. Tell Ritchie you've enjoyed Shropshire, but you've had enough of your friends for the time being—you want him. Let him think hearing his voice has persuaded you of it.

He would believe it. He was enough in love to believe it. People in love were so very apt to believe what they wanted to believe. Her hand was on the receiver again, but only for an irresolute instant before she turned her back on the telephone and opened the cloakroom door.

Sir Hugh was standing in the hall.

"You had a good connection, I hope? These country lines—"

"It was excellent, thank you."

"You'll join me for coffee?"

"I seem to have a headache. I'm going to my room."

Sir Hugh let her escape without more than his perfunctory,

courteous hope the headache would pass, but as she climbed the stairs he waited at the foot of them, looking up, and she could feel his eyes on her until she had reached the top landing and started down the hall.

What would he do? Go sit in the library as usual with the fire and his dog and his brandy?

She could see him there, see the deep shadowy corners of the room, and, as he poked at smoldering logs, the glint of suddenly leaping flames on gilded leather book bindings and on the brass and steel of the swords and firearms that hung against the wall.

When she reached her room she tried again to read, and determinedly she turned page after page. Anything was better than going to bed, and lying there sleepless, thinking, thinking, with no hope of ever finding a way out of the maze into which she had so rashly ventured. No possible hope. Not unless the scapegoat she longed for, without reason or logic, materialized by some miracle and assumed the burden of Hugh Vane's guilt.

It was after midnight when she finished the last chapter, with no more conception of what the book was about than when she had started it. Because the room was icy, she began, reluctantly, to think of bed, where at least she would be warm, but before she started to undress she went to the windows. Pulling aside the curtains Pell had drawn when she labored up from the kitchen before dinner with the nightly hot-water bottle Cherry no longer bothered to fill, she looked out beyond the garden toward the stableyard. That pathetic, irritating child. Was she out there still with her dogs? It was foolish to waste your pity, though. Cherry Vane was her own worst enemy, wasn't she?

No Robin Soames, and no veterinarian simply because she wouldn't give in, wouldn't listen to the dictates of common sense. Well, Robin would go away and leave her, stuck here, and Court Lady would die, more than likely, as a result of her stubbornness.

At the same time, could she honestly say that Cherry was the only person she knew of who had deliberately shut her mind to sensible, normal behavior? Hardly. And in the girl's case there was a legitimate excuse—her youth.

Suddenly, impulsively, Margaret snatched her mackintosh from the wardrobe and thrust her arms into the sleeves, picked up the Georgian silver candlestick from the dressing table, lighted it, put the box of matches in her pocket, and hurried out into the hall, with her shadow ahead of her, black and elongated, on the bare walls where pictures and mirrors and tapestries had once hung. Tiptoeing down the stairs, she crossed the lower hall and the cavernous, dark dining room, and made her way to the kitchen. Fumbling in the larder, she found bread and half a cold chicken and butter, and in the pantry a knife and a plate. With the candlestick balanced precariously along with everything else on the plate, she let herself out the scullery door.

Try as she would to shield the candle, the wind blew out the flame when she turned the corner of the house, and with only a new moon in the sky, she groped through the blackness of the garden, trusting to the faint white gleam of statuary to outline a way along the cypress-hedged walk, to the archway in the wall that would lead her to the stableyard.

She was oriented, then, by the smell of the pony and of hay and of old harness leather and saddles long in disuse. Skirting the cobbled paving, she opened the stable door and went along its rows of empty stalls to the rear, where the glow of an oil lantern, swinging from a dusty beam, showed her Cherry.

In jodhpurs and a rough, patched tweed jacket, the ribbon that tied back her hair slipped loose, her face touchingly young and exhausted under the guttering yellow lantern light, she was asleep. Court Lady's head was in her lap, and she, too, was asleep, as were the puppies, which lay curled in a heap on a pile of old horse blankets.

A blanket that should have covered the bitch had slipped off her, and very quietly, very gently, Margaret stooped and adjusted it. For all her caution, the bitch stirred, and with an effort, lifted her head weakly, and then dropped it again on Cherry's lap, and immediately she was awake.

She stared up at Margaret's touched, compassionate face uncomprehendingly.

"I came to see if you were all right. It's very late. And I brought you a bite to eat."

"I'm not hungry."

"But you'd feel so much better. How is Court Lady?"

The girl felt the dog's nose. "It's not as hot as it's been all day." She glanced at the tucked-in blanket. "You covered her?"

"Yes."

Slowly, stiffly, the girl got to her feet and glanced at a leather-strapped wristwatch. "I only slept for half an hour," she defended herself, "but if she'd gotten cold or I'd missed the time for her dosing . . ."

Awkwardly, she hesitated. "Thank you." It was a struggle, and it came reluctantly. She glanced at the plate Margaret was holding, and then her pride made her look away quickly.

"You won't change your mind?"

"I told you, I'm not hungry."

She turned her back on the food and was busy at the shelf that held various bottles and pots and pans. Having heated gruel, she poured a little into a saucer. Gently she gave Court Lady a pill, massaging her throat. Then she set the gruel in front of the bitch, patting her and murmuring to her, coax-ingly.

The bitch lapped only once or twice, weakly and disinterestedly, and she went to sleep again.

"It's a good sign, isn't it, her eating, even a little bit?" Margaret asked.

"Yes, but if she hemorrhages again . . ."

The girl settled herself on the stall's straw bedding, bolt upright, her eyes determinedly wide open.

"I'll gladly stay with her, if you'll go in and get an hour's decent sleep or make yourself a cup of tea," Margaret offered. "I'd call you at once, if—"

"I can manage."

"You're sure? You must be very tired." Margaret hesitated. "What about a vet? You wouldn't reconsider?"

The girl looked at her sharply. "Chubb talked to Pell, did he? And Pell passed it on? She's a sieve, if ever was one."

"It was only because she was anxious about you and Court Lady." Margaret hesitated again. "We talked about it at dinner. Your father would gladly help with the vet's fee, if you went to him. I know he would. He'd be only too glad."

"Glad? He couldn't care less about my dogs. And I wouldn't take a sixpence from him for my kennel expenses."

"How have you managed so far? How could you afford to buy Court Lady in the first place?" Margaret asked with frank curiosity.

"I saved my dress allowance, and that's how I bought all this." The girl nodded to the shelf. "The pans and the stove and the food. I'm only taking the allowance until I've sold a few puppies and gotten started, and then I'll pay Father back. It's the shots, and the worming, and the vitamins, and now all the medicines that have got me in a hole."

"If you won't go to your father—and I think it very silly of you, not to—wouldn't you let me lend you the vet's fee?"

The girl's wan face flushed, painfully.

"I wasn't asking for money," she exclaimed with furious resentment.

"Of course you weren't. Don't be a little ninny!" Margaret's retort was impatient. "I happen to be very fond of dogs, and anyone with eyes in his head can see Court Lady needs proper looking after." Her voice was gentler then. "Please, won't you let me lend you the fee? Consider it an investment. You've already spent so much. And you can take as long as you like to pay me back. If—if I leave, soon, as I expect I shall, you can send the money to me in London. I'll give you my address."

Cherry stared at Margaret consideringly, her enormous dark eyes as unreadable as her father's.

"I'd need at least six guineas," she said slowly. "These post-littering fevers can take more than one visit from a vet. And there'll be more medicines, and food for the pups since her milk gave out."

"Send me a bill for all of it until Court Lady is well." The briskness was back in Margaret's voice. "Keep an itemized account, we'll be businesslike." She reached out a hand and pulled the girl to her feet. "Go telephone the vet this minute. Have him come as soon as he can. I'll wait here until you get back."

"If it were for anything but Lady . . ." Cherry reached down and patted the bitch, her face carefully turned from Margaret.

"But it *is* Lady. So hurry. Get the vet before he has an early-morning call to look at someone's sick cow," Margaret said lightly and gave the girl a little push.

"I couldn't pay you back until next quarter."

"We can arrange all that later. Just go! And here, take my candle, and these matches." Margaret reached in her mackintosh pocket and tossed the box of matches to Cherry.

"If Lady weren't such a love—" Cherry's voice broke. "I'd not get another like her. But six guineas . . ."

"Please. It's all settled. Now run."

"Right-o. And thank you!"

It burst spontaneously from Cherry, and then she bolted. Margaret watched the tiny flickering flame of the candle the girl shielded with a hand as she ran until it was out of sight, and then she settled herself on the straw-covered floor, a horse blanket over her legs, her hands deep in her pockets.

The bitch and the puppies slept on, but an owl hooted from a perch high on a stable beam, and the pony, in a stall somewhere, stomped and whinnied, restless with the coming of dawn.

Margaret drew the blanket closer around her legs. She was positive that every rustle in the straw was a rat.

Cherry soon rushed into the stable.

"He's coming directly," she announced, relieved. "I caught him at a farm cottage not ten minutes away. There's a mare foaling, but he says he can leave for a little while and stop in for a look at Lady. Isn't it splendid? If he'd been at home and had to come all that way! And it won't be as much as six guineas either, I shouldn't think, with his being so much nearer."

She dropped down beside Court Lady, murmuring softly and ardently. "Did you wake up, beautiful? You are going to get well, hear me? You are. You are! You're going to get well, my good, beautiful, sweet dog!"

Margaret stood up. "I'm going back to the house as long as you don't need me. But I want to see you start eating that bread and chicken before I go. And don't say you're not hungry. You must be starved."

"It *has* been rather a long while since lunch," Cherry admitted honestly. She glanced at the plate on the shelf, and then with the same honesty she blurted awkwardly, "You've been jolly kind—"

"It was nothing. Good night. Though I ought to say good morning, since it's almost daylight."

Cherry, with Court Lady's head on her lap, was devouring the bread and chicken ravenously as Margaret left the stall and went back to the house through the gray, hushed, dew-soaked garden.

She let herself in as quietly as possible and made her way to the hall, but in the darkness that was far less penetrable than the grayness of the garden, she stumbled against the table where Pell put the papers each morning, and clutching at it to keep from falling, knocked over a brass letter box.

It fell on the rugless stone floor with an echoing clatter, and as Margaret leaned to pick it up, rubbing her banged knee and grimacing with pain, the library door opened and Sir Hugh was silhouetted by lamplight from his desk and by the last flicker of a dying fire.

"I—I was just going upstairs," Margaret offered weakly.

He isn't drunk, she thought, repelled and yet rooted, unable to take her eyes off him, but the brandy bottle would not be as full as it might, by a long way. Hours, he had been in there, hours. . . . His cold eyes were on her dew-wet shoes and thick wool stockings to which bits of Court Lady's bedding-straw clung.

"An article on British kennels, will that be another of your efforts, Mrs. Collier?"

He looked very tall in the doorway. He was standing rigidly straight, and Margaret wondered if the erectness was deliberate, to brace himself from swaying. Hours and hours he'd been sitting there, with his glass. Whom had he been trying to forget? A little boy ghost—or an Eurasian dancer—?

Margaret checked herself only just in time, but as though

to atone for the remissness of her faith, a fountain of pity welled in her. These sad, done-for Vanes, in their sad, done-for house; call the father a monster of selfishness, if nothing more, call the daughter a self-defeatist—but sad, movingly sad, all the same, both of them.

Through the dimness of the unlighted hallway, where dawn was yet only a hint, she faced the tall, thin-lipped man in the library doorway. "Why don't you go out to Court Lady's kennel, too?" she asked with simplicity and directness. "I would, if I were you, to please Cherry."

With her courage failing then, she moved quickly to the stairs, but on the first step she paused and turned, and daring the rebuff of Sir Hugh's hard, glacial silence, added gravely, "She loves you very much—in case you don't realize it."

TWENTY

"A bright start to the morning, madam—which isn't to say how it will end, so you'd best make the most of the sun while we've got it."

The deliberately dispiriting Pell offered her observations as she put down Margaret's breakfast tray. "And Sir Hugh wishes to know if you'd enjoy a pony drive about the place, the morning being so rarely fine—and not like to be again in a hurry. He'll be at the door in half an hour, madam, and it's my advice to take a raincoat."

Margaret accepted the invitation quietly and drank her tea, spread butter and marmalade on toast from the silver rack, cracked her boiled egg, and dressed as hurriedly as she could.

She was on the terrace, a little breathless, just as Sir Hugh in worn riding breeches and old boots, a yellow paisley scarf folded at the neck of his shabby tweed jacket, drove up from the stableyard in the Edwardian governess cart.

Margaret, noticing the scarf, was pleased; with a taste

for yellow, perhaps he liked her dinner wool, no matter how often he had seen it? It was so foolish, so inconsequential a question that she felt ashamed of herself, and could have wished too that the folded scarf, so much like an eighteenth-century hunting stock, accentuated less strongly the resemblance between Sir Hugh and the portrait.

"A drive won't bore you?" Sir Hugh asked courteously and without any tinge of his usual sarcasm or derision.

Margaret answered him simply and directly. "It was kind of you to think of it. I'm delighted to get outdoors."

"And so am I. The library struck me as a particularly musty old hole this morning, and though I've got desk work piled high, it can wait. And your cataloguing, as well. There will be plenty of wet days for catching up."

Margaret got into the cart, and when she was settled next to him on a sagging, worn leather seat, he gave the pony its head.

"We'll do the fields first, and then have a look at the cattle."

"What sort of cattle do you have, Sir Hugh?"

"Herefords. They are a hardy breed that winters well and they are good grazers. When we're through with finishing them off on our May grass for market, they'll be fat. With a bit of luck we'll make a profit on them."

"We? You have a partner?"

"No. Not a partner, a bailiff—a farm or ranch manager, as I expect an American would put it. The size of the place warrants an agent—he's a grander fellow than a bailiff—and costs accordingly. As it is, the bailiff's wages, and the wages of the herdsman and a shepherd, are what presently keep me so close to the ragged edge."

"With all those expenses I can see why you—you . . ." Margaret hesitated.

"Why I lose heart, and have those occasional misgivings

about whether there is any point to hanging on—or trying to hang on? But there's another side of the slate. When I've once got over the outlay for death duties that were payable when I inherited from my father—it meant selling off some fields—and when I get production going again, it will be a different story, I hope. There will be a living of sorts—even a little more if I'm lucky. And if time doesn't run out."

What did he mean by that last? Margaret queried, silently and uneasily. Had she imagined a shadow on his face?

"I saw a lot of young lambs in the lane the day I drove here. Are they yours? Do you raise sheep as well as cattle?" she asked brightly to silence her own thoughts.

"I've a few on an experimental basis. It's too early yet to know if it will prove economically sound."

She was glad for her own sake that she had made an effort to talk. The shadow, if shadow it had been, seemed to lift as though her question had come as a diversion.

Or perhaps the soft, beautiful morning was making things easier for them both, Margaret concluded, as the pony trotted out from under the dark driveway trees and through the iron entrance gates into the muddy, narrow lane where foxgloves would be tall steeples in the song-sweet hedges when summer came and brilliant scarlet fuchsias tumbled, and where violets and bluebells were now making their last appearance of the season.

"We'll go this way." Sir Hugh pointed with the cart whip, "if you don't object to a bit of jolting."

The pony, at the touch of the reins, turned off onto a still narrower and muddier lane, which in Margaret's opinion was no lane at all but only a rut and a succession of splashy puddles.

"It's a short cut between some of our farms and the highway into town," Sir Hugh explained. "We almost never use it, but I'm taking it to give you a closer look at our oats and wheat and barley, and at the maize—you Americans call it corn—that we grow for silage."

"This heavenly sunshine!" Margaret unbuttoned her cardigan. "And everything so green, everything smelling so good."

"Wait until the lilac comes on, if you enjoy perfume. Another week and the lanes and every cottage garden will be full of it."

"Just the smell of that lovely tilled soil is enough." Margaret sniffed deeply as she looked out on furrows and sprouting grain. "Such rich, deep soil. It makes me want to get out and crumble it in my hand."

"You sound a born countrywoman. Are you, Mrs. Collier?"

"No, I'm sorry to say."

"But you've lived in the country?"

"My husband and I had to live in the city because of his business, though we had a few acres in the country for weekends. I used to want to garden, but it had been my mother-in-law's place and was—well, untouchable." Margaret's reminiscent smile was a little rueful. "I hadn't the courage to get in and dig up what I didn't like, and plant what I really wanted. But summers, when I was a child, were perfect. My father bought a plantation so he could keep a few horses and hunt and shoot, and I was allowed to run wild. There were trees and fields and a stream—"

"Once you've had that, as a child, you never lose a love of the land. And speaking of shooting, the pheasants here on the place are going to be another source of income, once I've got our syndicate scheme working."

"A syndicate?"

"I'll rent the shooting to six or eight guns each season and sell the birds. They bring a pound or so a brace, and it's all highly profitable even with the cost of a gamekeeper, and the putting down, and the hatching of eggs."

"You certainly have a great many irons in the fire!"

The slow jog, jog, and the swaying of the little cart along the ruts, was a little like the lulling of a hammock except for a hard, jarring bump now and again when the wheels hit the bottom of a puddle. The sturdy pony, in mud above his fetlocks, plodded along so willingly that Margaret would have liked to give it a rewarding pat on its rough, patchy coat, not yet entirely shed from winter.

"Do English ponies like sugar lumps and carrots?" she questioned, laughingly.

"Immensely."

"I wish I'd asked Pell for a supply. I adore your pony."

"Would you like to take the reins?"

"Oh, wonderful!"

Margaret's hair, which Richard had described to himself as the color of sun-gilded creek sand, was blowing in a little breeze about her animated face, and her eyes, that he thought of as topaz, were pleased and interested.

"Tell me more about your farming plans."

"I could go on forever, Mrs. Collier. Best not to get me started. There's our reforestation program, for instance— large birch and larch plantings. There's a substantial tax relief for carrying it out, and government grants make it very much worthwhile to landowners."

"I shouldn't think your days were half long enough to get through with so many projects."

Sir Hugh looked faintly amused.

"I don't work by the clock. When any special push is on, I drive tractor, or run the harvester; I'd swill the pigs, if necessary—though with no real enthusiasm! And I still have to find time for the local Rural District Council meetings and to keep my books, and fill out dozens of forms to satisfy the Ministry of Agriculture. There are miles of red tape. A farmer doesn't have an easy thing of it in England these days. But if his land means everything to him—"

He broke off to smile, and again there was no sarcasm or derision in the question he put. "An article on British land-owners coming up next, Mrs. Collier?"

"No. No, I don't think so. My acquaintance with them is rather limited. I—I wouldn't feel free to generalize."

He glanced at her sharply, and then they jogged on in si-lence, with Margaret reflecting unhappily that next to her, so very close in the little cart, was a man to whom she could have given an enormous amount of respect and admiration if only—

Always, it was "if only . . ."

She stole a glance at Sir Hugh's hands. Good hands, well shaped and strong. Their palms would be hard; the running of a tractor or a harvester more or less guaranteed that. She could have respected his optimism, too, his "let's get on with the job" attitude that acknowledged difficulties but was con-fident of overcoming them by hard work and determination.

It was sad, the house having to wait for the coming of bet-ter days—better unless time ran out—whatever that implied. There was a vaguely sinister suggestion about the phrase that she didn't like. Margaret put it out of mind for a moment. "First things first" was sensible, of course, and naturally the land must be put ahead of anything else, but there'd be noth-ing left of Sir Hugh's house unless its decay was halted.

As the cart rocked along Margaret gave herself up to the sunshine that was warming her deliciously and indulged in wistful, absurd reverie. The blue-and-white Adam drawing room. Decay and desolation could be so easily routed. It would take money—but then she had quite a lot. Carpenters and plasterers called in. The boarded-up, rusty-hinged, peel-ing shutters painted, windows opened to sun and air. The dampness and the close smell, the chill of emptiness dis-pelled. Rugs and chairs and chandeliers chosen slowly and lovingly. Perhaps some of the original furnishings of the house could be retrieved from the antique dealers who had carried them off. And one, at least, of the Vane portraits could be rehung.

A restored house, it would be, to pass on proudly to future generations of Vanes. That is, if Sir Hugh ever had a son. She would do well, however, not to think about the house or the portrait just now. Margaret jerked herself forcefully from her daydreaming. Why let anything spoil the peace, the disarming peace, sweet as that which she had known on a day of cuckoo song.

A moment to catch and to fix in amber forever, if one could.

Dreamily she let thoughts of Monks' Court absorb her again. Her money wouldn't be all-important. It would count a great deal, but you could bring more than money with you, if . . .

She could bring aliveness, brightness, to Monk's Court. She would feel needed. At long last she would feel herself truly a woman. She'd be a woman offering understanding to Cherry, who was still only a child. She'd be a woman lightening a man's load with her willingness to share it. And she could soften his bitterness, whatever the deep-rooted cause of it.

With Allen she had been the kind of wife he wanted. A credit to him. Pretty. Well dressed. Responsive and acquiescent. Affectionate. Cheerful.

With Ritchie she would be gay. Every day would be a balloon ascension. She'd be a girl lucky enough to be cocktailing and dining and dancing all over the world with an exciting, adventurous companion. Ironic, though, if she should still be a Margaret Collier who was lonely inside, and who would never be her true self—a satisfied self—with Ritchie no more than with Allen.

She had chosen to stop thinking about life as Mrs. Richard

Page, and was drifting in wistful daydreams again, smiling a little, unconsciously, when Sir Hugh, with another glance, and one that caught her off guard, remarked quietly, "You look happy."

Startled, she took a moment to answer and then as quietly she told him, "I am—more or less."

"Reservations, are there?"

"A few."

"Is happiness ever total?"

"It could be."

"You believe that, Mrs. Collier?"

"I'd hate not to believe it—but I'm a romantic, unfortunately."

"What do you believe constitutes happiness?"

"It's difficult to express." Margaret hesitated. "A quiet heart comes nearest, and—"

"A quiet heart. I like that. You've put it very neatly."

"And—and just knowing you have found where you belong, found yourself, found the people who matter—and the moments of joy in belonging."

"To know where one belongs isn't too difficult. There seem to be fairly evident signposts. But as to the rest of it . . ."

"The orthodox romanticist never gives up hope." Margaret smiled, but a sigh escaped her.

"Even for a rich American life isn't perfect, Mrs. Collier?"

It was asked lightly, and there was no intentional sting to it, but Margaret's eyes clouded.

"Please don't. I wish you wouldn't," she ventured unhappily.

"Wouldn't what?" Sir Hugh asked, surprised.

"I hate it when you talk about rich Americans. It's insulting—and—and it's stupid. If you knew more of us—if you'd ever been to our country . . ."

"*Touché!* And let me congratulate you on your refreshing

frankness and honesty—which come as a welcome change. You should make a habit of them."

"You are calling me a liar, aren't you? I could call names too!" Margaret bit her lips. "Hadn't we better go back now?" she asked miserably. "I was—I was enjoying myself, but if we're going to wrangle . . ."

"You have had enough of me? I'd be sorry to think so."

Margaret's cheeks were scorching as Sir Hugh stated it.

His smile, then, was no more than the cold, narrow curve of thin lips she knew too well and dreaded, and the gray eyes holding hers were hard.

"I had not intended to shorten our morning together, Mrs. Collier. Not only do I find your company delightful, but you interest me; you interest me greatly. It follows, doesn't it, that the more time I spend in your company, the greater my opportunity for exploring the complexities you present? I can see an article of my own coming out of it—and, though not necessarily for publication, quite as fascinating—'The Stranger Within My Gates.' "

TWENTY-ONE

Margaret, on top of the library ladder, blowing dust off a copy of *War in India* and volume two of the *Treaty of Utrecht*, found it impossible to concentrate on a list of books. All her thoughts were on the previous day. Yesterday's drive with Sir Hugh had only compounded the difficulties of her situation here. But let Sir Hugh have his suspicions, his deepening distrusts, his growing curiosity; for her, there was an even stronger determination to seek out X. If only, oh, if only Jarvis Vane . . . Even as she sighed her useless wish for him to have lived, she was suddenly giddy on the ladder with the springing up a new, wild, illogical hope. Jarvis Vane could still be alive. He could. He could! Swiftly, eagerly, she bolstered the fantastic argument.

Take it step by step. Think of Jarvis Vane as the black sheep of the family. Think of Sir Hugh's extricating him time after time from disgraceful scrapes of one sort or another. In the Orient a man could sink to the lowest possible depths.

Think of Sir Hugh's wresting a promise from Jarvis Vane to stay out of England—paying him to stay out of England, perhaps—and then writing home announcing his brother's death. To an honorable man, a man of any integrity, a brother declared dead would be a thousand times more to be desired than a brother alive, and a scoundrel.

And next—? The black sheep, who could have known Honorine Duclair in China, had followed her to London. And on that night in Mount Street . . . Was it probable? No. You knew that. Possible? Just barely, and only if you could get around the fact of the memorial plaque and the record in Somerset House. Think again—think of something, anything. A forged death certificate. And if there had been no grave to dig, no body to dispose of, how simple to arrange for the affixing of that bronze plaque to a wall. "All manner of expenses," Sir Hugh had said. Payments to his brother, blackmail, in effect, he could have meant. Or so your unchecked, madly galloping imagination told you.

It was all farfetched and pitifully contrived. She had tried too hard, overreached herself. Knowing it, and sunk in a morass of depression, Margaret endured the morning and a solitary lunch, but afterward, when the library clock struck a quarter hour, reminding her that teatime was approaching, she got down from her second session of the day on the ladder and went to the kitchen in search of Pell.

"I'm going into the garden. I need some fresh air. Don't bother with tea for me—unless the others will be having it?"

"There will be just you, madam. And if you're not wanting tea in the library, would a thermos and sandwich suit, brought out to you?"

"Beautifully."

Pell's eyes were perceptive. "A headache, madam?" she asked as she put a loaf of bread into the oven.

"The beginning of one."

"A cold and chills could come on fast, with the weather what it is. Fine, as we had it yesterday, and now, look—all bluster and clouds—and no way of telling what's in the wind. You'll remember I said before, madam, there's other places, pleasanter, for a stay just now than hereabouts."

"I remember, and I'm sure you're right."

Pell at it again. Pell saying, "Leave, while there's time."

On the terrace a survey assured her that Chubb was nowhere in sight. Remembering a dead rat and icy lake water and the honk of vicious swans, it was pleasant to feel safely free to explore a little beyond the boundaries of the kitchen garden and the cypress allée without dreading his disagreeable surveillance, and wondering what horrid trick he—or his master?—might be mulling over now.

Idly strolling, she had passed a potting shed crammed with garden tools and flats of seedlings and pots of wintered-over house plants when she came on a small, brick-walled enclosure that took her eye.

In summer the walls would be wreathed with old-fashioned roses and clematis in full bloom. Already along bare branches, drooping racemes of wisteria showed a hint of white and purple. A picking garden it had been once, she judged as she went through a wicket gate, and the hedges of lavender that were dying out now would formerly have supplied fragrance for all the linen cupboards in the house.

As she walked leisurely up and down between the borders, Margaret pictured what the garden's past charm must have been, and could be again. Stooping now and then to pull a particularly deep-rooted and encroaching weed from some half-smothered but still surviving plant, she could see armfuls of heliotropes and blue lupines and pink Canterbury bells; maroon and buff sweet peas, white daisies, yellow columbines; sweet williams and dahlias; and chyrsanthemums and roses of all colors, cut to fill vases in every room of Monks' Court.

The weeding was not helpful to a manicure, she soon realized. Gloves were what she needed, and then, if she got down on her knees and went after the weeds seriously, she would feel like the heroine of the Secret Garden who had brought much the same sort of neglected little walled-away place back to life.

The fancy pleased her. Going back to the potting shed, she helped herself to a pair of gloves belonging, she supposed, to Cherry Vane. When she had pulled them on, she began to weed around the roots of peonies whose swollen buds were ready to burst open, and around crowns of delphinium and the grasslike blades of lily shoots and the matted sprawl of clove pinks.

A pile of weeds accumulated on the garden path. Margaret was working with a simple, and for the moment, unalloyed pleasure. Her depression had been thrown off, when, without warning of footsteps, a shadow was cast, squat and thick and humped, on the wet dark earth she had cleared.

Chubb. She knew it before she reluctantly looked up.

He was holding out a basket, a round, yellow-straw egg basket, spread with a napkin and packed with a thermos, a tiny milk jug and sugar basin, sandwiches, and sweet biscuits.

"Your tea, ma'am."

"My tea?" She looked her surprise. "Pell sent it?"

"She's got pastries to roll out. And I was handy, having my own cup in the scullery."

Margaret stood up. She looked toward the pile of weeds. "I hope you don't mind?"

"Them'll come thick again, with a new lot up by tomorrow," was his grunted answer, and when she had pulled off her gloves and taken the basket from his old, veined hands that were like knotted roots, he shuffled away toward the potting shed, his broad, short body a twisted tree stump.

There was a bench against one of the brick walls and Margaret sat down and unpacked the basket. Unexpected, certainly, having Chubb bring it. Pastries to roll out or not, it was completely unlike correct Pell to press into service an uncouth brother like Chubb. Those black, broken fingernails, that unwashed dirt grimed into cracked, rough skin. And how extremely pungent the smell of earth and manure and sweat and barn and chicken-run he gave off.

She mustn't forget that Chubb was a hard worker. With a reminder to herself that Monks' Court stableyard quarters were not likely to boast much in the way of modern bathing facilities, and trying to be fair and unprejudiced, Margaret unscrewed the thermos top, filled a cup, poured milk and spooned sugar.

Part of being fair was to remind herself she had nothing concrete against Chubb. She had done a lot of guessing, nothing more. And tea was welcome, whoever brought it. Good strong, boiling hot tea. And this *was* strong. No smoky bouquet to it, not at all the same fragrant steam given off by the choice, delicate tea she had drunk in the libary on other afternoons.

A less expensive brand, was it? A "staff" tea that Pell and her brother drank and that Pell inadvertently had put in the thermos? Margaret lifted the cup, and because the tea was so hot, took a cautious sip, and then before she swallowed, she was spitting it out. A poisoned tea!

The awfulness of the suspicion shocked her into an inability to move. For minutes she sat on the bench, the cup still in her hand. Chubb. The instigator—or the tool? Whichever he was, a Chubb craftily presenting himself in the kitchen at just the right moment, and after that, needing only to stop for an instant at the potting shed.

Still in a state of shock, she repacked the basket, put it over her arm, picked up the gardening gloves and walked to the potting shed. The door was open. Chubb was rubbing rust from a spade with a rag torn from an old undervest and dipped in oil and emery.

"I brought the gloves back."

Margaret tossed them onto a shelf, and looking around her at bottles and cans of sprays, she brought out in a strained voice, "Gardens everywhere seem to be the same. In my country we have all sorts of pests, too. And all sorts of poisons . . ."

The black, bright eyes fastened their unblinking gaze on her. "Here, we do say that it's the keeping after it does the job, when there's something needing to be put out of the way." Snuffling and hawking, he put down the rag and hoe. "There's a second cup due me in the scullery. I'll take the basket back with me, ma'am."

Margaret gave it to him.

"Would you know if there's dregs left, ma'am?"

"It's almost full."

He unscrewed the thermos top, and Margaret watched him pour a dark strong stream of still steaming tea around the base of a potted fern.

"Is tea good for plants?" Margaret said in a voice she would not allow to quaver, but with a fascinated, sick conviction the fern would immediately droop and shrivel.

"There's some as is, and some as isn't."

Chubb put the thermos in the basket. He could so easily wash out the thermos at a garden faucet before taking it into Pell, if he had poisoned the tea.

Left alone in the shed, she looked again at the fern, again at the array of sprays and powders. But in all probability she had imagined the queer taste and bouquet. Even if she hadn't the tea need not necessarily have been dosed with anything deadly. Had she drunk it, she might only have been made unpleasantly ill.

Chubb or—or someone else. Were they only trying to frighten her away from Monks' Court, merely carrying on a war of nerves? But would her leaving satisfy them? Were they bent on something more final? An end put to her by poison?

And on that other day, had they intended her to drown or to be pecked to death by those stretched-necked swans? The rocks tossed from the bushes could have been meant to further enrage the honking, hissing birds instead of to save her. She hadn't thought of that before. Now it so clearly loomed as a possibility. But how was she to know? And with her questions unanswered, how long could she bear the cold, creeping, thickening fog of uncertainty?

Then why didn't she pack her bags and drive away? Margaret was still asking it of herself later, in her bedroom, as she dressed for dinner, and it was no more explainable than why, why, she had not been able to wrench her eyes from the eyes of a portrait that had drawn her, magnetized, caught and helpless, from the moment their glances had met. In front of her mirror, Margaret tried to laugh at herself. Caught? An overdramatization. She was entirely free to leave at any time she chose. And it might be well to make it soon! She went downstairs with her nails freshly manicured, her hair brushed to a sheen, her mouth carefully lipsticked, and after sherry in the library there were three of them who sat down at the table in the barren, frigid dining room.

Sir Hugh was withdrawn, but punctiliously courteous. Cherry, too, was quiet and remote. She was civil enough, however, and when Margaret, making an effort to end a dragging silence, inquired about Court Lady, she was quick with a reply.

"She's better! The vet says she'll pull through if I stay with her again tonight, for feedings and drops and to keep her warm."

"And the puppies?"

"I shall have a job, weaning them, but the vet promised he'd come often and keep an eye on them. And he knows where I can sell two of them, if they get on well."

She glanced at her father, and then decided against what further reports she was about to make, but when dinner was over and they got up from the table, she asked, awkwardly, "May I see you a moment, Mrs. Collier, before I go out to the stable?"

"Of course." Margaret turned to Sir Hugh. "You'll excuse me?"

"If you'll get through with it, and join me to pour coffee. With neither you nor Cherry for company I'd be at a sad loss."

Margaret reddened, stung by the sarcasm, and, annoyed at her hot cheeks, followed Cherry to a small entryway at the side door into the garden where wet weather clothes and an assortment of outdoor wear hung on brass hooks, umbrellas and walking sticks stood in a tall blue-and-white Chinese jar, and heavy shoes and boots cluttered the stone floor.

"It's about the money, Mrs. Collier. I shan't need to borrow it from you." Cherry blurted it as she changed her skirt for jodhpurs.

"Oh?"

Cherry kicked off shabby red slippers and tugged on a pair of fur-lined galoshes.

"My father has advanced it. I've made a business arrangement with him."

"But I thought—"

"Yes, but things are different now."

"Different?"

"Father came to see Court Lady this morning before he made the farm rounds, and—"

"How nice."

"I thought so." Cherry buttoned a warm jacket and tied a knitted scarf under her small, pointed chin. "It made me think things over. If I am to take money from anyone, it ought not be from a stranger. You do understand, don't you?" Her large eyes were a trifle anxious, more than a little embarrassed.

"I understand perfectly. You did the right thing."

"It's not that it wasn't awfully good of you. Well, cheerio! The puppies will be wanting their supper, the greedy little beggars." She lifted a small basket from a hook. "No starving for me either tonight. Pell has seen to that! Though I expect nothing will ever taste as good as that chicken and bread of yours."

Having made the concession, and being either too shy or too stubborn to enlarge on it, she bolted out the door. Margaret stood watching her race across the garden, past the statues standing mournfully in their niches under a gently falling rain that had threatened all day, and then she went along the hall to the library, dreading the evening that stretched ahead, shut in alone with Sir Hugh and the pretense of her cataloguing.

Leave, she thought. Leave, now, tonight . . . this minute! Snatch your raincoat and run, run to the stableyard and your car. Run, you fool! And never see him again?

The single instant of hesitation, the asking of the question, was fatal. Sir Hugh, standing by the hearth where the old pointer snored and twitched in his dreams as usual, turned with a glass in his hand. "The distributor of largesse," he said. "Were you disappointed by Cherry's decision?"

Margaret felt the hot red in her cheeks again.

"I trust not. My daughter told me of your offer, Mrs. Collier. Personally I'm gratified to find she had sufficient pride, on second thought, to turn it down."

"I only wanted to help."

"The Lady Bountiful. But that's enough of that. I have a question or two I'd like to put. First, though, will you have coffee? I've got mine. And perhaps you'll have a brandy?"

"No, thank you."

Margaret sat down in one of the wing chairs and filled a coffee cup with a hand that was not quite steady. Questions? What sort of questions? she wondered in panic. A thin silver spoon clattered in the saucer of the cup she was holding. Questions about what? And how would she answer?

"It is time, I feel, that you brief me a bit on the true reason for your coming to Monks' Court. I'm sure you've no objection?" Sir Hugh asked it with mockery.

"I explained why, when I first came."

Margaret lifted the cup to her lips. "I'm in for it," she told herself, with panic like a hand at her throat. "This is it. Oh, dear God—and I could have left. Five minutes ago, I could have left."

"Now back to your extremely ineffectual lies, Mrs. Collier. I repeat, they no longer pique my curiosity, nor interest me in any way. No more fables, if you please, about magazine articles. You quite understand?"

"I—I was touring. All American tourists enjoy old houses and gardens."

"Really, Mrs. Collier! I've been fairly patient, hoping you would volunteer a true explanation, but as you refuse, may I just show you this?"

Sir Hugh moved to his desk, and as Margaret gasped, and set down her coffee cup, and sprang to her feet, he lifted from

behind it the portrait of the other Vane, and carrying it to
the mantel, leaned it against the blank, outlined square on
the chimney facing.

"You had no right!" Margaret flung it at him with a spurt
of courage. "It was for sale, and I bought it, and it's mine!"

"Undeniably, and you shall have it back. I had Pell find it
for me merely out of the curiosity I have mentioned. It so
happens that Camberley's was holding the portrait on consignment. Shortly before its arrival here, I had a letter from
them along with their check, mentioning it had been bought
by an American woman. Then, the day a picture arrived for
you with the gallery address on the wrappings, I began to
wonder if, on the off chance, it was you who had bought one
of the Vane family's more mediocre portraits. And so it
was. . . . Which rather surprising fact, added to your curious interest in Monks' Court, makes explanations seem more
than overdue, I'm certain you'll agree."

"You don't understand about American tourists. You
don't understand about Americans' buying things. The portrait is Georgian—whether it's fine or not, it's—it's pleasing.
And I happen to especially like the Georgian period."

"That's quite enough, Mrs. Collier." Sir Hugh's eyes were
coldly contemptuous. "You are not a convincing liar. From
the first day you came here, I've waited, wanting to catch you
up. Now I shan't wait any longer. Let's say my curiosity has
gotten out of hand. And I insist, Mrs. Collier, upon hearing
why you chose to single out the Vanes for your scrutiny.
How, in heaven's name, could my daughter, a girl who was a
complete stranger to you, have brought you here, or how
could I, a man you had never seen before in your life until
you came to Monks' Court?"

"But I had seen you!" It escaped Margaret without warning. Her face went chalk white. Sick with terror, she gripped
the back of the wing chair.

"Seen me?" For an instant, Sir Hugh's impenetrable eyes showed surprised disbelief. "Where, Mrs. Collier?"

"In London—" Cowering, Margaret breathed it.

"How very extraordinary. I get there so seldom." The dark eyes that pinned Margaret were unreadable again. "Just when and where in London did you see me, Mrs. Collier?" Sir Hugh's voice was steel. "May I ask you to be accurate?"

"Last month." The words came in an anguished, torn-out whisper from Margaret's dry mouth.

"Be more specific, please."

"The night of—the night of the tenth—late—in a flat on Mount Street."

The words hung in the air, suspended. An ember from the log fell into the ashes on the hearth.

Sir Hugh's face was a granite mask. "The night of the tenth, you say? Interesting. But unfortunate. Unfortunate for you, that is to say, Mrs. Collier."

With incredible swiftness he seized her two hands, gripping them relentlessly as she cried out with a little moan of pain and tried, uselessly, to pull away.

"Let me go! Oh, let me go!"

"Not until you have gone into further detail, Mrs. Collier."

"I was at the window of my hotel—please, oh, my hands!"

"Go on."

"It was hot—the curtains hadn't been drawn—I could see into the woman's flat opposite."

"What woman's flat?" The grip on Margaret's hands tightened.

"Honorine Duclair's." She flinched, with another moan.

"You are trying to tell me you could see across the width of Mount Street distinctly enough to identify the persons in the flat, Mrs. Collier?"

"I had been to the theater. I had my opera glasses."

"What was I doing when you saw me?"

"Pouring wine—and then you closed the curtains."

To Margaret, whimpering it, with the pain of her wrists a goad, with a cold spring rain against the windows, the library seemed to dissolve into the painted backdrop of a sultry London night, of heavy, oppressive skies, of sooty city rooftops, with the crimson-curtained drawing room of a Mayfair flat imposed on its foreground.

"How did you know who I was?"

"I didn't—not at first. Not until I saw the portrait at Camberley's."

"How did you know it was Madame Duclair's flat?"

"A friend told me. He used to be a reporter. He was interested in reading the newspaper write-up and he saw the address of the flat."

"And then? The rest of it, please."

Unrelentingly he forced the story from her. All of it. The river trip to Greenwich. Richard Page's insistence that she go to Scotland Yard on the French boy's behalf. Her interview with the Inspector.

"And after your worthy and highly commendable efforts on behalf of the young Frenchman, what next, Mrs. Collier? And if you don't try to pull away, your wrists won't pain as much. After you had seen the portrait, how did you trace it here, to Monks' Court?"

"By the Vane and the Salop."

"I am afraid I don't quite—"

"They are painted on the portrait."

"Ah, yes. I'd forgotten. And you looked at it closely enough for that? What next, then? Neither Vane nor Salop could have meant very much to you as a help to identification."

"I—I went to Somerset House."

"The clever, ingenious American! But go back to this

friend, this Richard Page. You told him of my resemblance to the portrait?"

"No. That is—I mean—"

"Just what do you mean? You told him, or you did not tell him. Which?"

"I—I blurted it. The surprise— I couldn't help it. But he laughed at me. And—and I pretended to laugh at myself. After that, I didn't mention it again, not ever, to him. Not to anyone."

"Admirable restraint on your part, if true. I'm grateful. But why was it you didn't speak out? What made you keep so remarkable a coincidence to yourself?"

"Because I—" She faltered and could not go on.

"I am waiting, Mrs. Collier."

"Because I couldn't believe it. I didn't want to believe it." It was wrung from her as Sir Hugh's hold on her wrists tightened again. "I hoped there was some mistake and that if I came here, I'd find out, for certain."

"A fairly thin story. You can't blame me for doubting so singular a concern about a stranger's guilt or innocence? And sorry as I am to disillusion you, there is no question of a mistake. It was I in Madame Duclair's flat. And I haven't an iota of regret that she is dead. In fact I should very much like to have seen her die twice over."

"No! Don't say it! How can you be so brutal?" Margaret exclaimed it in revulsion and horror as she struggled desperately to free herself.

"I repeat, I am sorry to disillusion you, my dear Mrs. Collier, but it is you who are the sentimentalist, not I, and in all justice, Madame Duclair deserved far more than she got."

"They'll find you—you'll spend all the rest of your life in prison. And Cherry . . ." Margaret murmured brokenly.

"No, I think not. I propose to avoid that contingency." Sir

Hugh's mouth twisted in a hard, significant smile. "You may or may not have noticed my revolver?" He nodded to the wall where, in contrast to old, tarnished sword blades and hilts, the sinister gleam of a polished steel gun barrel glinted. "It happens to be loaded, as I haven't the slightest intention of finishing my life in prison, or even of being brought to trial."

"You mean you'd—" Margaret's staring, fixed eyes were aghast.

"Precisely." With a harsh laugh Sir Hugh dropped her wrists. Deliberately, he filled his glass from the bottle on Pell's carefully polished silver tray.

"You won't join me? You should, you know. You've had something of a shock, I see. My apologies. But you brought all this on yourself, you must admit, with those opera glasses of yours—and your penchant for Georgian portraits. I wonder—would it make you feel better if I gave you my reasons for being callous about Madame Duclair's death? It's rather a long story; I suggest you sit down."

Trembling, her legs nothing under her, Margaret sank into a chair, stunned and unresisting.

"I had a brother once. A brother four years younger than I." Sir Hugh began his explanations coldly, factually, as she rubbed her reddened, bruised wrists and kept on staring at him.

"Jarvis—or Jody, as we called him. He was delicate as a child, and he had a limp, a congenital limp—not an acquired one, such as mine. Our mother had died young, and he and my father and I lived here in a man's world that contented us well enough. I was good at games, and with horses. When he was little I used to take him in the saddle in front of me, or drive him about—that's he in the snapshot on the desk. He thought a good deal of me, looked up to me. 'You can do anything, can't you, Hughie?' he'd say. He believed it, and nothing could have made him think otherwise."

Sir Hugh swirled the brandy in his glass, silent for an instant. "Not then, he couldn't," he amended. He was silent again, and then went on, "His favorite pastime was playing soldiers. He'd set up castles and forts and men, and pretend he was a drummer boy hero of all the battles our family had ever fought in. A revolt against his semi-invalidism, they'd call it now. Incidentally, that's one of his toy drums on the wall. He'd like it there, I thought."

In a long pause, Margaret, with the sound of rain in her ears like a steady tattoo, shivered, and felt the hair rise on her arms as it had risen at the sound of rain on another night, when she had listened for the sound of a child's footsteps, dragging a little, along a hall that led to a nursery.

"When the war came, Jody was too young for it, even if the services would have had him with his health record, and I saw only the last year of it myself. Then I married. After my wife's death I was at loose ends. I felt no immediate obligation to settle down here at Monks' Court as my father was still living, and there was Pell for Cherry, and later there would be a governess and then school. When some time later I decided to approach the British Intelligence Office for a job, Jody was madly keen to join up, too. To him, it would be a way of holding his own with Vane traditions—his way of doing his duty to his country. At any rate, we got taken on, and trained, and eventually shipped out to Hong Kong. When the Intelligence people had carefully planted that we were Communist sympathizers, and the word had been noised around the city, the opportunity they'd hoped for came along. We were hired by a big Soviet-controlled firm that manufactured and sold fittings for the hydroelectric dams the Red Chinese were beginning to try to install along their rivers with the help of Russian engineers. Our job was selling to the purchasing agents in Canton, and acting as complaint adjusters at the installation sites. It meant frequent crossing of the border and travel in the north, and when we'd learned to speak the Chinese of the provinces, we were in a position to send back a good bit of information to the Intelligence people regarding the Red's progress along industrial and other lines.

"We weren't always on jobs together, and after one of the trips I had made alone I got back after some weeks to find Jody more than eager to get out of Hong Kong himself, for a time."

Sir Hugh's raised brandy glass caught a flicker of firelight.

"He confided to me he had gone off the deep end over a dancer he met while I was gone. A Eurasian."

Margaret's throat constricted as she tried to swallow.

Sir Hugh gazed deeply into his glass. "He was in many ways only a boy still. Shyness and a self-consciousness about his limp had kept him away from women. And he was an idealist. When he found the woman had slept with half the men in Hong Kong, his disillusionment was shattering. It was a relief to us both to be sent to a new dam site on the Hwang River.

"But three hours after we started, Canton guards stopped our train somewhere in the middle of a sandstone wilderness and took us off for interrogation. The Eurasian was with them. She had been employed by the Reds to check on us and had reported that we were very probably British agents. She had been consummately clever. And when they finally dragged us into a disused freight depot and put us through the farce of a hearing, we hadn't a chance against her testimony. They began their devil's work with Jody, and she sat and watched while they tied him in a chair and tortured him for details of our activities. They had already clubbed him and smashed my thigh with a bullet when we had first tried to make a break for it. Then they tied me up and forced me to watch their special Oriental tortures while I waited my own turn as Jody's accomplice."

Margaret's white face took on a greenish tinge.

"I shall spare you the details, Mrs. Collier." With a glance at her, Sir Hugh continued tonelessly, understatedly. "It was a long morning. You see, my brother wasn't giving away a thing. Not Jody. When it got too much for him he fainted, but they brought him around. He was half out of his head by that time, and was begging me to call them off. 'Stop them, stop them, Hughie. You can, Hughie. You can do anything.' A very long morning, indeed. After that he became useless to them, and I myself fainted."

Sick and mute, Margaret could not tear her eyes from Sir Hugh's impassive, granite-hard face.

"The last thing I remember was a kick in the groin with a heavy boot and hearing the woman laugh. When I came to I was still trussed, lying in a puddle of blood; they had put another bullet through my chest, as a parting gesture. Jody was in his chair. Dead. The others were gone."

With a steady hand Sir Hugh lifted his glass and drank, and then continued in his uninflected, emotionless voice.

"As I was to hear later, they had reboarded the waiting train and it got underway again. They had left me for dead, of course—understandably. And I would have died had it not been for a Buddhist priest who came along. He was an old holy man living in a hillside hermitage. He had seen the train stop, and our fracas, and curiosity prompted him to investigate. He cut me loose and tourniqueted my leg, and packed the hole in my chest with rags he tore from my shirt. He got me to his quarters—a deserted monastery—on a sled he contrived out of bamboo matting off the depot floor. Then he went back and fetched Jody. He hadn't the strength to dig a grave; he walled Jody's body in one of the monastery cells—they were all carved directly out of the hillside—and he hauled small loads of loose sandstone shale to seal the door."

Margaret was sitting forward on the edge of her chair,

grasping its arms, her own fear forgotten for the moment.

"He fed me for a month, with his own rice bowl going short more often than not, and dosed me with herbs, and poulticed my wounds with wet tea leaves. I could walk, in six weeks or so, and when I told him I had to get south—inconspicuously—he shaved my head, and stained my face, and gave me a priest's yellow robe and hood and sandals. He started me off, with some bean cakes and a leather skin of rice wine and a map he had drawn, toward the nearest waterway where I'd have a chance to get passage on one of the melon boats that supply the Canton summer markets. A holy man, like himself, on pilgrimage. Solitary, and observing a rule of silence. It worked. At the end of another month I reached Canton and got across the bridge into Hong Kong again. And as my value there to the Intelligence people was over, they immediately sent me home, and to a London surgeon for a necessary leg operation."

Sir Hugh picked up the iron poker and stirred the log until it flared into leaping flames.

"My father died. Jody's end was largely responsible, although I softened my account of it as much as possible—and lied, outright, to Pell about the whole affair. It seemed kinder. I was back here, trying to make a go of it after I came into the Vane title, when I saw the Eurasian woman's picture in last month's London papers and the announcement of her dancing engagement. I could, of course, have turned her in to the Intelligence Office. They would have seen to her deportation. But I preferred to even my score personally—and more finally."

"Why? Why?" It rushed past Margaret's lips, in anguished and futile protest.

"I was convinced I owed it not only to Jody but to the other agents she was responsible for wiping out. There were three men besides my brother working out of Hong Kong who never got back from their missions those months I was away and unable to report on her."

"But it was all past—done with—when you saw her picture!"

"To me it was only yesterday, Mrs. Collier. One look at that face again and my only hesitation about killing her concerned ways and means. At first I considered poison, and then decided to let a feasible method suggest itself when the moment arrived."

His pause this time was longer, before he went on, "It was strangling that did for her, as you know. Simple, and effective."

"Don't! Don't! I can't bear it."

"It is not an agreeable story, true. But may I again remind you that if you had not taken so incomprehensible—even though exceedingly flattering—an interest in an affair that was none of your concern, you would not now have had to listen. And if you feel you have heard enough . . ."

"Go on." It was a faint, helpless whisper.

"After my plans were made, I went to London on what ostensibly was a necessary call on my bankers," Sir Hugh continued, "and when I'd found from the theater where the woman was living, I telephoned her. I had guessed enough from my brother's confidences that she had been known in Hong Kong as a nymphomaniac, and I was trusting to luck that rather than having lessened, her weakness had grown. I introduced myself as an admirer of her dancing and asked if I might take her to supper one night after the performance. She reacted exactly as I had hoped, and suggested I come to her flat, instead of our going to a restaurant. It was arranged I should meet her in Mount Street. I was stopping at my club, having been careful in every way not to deviate from my usual custom when I was in town. I changed into evening things, as was again my habit, and after several drinks at the

Ritz bar, where I am known, I dined late, and alone, at the Berkeley. This also was customary; the waiter who looks after me was born in our village, and his father was my father's butler, and we enjoyed reminiscing. Later still, I walked over to Mount Street and rang the bell at the flat and Madame Duclair let me in. She wasn't the sort to want a servant about in the evenings—which was one more thing I had banked on."

"She didn't recognize you?"

"Would it be likely?" Sir Hugh asked it expressionlessly. "Her one sight of me had been at the train stop, after a mauling that had left my face bruised and swollen and blood-smeared."

TWENTY-TWO

Margaret put a hand before her eyes as though to shield them from too vivid a picture, but the level voice went on. "You saw me pour the wine and draw the curtains, Mrs. Collier. Why you would be interested in my further procedure, I am not at all certain, and in fact I find myself very much at a loss; just how deep does this improbable interest of yours in my private life go? It would be interesting to know—but at any rate, luck was with me when I left Madame Duclair's. No one from the other flats was in the lift as I went down, and no one saw me go out the street door. I walked back to St. James's Street, where I spent the remainder of the evening at my club. In the morning, after a stop at my bank and my tailor, I took a train north. Chubb met me at the local station, and I got back here with the entire journey to and from London seeming commonplace and unremarkable—in the eyes of everyone but myself."

Sir Hugh's mouth twisted again in its brief, unpleasant

smile. "Rather too bad, after all my careful planning, for you to have been at your window, Mrs. Collier. You can understand it presents something of a problem to me?"

"If only you'd closed the curtains earlier." Margaret's whimper was an agonized reproach. "Why didn't you? Oh, why?"

"I suggested drawing them the moment I walked into the flat. Surely you don't think I wanted them open? But Madame Duclair insisted it was too hot to draw them—yet—when I suggested it—and intimated I was in too much of a hurry for privacy. Champagne, first! I was afraid to make an issue of it, one who plans murder must be cautious, and my first chance to get at them was when I went over to the sofa. She thought I was about to start the preliminaries of one of her usual evenings."

Another pause, made more unbearable to Margaret by the incessant rain against the windows. A drumming? Or a tapping, soft and insistent, of someone wanting to come in?

"Is—is the little boy who comes back, Jody?" she heard herself whisper, the palms of her icy hands wet.

"Clever you, Mrs. Collier! Fancy you guessing."

"Does he come, often?" Margaret's eyes were enormous in her white face.

"Often enough, but don't be alarmed. You won't see him. As I told you, Jody was always shy."

The rain. The rain. The little boy wanting to come in and beat his drum. A little boy proud of having his drum on display among the family's battle trophies.

Sir Hugh tilted the brandy bottle again.

"Has it occurred to you how difficult you could make things for me should your conscience send you running to Scotland Yard a second time, Mrs. Collier? Have you thought it through? You see, even though I don't go to prison, the simple fact of its being known I was in Madame Duclair's flat that evening would completely destroy my daughter's future. Our British newspapers are not any kinder than yours. Less so, some of them. Scurrilous. And there is nothing they more enjoy than a chance to tear down a man of title, no matter how obscure or unimportant he may be. Gutter writing. And that, for a young girl to be dragged through? Not if I can prevent it. Failure though I have been as a father in many ways, when I planned this I was entirely aware of a fundamental obligation I owed to Cherry." There was deliberate mockery in his thin smile. "And lately, Mrs. Collier, with my sense of parental duty even more keenly aroused, thanks to you, I am more determined than ever there shan't be a Vane scandal." His glance went to the service revolver on the wall, its oiled barrel a blue, steely glint. "There's nothing like a friend in need. But look here, you need a drink, badly. I insist."

Sir Hugh put down his own glass to fill another for Margaret, and forced her fingers around it.

"I shan't tell Scotland Yard. I shan't tell anyone." Margaret got out of her chair, a hand again clutching its tall back. "Just let me leave."

"I'm afraid I can't, Mrs. Collier. I don't trust you. Why should I? And I haven't the slightest wish to end things for myself, except as a last alternative. It wouldn't be fair. I'd very much like to outlast old Prince, here, for instance—" Sir Hugh gestured with his glass to the dog, asleep on the hearth. "And there are Pell and Chubb to consider. It may sound feudalistic, but life at Monks' Court is all they know. It will crumble to nothing if the estate goes smash. Which it will, utterly and finally, should I die before I've built up enough savings to see Cherry through with death duties. She would have to sell. You Americans may think you have taxes!

And I can assure you that to find me here at my desk some morning with a bullet through my head would be the nastiest sort of jolt to all of them."

"Suicide? And you said there wouldn't be a scandal. You'd do that to Cherry?"

"The verdict would be 'Death by accident.' I can count on the village coroner for that. He has known me all his life, and our grandfathers knew each other. We are friends. He would make things as easy as he could for Cherry. And the village will be loyal. No gossiping to outsiders. But all that is beside the point. There's a present problem at hand."

Sir Hugh's eyes narrowed thoughtfully. "I wonder. . . . You are in England alone, quite on your own, to all appearances, and from what I have gathered in conversation with you. You did have a telephone call, I remember, but only one, so far as I know. And I've made inquiry of Pell. And accordingly I shall proceed on the premise there is no one close enough to you, anywhere, to be immediately concerned if you drop out of sight for a time, and I shall ask you to stay on here until I can evolve some way or other to make entirely certain you won't talk. Neither now, Mrs. Collier, nor in the future."

"No. You can't keep me."

"I can quite easily."

"I told you I wouldn't give you away."

"Ah, but liars make it so difficult for themselves; people so seldom are willing to trust their word, Mrs. Collier."

"I swear it, I swear it!"

"A fairly melodramatic statement."

He was mocking her again. "I haven't a Bible available, but in lieu of one would you be willing to give me your hand and take an oath, Mrs. Collier?"

There was no escape from it. Margaret nodded, mutely.

"And if you will repeat after me, 'I do solemnly swear in the sight of God . . .'"

Her limp hand lay in his, inert. Words, repeated after him, were barely more than a moving of stiff white lips.

"Done. And very sensible of you. Not that it means I shall be letting you leave."

Sir Hugh lifted his glass and drank reflectively. "You may have the freedom of the garden . . . you'll enjoy a breath of air when the weather improves . . . but don't attempt to go beyond either the stableyard or the cypress hedge. Naturally, you won't go near your car. I trust things won't be too dull for you, here in the country. I am sorry both for your sake and mine that cataloguing was only a pretended interest. But perhaps you will join me in the evenings, anyway, to share my fire, and read, or do your needlework?"

The mockery vanished then as Sir Hugh added gravely. "I should very much regret any foolish try on your part to leave without my express consent. I gave considerable thought to drastic action once before, not too long ago, you may remember; whether I would again, is extremely doubtful. But don't put me to the test. I am determined to protect Cherry at any cost. She comes first. The point is, Mrs. Collier, if a choice were necessary between your being silenced and Cherry's future, I can only remind you that blood is thicker than water. And I most sincerely hope you won't forget it."

He limped on his stick to the library door and opened it.

"Shall we say good night? In the morning you shall have your portrait back. Though why you want it strikes me as singularly mystifying. Will you be less interested in it, I wonder, when I tell you my Georgian ancestor once entertained the same reprehensible desire for revenge, the same determination to even scores as I?"

His mouth curved sardonically.

"He and I have more than a physical resemblance; he, too, was involved somewhat unpleasantly with a woman. In his case, a sword thrust, occasioned by his wife's infidelity, necessitated a rapid departure to the Continent. A bad lot, as you can see, some of us Vanes. Though he was rather luckier than I. The lady who was responsible for his lack of self-control was obliging enough to survive. But it's too late an hour for recounting another tale of violence. So good night again to you, and may I suggest you take your drink with you? It will help you sleep."

TWENTY-THREE

The dimly lighted, winding stairs seemed unending to Margaret as she climbed them, and with the long, lonely hall at the top reached, finally, she hurried to her bedroom, bolted the door after her, and switched on the lamps. Later, when she had gotten into her nightclothes and pulled on her dressing gown to go along the hall to the bathroom, she did not dare look toward the nursery passageway. Scuttling back, she bolted the door again, and got into bed with the lamp left burning.

The rain. The rain. So soft, and yet so insistent.

"You can do anything, Hughie."

"Hughie." A boy with a black temper. A boy who threw toys in sudden, uncontrollable rages. Afterward, he had been sorry. But the man he had grown into wasn't sorry. Not the Sir Hugh who had carefully thought things out, and waited, and then had committed murder with vindictive deliberation.

Murder. Margaret repeated it, dully. No lack of faith or of

loyalty now, in saying the word. Not now, with her eyes opened to the truth.

And so this then was all there was to love—this hurting, this ache? And what about tomorrow, and all the other to-morrows ahead? What would he do with her? How would he rid himself of the threat she had become? Uncertainly, Margaret considered escape. Her sworn oath would not stand in the way. A promise made under duress was no promise. A lack of courage was the problem. She had so little. . . . Enough to slip out of the house some night and creep through the dark driveway trees to the lane beyond the gate, and along its lonely miles to the highway leading to Ludlow? It would have to be at night. By day, Chubb would be watching her every move. Sir Hugh would have seen to that. And even if there were the remote possibility of an inherently kind, good Pell asking awkward questions, Sir Hugh could so easily claim a right to keep the American lady in custody. The American lady who had been taken ill, and was not quite herself—a mild breakdown. The unfortunate American, without family or friends, who must be taken in charge until she recovered.

Pell would believe him. Poor madam, in a bad way. Madam, without family or friends. Too true. Too terrifyingly true. Margaret drew in her breath and flinched. The stark realization of her utter aloneness was like a physical blow.

Lawyers and bankers and hotel porters; that was what she had narrowed her life to, with common sense thrown to the wind. Friends? Left behind, an ocean away. The bank at home would not be alarmed for months by any absence, nor would her attorney; she had arranged to be gone indefinitely. The car-hire company? They would expect her when they saw her. The hotel in London? She had paid her bill, and left her luggage in storage, and said she would write when she was ready to reserve accommodations again. The hotel in Carlos

Place was used to traveling Americans, here today and gone tomorrow, and back another day, as the whim seized them.

No one in the world who would give a thought to where she was, or how long she stayed. Unless Ritchie still cared . . . ? Only that one telephone call, and no letters. For all of which she had been thankful. But now—now was different. She didn't deserve him, but oh, Ritchie, Ritchie, come get me! She implored it without hope, imagining his patience at an end, his ardor cooled.

Or was there the faintest chance of his being at the window of his flat, looking out on London, wondering where she was—in Shropshire, still, or gone off, somewhere else?—as she herself had once looked out over London to wonder about a tall, limping Englishman, and to vow she would find him?

It was childish to hope it. Ritchie must be through with her. But did she want Ritchie to come after her? Did she want her freedom? In the small, trying hours of the night, lying awake, and tossing, could anyone be certain of anything? She remembered her hand in Hugh Vane's, the hardness and the warmth of his palm. Suddenly she was weeping, wildly, uncontrollably, and sobbing, "He couldn't have. He couldn't have. I won't believe it. I won't."

Over and over she defended him. "Not he. Someone else. Not he."

Exhausted, and badly in need of a handkerchief, she raised up on a soaked pillow and reached a hand to the bedside lamp. The switch clicked uselessly, and she realized that this was one of the times Pell had warned her about when the electrical system of Monks' Court failed.

In a rush to light the nightstand candle, she fumbled for matches. The head of the first match she struck broke off at her hard, quick scratch against the side of its box. The second match, damp from too long a stay in the closed, disused bedroom, sputtered and fizzled out. Her hand was shaking a little as she tried again.

Such a very dark bedroom.

When she was successful, and when she had made a sopped, crumpled ball out of a handkerchief, she stumbled out of bed to the dressing table. Lighting a second candle, she picked up the brandy glass Sir Hugh had pressed on her and took a throat-burning, shuddering gulp. Anything to shorten the night and make morning come.

A wind had risen; she could hear it soughing and moaning in the trees along the drive, and hear the oak flooring and wainscoting and stairs of the old house creak ominously. Pushing aside the drawn curtains, she looked out; it was raining harder than when she had come upstairs; it was a gush and gurgle in all the lead gutters and spouts of the house, and from their gargoyle mouths onto the bricks of the entrance terrace. The drumming, drumming rain.

She was turning from the window when she froze, with a gasp of terror. Not the sound of rain—the beating of a real drum, distinct, unmistakable, above the wind's moaning. Sweat drenched her nightgown. Little Jody, playing at gallant drummer boy; he was out there, in the passageway, marching with the bravest of them.

Nothing, she was certain, could have persuaded her to take so much as a single step toward her door, yet seemingly nothing could keep her from it. Dragging her dressing gown from the foot of the bed, and with her satin mules clattering, she moved to the door like a sleepwalker, a candle in her hand. Unbolting the door and unlocking it, she stood peering out into the utter darkness of the hall.

It wasn't Jody. It couldn't be Jody. To think otherwise would be to know yourself gone entirely mad. Slowly, she went along the hall to the nursery passage, drawn irresistibly, her candle throwing grotesque shadows on the walls, now elongated, now shortened by a draft from the stairs and by the unsteadiness of her hand that set the wick to flaring wildly, then threatened it with a feeble flickering.

Now the drumming was closer. It was not a loud beat. Far more heart-stopping, far more heart-breaking, it was a steady, muffled roll. The door of the nursery was open, narrowly, and a candle had been lighted here, too, she saw as she stood on the threshold, staring, blankly.

The rocking horse. The toy soldiers. There they were. But there was Sir Hugh also, standing in front of the cold hearth where for so long no fire had burned to keep two little boys warm. The gold and scarlet cords of an infantry side drum were slung across his shoulders, and sticks in hand, he was beating a dirge.

Abruptly, at his sight of her, the slow cadence ceased.

"To wake the dead is one thing, to disturb the living inexcusable. My apologies, Mrs. Collier. I had thought the wind and the rain loud enough to silence my eccentric pastime."

"I wasn't asleep—"

"And curiosity brought you down the hall? That invincible, indestructible curiosity of yours? And now that you've seen what I'm up to, I expect you are saying to yourself, 'He's drunk'?"

"A little brandy does seem to go a long way—a very long way—at least I find it so."

"And I had more than a little, in your considered opinion? Perhaps you are right. But under the circumstances. . . . You see, Mrs. Collier, I had never told Jody's story to anyone but the Intelligence people until this evening and going over it was a mistake, I am afraid."

A mistake indeed. The tearing of a scab from a raw wound.

Thinking it, Margaret averted her eyes from Sir Hugh's face, hard as granite, yes, but gray as granite too, and with deep lines carved on each side of his mouth.

"Jody would have gloried in a battlefield death."

Margaret winced at the bitter, painful laugh.

"A last bivouac after Blenheim, let's say, or Mons. Or, for that matter, tattoo sounding for him in the Guards' chapel after that Sunday morning blitz during the war. Lots of jolly company, he would have thought, and a very decent show, the memorial service. But all he got was—what he got. And this evening I—"

"Go to bed, Sir Hugh." Margaret interrupted him gently. "Do go. Your coming here like this, isn't—isn't sensible, isn't right. Your brother wouldn't want it."

Sir Hugh's dark eyes studied her tear-reddened eyes, her hair tumbled loose on her shoulders, the trail of pale-blue nightdress showing below her hastily tossed-on robe.

"You were extremely kind, Mrs. Collier, to give me the pleasure of this unexpected little visit, and your sterling words of advice. However, if I choose to drum, I shall drum. But is it quite safe for you to be here, alone with a murderer? And isn't it a bit chilly for you?"

Margaret colored and drew her robe close. It was futile and silly to waste her pity, she knew—and knew as well that she had been dismissed.

The beat of the drum, slow and hollow and macabre, followed her along the nursery passage and into the guest-room hall. She could still hear it when she had blown out her candle and gotten into bed.

Sir Hugh at his mocking worst, she told herself, curling small under the blankets and eiderdown, and wishing the chill of his rebuff could be as easily forgotten as the cold breath of the drafty hall.

Lying awake, listening, fear seized her again when above

the soughing wind, the hard downpour of rain, the drumbeat
of a dirge was suddenly abandoned for a tempo so wild and
furious and passionate that she stopped her ears. Sir Hugh,
being swept to madness by the towering waves of his black
and terrible moods. And she was a captive in his house.

It was almost dawn when her eyes finally closed. She slept
heavily and late, and when she woke again, her breakfast tray
was on the bedside table, the brandy glass had been taken
away, and the curtains had been pulled aside to let in a watery, uncertain sunlight.

Her head aching, the pallor of her face smudged under the
eyes with dark shadows, she sat up against the pillows and
poured a cup of tea, and was drinking it as a knock at the
door brought Pell on her second morning trudge upstairs.
This time she was bringing the portrait.

"Good morning, madam." It was properly polite, but a little stiff, and Margaret wondered if her imagination was carrying her away, or if there was something of reserve in the
greeting, something that suggested the uncommunicative
prison wardress? It could, of course, be merely that Pell did
not approve of a so-called lady drinking brandy in the seclu-
sion of her bedroom.

"Your picture, madam. Sir Hugh gave orders it was to be
fetched up to you."

"Thank you."

"Where is it to be put, madam?"

"Just stand it anywhere. And you may take my tray."

"The egg isn't to your liking, nor the bacon, madam?"

"It's a lovely breakfast." Hastily, Margaret was placating.
"But I've a headache, and I'm not hungry." She flung the
bedclothes back and got up. "I'll feel better after my bath
and when I get out into the garden."

"There's nothing like fresh air, I always say, madam, if
one's feeling a bit peckish. You'll need stout shoes, though.

And it's best, I should think, to stay on the garden paths; there'd be nothing but bog after last night's rain if you tried the path to the lake or the stream."

Was it a reminder of boundaries, a warning?

"I'll keep to the gardens." Margaret was quietly acquiescent. "Where is Miss Cherry?" she asked. "At the stable, I suppose?"

"Yes, madam."

"And Sir Hugh?" He was to be avoided at all cost, Margaret was telling herself.

"Gone to the farms, madam."

"Will he be back for lunch?" It would make a difference to her own plans for the morning. She would ask for a sandwich, or cheese. Anything. And she would eat it in the garden, rain or no rain, rather than face him until her temples had stopped throbbing, until her thinking had cleared. And until the color was back in her face, she thought, with a glance in the dressing-table mirror as she picked up her brush, and until her eyes looked less obviously wept dry.

"You're not well, madam?" Pell's black eyes were on her observantly.

"Well enough."

"A change of air does wonders, madam—some place warmer, perhaps? It's a bleak spring we're having here. There's nothing like a change for a tonic, if Madam isn't feeling quite the thing."

"You don't think I wouldn't leave, if I could?" Margaret turned on her furiously. "I'm not staying from choice!"

"I was only suggesting you go, madam. And like as not, if you'd think on it, you could . . . but there, it's not for me to say. It's quite up to you, madam." Pell's mouth closed firmly, but she looked troubled, and uneasy.

What was she getting at, with her broad hints? Pell was a wardress, wasn't she? Or was she? Only one fact was plain.

Pell herself, for some reason of her own, wanted Margaret to leave.

Was it because she was disapproving and fearful, sorry for Margaret, caught like a fly in a spiderweb? Were there plans she knew about that Sir Hugh had in mind, and Chubb would carry out? It was all too frightening, too bewildering; to attempt thinking it through only made her head throb harder.

Abandoning the puzzle, Margaret repeated a question. "Will Sir Hugh be in for lunch?"

"It will be just you in the dining room, madam. Miss Cherry asked for a basket lunch, and Sir Hugh will be eating in one of the cottages, so he told me."

"Oh. I see."

A deliberate staying away, was it? Would she see him at dinner, or was this the beginning of a solitary confinement? The thought was a stab. A longing to lose herself in private contemplation of the portrait took forceful hold of Margaret. She rushed through her bath and her dressing, and waited impatiently for Pell to finish putting fresh linen on the bed and get through her slow, conscientious plumping of pillows, her morning routine of dusting and mopping.

On edge with thwarted eagerness, she wandered restlessly to the windows overlooking the terrace and the wet, melancholy garden to which her parole would keep her prisoner. To have the courage to break it! To be less of an abject coward. No. More than that. To have the will to tear herself away.

Staring out, drearily, she saw a small mud-spattered car wallow through the puddles and bump over the deep ruts of the driveway to stop at the stableyard archway. In spite of her low spirits she watched with interest as Robin Soames unfolded his long legs from under the wheel.

Another chance being offered Cherry? Lucky, lucky girl. "I'm glad, so glad. The best of everything, you two." As Margaret sent off her silent good wishes, blurring tears were near the surface. That elusive thing called happiness was so plainly meant for some people, but not for everyone.

Hearing Pell close the bedroom door after her with a correct, "Thank you, madam," she turned swiftly to gaze at the portrait propped against the wardrobe.

Sir Hugh's double. Or would be, if ever Sir Hugh's mouth would curve with that hint of tenderness rather than with sarcasm or bitterness, and if there were warmth to his eyes instead of that dark, glacial aloofness.

She had traced the mouth of the portrait once before; now she was withdrawing her hand quickly before it touched the canvas. Why, why allow herself to be tormented? Why degrade herself? And where was her pride? Her self-respect?

She thrust the portrait into the wardrobe as far back as it would go behind her clothes and suitcase, and jerking her raincoat off a hanger, she ran down the stairs to the lower hall, and through the side door to the garden. The sad, neglected allée of dark cypress, the niches with their blank-eyed, dripping statues stained with mold, blotched with fungus, and the broken, leaf-clogged fountain basin added an intolerable burden to her depression.

Up the allée, and down again. Up again, and down. This was to be all, this gray, dreary monotony, day after day, day after day, for how long? Up and down. Up and down. Or if not this, her bedroom, until books put her eyes out, or until she lost her mind thinking about a little boy whose footsteps she had heard, and whom she would see unless she got hold of herself. Any day now she might meet him limping toward her out of the nursery-passage shadows. And if ever she heard a man's voice pleading, "Hughie, Hughie . . ."

With her hands clenched in her raincoat pockets, Margaret fled from the cypress garden and fairly ran through the archway to the stables. Someone alive to be with. Anyone alive.

Cherry, in the stable, was sitting on spread-out horse blankets, with an old saddle for a backrest. She was dividing her attention between the sleeping puppies, their stomachs distended with mid-morning milk and gruel, Court Lady, using her lap for a pillow, and an account book and pencil.

"Good morning—do you mind if I visit for a moment?" Margaret asked almost beggingly, and Cherry, glancing up briefly, moved over on the blankets, and as Margaret sat down, began to do scribbled sums.

"I knew it!"

"Fifty pounds ahead of the game." She announced it triumphantly, more to herself than to Margaret as she turned a page and jotted down a final figure. "Fifty whole pounds if I can sell nine of the puppies. And with five spoken for already, and inquiries about three more . . ."

"Ahead of the game? You mean, it's fifty pounds profit?"

Cherry's usually passive or sullen face was alive and glowing, and Margaret found herself softening. The least you could do was make an effort to share in her pathetic little moment of success. "After all expenses? How splendid!"

"It means with Court Lady bought, and the puppies' inoculations and worming, and Father paid back, and stud fees for the female I'm going to keep and breed to Beaumont Champion. Beau has more field-trial ribbons than any dog in Shropshire."

"You would rather go on raising puppies than go out to Naasam? You'll be happier?"

It fell from Margaret's lips unexpectedly. "I'm sorry! I was thinking out loud." Her apology came swiftly as the excited aliveness vanished abruptly from Cherry's face and her gray eyes darkened ominously. Gone was any tentative willingness to accept Margaret, and gone so much as a pretense at civility as she asked contemptuously, "You are not terribly quick at taking hints, are you, about keeping out of other people's affairs? Are all Americans the same way, Mrs. Collier?"

"Most of us try to be kind," Margaret retaliated sharply. "And can't you give me the benefit of the doubt and believe I sincerely want to help you?"

A scornful little smile spoiled Cherry's mouth. "That's likely. You never saw me until a week or so ago. A tourist, barging in. I'm nothing to you. Why would you want to help me?"

"I don't know why, actually," Margaret admitted simply. She hesitated and then went on slowly, "Perhaps because I am older than you; it all seems such a waste, this throwing away of your girlhood and your prettiness—because you *are* pretty, that is, when you're not going around looking like a thundercloud. And Robin Soames is as attractive and nice a boy as I have ever seen. I hate to think of your losing him."

It was useless, any argument of that sort, Margaret saw; a butting of her head against a stone wall. Another tactic, would that work? It was worth a try, and nothing would be lost, with the girl already so irked and resentful. It would be ruthless, it would hurt, but . . .

"You are too devoted to your father, Cherry," she went on. "No normal girl—of any maturity—wants to make a parent the center of her life. If you can't see that for yourself, it's time you grew up! I beg of you, take your nice, adoring Robin, and get away. . . ." Margaret's voice broke with intensity. She put a hand on Cherry's shoulder and gave her a little shake. "Go away, while you still have the chance! You'll be so terribly sorry some day, if you don't."

Cherry pulled away, her mouth set stubbornly, her eyes furious. "You've no right!"

"No, of course I haven't." Margaret acknowledged it honestly, and then she shrugged. "And what's the use of me talking to you anyway? But you are being stupid, just plain stupid —and immature, and silly—yes, and greedy—always demanding more from your father than he is ready, or able, to give. Don't you see? You've managed things all wrong! You both could have jogged along perfectly well together since you've been out of school if you hadn't asked for so much. As it is, you only trouble and vex him. He doesn't know what to do with a daughter on his hands—a daughter without a mother, who might become one of those pathetic women whose only interest is dogs. Very few men would know what to do. But whether you believe it or not, he's got your interest at heart. He'd like nothing more than to see you happily settled with someone like Robin Soames. To say nothing of seeing you smile occasionally instead of scowl. A girl with the name of Cherry ought to be gay, ought to laugh, ought to have learned how to love a father like yours with—well, with lightness. With a sense of humor. And you never show a speck of humor. . . ."

Cherry jumped to her feet.

"You are the most detestable, most impossible person I ever hope to meet. And when I think how you've gotten around my father—how you've settled in here!"

"You'd send me off, I know, if you could, and I shouldn't blame you. And I shall be leaving as soon as—as soon as it is possible, I promise you. For the moment I can't say when exactly—something has come up."

"Father's books, that cataloguing. Oh, I know how you've edged your way in!"

"The books aren't keeping me. It's just that . . ." There was no explanation possible to make. Margaret's stammered attempt trailed to nothing, and then her eyes were sorry as she went on gently, "To hurt you seemed the only way. Try to forgive me. But even if you can't, go away with Robin. Please, please!"

She got up from the blanket and walked out of the stall, and with Cherry's resentful, angry gaze following her until she had crossed the cobbled stableyard, she went through the archway toward the garden.

Once more she was pacing up and down, up and down, the length of the cypress allée. Chubb was weeding the paths. Had he been put at the task primarily to spy on her?

"Good morning, Chubb."

" 'Morning, ma'am."

Up and down, up and down. The dark drip of branches. The squelch of her shoes on wet gravel.

Old Chubb, toadlike and malevolent, blowing his nose again and again in a disgusting handkerchief as an excuse to look up from his weeding and keep his bright black eyes on her.

At noon Pell came into the garden to announce lunch and Margaret followed her back to the house. The nightmarish craziness and incongruity of it all. To sit down to a table set with lovely old silver and china and linen, to help yourself to forced strawberries and clotted cream—and know you were a prisoner.

Pell's eyes were on her as sharply as Chubb's had been, Margaret was convinced. And there would be meal after meal eaten alone in the cold, blank emptiness of Sir Hugh's dining room, she didn't doubt, and day after unending day to be gotten through, unless somehow she mustered the willpower, gained the self-respect, to sever the chains binding her to Monks' Court.

With desperate resolve she pushed herself to a decision. Tonight. Do it before she weakened again, before she sank any deeper in the morass of her illogical, ever-springing hopes, the quicksand of her recurring doubts. Do it while the portrait was still at the back of the wardrobe, with those eyes, that mouth, out of sight.

Wait until after dinner, when Sir Hugh would be in the library with his brandy, Cherry gone to the stable, Pell asleep in her attic room. Tiptoe down the stairs, lift the bolt of the side door, quietly, quietly. Don't attempt to take the car. There was no telling whether or not Chubb had been delegated to stand a night watch. And there were the dogs to bark. She could arrange later about the car's return to the hire agency. Luggage, too, could be arranged for. Don't burden yourself with your dressing case, even. She would have the longest walk of her life ahead of her to Ludlow. Margaret pushed aside her plate of strawberries, her mind made up, her course determined.

"You are going to your room, madam, if Sir Hugh should inquire?"

"Yes."

A check on every move she made. Her whereabouts known every minute of the day.

In her bedroom, Margaret took her handbag from the dressing table drawer. Yes. Her letter of credit, and plenty of cash. Much more than enough to hire another car in Ludlow to get her back to London and to pay for a telephone call to her hotel for reservations and for a call to Ritchie. Just to hear his voice!

Lovely, lovely, if she could persuade herself into caring enough—caring all the way. Caring terribly. The way she once had. Lovely to think he might still be her friend, and her haven, now, her lifesaver, literally. Ritchie, if he took her back, would never, never let Hugh Vane get at her.

She was thinking then of a Knight Crusader, lying in his armor next to Catharine, his wife, in the Vane chapel. Catharine had gone through with things to the bitter end. How much lesser a creature she was, turning away now, shrinking from pain and horror, finding her love and her trust too impossibly difficult a gift to give another Sir Hugh Vane. But forget Catharine. Forget the knight in armor, with the sweet curve to his same lips.

Forget the mouth and the eyes of a Georgian portrait. Above all, forget the eyes and mouth of the last of the Vanes.

She could, if she tried hard enough. Anything was possible —almost anything—if you put your every effort to it. She had romanticized them all. Real life, the good life, was a life with Ritchie.

The bedroom was icy, and as Margaret sat down to wait out the afternoon with her tapestry, she wrapped the worn, pale-yellow silk puff from the bed around her shoulders.

Yellow. Her favorite color. And this was her favorite bedroom, of any she had ever been in. The dust covers would go on again, she supposed, after tomorrow. Say good-bye to the whole, heartbreaking, beautiful house you had chosen to leave.

The afternoon dragged on. Time after time she rethreaded her needle with stiff, awkward fingers. So cold a house. At four o'clock it began to rain, and she turned on the lamp.

Had he come in yet from the farms? Had Pell brought the tea tray into the library? Was the old dog asleep on the hearth? The shelves crowded with musty-smelling books. The cabinet full of curios. The walls covered—except for that bare, stripped square over the mantel—with swords and firearms, including a World War II revolver, its blue steel glinting in firelight. But forget the library, as well as the chapel. Forget. Forget. Forget. It would be like the steady, constant tick of a clock, always, that *Forget, Forget, Forget.*

When Pell rang the dressing-bell, Margaret forced herself to change into her yellow wool with hands fumbling at its fastening.

In the passage outside, shadows would have gathered. Try not to listen. There were only a few more hours to be gotten through. Ludlow, and a car, and then London and Ritchie. Free. Never again to be enslaved. And never again to be afraid of either a living or a dead Vane. To be Margaret Collier once more. The real Margaret Collier, wakened at last from a sequence of nightmares. When the gong reverberated again for dinner, she made herself open the bolted bedroom door and walk to the top of the stairs and go down them with her hand on the banister for the support it so often had given her.

Sir Hugh was waiting for her in the hall below, his dark eyes as imperturbable as ever, his "Good evening, Mrs. Collier," smooth and even.

"I have told Pell to hold dinner until you have had a sherry and a few minutes by the library fire. I am sorry we don't run to central heating. You Americans find our houses beastly chilly, I expect."

He was waiting for her to cross the hall. There was nothing to do but obey. The fire was burning with a rush of flame up the chimney, and for a moment Margaret was conscious only of gratitude for the warmth. A lovely fire! She stood by the hearth where the old dog slept and held her hands out to the blaze. This could have been all she would ever want—this room, this fire—this man. All. Nothing more for the rest of her life.

"Sit down, won't you?" Sir Hugh drew a wing chair closer to the hearth. "Now then, your sherry." He limped toward her.

That glass in his hand again. Another nightmare, terrible as a struggle in quicksand. This time, the shabby brown leather chair had become, to her horror-widened eyes, a crimson damask sofa.

This time, it would be *her* throat. Margaret Collier's throat. With a hand that shook, she accepted the sherry, and then it was spilling over the rim of the glass onto her dress in a dark stain.

Blood. Blood on a white rug. She could see it as she stared.

TWENTY-FOUR

For the first time since she had known him, the ice-gray eyes lost their enigmatic aloofness, their cold detachment. Filled with a dark melancholy, and with infinite regret, they looked down at her.

"You are frightened, Mrs. Collier? I am everything that is repulsive in your sight, and menacing? It's the greatest pity—even though understandable. And nothing to be done about it, I am afraid. But before I attempt anything along that line, may I just say I'd very much like to call you Margaret? Mrs. Collier sounds a bit ridiculous under the circumstances. But give me your glass."

Margaret relinquished her glass wordlessly, and when he had set it on the tray he said quietly, "You shan't be hurt. You may leave Monks' Court whenever you choose. I couldn't possibly detain you. Not now. Not after I have waked to what has happened to me. The sooner you go the better, for that matter. Having you about won't be easy—

things being as they are. Unfortunately, I care much too much."

Margaret stared at him, dazedly. "I—I don't understand?"

"Nor do I, God knows. It's a blow, and a fairly shattering one."

"But?" Margaret's heart lurched. "You can't mean—?"

"I mean exactly that. Though how I have come to care for a woman, really care, after all these years, is beyond me."

"Care—?" Margaret repeated it, stunned, and then her attempt at laughter held a note of hysteria. "Is it part of the two-shilling tour, along with tea and cakes?" The laughter ended in a kind of sob. "It's not terribly funny—a poor sort of joke."

"It happens not to be a joke at all." Sir Hugh stated it gravely. "It happens to be a statement of fact. My marriage to Cherry's mother came about naturally enough," he went on slowly. "She was pretty, we were both very young—and there were the urgencies of wartime. How long she would have been happy here I don't know. She looked on Monks' Court as an empty place, finished and done for. She neither got the feel of it nor learned to see in it the possibilities I saw for the future when I would inherit it. She tried, but . . ."

Again Sir Hugh continued with his quiet recital. "When I got back from China, I hadn't the time nor the heart for anything but work. And after I—I had been to Mount Street, I knew I could never think of love, much less marriage, again. But last night when I saw you with that candle in your hand, and your bright hair loose, you made me think of a candle yourself, shining against the darkness of my house. And—well, there you have it. But when I think of the rotten, beastly luck that brought you here—the frightful muddle you have walked into—"

"I'll wish all my life that I'd never seen your gates." Margaret whispered it brokenly.

"And I'll wish you never had. To be alone here behind the gates of Monks' Court is all I've wanted—it is all I have a right to. But Margaret, Margaret—just this once."

Sir Hugh's arms were around Margaret, his hard mouth on hers.

Passively, at first, she let him have his way, and then she was clinging to him. Returning kiss for kiss, she thought dazedly, "From all across the ocean, London calling to me for this. London giving him to me. . . ."

Lost, she clung the harder when Sir Hugh pushed her from him. "No, Margaret. No. We've gone too far already. And Chubb will drive you to town. You are leaving this evening. Leaving now."

"I won't. I won't."

"Ah, but you shall."

"I'm staying. I'm staying." Margaret's cry was passionately rebellious.

"You have forgotten what Scotland Yard will call me? What I chose to attempt, deliberately, and in cold blood?"

The word "murderer," which she had so often tried to check unspoken on her tongue, hung in the air between them, and Margaret collapsed in her chair again, huddled and weeping.

"Last evening I shocked and horrified you with my story. Nothing has changed since then. Not fundamentally. What importance is there to the touching of our hands and mouths? None, balanced against all the rest of it. If you knew how I loathed myself. And I've good reason to, wouldn't you say?"

His mouth was bitter. "To be sorry would be the decent thing. But I am not sorry. I am glad. I wanted the Duclair woman to die, and I have planned how I might manage her death for years. Years, Margaret. The wish itself constitutes murder, with or without the act. In my mind, all those years,

I took her life a hundred times over. And that admission
alone should make you realize it is impossible for you to stay
on or for us to have any sort of shared life. God knows, it is
difficult enough for me to live with myself."

He knelt down by Margaret's chair and took her cold hand
in his. "Don't cry. I am not worth it. Think of me as I am—
think of me realistically, in a true light. A man who longed
for years to get his hands around a woman's throat. Who
dreamed of it, who lived with the hope, day after day, night
after night."

"I can't bear it for you. I can't bear it."

"You shall have to bear it. It is done. It is water over a
dam. And don't waste your pity on me. I tell you, I am glad
she is dead. I wouldn't want her back, not even to save what
you and I might have had together. Or what I might have in
the future with Cherry. She deserved what she got. She was
let off far too long—and at the end too easily. Minutes for
her. Hours, for Jody. But you haven't been let off anything,
have you?"

He put Margaret's hand against his cheek.

"My only regret is your involvement. And I shall ask something more of you than to stop crying. Put me out of mind.
Forget me. You can, if you try. What have we had of each
other, but a few short moments? And you have years ahead of
you. You are a very charming woman. You are warm and
responsive. You love life. And there will be someone."

"No! No."

"And I say yes, again. Come, get up. You are leaving—at
once. Instantly."

Sir Hugh pulled Margaret to her feet.

She fought him stubbornly, despairingly, and as he attempted to free himself from her clinging arms he was as
oblivious as she to the sudden opening of the library door.

"Father—"

Sir Hugh turned and stiffened. Margaret, with a gasp, drew away from him.

Cherry, in her raincoat, with the hood over her head, seemed unaware of any awkward blundering on her part or of the tension that almost palpably filled the shadowy, fire-lit room.

"I am going to the Vicarage for dinner, Father. And I shall stay the night. Robin is stopping by for me. I thought I'd just tell you."

She stammered to a halt, self-consciously, with bright, hot color flooding her cheeks that deepened as Sir Hugh raised a questioning eyebrow.

"Did you also have in mind to tell me that you might possibly be considering Naasam with Robin—as well as dinner? You will be off with him, will you, when he leaves?"

"Yes."

"Extremely sensible of you. I highly approve." Sir Hugh made a formal little bow to his daughter. "Robin is a very fortunate young man. My congratulations to him. And will you tell him I shall want a little chat with him? Tomorrow, say?"

"Yes, Father."

Her shy, inhibited inability to say anything more, and Sir Hugh's diffidence and restraint were painful and pathetic to witness. In a surging tide, Margaret's pity went out to them both. Each straining, groping, toward the other, each face to face with a barrier, built mutually through the years. But perhaps when Cherry grew up a little more, perhaps if her father could learn to unbend a little . . .

"And now I expect you would like to be on your way, my dear. We shan't keep you."

It was a dismissal, and Cherry, recognizing it, with a quick glance at Sir Hugh and then at Margaret, was apparently conscious, if only uncertainly, of currents and cross-currents running between them.

"Good night, Father." She said it hastily.

"Good night, my dear."

"My dear." Could anything have been more reserved, more understated, Margaret wondered? But Cherry's face was all at once vividly alight, her eyes glad, and with her hand on the doorknob she turned.

"Good night, Mrs. Collier."

"Good night, Cherry. It's wonderful."

"I was thinking—that is, as long as you are fond of dogs— would you like one of the puppies, Mrs. Collier?" She asked it, haltingly, with jealousy and resentment still struggling in her, but going down to defeat before her newfound joy, a humbling gratitude. "You may take your choice. . . . And oh, I forgot, there was a telephone call for you a few minutes ago. Pell took the message."

"A telephone call? For me?"

"It was a Mr. Page from The Feathers in Ludlow. Pell told him you were just going in to dinner and he said he'd call back later."

Cherry was gone then and Margaret was clinging to Sir Hugh again, stricken.

"It's my London friend! The one who told me whose flat—"

"How did he know where to find you?"

"Through my London hotel and the car-hire garage. He telephoned once before, from London, and The Feathers transferred the call to Monks' Court. But now, if he's come all this way, if he's followed me, it means he's found out something. I knew he would. Hugh, Hugh, I knew he would." She was babbling incoherently. "He'll bring the Inspector. You'll go to prison!"

"Hold on, Margaret. It will never be prison for me, nor even a trial. I thought I had made that clear? And why need we anticipate the worst? You told me you were positive that Page didn't see the name Vane when you both looked at the portrait. Well then?"

"You don't understand!" Margaret cried, frienzied. "It isn't what Ritchie saw, it is what he heard—'the man in the flat.' I tried my best to cover it up, but if he thought back, if he remembers the way it slipped out, if he has been curious enough to think it over—don't you see? Ritchie was a newspaperman once, I tell you. And if he guesses there's any kind of a story, he'll never give up till he's onto it."

"Did he sound suspicious when he called before?"

"No."

"Then isn't it far more likely he has come up to Ludlow only looking for you, Margaret, rather than for me? You say he is a friend; is he more than that? Is he in love with you?"

"That's not why he's here—not the only reason. I know it isn't! He had begun to think there was something I was holding back, keeping quiet about, even before I left London."

"What makes you think so?"

In Sir Hugh's arms she poured out a jumbled, frantic description of her last few days with Richard. Richard looking at her oddly. Richard continually asking her if she were tired. Richard noticing she was distraught, noticing her withdrawal from him.

"An affair, was it, between the two of you?" Sir Hugh asked quietly.

"An old attraction and perhaps a new beginning. Nothing more."

"I don't like his coming here any more than you do, but turning up doesn't at all mean I'm in for it. I'm not the one he is after, my dearest girl."

"But you are, Hugh, you are!" Clinging to him, Margaret insisted it.

"Come now. The prospect isn't at all that grim. We've only got to sit tight and wait to see what his next move will be. When he rings through again, this evening, you perhaps can feel things out a bit."

"Wait? Wait, and not know? I can't, I can't, Hugh! It's been so long already. So terribly long. The awful worrying . . ."

It was wrung from her, and then, as he smoothed her hair and attempted to calm her, she declared in a shaking voice muffled against his shoulder, "I'm going to call him. Now. Right now. I'm going to find out why he came."

"And I'm to skulk while you do the maneuvering?"

"Don't, Hugh. It has to be this way. I've got to know." She drew away from him. Going toward the door, she paused at Sir Hugh's desk and picked up the silver-framed snapshot. "Your poor Jody. Poor little drummer boy. Why did God ever let him grow up? Why did He let such awfulness happen to him?" She questioned it through a quick, blinding shimmer of tears.

"You think I haven't wondered the same thing?"

"So many 'why's,'" she murmured, bewildered, as she put the snapshot down. "Why did I choose London? Why did I look out of my hotel window that particular night? Why . . . ? But still worth it. Worth it a thousand times." Her voice shook. "How could I have said I'd be sorry, all my life, that I'd ever seen your gates?"

He caught one of her hands and laid it against his cheek, without words. She freed it, struggling to keep back the brimming tears, and went out to the hall and the telephone closet.

When she had been connected with The Feathers and was waiting for Richard to be put on the wire, she reached out for a sleeve of one of the rough outdoor jackets.

Hugh near her, she would pretend. Hugh helping her to steady her voice. Hugh helping her to sound herself—natural and unalarmed—helping her to allay any of Ritchie's suspicions and to go through with whatever might now be asked of her.

". . . Ritchie? It's Margaret. Maggie."

"Well, well, little Mag, out of the blue! How's life with the landed gentry these days?"

"Fine."

"Glad to hear it. You're not much of a letter writer, would you say?"

"There's not much to write about."

"No? A quiet country existence with no divertissements? Sounds nice and healthy anyway. But I'd have thought you'd have time on your hands to send me love and kisses even if you *were* hard up for real news. You haven't forgotten yours truly, I trust? You haven't, have you, Mag?"

"You'd be pretty hard to forget. But when did you get in, Ritchie?"

"Half an hour or so ago."

"How long are you staying?"

"I don't know. That's up to you."

"Up to me?" Margaret clutched the coat sleeve harder. "What have I to do with it?"

"Everything. Because I'll be here until you say you are ready to come back to London. Back with me, that is. And to stay. And I mean *stay*."

"Now, Ritchie, if you are going to start that kind of nonsense again—"

"We'll talk it over tomorrow. Either you meet me here at the inn, Mag sweet, or I'll be dropping in on you at the Vanes'."

"I'll come to town."

"What time?"

"In the afternoon."

"In time for a cup of tea? No, you don't, Mag. We'll have the cuppa, but you're staying on for dinner. Understood?"

"Yes."

"You wouldn't want to go all out, and say you're looking forward to it?"

"Of course I'm looking forward to it."

"And in the meantime you'll be remembering I love you, sweet?"

"Yes."

"Then I'll sign off."

A receiver in Ludlow clicked on its hook. Margaret let go her hold on the jacket sleeve and went back to the library.

"Well?" Sir Hugh was leaning against the mantelpiece, an arm covering his face.

"I've promised to meet him at the inn tomorrow." Her voice broke. "He is a friend—whatever else he is, he is that— and I acted out a lie." Bewilderment was in her face again. "So many lies since that night. And I always used to tell the truth."

"Start telling it again, I advise you, Margaret." Sir Hugh's voice was harsh. "When you see him tomorrow, tell him everything. I am the last person in the world to want you to live with a guilty conscience. You won't find it pleasant."

"Tell? You think I'd tell?"

"Why not? I've explained, and more than once, how I'll manage. And Cherry has Robin now."

"And I? Whom would I have?"

He ignored her question.

"You haven't told me. Is he onto anything?"

"It didn't sound like it," she admitted slowly.

"You see, I was right. A false alarm. And by tomorrow you'll be out of here, and the whole wretched business behind you."

"No, Hugh. I'll have to stay on here for a while at least."

"Why is that?"

"If I leave Monks' Court just when he has arrived in Ludlow, he'll be certain to suspect something, even if he hasn't already. He'd be all the more curious as to why I came here at all, and he'd wonder and wonder why I was hurrying away. He'd be sure to suspect I didn't want him coming out to Monks' Court or meeting the people who live here. I *must* stay, Hugh. Just let me satisfy him tomorrow with some sort of explanation for my visit—I'll think of something. And I'll see him the next day, and the next, if I have to, until he's persuaded there's no story here after all. And when he's willing to go back to London, I'll go back, too. I promise, Hugh —if that's what you want."

"What I want?"

"Meanwhile, I'll be the unchaperoned Mrs. Collier—one of those impossible Americans." Margaret's pitiful attempt at a little joke came unsteadily. "Think how highly improper— you and I, alone here, when Cherry goes." Her voice caught in a sob. "Not that right or wrong seem to matter to me any longer."

"I envy you. I wish I could say the same. Unfortunately, black is still black to me, and white is white."

"No shadings?"

"No shadings."

He swung around from the fire.

"Shall we go into dinner?" he asked formally. "I'll have Pell fetch up a special bottle for us, and we'll drink to Cherry, that *rara avis*, that solitary survivor of a perished breed—a happy Vane."

TWENTY-FIVE

Margaret, ready to leave for Ludlow, and standing on the terrace with Pell, watched Robin's car start off for the Vicarage. It was followed by the old, battered Land Rover, and she waved again to Sir Hugh and to Cherry beside him before it disappeared around a curve of the driveway.

It had been Cherry's choice to ride with her father instead of with Robin.

"Father might like it," Margaret had heard her explain in an aside to Robin, who had brought her back to Monks' Court early that morning to get on immediately with hurried wedding arrangements.

Margaret had seen Robin's quick, approving nod. Plenty of time ahead for those two, she had thought wistfully. All their lives. They could afford to spare half an hour apart, now. Lucky Cherry. Lucky Robin.

She was sincerely and deeply glad for Cherry's happiness,

and for the support and the comfort that would be hers, no matter what lay ahead for her father.

And such a new Cherry, emerging as though from a chrysalis! Marveling, Margaret had seen it happen overnight. The sullen look had vanished from her eyes, and she was no longer on the defensive. All morning, and through lunch, she had made awkwardly shy but eager little advances both to Margaret and her father, and Sir Hugh had done his best, in a stiff, difficult way, to meet her halfway.

Call it only the establishment of an entente; it was more than enough for the present, and there was not likely to be a future for Cherry's father.

By mutual, unspoken agreement Margaret and Sir Hugh had avoided any further discussion of their own situation. The morning had belonged solely to Cherry and Robin, and to their hastily scribbled lists.

A license. Passport and visas and inoculations for Cherry. Plane and hotel reservations. All arranged for. Shopping. A white dress and veil. Packing. A bouquet ordered.

The culmination would be a tiny wedding in the parish church, with Robin's father reading the service, and a bubbly punch and a wedding cake afterward at Monks' Court.

White ribbon bows for the collars of Prince and Court Lady, as would befit the occasion. Last-minute hugs for the puppies when Cherry had changed into her new traveling suit, with Robin's mother ready to take them home with her.

A last hug to Pell. Handshakes with Chubb. A hug for her father? Almost certainly. And some little special, awkward good-bye proffered the American.

Margaret swallowed a lump in her throat. A young, sweet wedding, the wedding of two gay, tender children, so caught up in happiness, was heart-wrenching enough to watch at any time. But this one, now!

How would Sir Hugh get through it? How would she herself get through it? Don't ask. Don't think about it. Just take each hour, each minute of each hour. It was time she realized there was no hope of a shared future, ever, for her and Hugh.

As the Land Rover disappeared from the driveway, Margaret was struggling against the tide of uncertainty and fear that had washed over her in swamping waves all morning, and to divert her thoughts she turned to Pell. "Such excitement, all this, about Miss Cherry! It's lovely, isn't it?"

"You don't half know how pleased I am, madam. It's sun through a cloud, that's what it is. And if . . ."

"If what?" Margaret asked quickly, and told herself it was only a little stir of chill wind that had made her suddenly shiver.

"I shouldn't like to say, madam. It isn't my place."

"What was it, Pell?"

"It's only that I was wondering, madam, if you'll be staying on now, or with Miss Cherry gone, would it be me and the master alone here?"

"I'll be leaving—very soon." With a glance at Pell's face, Margaret added quietly, "You are glad, aren't you? You want me to go. You don't like me, do you?"

"Like you, madam?" Pell considered it. "Put to me like that, a straight answer isn't easy come by. And I'd be sorry, I can tell you, madam, if you took offense."

"You won't hurt my feelings. Tell me the truth, Pell. Go on."

"It's the mists settling in, like I said before, madam, only heavier every day, over Monks' Court. They make me wish we could see the last of you."

"The mists?"

"The same as I spoke of, madam, one morning over breakfast, if you'll think back."

Pell looked toward the Welsh hills, beyond the terrace to the west, their peaks lost in sullen clouds, their base all but obscured by swirling gray vapor.

"Mists too thick to see through, madam, except enough to warn you of crags, and gullies, and steep, rough climbing ahead, with deep glens to lose your way in, and black tarn water, with no bottom to it, if your foot slips. Terrible mists, madam. There's some as say the devil keeps a cauldron on the boil. . . ."

"But what have I got to do with you and your mists? And you still haven't said why you don't like me."

"It's this way, madam; though it's true a chill and a darkness has lain heavy on the house for years back, the cold and the thickness of it has worsened ten times over since your coming here."

"And some of it would lift, if I go?"

"So it would, madam, to my thinking."

The bright, black, Celtic eyes had a queer, faraway look. "Someone, or something, has brought a new trouble here, madam. And it is coming closer, led by you, as I see it. There's that much plain as day to me, no matter how much else is hid. You, leading trouble by the hand—and a darkness falling."

"So that's why you and Chubb have tried so hard to get rid of me?"

"I longed for you to go, madam. But it was Chubb who was up to tricks." Pell twisted her apron. "He's simple, madam, if you know what I mean." She confessed it sorrily. "But he's got the same knowingness that has showed me trouble ahead—he sees it as a storm—and nothing would do these last weeks but he must be playing his daft games, try as I did to talk him out of them."

"The boat?"

"And the rat, madam."

"And the tea? Did you know about the tea? Did you know he tried to poison me?"

"It was only to make you ill. I shouldn't ever have let him put hands on that thermos, madam. I was baking, and there he was, in the scullery, and me never dreaming he'd take it into his head. He told me, after. Came to me with the tale, he did, and as disappointed as a child you'd seen through his foolery. A plant-food tablet it was, nothing more. Like I say, madam, he's simple, he's not got the wits of a hare, nor one of Miss Cherry's fowl. But he worships Sir Hugh, madam. In his poor way he was trying to help matters here. And if you could find the goodness and the kindness not to have him punished, madam . . ."

There was a long silence, until Margaret, with her eyes on the mist-veiled dark hills, promised in a small, strained voice, "He won't be punished. And I'll go away, and stay away, for always, as soon as I can, Pell."

"I wouldn't know how to say a proper thank you, madam."

The relief on Pell's face spoke for her, and then she was a correct, controlled servant again. "If you're to be in for dinner, madam, would a grilled cutlet suit, and some lettuces, and a strawberry tart?"

"I won't be back until late. There will be only Sir Hugh for dinner. Miss Cherry and Master Robin will be at the Vicarage."

Margaret moved toward her car, which had been brought up earlier from the stableyard by Sir Hugh and parked in the driveway for her. But on second thought she turned back to the house, and waiting until Pell had disappeared in the direction of the kitchen garden, she let herself into the front hall and hurried along to the library.

Carefully she lifted the revolver from the wall and put it in her handbag. A moment later, after she had transferred it with gingerly caution to the glove compartment of her car, she drove off, the thought of the gap left in Sir Hugh's fire-arm collection comforting to her.

Always a way out, he had said. And just how disturbed was he, under his surface calmness, about Ritchie's arrival?

"Death by accident."

And she herself to blame for the "accident." She, leading trouble by the hand. Her fault, because she had looked out of a window, had stared at other people's private lives. Her fault, because she had whetted Ritchie's curiosity.

Hugh coming back this afternoon to his lonely, melancholy house, might so easily think, "Cherry is taken care of. Margaret will be better off without me." But the gun would be gone, his depended-upon, readily available gun, and perhaps on finding it gone, Hugh would guess who had taken it, and think twice before selecting and loading another.

At the nearby stile she waited while a shepherd, climbing over, crossed the lane to join his dog, barking at the heels of a flock of new lambs in a field opposite. Rather than fleecy toy lambs or Staffordshire figurines, they looked like animated mud pies, Margaret thought, or dripping, dirty sponges on stilts. They should have made her laugh with their absurd gamboling, she supposed, unhappily. How delicious it would be to laugh again. Really laugh. Was it possible that laughter had ever come easily to her? And how would she manage at tea and supper with Ritchie, if he were his usual light, amusing self, expecting gaiety and fun to be tossed back to him like a ball?

The lane, its hedgerows pink and white with hawthorne, came to an end. A road only a little wider, a little less rutted, took its place. Then there was a signpost, and the main high-way, and eventually the river to cross, the Castle to pass, and the Church of St. Lawrence.

The courtyard of The Feathers was full, she found, but she squeezed her little car into the curb a few yards from the inn, and then going in through the street entrance to the Ladies' Parlour, she took off her driving gloves and washed her hands and combed her hair, outlining her mouth with fresh, bright lipstick while she gathered courage to meet Richard in the lounge.

How foolish to be so afraid! This would be Ritchie waiting, she reassured herself, dear Ritchie, her friend. But wanting to be more than that. Much more.

And why not let it all work out that way? Why not say to him, "Look, I ran away, and it was inexcusable of me, and silly. But now I want to come back, if you'll have me, and if you won't ask questions."

Would he agree to the bargain? It was worth a try. Anything was worth it that might put an end to Ritchie's fox-hunt.

Amare est donare. . . . . A hurt, for a little while, and then a sensible, normal going-on with life—no real mutilation, nothing like two hands offered.

There was a vase of white lilac on the dressing table, under the mirror where Margaret was facing herself. Absently she bent her face to it, and drawing a deep breath of fragrance, was back in a summer tent of green, heart-shaped leaves where she and Ritchie had once spent so much of a long summer.

Shyness, her first, innocent, frightened awakening. What was it, what uncertain, girlish emotion had made her draw back?

Girls so often muddled their lives. If she had let herself go that summer, perhaps there would have been more for her with Ritchie than she had ever found with Allen. And wasn't it true that in London, a giving in to Ritchie had seemed not only inevitable but desirable until that sultry, disturbing night when she had looked across Mount Street into a lighted flat? How utterly all that had been changed.

With a little hopeless, resigned shrug. Margaret broke a sprig of lilac and put it in the lapel of her jacket and went to meet Richard. He was sprawled in an armchair in the low-ceilinged lounge that was all oak and pewter and brass, and stuffy with the fumes of stale beer and tobacco and coal smoke, his pipe lighted, a glass on the magazine-littered table in front of him, his eyes watching the door.

"Hi, Mag."

"Hello, Ritch."

Both of them were carefully casual, but Richard's eyes told a tale, and Margaret, bewildered, wondered if she were two women, one who belonged heart and soul to an Englishman, the other too honest to deny a rush of undeniable affection and excitement at sight of this tall, broad-shouldered, breezy American in new, expensive tweeds, this American with thick red hair and a cowlick, with clear, ardent blue eyes.

Nine women out of ten would envy her. Nine women out of ten would find it the easiest thing in the world to do what she was going to do.

"We can't talk here, it gets jammed a little later, so what about a spot of tea, al fresco, for old times' sake?" he was asking. "We picnicked in St. James's park once, remember? And shall we go all out touristy and walk to the Castle? The porter tells me there's a gatehouse we can huddle in if it starts raining."

"Whatever you say, Ritchie."

"Then I'll have a word with a waiter."

Ten minutes later they left the inn, with Richard carrying a basket Margaret recognized as his extravagant purchase from Fortnum and Mason.

He saw her glance at it.

"Brought from London with the happy hope we might be doing just this," he explained. "My best girl and I, rusticating in Salop."

"Salop?" Richard had stressed it, meaningly, if lightly, and Margaret's question came quickly.

"Yes. Salop. You asked me where it was that day in the park, need I remind you? At that point I'd have sworn you hadn't even a bowing acquaintance with the English countryside, or with any of its inhabitants—much less its landed gentry. Evidently I was mistaken. Or else you are a damned fast learner."

She chose to ignore the sarcasm, and neither of them spoke after that until they had walked down the narrow, crowded street, past the close of St. Lawrence's Church, where the choirboys were practicing, their hymns floating high and sweet, and reached the Castle's admission wicket. Richard bought tickets, and they crossed the grassy Outer Bailey and passed over the moat that led to the Keep.

When they came to the ruins of the Council Hall they sat down with their backs against a stone wall cushioned by the new green of wild fuchsia and valerian that sprouted from every crack, and by a thick mat of buttercups. Richard opened the picnic basket.

"Cucumber and anchovy-paste sandwiches, tea in one thermos, hot water in another, and milk and sugar," he announced after a thorough rummaging. "And sliced bread and butter. Gad—what's this sticky stuff, honey? One break we get, this foul English climate is too ruddy cold for ants."

As he unscrewed the top of a thermos, Margaret, reminded by the stone wall of a heap of rubble at Monks' Court, and thinking of a silver tea tray and a fire-lit library, scarcely heard him.

"Woolgathering, Mag? Here. Take your cup."

Richard filled a cup for himself and chose a sandwich. "Let's get down to brass tacks now, shall we? I've got a few questions to ask, as you may have guessed. Number One, what's the lowdown, sweet? What really made you run out on me?"

"I wasn't tied to you, Ritchie. I had every right to leave, if I chose."

"That's no answer. But we'll skip it for now, and go on to Question Two: Why Salop—if that's what you want to call it—for a hideaway?"

"I—I just thought I'd like it. And it isn't a hideaway."

"No? Aw, Mag, come off it. Who do you think you are fooling? And Question Three, a triple-header, coming up: Who is this guy, Vane, and why are you staying in his house, and what connection has he with that portrait you bought?"

"Portrait?"

"Don't try to pull that innocent stuff, sweet. It may interest you to hear I spent a lot of time thinking about a lot of things after you left London. You'd be surprised. Talk about ships and shoes and sealing wax. . . . And after I'd done a little backtracking I remembered the afternoon we stopped in at that antique shop in Albemarle Street. I was pricing a pair of dueling pistols when you came out with something weird about one of the portraits you had been looking at being a ringer for the man you had seen in the Duclair woman's flat the night she was murdered."

"I—I couldn't have said that, Ritch."

"Don't try to get out of it, Mag. And don't try to deny that from that afternoon you weren't yourself. I can't pinpoint the difference, but there was a difference. It wasn't only that you began to cool off on me; you were jumpy, and queer—and trying to cover up something, I decided, when I'd thought it over."

"I never heard such rubbish. You're imagining all that." With difficulty, Margaret swallowed a bite of sandwich that had needed a gulp of tea to get it down.

"Imagining? Maybe. But when I went back to the shop to have another look at the portrait out of sheer curiosity, the man in charge remembered us coming in before, and told me you'd telephoned down from Ludlow to buy it. That set me to thinking again, I can tell you."

Richard chose another sandwich. "Have you ever tried to put together one of those giant-size jigsaw puzzles that take two bridge tables?"

"What if I did buy a portrait? Lots of people buy them."

"Right. But why you wanted this one, in particular, is what interests me, and why you had it sent on to this Monks' Court place, where you are staying, instead of having it held in storage, if you didn't want it shipped home yet."

"How do you know it's at Monks' Court?"

"You can dig a lot of information out of a porter with the help of a few shillings. And I've been wondering: Could it have belonged originally to this fellow Vane, by any chance?"

"Why should it have belonged to him? Hundreds and hundreds of English people have owned family portraits."

"Right again. Just the same, I'd like a look at this one— and at Vane. Think it could be arranged?"

"The English don't like strangers barging in on them. And anyway, I don't see the point."

"Neither do I, as a matter of fact," Richard admitted with a considering frown. "Damned if I do. Not clearly, that is. But there's a glimmer. And the first lesson I learned as a cub reporter was to follow a lead and not worry about blind alleys till you came to them."

"A lead?" Margaret repeated it in a small, stricken voice that caused Richard's glance to fasten on her with quickened interest and curiosity. "What do you mean? What connection could there possibly be between a portrait I happened to buy and Sir Hugh Vane?"

"You tell me, sweet. It's exactly what has me guessing, though, as I say, there's a glimmer—light where there was no light. Too bad you're such a stubborn little devil, and have dug your heels in so hard. Sure you won't change your mind and give me the lowdown, the real scoop? I've a feeling it's big stuff. And if I could get my hands on it . . ."

There was a kind of avidness to it, and Margaret, remembering a phrase too often in her mind—"once a newshound, always a newshound"—shivered.

"Cold?" Richard asked, concerned.

"No. No, I'm all right."

"But you aren't talking? OK, OK, if that's the way you want it."

Richard shrugged, but his eyes were bright with annoyance for a moment, and then he was looking amused. "Speaking of a connection, there's one tie-up, at least, in this whole business, that's fairly safe to bet on."

"Oh?"

"The squire of your portrait and the Mayfair type you said was his double had wenching in common if nothing else, I'd say. Those Georgian boys got around quite a bit, from what I've read, and so did the bloke you saw—judging from the company he was keeping that night." The amusement was tinged with a faint contempt. "Not that I think much of his taste."

The question he put then was jocular, on the surface, but to Margaret a hard core of purpose lay behind it.

"This Vane, what about *his* private life? Is he one to like the ladies, too? And does he get down to London, ever, for a fling?"

"London? How should I know whether he goes to London?" Margaret's hands gripped tightly together. "Sir Hugh has a daughter who raises dogs—she has a kennel—and . . ."

"And it was only because of the daughter and her dogs that

you ran out on me? The daughter was your reason for buying the portrait?"

"Stop third-degreeing me, Ritch—I won't have it. It's horrid of you—and it's all so silly. You are making something out of nothing. And why should it matter to you, the portrait, or—or anything else?"

"Anyone else, you mean, don't you? And haven't you ever heard of jealousy? God, if you knew how I've missed you . . ."

He snatched her to him, and she was submissive as his mouth sought hers, hungrily. Let him kiss her. Let him take her. What difference did it make? It was going to be Ritchie from now on anyway, wasn't it? Ritchie, for Hugh's sake?

But oh, not yet. Not so soon. Not when only last night . . .

She began to struggle and beat at him with her fists, and instantly, he let her go.

"I prefer the willing type. I've never gone in for wrestling matches," he commented with a short laugh.

Margaret had opened her bag and was glancing in the mirror of her powder compact and touching a handkerchief to her mouth as he began piling cups and plates into the Fortnum basket.

"I could use a drink. Let's go back to town. And you know something? I'd drop that Vane fellow if I were you, and fast, Mag." It was suggested without emphasis, but it was an order, and Margaret snapped the compact closed and turned to him with a flare of anger.

"You and your bossiness, Ritch! And you needn't refer to Sir Hugh as 'that fellow,' either." The anger was gone then, as quickly as it had come, and her eyes filled, and she put a hand on his sleeve humbly. "You deserve an explanation. I wish I could give it. I'll never be able to. But if you still want me—and if you'll let me have a little time—let me work things out, my way. . . ."

"I still say, drop him fast. And you'll be sorry if you don't. Because if a hunch of mine turns out— We'll skip that for now, though. And as to whether I still want you or not . . ." The blue eyes that looked down at her were steady and confident. "I not only want you, I intend to have you. Things would have to be loused up a whole lot worse than they are now between us before I'd be willing to call it quits. So put up your mouth, sweet. You'd like it, if you'd only let yourself get used to it. That's my girl. That's my Mag."

TWENTY-SIX

Richard, heady and exuberant with triumph, did all the talking on the way back to the inn.

". . . a villa on the Mediterranean for a few months? Would you like that, Mag? Let's live it up! Or the Italian lakes? Name it, and we'll settle for it. I can work anywhere, as long as I've got my typewriter."

Margaret gave all the appropriate, interested answers at each appropriate and indicated moment. Begin now, here and now, to play your part, she was admonishing herself dully. Your bargain is made, now live up to it.

Poor Ritchie, so completely convinced he had won her over at last. Contriteness and a sense of shame bothered her fleetingly, and then she was immediately defensive, with passionate fierceness.

For Hugh. The only possible way to save Hugh. Ritchie would forget Hugh now, or so she prayed. He would abandon the chase, caught up as he so obviously was in his exultant happiness—his gloating happiness.

With distaste, Margaret wished some other adjective had been her choice. But that was Ritchie for you. He had always been determined to carry through his projects, whether large or small, and he had always crowed over his successes.

How impossibly difficult it would be for him to face any major defeat, any real blow to his ego. Much, much more difficult than for most men. And how well, fortunately, she understood him. She ought to, by right; she'd known him long enough.

Which simplified things, because from now on all she need do was adjust to his ways. Merely make up her mind to do just that—adjust.

To begin with, concentrate on his wit, his talent, his generosity. Tell herself life with Ritchie was going to be full of excitement and interest, of fun, of color. Remind herself, with gratefulness, that lonely widowhood would be behind her. Be honest, and admit that Ritchie could oh, so easily stir her to pleasurable physical excitement, if once she let the bars down between them, if she let herself relax, if she told herself, "I have waited more than long enough, and I am lucky Ritch came along again."

It shouldn't be too difficult. Not if she were sensible. Not if she firmly, determinedly suppressed the odd, unreasonable antipathy that had held her back from surrender so many times before. She might have to work at it; she had tried to be sensible, tried to be firm with herself before, on various other occasions, and failed miserably.

But this time it would be different. This time it would be for Hugh.

She was adequately if quietly responsive, and she had the right smile at the right moment for Richard as they walked along, Richard with an arm linked in hers possessively, the picnic basket swinging from his right hand and bumping against his long legs.

His stride was free and buoyant, his head high, his casual brown felt hat, so right with his tweeds, jammed a little rakishly on his thick red hair. He made all the other men walking on King Street seem smaller, it struck Margaret, and he gave the impression of elbowing people out of his way.

At The Feathers, when he had found chairs for them in a secluded corner of the lounge and ordered sherry for Margaret and whisky for himself, Margaret, as though from a long way off, heard him make plans, briskly and efficiently, and was conscious vaguely of relief that someone was now running her life.

". . . We'll have an early dinner." The planning was as thoughtful as it was detailed. The early dinner would enable Margaret to drive back to Monks' Court before dark; in the morning, with her luggage, she would rejoin Richard at the inn for breakfast. Her car would be left with the local branch of the hire agency, and their return to London would be in the new car of which Richard was so proud.

"Looks. Power. Speed. It's got everything. And I told you we'd be going places in it this spring, Mag."

Once in London he would see to all the necessary wedding arrangements; he had a friend at the American Embassy who knew the ropes. But first of all he would buy her a ring. Not a diamond—a topaz. A big, dark Brazilian stone, the color of her eyes. There was a shop on Bond Street. He had taken a look. And she did know her eyes were topaz color, didn't she?

He had another whisky and Margaret another sherry, and then they went into the dining room and Richard ordered a bottle of the best the wine list offered.

He raised his glass to Margaret, and then jubilantly, confidently, raised it again. "To us." And Margaret, finding it easier by far to drink than to eat, drank with him, and let him refill her glass when it was empty, even while she wondered, uncomfortably, if she were encouraging Richard to empty the bottle too soon. He was getting a little beyond himself. Overexuberant. Overelated. "Riding high," would be his expression for it.

It was toward the end of dinner that he reached across the table and put a hand over hers.

"A little more willing now, by any chance, to talk about Vane?" he asked unexpectedly. "For instance, you are sure you don't know whether or not he was in London lately—say, around the end of last month? Still keeping quiet? What's the point? I can always check. And if it turns out he *was* in London, his number is up, sweet. Better face it."

The surprise attack was jarringy disconcerting and alarming, and something nakedly brutal about his assertiveness, his assurance, made Margaret shrink, involuntarily.

"I could almost be sorry for him." His mouth stretched in a smile. "That bitch, with her stink of frangipani, and her lacquered hair, and those jade-green pajamas—those made-to-order, Thailand brocade pajamas—wasn't worth it. But he'll have to sweat it out, as far as I'm concerned. It won't be yours truly who lets him off."

Margaret looked down at her plate where new peas and salmon, congealing in white sauce, had scarcely been touched. Ritchie, across from her, with that mirthless, vindictive smile, that dreadful smile? It couldn't be, she tried to tell herself. And then, with a slow, faintly dawning comprehension of what he had said, of what his ugly sneer might treacherously have revealed, she was staring at him with stunned incredulity.

"Frangipani?" she questioned weakly.

"Those Oriental women always go in for that heavy stuff."

"Made-to-order pajamas? Jade-green Thailand brocade?" She was in deep water, now, and she knew it.

"Isn't that what the papers said she was wearing?" It came quickly, smoothly, but to Margaret, the dining room had begun to revolve, the table to pitch.

"The papers said 'green silk—and—and a tropical scent'— not the rest of it. They wouldn't have known. No one would know, I should think, unless—"

"Unless he were on the inside, like your Englishman? Not so, sweet. Where have you been, all your life, not to have heard about labels in clothes, or perfume bottles standing on dressing tables? Reporters can read, can't they?"

"Yes. Yes, of course, but—"

"But what?"

"Wouldn't a perfume bottle just say 'Nuit tropique'— something like that? And labels aren't marked, 'made to order.' "

"Who laid down that rule? Dior?" Richard laughed and felt in his pockets, and brought out a package of expensive cigarettes. "You don't, do you? Any objection if I light up? I shouldn't, at dinner—but we all have our little vices."

He was all Ritchie, and not a stranger to her as he struck a match with breezy nonchalance. Unless he was trying just a little too hard? Unless she could say his eyes were a little too interested in the match flame?

"Green silk, highly perfumed lounging pajamas"; ". . . the body in garish, green silk pajamas." That was the way it had been written up, with variations, in every one of the papers she had devoured. And never, not once, any mention of frangipani in particular, nor any mention of made-to-order or of Thailand, nor any descriptive use of the words jade or brocade.

Only someone who had known her—known her inti-

mately. Who had perhaps pocketed the bill for the specifi-
cally ordered jade brocade from Thailand, or in front of
whom she had preened and boasted of those exotic, alluringly
fitted, custom-made pajamas.

Ritchie noticed women's clothes. Ritchie had an eye for
them, and Ritchie was interested in them as a writer, observant of all details. And don't forget—Ritchie had been in
Bangkok . . . he'd have seen silks. . . . Something else—
Ritchie on the subject of lacquered hair, once. "Hair lacquered like a Japanese doll's," he had said. He could have
been thinking, ". . . like a Eurasian dancer's."

Margaret lifted her goblet and wet her dry mouth with
wine, and when she had set the goblet down again, carefully,
she stood up, holding to the table edge. "I—I need to powder
my nose." She spoke through stiff lips. "Excuse me, please."

Her napkin had fallen from her lap to the floor. For the
benefit of an approaching waitress she had an automatic
"Thank you."

"Will it be the sweet, or a savory next, madam?"

"Neither."

"Coffee in the lounge?"

"Nothing." Unsteadily, Margaret was on her way to the
door.

"Something more for you, sir?" The waitress, looking surprised and curious, had turned to Richard.

"No." Richard was already on his feet, pushing past her
and crossing the dining room. Seconds ahead of him through
the lounge, and with the door of the Ladies' Parlour closed,
Margaret sagged against it, with a rush of thankfulness she
was alone in the room.

Ritchie, instead of Hugh? Hugh innocent? Ritchie the
killer? But how could it be? Ritchie had been with her, that
night. The theater. Supper. Dancing. A drive. Then back to
the hotel, good nights at the lift. She in her bedroom, then.

And across Mount Street, Hugh. But later, after Hugh left
. . . Had Ritchie been waiting?

Hugh innocent. Ritchie guilty. To grasp it was impossible.
Dazed by the mingled shock of her wild, unbounded relief,
the shock of her horror, and terribly afraid, Margaret moved
unsteadily to the washbasin and ran cold water, and held a
wet towel to her face until her trembling and vertigo lessened
enough to let her think with some approach to clarity.

If it was Ritchie, why had Hugh let her go on assuming his
guilt? As she searched, bewildered, for an answer, remembered words sprang to mind and took on enormous import.
Hugh had said, "I wanted her to die." Hugh had said, "She
got what she deserved." Yes. But Hugh had said also, "The
wish itself constitutes a murder, with or without the act."
And Hugh had never, never, said, flatly, "I killed her."

Only his terrible wish to kill, his seizing of the first chance
offered, had been confessed. Could it mean that Hugh, in
self-revulsion, considered himself a murderer, even though
he had stayed his hand in time and left the actual killing to
Fate? Fate, who was Ritchie? And was Hugh, tormented by
his conscience, and living with a sense of guilt he couldn't
throw off, trying now in some pitifully twisted way to pay for
that guilt? But how could any questions be answered, any sup-
positions affirmed, until she went to him, begging for the
truth? Don't try to unravel tangled skeins here and now. All
along, from the beginning, she had, in her heart, refused to
believe him a murderer, and now, to have her faith justified,
she had only to wait a little longer.

So soon, so heavenly soon, she could be with him. Don't
wait, now, to ask yourself questions about Ritchie, either.
Push the horror as far from you as you can. Just get back to
Monks' Court, and Hugh.

Hugh. The pull toward him was once again as irresistible as

it had been the first time she looked into the dark eyes, painted on canvas, of another Vane.

Hugh, my love, my love.

Again, she tried to think clearly. How would she get to her car, if Ritchie was out there, waiting for her? If he had even faintly guessed what she suspected, he would never let her get back to Hugh. He would never let her give him away to anyone. Not Ritchie, who had always to be at the top, who intended to stay at the top.

Very quietly, Margaret opened the door a crack, and then quickly closed it. Richard, just coming out of the bar, was taking up a position in the hallway. Logic tried to tell her, then, to walk on out, calmly, to the telephone at the porter's desk, and then to sit quietly, securely, in the lounge, surrounded by people, until Hugh came for her. The pull toward Monks' Court was too strong.

The street door! How could she have forgotten the street door? Every vestige of common sense, all caution deserted her as she ran to the door through which she had entered the hotel that afternoon, and in seconds she was out of it and onto the sidewalk, racing to her parked car, oblivious to stares as she rummaged frantically in her purse for its key.

Sliding under the steering wheel, she switched on the engine. It sputtered, and failed, sputtered again, and caught, and with a clash of gears, and her foot hard on the accelerator, she shot from the curb into the early-evening traffic of the Bull Ring.

Horns were honked loudly. A truck driver leaned out of his high cab to swear at her. Narrowly she missed a boy on a bicycle. Someone shouted at her.

It was the boy's frightened face that brought her to her senses momentarily and made her slacken speed and endure the congestion of King Street.

Too late she began to regret her foolhardiness. Ritchie would not wait very long for her outside the hall door of the Ladies' Parlour. Realizing even by now, probably, that she had run away, wasn't he already after her in that new car of his, red and shiny as a Christmas toy?

Easily he would guess where she was going. Easily his Jaguar could catch her little car. Easily, easily he could force her off the road.

One way or another, he could get rid of her. People murdered other people every day.

Accomplished Ritchie. An old hand.

Think about Hugh. Don't think about Ritchie. Make yourself believe that Hugh, in the library, waiting for you, is trying to get through to you, trying to tell you to use your head.

Make yourself believe that Hugh, with his own drop of strange Welsh blood, like Pell, had a knowingness. Let him help you concentrate on your recollection of the way back to Monks' Court. Believe that he can. Don't be ashamed to believe.

Those veiled, purple mountains looking down on Monks' Court were not ordinary mountains, remember. They were Welsh. They were mysterious. Anything at all could be brought about in their shadow. And for good, as well as for evil.

Now concentrate. And be glad you have twilight on your side instead of night-time blackness.

As though she were looking at a spread-out map, Margaret began to visualize the road that lay ahead of her across the river.

A turn here, and another there. A signpost. A branching. Another turn right. But hadn't there been a lane? Or not a lane? Hardly that. A cart-track—the lane she had jogged along with Hugh, behind the old pony!

Her single chance of outdriving Richard was shown her clearly. To a stranger like Ritchie, needing to ask the way to Monks' Court, a route with the maximum miles of smooth highway, the minimum of rough, muddy, deep-country driving would be recommended. The Jaguar would eat up those miles like nothing, but if she herself turned off the highway and took to the cart-track until it led into the Monks' Court lane, she could keep well ahead of him. And the thing, now, was to get out of sight as fast as she could.

Recklessly, Margaret pulled over to the wrong side of the street and swerved into what was little more than an alley that ran between two of the Jacobean houses whose shop fronts lined the curb. Praying it wouldn't be a cul-de-sac, she dodged through another welter of trucks and vans. Her hands were slippery on the steering wheel when at last it opened onto a little cobbled street recognizable to her only because the Church of St. Lawrence towered directly ahead of her. If she kept straight on, she would pass the Castle, and then, with the bridge crossed, she would be on the main highway.

When the bridge was behind her, and a glance in her rear-view mirror satisfied her that she had, so far, eluded Richard's certain pursuit, she began to drive faster than she had ever driven in her life before.

She was fifteen miles or so out of town when the twilight she had counted on as an ally failed her. The heavy, full clouds that had threatened most of the day emptied. Automatically, she slowed to roll up the windows of her car and reached a hand to the dashboard. First, the windshield wiper. Next, the lights. No. Not the lights, she decided quickly. To turn them on would be to make the taillights twin beacons for Richard if he was behind her.

Faster, now. Still faster. Push the car to its limit. And now begin anticipating the Monks' Court signboard, strain ahead to see it, and watch for cart-tracks, just this side of it.

She forced the little car on until, through the rain, the white-painted signpost was an indistinct glimmer, and then wrenched it sharply to the right, off the asphalt into the jolting ruts of the short cut. The car could only crawl after that, but eventually the cart-track merged with the hedgerowed lane that led to the Monks' Court driveway.

Hugh—only minutes, now. Her heart was crying it out just before the little car, slithering in mud, went into a ditch, and from behind her, coming around a curve in the lane, rain-blurred, diffused headlights struck a wavering reflection in her own car's streaming mirror. The Christmas-red Jaguar had caught up. Or almost.

Panic-stricken, Margaret sprang from her car. If she could push through the hedgerow before Ritchie's headlights silhouetted her, she could race to the house under cover of trees and tall bracken.

Run. Run. But how run, with every briar and bramble of the hedgerow clutching, clawing, to delay her? Distraught, Margaret yanked at her tweed skirt to free it and tore away strands of honeysuckle looping like thick rope around her ankles. The headlights had come closer; to the driver behind them, the little abandoned car and the trampled grass, the gap she had forced in the hedgerow, would tell a plain-to-read story.

She heard the car brake, and a door slam. As though in a frustrating dream in which she could only stand still instead of move a step, she felt the sopping wetness of grass, the sting of nettles. Wet leaves slapped her face. Blackberry runners snagged her stockings, raked her legs. Tripping, then, over the knobby surface roots of clumped trees, she groped for something to support herself, and her hands touched cold, hard stone.

Stone? A piece of the rubble of a ruined Saxon tower? If

it was, the chapel of Monks' Court was close, miraculously close.

Behind her she heard someone scrambling through the hedgerow as she had done, clutched, as she had been, by briars and brambles and ropy vines.

"Mag? Mag?"

He was playing the beam of a pocket flashlight in a wide arc. "Mag?"

Did he think she would answer, think she would wait for him, and listen to whatever explanations he might choose to make? Silently, vehemently, Margaret repudiated him as she stumbled on through the rain. "No, Ritch, no. And don't call me Mag. I'm not your Mag. I never was. Not even in the beginning. You know I wasn't. I couldn't be. I wanted to, but I couldn't. Always, something holding me back—something . . ."

"Mag. Mag!" He called it out triumphantly, this time. The flashlight had focused on her just as she gained the ivy-hung chapel. With her last reserve of strength she threw herself against the chapel's heavy door. Then she was groping through almost total darkness to the Vane vault. Fumbling for the big, rusted key, she turned it. The grilled door swung narrowly inward. With the key in her hand, she slipped through, clanged the door shut after her, turned the key again, and pulling it from the lock, and clutching it, she dropped down on the damp, grave-cold floor between two stone figures asleep, in effigy, on their biers.

The pound of her heart was loud in her ears. Each panting breath she drew, coming hard, tore from her throat like a sob. Richard was at the chapel door. Without haste, he moved into the nave and then paused, and with the narrow yellow beam of the flashlight a searching pointing-out finger, he called, loudly and clearly, "You are here somewhere, Mag, and don't think for a moment I won't find you. And there's no reason to make something big out of this little matter. So why not be sensible, and say you'll talk things over with me? Won't you, Mag?"

He waited, with his question loud and hollow sounding in the unanswering gloom. "No? As I've said before, you were always a stubborn little devil." Slowly Richard moved forward, the inquisitive yellow beam circling the base of stone pillars, exploring under old, worm-eaten oak benches set against the walls. He was at the altar rail. Margaret, shutting her eyes tightly, not to see him coming closer, crouched lower, and began to pray.

"Dear God . . . our Father . . . don't let Ritchie find me. And keep Hugh safe. I pray Thee, Lord, his soul to keep . . . and his body, too, God. . . ."

As the jumbled, incoherent phrases repeated themselves, imploringly, an owl, perched on a rafter over the vault, hooted, and out of the icy darkness, with its smell of damp mold and of ancient dust and bones, a bat fluttered close and brushed her hair. Too late, she tried to catch back a gasp, and then Ritchie's flashlight had picked out the grilling, and the yellow finger, pointing, showed her crouched.

"So there you are, you damned little fool." The flashlight he held was not entirely steady as he played it over her chalky face, her eyes, which were open now, wide and terrified and half blinded by the beam, her rain-wet hair straggling, her tweeds soaked and muddied, her sheer stockings shredded. He laughed, his eyes overbright, his face a little flushed. "You didn't really think you could give me the slip, did you? And now we're cozily together again, let's settle down to a little confab. Out with it, Mag. Let's have the real reason you pulled this stunt, this crazy running away from me again."

"You don't know?" Margaret's voice shook.

"A little clueing in would be a big help."

"It was because—because you had never told me you knew the Duclair woman, and—"

"And if I did, so what?" In the glare of the flashlight he was only a voice, cool and unperturbed.

"You kept it from me—you made a secret of it—and this evening, at dinner, I could tell you hated her. The things you said. The way you said them. And you knew about her clothes —the clothes she was wearing—that night."

"A lot of men could give you the scoop on her wardrobe." His laugh was ugly. The flashlight wavered, and she could see his eyes, very blue and hard. "But you've been getting ideas, have you? And playing guessing games? I was a little afraid of that. It seems Old Big Mouth Page let a few things drop over the dinner table. Well, that's that. If you've caught on, you've caught on. But you hadn't planned to blab to anyone, had you, sweet?" He moved a little closer to the grilling. "It wouldn't be wise."

"How could you, Ritch! How could you? And why—?" It was a passionate, horrified reproach, a shocked, bewildered begging to be given any answer at all.

The smile Margaret had seen before turned him again into a stranger. "Why? She got in my way, that's why! Her big mistake—you'd like the lowdown on it? Here's the gist. We played around in Hong Kong one winter when I was out there free-lancing. Then when she came to London in this revue of hers, and got smart about me being worth looking up, she did her best to hook me again. She knew she wasn't dancing as well as she used—or getting any younger. It was time she latched onto a good thing. I'd been trying to shake her for weeks before you showed up, and then after you came, I wanted out more than ever, and so I—"

"Don't tell me! I don't want to hear—"

"I hadn't planned it that way. Things got out of hand. She asked for it—" The dreadful smile that made him a man she didn't know was back as he lurched a little, and then straightened himself, carefully. "If you think I was going to let that so-and-so spoil my second chance with you . . ."

"How could she have spoiled it?"

"She saw us at the Savoy one night, and then somewhere else, and somewhere else, other nights. She came around to my rooms after one of those nights, late, and threatened me with a paternity suit if I ducked out on her. That sort of blackmail is tired old stuff, but all the same, if she'd brought charges she might have made them stick. She has a child in Hong Kong— It could belong to half a dozen other men, but there'd have been the dirtiest sort of rotten mess raked up."

"But you could have told me, Ritchie. We were friends! Old, old friends."

"Told you, and lost you? You were always a Puritan, Mag. You pulled away from me once before, remember? I wasn't risking it a second time. Christ, what a lousy joke! Me thinking, 'Here's Mag back. Mag to top off all the rest of my good luck. Mag, the flag on the peak.' I'd arrived. Really arrived."

"And yet you went to her, that night, after you left me?"

"Only to tell her to go to hell with her threats. I crossed over from your hotel, but when I saw the lights on in her flat, I guessed she'd brought someone back with her after the revue, and I walked around for an hour. I had a drink or two at a bottle club—a drink never hurts, a quickie, or a couple, when you need souping up—and then I went back. She was alone by that time. I'd figured her big talk was ninety-nine per cent bluff, but when I began to find out she was playing for keeps . . ."

He shrugged. "As I said, it was her mistake. You can see for yourself I had to shut her up, can't you, Mag?"

He asked it with a terrible matter-of-factness. "Because the

point is, from now on in, a whole lot is going to be up to you.
I thought it out, driving over here. You either give me your
promise to keep your mouth shut, and you admit to me it was
that fellow, Vane, you saw in the flat, or you'll be through.
Washed up. Kaput. Finis. Dead. I won't enjoy what I'll have
to do—I'd much, much rather not—but you do understand,
don't you, that I'm in an awkward spot?"

He didn't mean it. He couldn't mean it. Margaret, staring,
and shaking, huddled in the farthest corner of the vault, told
herself she knew he didn't mean it. This was Ritchie, looking
and acting like a stranger, perhaps, but still the old Ritchie,
who loved her. Unless he was a Ritchie gone mad. Oh, God
. . . that ghastly reasonableness.

"Tell me you understand, Maggie girl. And don't take all
night about making your choice. It's too cold in here for
hanging around, and you in those wet clothes."

Mad. Entirely mad.

"Well—? I'm waiting."

The flashlight was suddenly in his left hand, and his right
was reaching through the grille for the key to the vault.
"Took it out, did you? Atta girl! Right on the ball. But you
haven't stopped me yet, sweet." His flashlight searched the
chapel again, and this time the beam found the oak benches
that lined the walls.

"How true it is that where there's a will, there's a way.
Bench on top of bench, and over the grille I'll go. Though
there's still time for that promise, and the truth about Vane.
And by the way, how's he taking my arrival? He knows you
met me this afternoon?"

"Yes."

"And doesn't like the competition, I expect. Well, I don't
like competition, either. I wanted that French kid the police
were holding to get off—I hadn't a thing in the world against

him—but when it comes to Vane taking the rap for me, that's another story. I'll enjoy seeing that guy in a prisoner's box."

"He'll never go to prison. He'll never stand trial. He'd kill himself first. He wouldn't put his daughter through it."

"Family honor? The *noblesse oblige* stuff? And you believed that tripe? Don't make me laugh."

"I believed every word of it!" Stung by his jeering, she rushed headlong and unthinkingly into her quick, trembling-voiced declaration, "I believed it enough to take his gun from the house when I left this afternoon. . . ."

"You're trying to get me to lay off Vane? Trying to tell me I won't gain a thing by turning him into the Yard? Any day I won't."

There was the heavy scrape of wood on stone as he dragged one of the benches in front of the grilling. He was dragging a second when he stopped short. "Vane's revolver. It wouldn't be in your car, by any chance? Well, well, well. There's an idea. To tell the truth, I hadn't been looking forward one bit to twisting your pretty neck, much as it has to be done. But just to take aim and pull a trigger wouldn't be half as unpleasant a chore. So if you'll be patient, I'll whip out and see what I can find. I won't be half a minute. Never keep a lady waiting—isn't that what all the rules say?"

He wasn't only mad. He was drunk. He must be drunk. It was the only explanation for the volubility, the macabre banter.

"Ritchie—please, please, Ritch—!"

"It's too late to soften me up, and don't try skinning out of here, either, once my back's turned. It won't work. I intend to lock the chapel door when I go to your car. And even if you knew another way out, you'll never find it, sweet. You couldn't see a foot in front of you without a light."

He was right, she acknowledged, sick with terror. Any frantic search for another door would be useless. The blackness to which she would be abandoned when he left with his flashlight would be impenetrable. Outside the chapel, out in the safe, normal world where safe, normal people lived, nightfall, by now, she could guess, had blotted the last of twilight from the sky, and in here, darkness, thick and suffocating, would be like a sack over her head.

The chapel door closed heavily behind Richard. Now he would be making his way through the briars and brambles. Now he would have pushed through the hedgerow and be trampling the last of the bluebells by the side of the lane. He would open the car door. Hugh's gun would be his gun.

Again Margaret heard her hard breathing, the irregular pound and thud in her breast, and wondered, dully, if ever her heart would beat like other people's hearts again, her breath ever come quietly.

When Richard was back, the flashlight was in one hand, the revolver in the other, its polished steel glinting as she had seen it glint before, in firelight. But the gun didn't mean a thing. It couldn't possibly mean anything. Ritchie was only trying harder and harder to further terrify her into promise-making and to an indictment of Hugh.

"Here I am, sweet. I told you I wouldn't be long. And now for our little get-together."

Cruel Ritchie—no, no, cruel, crazed stranger—

"I could take a potshot at that lock to get at you, of course, but it seems a shame to blow up all that old ironwork. I've a great respect for antiquities, I'll have you know. Besides, your god-damned Englishman seems to have a pretty high opinion of his marksmanship—there's only one bullet in his gun. So it's on with scaling the heights."

He put the flashlight and the revolver on the floor and dragged again at the second worm-holed bench he had hauled from against the chapel wall. Settling it to his satisfaction was difficult. It proved too heavy and cumbersome for him to place squarely and firmly on top of the bench he had already shoved in front of the vault door. He was forced to compromise by propping it at an angle, slanted like a gangplank.

"That'll do it." Frozen, wordless, Margaret watched him pick up the revolver, thrust it into a side pocket of his jacket, grasp the grilling, and pull himself up to a precarious footing on the oak incline. He was just ready to swing a leg over the top when, with a giving way of old, desiccated wood, the bench his left foot still rested on tilted, slid, and collapsed.

Margaret heard him curse, saw his grip tighten, and with his jacket caught high, close to the collar, on the arrowpoints of the paling, saw him kick out to free himself, and then his suddenly shifted weight had swung him heavily against the grille.

The gun in his pocket went off with a shattering reverberation in the small, shut-up chapel. For a moment he hung, a deadweight, suspended, and then there was a soft tearing sound of cloth, and as Margaret screamed out his name— "Ritchie!"—the impact of his body against stone.

Stunned, incapable of moving, she stayed crouched, with the chapel silent again, until a faint, questioning "Mag?" brought her out of a vacuum of horror.

"Mag—?" The insistency of it got her to her feet. Unlocking the vault door with hands that shook, she clambered over the barricade of benches, stumbled to where he lay, sprawled in a limp, bloody heap.

"Mag?" Weakly, he caught at her hand.

"I'm here, Ritchie. I'll bring a doctor. You'll be all right."

"Sure, sure, I'll be fine." It was a faint derisive whisper she had to bend lower to hear. His eyes opened. "I couldn't have done it to you—couldn't have gone through with it—say you know I couldn't. . . ."

"I know."

"And don't look so sorry. A hell of a good break—for both of us—the way things are."

The flicker of the brief smile he forced was brilliant and extraordinarily sweet. "The Savoy and the Ritz and Mirabelle's—you in that floating, black rag . . . 'Gladly I lived, and gladly I lay me down to die . . .' Corny, but anything for my Mag—anything at all to be of service. . . ."

A scarlet, choking hemorrhage silenced him. The blue eyes went blank. His mouth slackened. His jaw dropped.

Beyond tears, Margaret stood up. Ritchie, lying there, dead. Ritchie, of all people, dead. Ritchie who wanted the world, and so briefly had possessed it. Ritchie who had loved her when summertime meant a tent of leafy lilac, and who now, at the end, had loved her enough to be glad that roiled and muddied waters would settle and clear for her.

Before she left him, she unpinned a wilted but still fragrant white sprig from her jacket and stooped again to put it in the hand that had reached out for hers. He was lying as quietly as were the two stone effigies in the vault, and with nothing more to be done for him, she turned to the chapel door.

Hugh, waiting. Hugh to be told. And after that—? All of it could wait. The rain had stopped. The briars and brambles and knobby roots were nothing as she ran. There was the lane. There were the gates, and the driveway. And now, the house and the mountains beyond, shrouded in mist. Hugh's house. The house of the Vanes. Hers now the right, and the joy at last, to share it with him. She would belong, now, like Catharine Vane. And Cherry wouldn't mind. Not any more. Cherry, who had Robin, would be generous. And Jody? What of Jody? Love could be trusted to exorcise the bitterness and pain of the past. And who, then, could object to a little boy ghost playing happily with his drum along a passageway?

Pell, with her knowingness, would see the trouble and un-happiness, which had weighted the house so heavily, dissolve as surely as all chill, all melancholy would soon vanish from its every room, as surely as other springtimes come, bringing the call of a cuckoo again.

Margaret reached the moss-grown steps of the terrace. "Hugh—!" In answer, a tall man limped toward her through the warm lamplight of an open doorway. As she ran to meet him, the mist lifted from the mountains that reared above Monks' Court.